I0651017

Rise of Hawk

Rise of Hawk

by
Ke-Yana Drake

Ke-Yana Drake
Thames, New Zealand
2013

The Time Speaker Series:

#0 Rise of Hawk (prequel)
#1 Time Speaker

Copyright © 2009-2013 Ke-Yana Drake
All Rights Reserved.
http://www.keyanadrake.com/

Published in New Zealand
First Edition

ISBN: 978-0-473-23878-0

Set in 10.5/12 Georgia – R2 2013/03/24

A Dedication

Rise of Hawk is dedicated to Mariusz Gospodarczk.

When depression had me in doubt about whether I
could do this, you were there with your enthusiasm
and joy to tell me I could. At times, your passion for
Rise of Hawk and its characters were the only fuel I
had to keep going—I couldn't stand to disappoint you.
I hope by giving you your own character in this story
that you live forever with my precious Rebels.

Bāshana mā
(You are precious to me)

Acknowledgements

First and foremost I'd like to thank Rick, without you I wouldn't have published one book, let alone two! I hope one day to have as many books published under my belt as you do today.

To my brother, Adam, you're a pain in the ass sometimes (as I'm sure I am too), but I want to thank you so much for all your brotherly annoyances, and your unwavering faith in me and my crazy-ass dreams.

Thank you to Heather Watson for again doing an amazing job on my cover art. I hope I can always have you as my epic cover artist and good friend!

I'd also like to thank my friends who loaned their names and a little personality to my Desert Kids: Xak, Liz, Nick, Jai and Shay, I love you all. My conlang friends, deviantART friends, and fellow Indie Authors on twitter, facebook and blogs, thank you all.

Also, thank you, new reader. I hope you enjoy Rise of Hawk, the prequel novel to Time Speaker, and may you enjoy the many more stories to come in the Time Speaker Universe.

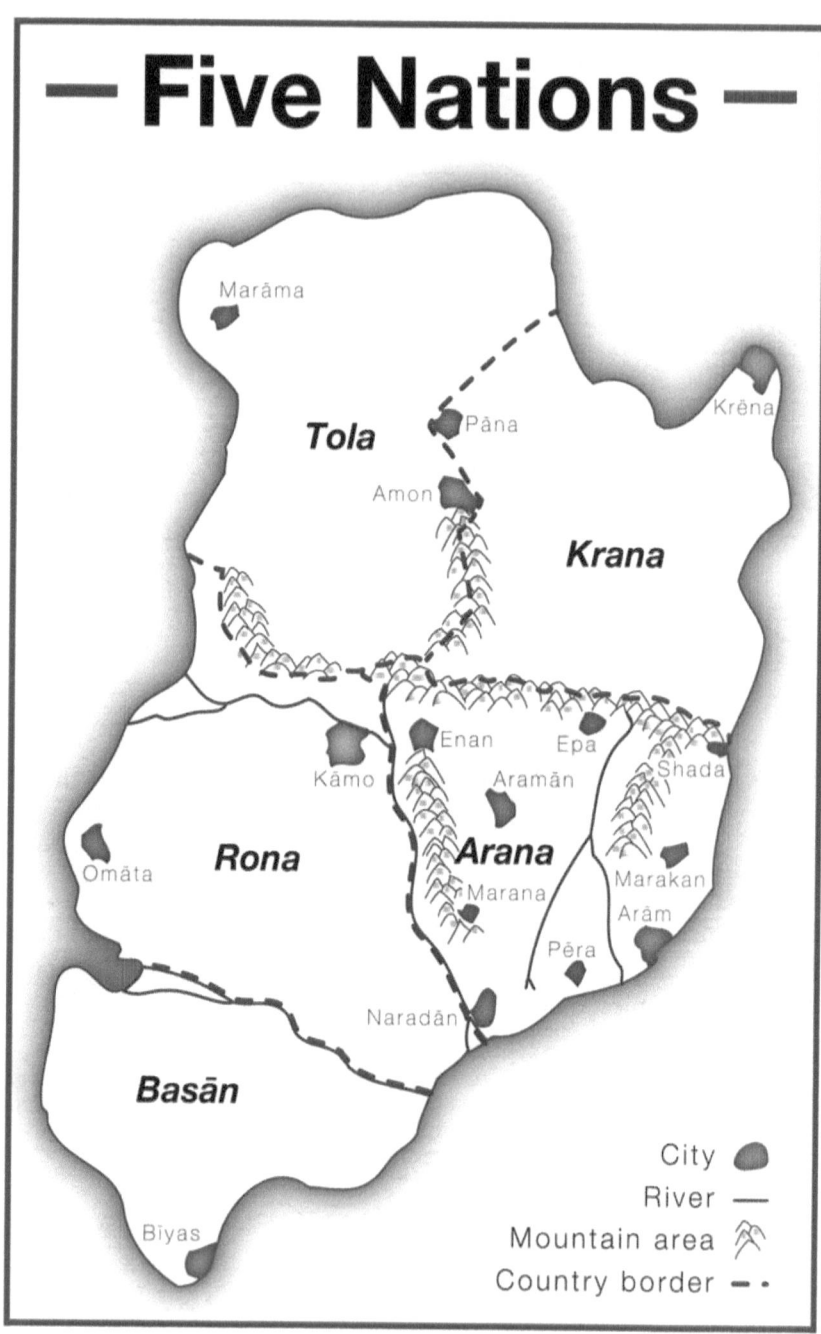

Planet Shadow, an introduction

It is believed by the humanoid inhabitants of Planet Shadow that they were once divine beings living in the heavenly realms of Light. The story is that three thousand years ago, the people fell from the Light into the Darkness and Chaos of the physical world. One of the people, a chosen messenger of the Divine forces, rose up as a leader and brought order to the chaos. He was the Founder.

The Founder split the people into Five Great Nations. Rona, the ebony giants of the west coast; Tola, the tall ochre artisans with violet eyes of the north west; Krana, the dwarfish crop farmers on the north east coast; Arana, the cream linguists and politicians on the east; and Basān, the yellow tinted scientists who live in the earth under the southern rainforests.

The Founder taught the people how to make their own light with fire and how to live safely in the darkness. Afterwards, He left the people, and his wife and children to find a way back to the Light. He promised that one day he would return and take them back home to the heavenly realms.

As the years and generations flew by, the nations eventually came to be ruled by seven Great Families. About two thousand years after the Founder, the Great Families and the priests of the Old Temple had become corrupted by power and greed.

Twelve great leaders, the Patrons, came together and united their forces to overthrow the priests of the Old the Temple, and the corrupted Families. They waged a great war, called the Reformation. Once the war was won, the surviving Patrons reformed the old Temple into the modern Church of the Founder, and established a democratic government in each of the Five Nations.

In the year 2911, an Aranan scientist by the name of Freyan Rena discovered the genes that marked those with psychic abilities, and in an effort to control those individuals who could pose a threat to the government, the Agency was born.

The Agency conscripted not only those who were an immediate threat to the government, but every single Psi and gifted Talent in Arana. Over the three generations since the Agency was created, over a third of the population was taken or executed for treason.

With every gifted person afraid of the Agency, economic development slowed to a halt and a great financial and cultural recession descended on Arana.

The Hundred Years Depression left most Aranan cities with entire suburbs of abandoned factories and property. Such buildings filled over time with homeless squatters, and illegal Psi and Talents hiding from the Agency. The only industries to thrive in Arana were an international mega-corporation running the basic civilian infrastructures of each country, and the criminal underworld.

But in the year 3000, the hope for an end to the suffering in Arana at the hands of the Agency came in the form of a mysterious man known only as Hawk...

Pronunciation Guide

I have created a fairly large and complicated artificial language called Ranqa (pronounced "Raan ka"), for the Time Speaker universe. Many of the character names, city and country names, and the swear words are written in this language.

- A vowel with a macron, e.g.: "Lilān" (as with Te Reo Maori), means an elongated or stressed vowel. A double vowel, e.g. "Triian" means exactly the same as a macron vowel.
- The "a" sounds are generally the same "a" as in "father" *not* "cat.
- The "o" sounds are generally the same as the first "o" in the word "Boston" or "sock", and not the "o" that rhymes with "toe".

Some swear words:

Hai da! Or Hai di'chena
This has the same meaning as "the shit has hit the fan." In a general sense "hai da" is a replacement for "shit!" when something is going wrong.

Nūthen or Nuth
This is essentially a replacement for "hell" or "hades" or any other place that's particularly unpleasant for the dead.

A'kenān, a'kēna, a'ken
This is essentially a replacement for "bastard", "bitch", and where "shit" is used as a noun (e.g. "you little shit").

Kitāsa-faced
This replaces "shit-faced" and can only be used in the context of "shit-faced drunk" or "out of your mind" on drugs.

Mārā
Literal meaning is "this moves me", but it's used like "holy" in "holy cow", or where you'd use "wow".

Mamon

Is a replacement for "bullshit", but only in the context of describing something as a lie or rubbish. No other context.

Preta

Is the name of a vegetable shaped like a cucumber, so it's a replacement for insults such as: dick, knobhead, dickhead, prick, etc.

So'then

Is essentially a replacement for "fuck", except that it can only be used as an expression of anger or surprise, not as an insult for someone.

Abe Kashān

This is a replacement for "oh my god". The "abe" part is pronounced as two syllables. It essentially means "by the Founder!"

Tokāto

Is the older version of "oh my god". Tokāto is the ancient word for the Divine. This is used exclusively by those few followers of the Old Temple of the Founder.

If you are interested in the correct pronunciations of names, swearwords and other Ranqa sentences please come to the website (www.keyanadrake.com) and look up the SquareBracket Glossary.

Dramatis Personae

Amana Enan—Original Rebel. Older sister of Tolan Enan, and high rated Telepath.

Ana—Agency Engineer, friends with Hiran.

Araian Cowdy—youngest child and only daughter of Jaran Cowdy senior, Dobid's younger sister, mother of Boe EeYan, best friend of Asha's. High rated Kinetic.

Asha Kān—Taelin Kān's younger sister, Tempa Kān's mother, fugitive from the Agency.

Ayren—Third in charge of the Rona-Abān. Younger brother of Jodina.

Bana Malar—Ao Agent, husband of Liina Meel, father of Gusa Meel.

Bez Ezita—Original Rebel. Husband of Ella, father of Jena.

Boe EeYan—Araian's young son.

Brān Maren—Original Rebel, mid-to-high rated Time Psi.

Cassandra Cowdy—daughter of Gwen, niece of Dobid and Araian Cowdy.

Cheetah—Agency assassin. Enemy of the Rebels.

Dela Malar—Bana and Hoyal's sister, Gusa's aunt, Wolf's mother. High rated Ao Agent.

Dobid Cowdy—youngest son of Jaran Cowdy senior. High rated Ao Agent.

Ella Mehn—Original Rebel. Cousin of Kala Mehn, wife of Bez Ezita and mother of Jena and two younger sons.

Enigma—Agency spy, under cover as Naethan Amon.

Father Andrew—Head Priest of the Arām Cathedral of the Founder. Friend of Nama's and the Rebels.

Father Owen—Priest, friend of Father Andrew.

Fritz—Ayala Spades. Gangster, slaver, the one responsible for the death of Nalana's mother, Rita Yen.

Goid Malan—Mena's youngest brother, second in charge of the Rona-Abān.

Gusa Meel—Bana Malar and Liina Meel's young daughter.

Gwen—Gwenith Rena, daughter of Triian Rena, married to one of Jaran Cowdy's sons and mother of Cassandra Cowdy.

Hawk—Enigmatic figure.

Hetera Beu—Rebel, mother of Timān Beu, friends with Nama Ree and Taelin Kān.

Heth Pallen—Ao Council member, Head of the taskforce searching for Hawk.

Hilla Norman—wife of Krena Ree, Leader of the Rebels by proxy.

Hiran—Computer Talent, friends with Ana.

Hoyal Malar—Bana's older brother, vice-Head of the Ao Council, good friend of Jaran Cowdy senior. Psycho.

Jaichi—Friend of Xak's. Mid-to-high rated Kinetic.

Jaran Cowdy senior—The head of the ruling body of the Agency, the Ao Council. Asshole.

Jena Mehn—Original Rebel. Daughter of Ella Mehn and Bez Ezita.

Jodina—Ayren's older sister. RA member.

Kala Mehn—Original Rebel. Nama's wife, cousin to Ella. High rated empath.

Karen Frene—Triian Rena's daughter, doctor and friend of Hawk.

Kita Oran—Rebel, an ex-telepath Interogator for the Agency.

Krena Ree—Original Rebel. Leader of the Psi Rebels in the year 3000. Wife of Hilla Norman.

Liina Meel—Ao Agent, wife of Bana, mother of Gusa.

Lilān—ex-Rona-Abān, on the run from the RA, the Ronan Guard and the Agency. One person army. Explosives expert.

Marius Adarān—Tolān man captured by Fritz, held captive to fix the casino gaming machines.

Mena Malan—Leader of the Rona-Abān. Egomaniacal sociopath.

Naethan Amon—aka Father Owen. Rebel, ex-priest, ex-army. Agency spy.

Nalana Yen—15 year old street kid, healer and empath.

Nama Ree—Original Rebel. Younger brother of Krena Ree, grandson of the first Rebel leader Jerna Ree. Husband of Kala and childhood friend of Asha and Taelin Kān. Ex-Taskforce Agent.

Naomi—five year old Aranan girl, kidnapped by the RA.

Nick—Friend of Xak's. Mid-to-high rated Kinetic.

Old Ana—Crazy old Ronan lady, homeless. Time Psi Prophet.

Old Ren—aka Renada Yen. Original Rebel. High rated healer and the oldest Rebel. Only son of Isa Zuru, uncle to Nalana Yen.

Raen—Rebel, low rated Telepath, cleans out chimneys because he likes hot food that much.

Rahan Aria—unwilling Agency guard, high-rated Computer Talent and cousin of Toma Aria.

Rān and Ridān Ree—Original Rebels. Twin sons of Krena Ree.

Rega—psycho bully kid in the same desert training base as Xak and seems to have an obsession with killing/beating Xak.

Risa—leader of a small Rebel cell of Illegal Psis who raid places for Rebel supplies. Originally from the desert regions of Arana.

Taelin Kān—Asha Kān's older brother, best friends with Nama Ree and the Orignal Aranan Psi Rebels.

Tempa Kān—Asha Kān's baby girl.

Timān Beu—Hetera's baby son.

Tiras Malar—Ao Operative Agent, cousin to Kita Oran and Bana Malar. Triian Rena is his great aunt.

Tolan Enan—Original Rebel and high rated kinetic. Younger brother of Amana Enan.

Toma Aria—cousin of Rahan Aria. Dobid Cowdy's personal assistant.

Triian Rena—Ao Councilor in the Agency, one of the good ones.

Levi—friend of Xak's. Electromagnetic Talent.

Liz—friend of Xak's. High rated Kinetic.

Wolf Malar—Son of Dela Malar, the boy from Xak's vision. High rated Telepath, Empath and Time Psi.

Xakarii Kane—aka Xak. 15 year old boy trapped in a desert training base. High rated Time Psi, sees visions of Hawk.

———-

Jerna Ree—the first leader of the Aranan Psi Rebels, grandfather of Krena and Nama Ree.

Isa Zuru—Nalana's grandmother, Ren's mother. First generation Psi Rebel. Time Psi Prophet.

"Victory is not as simple to define as you'd expect. It's not just a case of win or lose. Sometimes, the greater the victory, the greater the loss in achieving it."
Toma Ree, Jerna's Father
Jerna Ree, the second leader of the
Aranan Psi Rebels
The Year of our Founder 2911

"My grandmother once told me that the Great Fates; the Great Guardians of Time, are weavers. What they weave is a huge unfinished tapestry that is Time, and each thread is one person and their lives. A Time Speaker is a thread that the Fates have put into the weaving deliberately to moderate those threads around them, and keep the tapestry from breaking apart. Through the Time Speakers flows the intention and power of the Fates.
Nalana Yen
The Year of our Founder 3004

Part One

19 Aracan 3000
City of Arām
Country of Arana
The planet Shadow

A cobbled ochre footpath led in curving spirals across the road and into the northern entrance of Star Mall. Waiting for the cross signal, Asha glanced warily up and down the street. There were neither cop cars nor Agency vehicles on the road, and no visible Blue Suit Agents on the footpaths either. It looked like just another normal autumn day in Arām. The traffic light buzzed above her and she stepped off the curb, crossing through the paved spirals to the mall entrance.

She touched the baby's back through the material of the maternal sling she wore. It was quite a risk for them to go into a public mall, especially unarmed, but it couldn't be helped. Baby Tempa needed a diaper change and feeding, and Asha couldn't do that in the street.

The automatic doors opened and as she stepped into the warmth, she looked around. Inside was busy and brightly colored. There were flashing screens everywhere advertising various name brand products, and people walking in all directions over the shiny stone floor. For a moment it was disorientating after the quiet coldness of the street.

To her right, an escalator rose up to the next level. On her left, the smells of coffee and food wafted towards her from a cafe and made her stomach grumble hungrily. Ahead of her, lines of clothes and shoe stores filled much of the mid distance, and further ahead, where the walkway curved out of sight, she saw a blue oval sign hanging from the ceiling with "Baby World" written on it in pink. Dodging shoppers, she strode towards the store while keeping a wary eye out for security.

As she neared the baby store she smiled. Lady Luck—Krena the Summer Patron—must be watching her back. In front of the store entrance, a wire specials basket held packs of diapers of all sizes—making them much easier for her to steal. And even better, some careless shopper had dropped a smaller sized pack on the ground.

Excellent, she thought.

Hooking the plastic-wrapped diaper pack with her shoe, she kicked it out of visual range of the counter and bent to grab it. As she stood upright again, she felt a wave of prickling static travel from her feet, up her spine and over the back of her skull, leaving in its wake a deep sense of dread and danger that pointed behind her.

Dropping the diaper pack and putting her hand over the baby's head protectively, she vaulted sideways over the middle aisle of seats and potted plants, and landed behind the cover of a large palm tree. There was a Blue Suit Agent and his weapon was already aimed.

With her "normal shopper" cover blown there was no reason to hold back. She kinetically gripped the palm tree in front of her, lifting it off the floor so that it hovered for a moment in the air between them. Using her rage to fuel the thrust, she threw it hard at the Agent. He fired his weapon and shattered the crockery base, but it wasn't enough to stop him from getting a two meter tall palm tree to the head. The Agent and plant fell back onto the stone floor. Dark earth was spread over the white marble and the man landed hard with his head at an odd angle.

She turned around, sprinting for the crowds of people at the entrance of a large department store. As she ran, she put her hand under the baby sling to touch Tempa's back and very gently ducked into her daughter's mind. It was sensible that she had to use a telepathic sleep program, but she still felt a little stab of guilt. If their lives weren't at stake, she wouldn't force her daughter to do or be anything except herself, but combat was no place for a young baby to be awake, least of all a sensitive untrained empath.

Asha headed through the store entrance. Inside the department store, crowds of people moved slowly with trolleys and children running around—all seriously complicating her ability to move quickly into the middle of the store. She got half the distance she would have, had the place been empty, before gunfire sounded behind her at the entrance. Asha ducked under the cover of shelving and glanced behind her.

In their panic to get out of the way, many distressed shoppers pushed uselessly against each other. Some fell, others clambered over the fallen and all half-blocked the entrance with chaos and civilian bodies.

Asha grinned. Agents weren't allowed to kill civilians, so this situation would complicate things for them. Turning away, she ran while adeptly dodging people and random displays, making a bee-line for the nearest wall and hopefully the staff exits. A weapon fired from behind and towels fell from a shelf right next to her head. She flinched and jumped sideways behind the cover of a tall metal display of white crockery platters.

Icy calm and focused, she waited.

She sensed two Blue Suits as they ran towards her— their fear made them easy to sense without looking. With such poor emotive control they had to be low rank Agents.

A playful smile twitched around the edges of her mouth. *Easy to take out,* she thought.

As they neared her location, she held the baby with one arm and gripped the top of the display with her free hand. Asha used her kinetic ability to lift her up, flipping sideways over the top shelf, and landed right between the two Agents. They cried out and stepped back in an attempt to fire their weapons, but not fast enough. She took one man's gun as she dumped him on the floor with a little twist of his wrist, and turned to throw a forceful palm blow to the second one's sternum with a satisfying crack.

The two Agents lay on the floor, both unconscious, defeated. For a moment she looked down at them. A dark expression drifted into her blue eyes. Lifting the Agent's weapon, she put a bullet in both of them. Dropping it next to their bodies, she continued her dodging sprint across the marble store floor.

She didn't get far before a store security guard ran towards her down the aisle with a stick in his hands. Without pausing for even a second, she disarmed him and, pulling the guard into a throw, she initiated a telepathic sleep program into his unprotected mind.

She shoved his half-conscious body onto a pile of towels out of the way and continued running.

Gunfire sounded to her left and she ducked right behind the cover of another tall metal shelf. Eyes flitted around her, frantically looking for an escape route and upon finding none, she looked above her.

Asha skipped up the levels of metal shelving using her kinetic ability, and flipped sideways onto the top shelf with her back close to the ceiling and baby still tucked carefully into the sling across her chest.

Careful not to knock the three meter tall shelving over as she changed her position, she hooked her fingers under a ceiling panel, lifted it and pulled herself into the roof space.

* 2 *

After clambering awkwardly with the baby through narrow roof-space access ways, Asha came out into the fresh air on the angled metal roof of the mall. Standing up in the wind and air, she paused to catch her breath. The wind was strong and tugged at the piece of string keeping her long hair out of her face. After a few good pulls, the wind got what it was after and the string flew up into the air. Her freed hair surrounded her in an ocean of curly black threads, flowing around her face and body as if she was under water. A smile twitched at the edges of her mouth; it was nice to have the wild air in her hair again.

She brushed her locks back from her face with one hand, and turned to look around her for a potential escape route. Of all the directions she could go, there was only one building close enough to the mall roof to jump, and it was on the back-end of the large building.

Letting go of her hair again, she ran the length of the sloped roof and leapt into the air with a carefully calculated kinetic push. It felt like she was flying for several seconds and then the next building's roof came up to meet her. Steadying the baby with one arm, she landed into a shoulder roll and flipped back up on her feet.

She stopped to catch her breath and telepathically sense out the nearest Blue Suit Agents. Some were very close below her, but they seemed to be traveling towards the mall and had not yet been ordered to set up a street cordon. That meant that they thought she was still inside and this was good.

A rusty fire escape ladder led down the building, into an alley hidden from the street. When her feet hit the concrete again, she knew instinctively that she had escaped this time. Despite this instinct, she wouldn't completely relax until she was far away—the Agency trained people to be persistent.

The alley was "T" shaped, to her left and right led out to the street and ahead of her, a long narrow space cut between two large buildings. Asha ran straight ahead.

She knew much of the alley system of Arām after being on the run for three months and she followed that knowledge. Instinctively shooting up and down narrow paths, cobbled lanes and driveways, and avoiding main streets and areas where there were cameras, she got as far away from the trouble as she could. The further she got from it, the calmer she became. Finally, several kilometers from the mall, her pace lessened to a walk.

She turned and entered a fairly long gap between two tall brick factory buildings.

Right, where to next? she thought.

She couldn't go and find the Rebels or her brother Taelin without the risk of bringing the Agency down on them, but this living on the street wasn't working either. They would send A2 assassins after her soon and that would be worse. There had to be some other way to survive this. Others had escaped the Agency from the high ranks and managed to survive—surely.

Still focused on her thoughts, she got within a meter of the alley exit and a male figure stepped inside from the street in front of her. She was forced to back up, just to keep from bumping into him. In the dimness, she didn't immediately recognize the face that stared across at her. When she did, she took a sharp in-breath and stepped back.

"No!"

"Asha, wait." His voice was gentle, almost a whisper. Behind him she heard the sounds of sirens, and a number of Agency vehicles shot past the alley at high speed.

When the street behind him was quiet, he spoke again. "I'm here to help you, Asha. You trusted me once, will you trust me now?"

Fighting her instinct to run again, she swallowed. "That was a long time ago."

"That's true," his voice was sad. "But I offer you and baby Tempa safety from the Agency in exchange for your help."

She snorted. "How could I possibly help you?"

"Do you remember where the Rebel building is located?"

"I'll not help you kill the last of them." She turned and strode away from him, but he followed after her. A firm hand grabbed her elbow, pulling her back around to face him. She wondered if she should risk putting him on his ass so she could get free, but then thought better of it.

His voice was still gentle. "No, that's not what I want. Will you please hear me out before you disappear?"

* 3 *

Taelin was sleeping, curled up in a ball in one corner of an empty, dusty apartment. His face twitched and fists clenched and unclenched under the stress of reliving the horrific memories of his past.

Sixteen years old, he sat under the kitchen table where his father had left him. The lacy decorative cloth covered the view of his surroundings completely. There was a terrible noise around him but Taelin couldn't think, he couldn't feel and couldn't move.

Gunshots. Screaming. Crying.

Then it all went silent for a very long time.

No thinking. No feeling. Just stillness and silence.

Sometime much later, a hand moved aside his mother's embroidered table cloth. Yellow-brown eyes came into view and someone spoke his name. The person touched his face with chilled fingers. Fear and grief flowed through their skin and into him. It hurt:

the touch hurt. Someone spoke but his mind could not understand the words.

There was a mental pop and he blinked.

"Taelin! Are you OK? Taelin?" Krena Ree was there, her square face covered in tears and her wide eyes were fearful.

Fighting against the silence in his mind, he lifted his arm from the floor and took her hand from his face.

"Please..." it was nearly impossible to speak, but he pushed through it. "Please, don't touch. It hurts."

Krena nodded and shuffled back so he could get out from under the table. There were puddles of blood on the kitchen floor, and people-shaped figures lay underneath the sitting-room throw rugs. He couldn't see his parents or his little sister.

He struggled again to speak. "Whe... where are they?"

"I'm sorry, Taelin. They took Asha. Your parents are dead." Tears lifted into her eyes.

He wondered why he couldn't feel anything. "What... what is wrong... with me?"

Krena sighed and shook her head. "I don't know, I think your dad did something to keep you safe—"

A noise sounded outside and they both looked towards the front hall. "We've got to go. I'm so sorry, young Taelin."

"Police! Open this door!"

Taelin jumped up, flinching violently out of his dream. He came to full consciousness as he landed on all fours, with his back to a corner and staring at the only door in the empty room. It took him several moments to remember where he was; it was a condemned apartment building. Many street kids lived in its unlocked rooms, and he had been lucky to get his own room away from the cluttered psychic noise of sharing personal space with others.

Outside his space, someone yelled fearfully and he craned his neck to listen. Numerous firecrackers popped downstairs and he tensed. It wasn't close enough to Winter Solstice for crackers. That had to be gunfire, which meant there were intruders in the building.

Could be Spades' slavers looking for street kids and Illegals. But if it isn't the Spades— mid-thought he stopped and listened again.

Someone was outside his room and, based on the deep sense of ill-ease that had suddenly dropped into his belly, he figured they were not friendly. He had to get out.

Being as quiet as he could on the bare wood floor, he crept towards the nearest window. There was a fire escape; if he could unlock the window he'd be able to get away.

Carefully, he fiddled with the old-fashioned turning clip-lock. Heavy footsteps came closer down the hall towards his door, and more gunfire sounded below him.

The lock slid out of place and he put his fingers under the window edge. But after a gentle pull, it didn't budge.

From across the room, he heard someone turning the door handle. There was no lock on his door, but there *was* a chain across it. The door opened stopping at the length of the chain, but thankfully they couldn't see him because of the angle of it. Through the gap in the door, he heard the sound of radio static and knew at that moment it wasn't Spades Slavers.

"This is the Agency! If you co-operate you will not be harmed!"

Taelin swallowed down his fear. He couldn't be captured and taken by the Agency, not like his little sister Asha. He'd rather die fighting like his parents, instead of being forced to become an Agent simply because he had Psi genes—and useless locked Psi genes at that.

Getting a better grip on the edge of the window, he pulled up with a quick and hopefully efficient yank. The window flew up and open. He rolled out onto the metal fire escape, slipping and half-falling onto the ladder. He released the rusty catch, and gripping the metal bar tightly, he and the ladder dropped down to a jolting stop.

He climbed to the bottom rung, let go and landed on the concrete below. Above him, there was a loud bang and he realized that the Agent must have broken through the door chain.

He looked around him at the narrow lane. Going down to the street would likely lead to their vehicles and armed Agents ready to corral him into custody. Up the lane looked like a dead-end, but there was a hidden path between buildings that led out to the next block over. If he could get there, it would be an easy unexpected escape route.

Turning, he started to sprint.

Gunfire sounded from above and bullets hit the concrete behind him. He flinched but kept running. At the end of the drive was a waist-high concrete fence, which he vaulted. Another volley of gunshots fired and as he passed into cover, he felt the impact of a bullet in his right shoulder.

Swearing, he stumbled but did not fall. The agonizing pain radiated through his back and right shoulder-blade into his lungs. The world spun nauseatingly, but he kept running. He had to get as far away as he could before he would rest. Agents were persistent chasers and if he didn't fully get away they would find him again—as they had others he'd known and lost on the streets. Taelin flew out through the narrow gap and crossed the street to the next alley.

Which direction should he go in now? He doubted that he could get the bullet out on his own. Even if he had the right equipment, agony wasn't conducive to sewing stitches in one's own skin. But, he didn't know any safe street doctors, and any official medical facilities were a one-way ticket to the Agency.

Heading in a southerly direction, he knew there was only one option; he had to try and get to the Rebels and to Ren, their healer.

Running up the next street around pedestrians, he searched for another alley or side access-way. He had to get under cover and stay under cover, as much as he could. There were government cameras everywhere, as well as cops.

The pain in his back was sharp and permeated him with every beat of his heart, but he stubbornly focused on his goal. This wouldn't be the end. It couldn't. Another alley presented itself to him and turning, he shot straight for it.

He ran for three blocks, zigzagging through narrow alleys and lanes before his feet started going numb.

Stumbling, but still upright, he passed into another lane and slowed his pace. He couldn't hear any Agency sirens nearby, so he figured it might be safe to slow down a little. Pushing off one wall with his hand, he kept moving towards the other end of the alley. It looked impossibly long and bent slightly sideways.

The world flipped around him like some demented roller coaster and he stopped to lean on the wall. It was too close to the Agents. He couldn't faint now, he had to keep going. He took a wobbly step, legs weakening under his weight, and he dropped slowly to the dirty concrete. Still fighting but losing, he kept his eyes open for as long as he could, even beyond his capacity to see any more. Finally, the pain and blood loss dragged him away from consciousness.

* 4 *

There was pain in Taelin's lungs. He coughed to shift the sensation, but only made it worse. A moan escaped and he opened his eyes to see fuzzy concrete in front of his nose. Someone had a hand on his back. The psychic chatter that came through their hand was nearly as overwhelming as the pain.

"What should I do? He might die but he could be dangerous." The touch on his back was prickled with shafts of static and slicing fear.

He moaned again and tried to move away from the hand. "Don't..." he mumbled. "Don't touch... it hurts..."

The hand lifted from his back and the psychic noise eased away, leaving only the pain of the bullet. A figure was crouched next to him and, as his sight cleared, it focused into a girl. She had deep brown eyes and long sandy hair that framed her almost heart-shaped face in messy uneven ringlets. The girl couldn't have been any older than fourteen or fifteen and she looked scared. But, with the rags she wore and the lack of shoes, she didn't look much like an Agent either.

Taelin smiled slightly. "Hi."

"Hello." The fear in her eyes lifted into the kindest smile he'd ever seen. "I," the smile dropped into a frown again. "What do I do? Should I find someone to call an ambulance?" There was an oddly familiar accent in her voice.

"No, don't." He lifted his left arm out from under him so he could use his elbow to push himself up. He remembered running, but he wasn't sure how far he'd gotten before he fell. He might be close to the Rebel building but he could be far away too. What he did know was that he was far too weak to get there on his own.

"Who... are you?" He felt stupidly drowsy and it made it hard to talk.

She seemed very unsure and this was reflected in the tiny voice that replied. "Nalana."

"Taelin." He frowned. "Shouldn't you be in school? There's no schools out here... not for ages."

"I... I had to run away... he was going to hurt me." Tears formed in her eyes. She was obviously scared of something, or someone.

He tried to smile. "So... you're in trouble too... huh?"

She nodded.

"Do you... know... how close the... Park is?"

She pointed down the alley. "It's not far, you can see it from the end."

"Other side of th' Park... are some friends of mine... they can help. We'll be safe there... for a while."

Her face tensed and he realized how dangerous it was for a stranger to ask a young girl to come home with him.

He smiled. "How 'bout... could ya help me... get to them?"

A burning shaft of pain stabbed through his body. He groaned and closed his eyes to ride it out. A warm hand touched his back and this time he had enough focus to block her psychic feedback from his mind. Through her touch, he felt a heat push into the pain. His breathing became easier and the agony in his back lifted into a much duller throb.

She must be a healer like Ren. But not as strong.

"How far from the Park are your friends?"

Leaning his head and good shoulder on the brick wall, he rested for a moment.

"Two blocks."

The girl stepped around him and offered a hand to help him stand up. Using the wall under his shoulder and her offered hand, he very slowly edged himself upright. She lifted his good arm around her shoulders, but this time her touch wasn't painful at all. She'd created an empathic wall between them.

As they walked out towards the street, he tried not to lean on her too much, but the world kept spinning slowly sideways and she was the only thing that was steady.

"Are your friends psychic too?"

A weak smile lifted the edges of his mouth. "Why... do you think I'm... a Psi?"

"Because you can block emotions, I felt it before. It's no wonder it hurts when someone touches you... all that sensitivity only in your skin. It took me years to learn how to block and I still can't do it very well... so... are they psychic too?"

He would've laughed had he been able. "They're... the Psi Rebels... so.... yes?"

They left the alley and stepped into a bright sunlit street. Squinting in the glare and sudden heat, he wondered when the day had gotten so hot. The nearby road traffic seemed to spin oddly around him and he fought with the vertigo in his head. Nalana lifted an arm around his waist to support him. With the movement, he felt a wetness down much of his back that could only be blood. He wondered how much he'd lost and he hoped it wasn't too much.

In a long gap of traffic, they shuffled slowly across the road and into the north-west corner of the partially forested City Park. The moment they came under trees, blessedly, the light dimmed and the temperature dropped down again.

Swaying slightly, the two of them walked for a short distance in between the massive park trees. He could barely see or lift his legs. A wave of nausea added another spinning motion to his perceptions and he felt heavy all of a sudden. Stopping, he put a hand on the trunk of a tree and closed his eyes for a moment.

"Wait..."

The pain in his shoulder and back seemed to fade from him a little. His legs started to give way and Nalana spoke, but his mind couldn't process the words. Then, dragging her with him, he dropped onto his hands and knees. There were tree roots in front of him and he put his hand on the wood, trying to gain more of a sense of reality, but it didn't seem to be working. She got out from under his arm and helped him lie on his side with his back against the tree roots.

"Taelin," her voice sounded desperate. "Where are your friends?"

"Other side of the Park," he panted. "Two blocks... after the playground... turn left," his eyes closed and he felt a warm hand on his face. "Metal doors..."

"Hold on," she continued to speak, but the sounds flowed over him as he spun slowly away.

His last thought was of eleven years ago: his little sister, Asha, only ten, in his arms and weeping. *"I didn't mean to hurt him! He just made me so mad!"*

* 5 *
At about the same time
Psi Rebel Building

Hilla brushed sadly at the messy strands of black hair around her wife's sleeping face. Krena Ree sounded like she was breathing through a tiny straw half-submerged in water; all bubbly and strained. She'd aged so much over the months of her illness. She was only thirty-seven, but now looked twenty years older.

Sunlight flowed through the floor-to-ceiling windows on two sides and heated the broad room around them just nicely. Behind her, the three youngest of the Rebel children filled the room with nearly constant laughter as they played "FLY ME" with young Tolan, who was a very strong kinetic. Adding a mischievous undertone to the joyous laughter, the two eldest children, Krena's twin teenage boys were huddled in the corner whispering and giggling—likely plotting their next practical joke on someone.

It was nice to hear the innocent (and not so innocent) laughter of the Rebel children, because it took the edge off the aching pain all of the adults were feeling. Sitting on the floor at Krena's feet, Tolan's big sister, Amana, looked up over her book and gave Hilla a pained expression.

Hilla swallowed and answered with a gentle smile. They all knew that Krena was dying, even before Ren told them. It was just a matter of time now.

A cold wind brushed past her, sending sharp prickles over her skin through the threadbare pants she wore. Someone murmured nearby and she stepped around Krena's cot towards the noise. Old Ren lay asleep on the floor with his back to the sun lit windows. His face twitched as if he was dreaming.

"Someone's at the door..." Ren grumbled, still asleep.

Next to him on the cot, with her words barely understandable between wheezes, Krena spoke as well. "Hil... la... get... the... door..."

Hilla stared at the two of them in surprised fear, and for a moment, she trembled in the grip of something cold and terrifying.

Amana got to her feet and asked what was going on.

Hilla looked at her, about to reply that she didn't know, but from the direction of the bathrooms there was a bang and someone swore. She swallowed back the odd sensation in her extremities and shook her head. Whatever it had been it was nothing. She made her way across the room towards the bathroom doors and called out.

"Are you OK, Brān?"

The old man stepped through the bathroom door and frowned at her. "Hilla, something's going on. There's a woman coming to our door and she needs to talk to you."

She blinked at him. "Wh... What?"

"Someone's at the door. They're here to talk to you and it's really important that you listen."

The noise in their vast living room silenced, and the creepy feeling she'd had before settled into her toes and fingers.

She shivered involuntarily. "Who... who is she? What does she want? Is she here now?"

"I don't know those things," he shook his head, scratching at his graying brown hair with one hand. "Just that there is a woman coming to talk to you, and what she has to say is important. The static wave was so strong it knocked me off the toilet."

The image of grizzled old Brān falling off the toilet, flashed across her mind. She managed to suppress the laugh, but not the smile.

He lifted one gray eyebrow at her and a wordless apology rose from out of her smile.

He sighed. "She'll be here soon, if she isn't already outside waiting. What do you want to do?"

Turning to face the others, she quickly fired off orders. "Tolan, put Jena down, I might need you. Amana, want to come down with me too? Everyone else, stay here." She turned to glare at Krena's twin teenage boys across the room. "And I'm serious you two! Stay here until you're given the all-clear. No games! Got it?" She used a pointed finger to emphasize her seriousness.

"Yes, Hilla." Their voices chorused together with that recognizable undertone of mischief. She knew they'd do as they were told, but she still gave them a stern look before turning away.

She, Amana and Tolan walked down to the base of the stairs, through the L-shaped hallway, past their barred prisoner cell, and into the dim ground floor area. She stopped a few meters in front of their metal entrance doors and waited apprehensively.

"What's going on?" Krena's younger brother Nama came out of the hall behind them, his deep voice echoed in the high roof. He must have been in one of the storage rooms.

"Someone's a—"

A double rap on the small wooden door-panel interrupted her explanation.

Nobody moved for several seconds. Hilla wasn't even sure if she wanted to answer it. There was a sigh and, ever the blunt let's-get-stuff-done person, Amana walked to the entrance and unlocked one of the metal doors. She opened it wide and lifted her weapon to aim it at the new arrival.

Hilla stepped forward to see the woman who stood there. A baby was strung across her front in a faded blue sling. The woman was tall, with long curly black hair that fell around her face and down her back, and she wore dark clothing. Her deep blue eyes spoke of wariness and apprehension, but also relief as if she recognized them.

"Um," she cleared her throat. "I am unarmed. I'm Asha Kān, and I have a message for Hilla Norman from a man called Hawk."

* 6 *
Across town in the Agency Tower building

Hiran waited at the ground floor entrance to Engineering. Around her, the spartan white-walled hallway was quiet of people and nothing seemed amiss.

Ana turned the corner and their eyes locked. Hiran brushed a stray thread of black hair behind one ear and grinned at her beautiful friend.

Ana smiled, lightening her blue eyes.

Hiran lifted her black neoprene laptop bag. "You got them?"

"Yes." Ana opened her fist, revealing the large ring of her mother's Engineering department keys hanging from her thumb.

Hiran brushed the laptop bag-straps over one shoulder and turned to watch as Ana unlocked the door. She walked after Ana, out of the crisp clean administration level of whites, blues and yellows, and into rough dark tunnels of rusted piping, dripping water and the occasional grease-covered engineer.

She followed Ana down a set of curving metal stairs, their footsteps echoed up into the high roof which also serviced one set of elevator shafts. A man in orange coveralls walked past them, a massive wrench resting over his broad shoulders. He tipped a yellow hard hat at Ana as they passed each other.

"Hey, Jon." Ana responded, sounding so very calm. Hiran was jealous that her friend could act so cool and collected on the day they were going to escape the Agency.

Hiran followed into a wide tunnel that had once been a sewer. The round walls were painted a rusted cream color, but where the paint dipped into the outlines of brick underneath, black stone showed through wide water-damaged cracks. Ana leaned back and took Hiran's hand.

"Be careful, the floor is slippery here."

In one section of the long curving tunnel there was a string of blown light-bulbs. They walked around a curve into the dimness and for a number of moments Hiran was in absolute darkness, with only the touch of Ana's hand in hers to know that anything else existed in that pitch black. They turned a corner, and the glow of artificial lights illuminated her way again.

Coming to a set of concrete stairs, Ana let go of her hand and jogged down, around to the next level below. It was level four of the basement and it was on this floor that neither of them were allowed to be. It was there that any trouble could snowball into both of them being caught and executed for treason.

At the base of the stairs, a long concrete hall led in both directions. Oblong lights sat on the concrete walls at head-height, like giant yellow glow worms.

Ana turned right and Hiran followed. At the very end of the corridor was a steel door that led to a disused furnace room. The building had long since had its environmental control system upgraded to the modern solar units, but the workers had forgotten to take out the old furnaces and the rooms which housed them. The abandoned space would give Hiran enough time to hack a particular electronic lock, and then they'd be free of the Agency.

Wires and piping filled the space above Hiran's head as they walked and a fan throb pulsed through the air from the older conditioning system.

Men's voices came towards them. She stiffened and looked behind her—it was too far to run back to the stairs. Ana grabbed her by the arm and pulled her sideways out of sight into an alcove lined with gray Psi suppressant concrete.

Hiran closed her eyes and willed the men not to see them. She squeezed Ana's hand, trying to tell her that even if they were caught and killed very soon, she was glad to face it with her. The voices came closer and the two of them huddled further to the corner trying to make themselves as thin as possible. Soon the men would pass where they were hiding and the Psi suppressant materials in the concrete would no longer shield them from being detected.

Ana lifted her lips to Hiran's ear and whispered. "I have an idea, just go with it."

Hiran frowned, about to ask 'go with what' when their lips met. She felt a strong arousal flow like water from Ana into her, and she breathed in sharply through her nose, with what would have been a gasp had her mouth been free. Ana's slightly cold hands lifted the hem of her blouse out of her skirt, and traced a tingling line from the skin of her waist towards her bra line. Hands plunged up into her bra and brushed very sensitive skin. Hiran shivered.

She understood that Ana was using her empath ability to make her feel aroused. She also realized that Ana was doing it to cover their fear. Kissing her back, Hiran un-tucked Ana's blouse from her pants and copied her actions. The kiss swallowed Hiran in an ocean of wondrous sensation for many moments, hands brushing sensitive skin and sending shivers of pleasure up her spine.

A call of surprise broke her sharply out of it and she opened her eyes. The two men had walked past and immediately seen what they were doing. Hiran blushed, not sure if she was supposed to have enjoyed that quite as much as she had.

Ana turned to look sideways at them. The change in expression in the two men suggested they recognized the four gold pins in her uniform lapel, and that she outranked their five and six pins.

"Could you give us some privacy please?"

The younger of the two men blushed and turned away. The elder looked confused for a moment, but followed his companion. When the men got to the end of the hall and turned out of sight, Ana looked back at her with a playful smile.

"That was close. Come on, let's get to the furnace room."

Hiran nodded. Mischief lifted one corner of her smile as she bit her bottom lip.

When they got to the door, Ana unlocked it with her Engineering Master keys and they stepped through. The warm dry air that met them reminded her of her mother's attic.

The dry heat and scents of metal and wood dust filled the air, and an uncovered light bulb lit the sparse oblong room with a barely adequate yellow glow.

Hiran set herself up on the dusty concrete floor in the middle of the room. She placed her laptop on its neoprene bag and took it out of sleep-mode with a single key touch.

The lock she needed to hack was for the second door in the room. It was a fire-door, permanently locked under several layers of security. The Agency had blocked it off because on the other side of it was an open path directly out of the building—a bad thing when you want to keep people in.

Her laptop beeped and asked for her login code, which she supplied. The screen went blank for a moment and then blue. In the middle of the blue a short note was typed in grey text, it held there for a few moments, and then flickered away to her main loading screen. She frowned at her computer. That wasn't supposed to happen.

"What's wrong?"

She looked up at Ana. Her fear and confusion were interrupted by thoughts of kissing her and how good it felt. She smiled impishly at Ana.

Amusement played in the edges of Ana's smile. "If you want we can explore that later. But, for now can we focus. What's wrong?"

Hiran swallowed. "Someone's gotten into my computer and left a post-login message saying to 'check the paint can'."

Ana lifted one hand to her hip. "Paint can? Is it an error? Should we abort?"

"I don't know." Hiran looked around the room, wondering what they should do. But, then she saw to the left of the exit, on the floor behind Ana and tucked away, was a paint can—one of the big ones.

A shot of fear flickered in her and she pointed. "Paint can."

Ana turned towards it and knelt down. Her hands came out of the tin and brought up a gun with a yellow sticky note on it.

The door in front of her opened, and Hiran didn't even have time to yell out. A security guard stepped in and lifted his weapon. It was obvious to him that she wasn't where she should be, and therefore she must be a traitor trying to escape. She knew exactly what came after this and closed her eyes.

A weapon fired but she felt no impact. Hiran opened one eye cautiously. The guard lay face-down on the ground, and Ana stood over him with the gun still aimed at his back.

In her shock, Hiran just blinked at her. Ana stepped over the guard's body and handed her a sticky-note. Written across the yellow paper, in tidy curling handwriting was: *"Jaran Cowdy AoCo112, 067152"*

"Will that open the door?" Ana asked quietly.

Hiran blinked at the sticky in surprise and laughed. "An Ao-level security login? So'then yes! No hacking required with that."

"Good, we need to hurry. The absence of that guard will set off an alarm soon."

Hiran's fingers flickered expertly across her keyboard. Windows opened and closed on her screen as she quickly shifted through the many systems masking the unlock command. It could all be a trap but they didn't have a choice now they'd killed someone. She put in the login codes and pressed enter.

Another window flicked up to tell her who "Jaran Cowdy" was, and the information made her heart skip a beat. "Hai di'chena!"

The fire escape door clicked, and stuffing her computer back into its neoprene bag, she got to her feet quickly. "We have to get out of here now. That code—"

On the other side of the fire door was a very dark, empty car-parking lot. Across the darkness was their escape.

Pausing in the doorway, Hiran swallowed. "That code wasn't just some random Ao Agent."

Ana started to run into the darkness. "Who was it?" she said over her shoulder.

Hiran followed. "The Head of the Ao Council."

Ana stopped mid-step to look at her in utter shock. "We'd better get out of here soon. If we get caught our deaths will not be quick."

Gunfire sounded from behind them and they both flinched.

"Run!" yelled Ana.

The fire escape door was one of those proper ones with a metal bar across the width of it that opened out onto the street. Together they sprinted for it, hit the bar and suddenly met sunlight and free air. There wasn't time to enjoy it. Unfortunately, they had to keep running.

* 7 *
Rebel Base

Hilla Norman stood with the two men either side of her. In front of Hilla, standing in the doorway, was Amana with her weapon aimed at the new arrival.

The woman stared back at three of them with a confused and fearful frown on her face. She cleared her throat again. "I am Asha Kān," she spoke louder, with more confidence. "I need to talk to Hilla Norman."

Swallowing, Hilla stepped forward. "I... I'm Hilla."

The last time any of them had seen Asha Kān she'd been a child and taken by the Agency, so her appearance could mean a number of different things—few of them good.

Asha warily eyed the weapon in her face, before her dark blue eyes lifted to Hilla. Asha looked very much like her mother had before she was killed, so, Hilla had no doubt that she really was Asha Kān, what she wasn't sure about were her intentions.

"I've been instructed to ask if you would agree to meet with Hawk."

Hilla frowned. "Who is Hawk?"

She seemed to choose her words carefully. "He says he wants to help the Rebels fight the Agency and survive what is to come."

"I... I don't understand, what's going on?"

Asha shook her head. "I don't know much myself. I only know that he'd like to meet with you and that he has guaranteed your safety."

Feigning confidence, Hilla put a hand on one hip. "And why didn't he come here himself? Why use you?"

"He wants to keep his identity a secret." Her voice was quiet and Hilla sensed a snippet of fear, but couldn't see what had triggered it.

"So, what?" Amana, re-gripping her weapon tensely, sounded cynical. "We're just supposed to trust him, and do what he demands because of what you and your parents meant to the Rebels?"

Hilla sensed confused fear in Asha and her deepening frown mirrored this. "I... no, you misunderstand me. He's not demanding anything. He's simply asking to meet her. She can say no and I'll go back and tell him."

Asha flinched as if she'd been bitten and looked behind her. A girl, perhaps thirteen or fourteen years old stood on the pavement.

"Um... hi," the girl stepped inside and glanced nervously at Amana's weapon. "D... do you know Taelin? He's hurt and needs help."

"I'll get Ren." Behind Hilla, Nama spun around and ran back up the hall to the stairs.

In the doorway, Asha looked sideways at the girl. "Is Taelin alright?"

"Um... I'm not sure, he's been shot and I can't carry him." The girl stared wide-eyed at those gathered in the doorway and locked eyes with Hilla. "Are you really the Psi Rebels?" She was frightened, but Hilla sensed she was also a little excited, as if they were celebrities to her. The girl had no empathic trace of being an Agent—she was far too open to be a spy.

A smile broke out on Hilla's face. "Yes, we are."

"Can I," fear flickered in the girl's dark eyes, "join you?"

Behind Hilla, came the sound of running and Nama shot back out through the hallway towards them with Ren in tow.

"Tolan," he flicked his head and the boy next to her stepped in behind him. At the door, Nama turned to give her a firm yellow-eyed glare. "Don't you go anywhere until I get back." Then Nama led the small group out of sight.

There was only Hilla, Amana and Asha left standing in the doorway. Looking back at their new arrival, Hilla wondered what she should do now. As far as she could empathically sense, Asha seemed to be the person they had all known as a child. There was no feeling of hostility or threat in her, and Hilla was certain that if Asha had been a threat to them she wouldn't have brought her baby with her. Upon realizing that it was likely she wasn't a threat, Hilla's instincts of hospitality insisted that if she wasn't a threat, then she was family, and she should let this woman inside.

"Please come in, Asha. Let's go upstairs. Are you hungry?"

Some of the tension lifted from Asha's face, revealing a genuine smile. "Thank you. I don't remember the last time I ate."

Hilla led Asha down the hall and up to the second floor. When they got to the top of the stairs, a room full of wide curious eyes stared tensely back at them.

"Everybody, this is Asha Kān, she's Taelin's younger sister. Ella, could you make some tea and see if we have any maka bread left?"

Asha walked slowly into the center of the room and stood there looking around her. There was a sense of peace in the woman, as if perhaps she was returning home again. When she turned around, Asha was smiling broadly.

A grin lifted into Hilla's face and she indicated the floor with one hand. "Please, pull up a floor."

They sat facing each other. The others crowded around them, close enough to hear and watch, but far enough away so that if this visitor was a threat they could scatter quickly. Amana sat to Hilla's left, with her gun placed obviously in her lap to let their guest know that they weren't completely trusting of her, no matter who she used to be.

With a tense sigh, Hilla looked up into Asha's oval face. "So, let's start again. This Hawk person wants to meet with me and he's sent you as his messenger?"

Asha nodded.

"Do you know what he wants to talk about?"

"No, he didn't tell me much of anything." Her voice was quiet, but Hilla sensed no deception—Asha believed what she was saying.

Amana snorted. "Then how do you know he doesn't want to kill Hilla?"

"He gave me his word." Asha's voice was calm and firm.

Amana made a scoffing noise, which was silenced immediately by Krena calling out from her cot. "Hil..la."

"Excuse me a moment." She got to her feet and when she reached her love, Krena's light brown eyes were open. A weak smile twitched at the edges of her mouth.

"Abe Kashān, Krena Ree?" The dark-haired Asha stood next to her.

"Yes, she's—"

"Hilla, go with Asha." Krena's mental voice was very weak, but clear even though Hilla wasn't a telepath.

She frowned at her. "Why?"

"Twenty years ago, Seda Kān said that a man called Hawk would come. He said his children would help this man destroy the Agency and save us."

"Dad said that?"

Hilla shook her head. "But, Krena, I don't understand—"

The wheezing was getting worse and Krena's eyes were closing again. *"Hilla... go... with... her."*

* 8 *

Taelin lay on his side under an ancient tree with its spreading root system splayed around him as if he'd been there forever. With a ball of fear stuck in his throat, Nama ran to his old friend and knelt down. There was an obvious bullet wound through the right shoulder of Taelin's black leather jacket. His skin was cool to the touch and there was no response from him at all. Leaning over, Nama put an ear to his chest. Taelin's breathing and heart beat were very slow and weak.

"Abe Kashān."

"Is he—"

"No," interrupting Tolan's question, he glanced up over his shoulder at the boy. "He's bad off but still breathing."

Old Ren knelt down next to him. "Help me turn him over so we can get a look at this wound."

He and Ren gently shuffled Tae onto his stomach and took one arm out of his jacket. A lot of blood stained his shirt down much of his back, but it was an otherwise fairly clean injury with no evidence of additional damage. Ren placed his hands either side of the wound and closed his eyes.

Taelin's breathing normalized and his body seemed to relax. A further few seconds later, a fairly un-mangled bullet lifted out of the wound and rolled onto the ground. Behind them, the girl let out a surprised gasp.

"Nama, he's lost a lot of blood," Old Ren's violet gray eyes were tense. "We need to get him back as soon as possible."

Together, they put Taelin's jacket back over the wound. With one hand resting on Taelin's arm, Nama looked sideways at young Tolan. "You think you can carry him so he looks like a drunk?"

The leggy sixteen-year-old laughed. "No problem."

The boy could kinetically lift a fuel tanker without breaking into a sweat so carrying Taelin wasn't a problem. The difficulty came from having to be subtle in public places. If they looked like a group of friends helping their drunken mate get back home, it would avoid having to fight their way through an Agency Task Force because some frightened civilian rang the hotline.

Nama helped the boy lift Tae onto his shoulder. Once Tolan had him in the correct position they started slowly back across the City Park towards home.

Ren fell into a rear-guard position, and Nama walked in front with the girl. She was shy and quiet, but at the same time the shyness seemed to be a defense mechanism and not a lacking in confidence.

Nama put a gentle hand on her shoulder to get her attention. "So, what's your name, kid?"

She looked sideways up at him and in the sunlight he saw a slightly red-purple undertone to the deep brown of her eyes. "Nalana Yen. What about you?"

"Nama. Nama Ree."

Her eyes widened. "Are you related to Jerna Ree?"

He smiled. "Yep, he was my grandfather. Heard of him?"

"Of course! My nan used to tell me stories about him and the first Rebels. They were heroes."

"So, you wanna join us to become a hero too, huh?"

She shrugged. "Naw, just wanna be safe. Couldn't be safer than with the Rebels."

"Well, you'll be fine for a while as our guest, but it's not my place to say whether you can stay or not. Hilla and my sister are the leaders of the Rebels, not me."

They walked over a grassy rise, and down towards the playground in the south-west corner of the Park. There were two blocks to go and they'd be home again. He wondered if Hilla would listen to him and stay in the base, or be defiant and make the decision without him.

Probably the latter, he thought cynically.

They came around a pair of wooden seats to see Amana running towards them.

"Nama!" Her mental voice was loud in his head, and he screwed up his face from the sudden sharpness of it. "Nama! Hilla's gone with Asha. I couldn't stop her."

"What?"

He stared at her and the tension on her rounded face tightened.

He lifted an eyebrow at her. "What else is wrong?"

The others walked past them, as Amana handed him a little yellow slip of paper. It read:

"Two Agency escapees will die soon unless Nama goes to the corner of Tara and Hiran Streets,
-Hawk"

A deep wary sigh escaped him. "You take them home, I shouldn't be long." He took one long last look at Taelin and his other family members, and sprinted east towards the roadside.

* * * * *

Nama didn't like being sent on errands for other people, especially when he suspected that the errand was engineered to keep him distracted and out of the way. If it was anything else he would have ripped up the note, but escaping the Agency was difficult at the best of times. If they were real escapees they would need real help.

As he got onto Hiran Street and continued sprinting north up the four-lane road, he heard a number of gunshots echo down towards him. The gunshots could easily be some Spades gunfight, but it could also be the escapees in trouble. It was only one more block north and as he neared the oddly abandoned intersection, he slowed his pace.

In the middle of the road a blue-suit Agent stood over two kneeling women. Nama walked onto the road towards them and lifted his weapon. The tall skinny Agent didn't react to his nearness at all, but one of the women stared wide-eyed at Nama over the gun in her face. Terror shifted to a silent plea in her eyes.

Nama made his voice sound very harsh. "Drop your weapon."

The Agent didn't move except to glance sideways at him. "This is Agency business. Go away."

Nama sighed. "Your funeral."

The bullet hit the man in the back slightly off-center between his shoulder blades. He let out a pained wheeze and crumpled to the concrete. Approaching his body, Nama picked up the Agent's weapon, flicked the safety and put it in his pocket.

He glanced down at the two women. "You two heard of a guy called Hawk?"

The closer of the two women shook her head, her gray eyes were wide.

"Well, then, d'you know anything about this?" He lifted the yellow sticky-note and showed it to them.

Surprised, they both got to their feet.

The gray-eyed woman lifted another yellow sticky-note from a pocket in her pants and handed it to him. Written across the paper in the same handwriting as his note, was an A0-level pass code.

Nama lifted an eyebrow at it. Whoever this Hawk person was, he sure knew how to engineer an escape.

"Come on then." He indicated with a throw of his head that they should follow him, and turned back the way he'd come.

A taller blond woman matched pace with him on one side. "I'm Ana."

"Nama."

The second woman stepped up on the other side of him. "Hiran. Do you know—"

"No, I don't know anything. Let's just get off the street first." He really needed to get back home as soon as possible to check on Taelin and start searching for Hilla.

This Hawk person better not hurt her, he thought darkly.

The road onto which their building entrance faced was long and wide. A hundred years ago the street had been crowded with working factories and other businesses, but there was only one factory still operating in South Docks, and that was five blocks up the road towards the city center. Every other building had been demolished or boarded up and abandoned. Rubbish spiraled about on the breeze that blustered around them. At random intervals down the street they passed cars that had been dumped on the side of the road, then stripped and burnt down to the metal. One could almost film a zombie movie on their street—it felt that dead and abandoned.

Carving a lazy diagonal line across the road, he headed towards the big metal factory doors of their building. Nama sensed the twin's mental chatter reach out to him before they opened the front door. Two young faces grinned mischievously at him through the gap, and he smiled at them.

"I'm sure that isn't my two nephew's breaking the rules!" he called out playfully.

"Rules say we can't go outside without someone else—"

"You're out here, uncle!"

Laughing, he pushed the door open and stepped inside. As he walked past them, he messed their dark hair affectionately. "Is Hilla back?"

"Naw," they both said in unison.

"Boys, this is Hiran and Ana. These two bundles of mischief are my sister's kids, Rān and Ridān. Come in." He closed and locked the door behind them and the two women looked uncertain, but he gave them a welcoming smile. "Come on upstairs and I'll introduce you to the other Rebels, then I've got to go find my wayward cousin."

* 9 *

The day was sunny and warm. Had Hilla not been so nervous, she would have enjoyed the three block walk with Asha through the mostly abandoned industrial area of South Docks. They turned off the street and down a driveway, entering the side door of a small wooden warehouse.

Inside, jagged dusty rays of sunlight reached through the shattered and dirty panes of glass above them, illuminating rubble on the concrete floor in odd flickering lines. Immediately above her head, running along the wall opposite the windows, was a rusty metal gangway. With no obvious access ladder, the useless gangway connected a series of small rooms above them, their doors open, some half off their hinges, revealing empty broken spaces that may have once been offices.

In the middle of the downstairs area on the bare dusty concrete sat a fairly modern-looking office chair. Asha led her to it, indicated that she was to sit down and once Hilla was seated, she crouched in front of her in the dust.

The younger woman gave her a gentle smile. "You can't look at him, Hilla. You have to look at me. It's dangerous for you to see Hawk's face, do you understand?"

She sensed that Asha meant she would be killed if she knew who he was, and her heart skipped a beat. She nodded slowly—it was too late to back out now. Behind her, she felt a presence and obediently kept her eyes to the front. Feet brushed on the dusty floor and Asha looked over Hilla's shoulder at someone as they approached.

The man had a distinctly blue empathic signature. His energy pulsed and burred in a strangely excitable way, even though she felt that he was also very calm. A warm hand settled on her shoulder and she fought her body's instinct to flinch.

"Thank you for coming, Hilla," his voice was deep and calm, almost gentle. "I have invited you here because I have a proposition to make, and I'd like you to hear me out before you make your decision. Do you think that's fair?"

Hilla found it difficult to keep her eyes on Asha, but she nodded. "Yes."

"From this day on, there will be a sequence of events that will end with the total annihilation of the Rebels by the Agency. To survive what is to come, the Rebels need greater numbers and a different strategy. They also need a Time Psi leader who can see what will happen, so that the Rebels can avoid as much of this damage as possible. I offer myself as that leader."

She made a noise of surprise and opened her mouth to speak, but he interrupted her.

"I need you to hear me to the end, Hilla. I think once you see what I'm going to show you, you'll change your mind. But I do promise that as the new leader I will do everything in my power to protect the Rebels—however large their numbers get." The man shuffled his feet and put his other hand on her shoulder.

"Asha?" His voice was barely a whisper.

Asha leaned forward on the ground and took Hilla's hands, as if in comfort. Her dark blue eyes were firm, but not at all afraid. "He's going to show you something telepathically and using Time Psi energy, so you're going to feel nauseous and probably as if your skin is itchy or cold, but don't panic and don't fight it because he might accidentally hurt you. So, Hilla, please relax, OK?"

Nodding, Hilla closed her eyes in an effort to calm her quick panicked breathing. She knew what kind of damage a telepath could do to a non-telepathic mind if they fought against an intrusion.

She felt it the moment he ducked into her mind. It was like a pressure in the back of her head and in her temples; a pressure that kept getting heavier. Something clicked and an icy wind flowed over her body through her clothing. It felt so much like the sensation from earlier and she realized it meant that whatever this was, it was bigger than just her and her family.

Another click sounded in her mind and images flashed past her eyes. She knew instinctively that these were of events in the future. They came quickly, flickering across her vision, and as one sequence ended another started. Those she loved were one by one hunted down, tortured and then killed by the Agency. Tears started to run down her face and she whimpered in distress. The final image was of Nama cornered and shooting madly at those who had trapped him. He was gunned down. The images stopped abruptly and she was back in the warehouse. It felt like her ears were ringing for a moment, but from the inside of her skull.

Behind her, his voice was very gentle and sad. "That is what will happen if you say no. Let me show you what we can do together."

The icy wind hit her skin again and she shivered. The second set of images was powerfully vivid, and she sensed the man's deep hope that this was the future that would come into being and not the first. What she saw was amazing. Over a sequence of many years the Rebel numbers expanded exponentially into hundreds, possibly even thousands across all of Arana. Images flashed of people escaping from various Agency buildings, and then together, later as a unified army fighting back against the Agency.

All of the images culminated at a massive explosion that ripped out of the Agency Tower building several stories above the road. She heard the thundering boom above her of the explosion and the sounds of falling glass hitting concrete like little bells. There was a mental pulse and she found herself back in the dusty warehouse free of his mental pressure.

She laughed. "You can actually win against the Agency?"

"Together, we have a better chance at it. I can not guarantee a total victory because the future is not set. But, yes, I will do my best to help the Rebels defend themselves and free others."

She sensed under the genuine intention of his promise that there was more to it than just helping the Rebels. "What is it you want in return?"

"You're a quick one, Hilla Norman." There was a smile in his voice. "Sometime in the future I will call upon the Rebels to help me with something much bigger. Until then, all I ask is that the Rebels trust me and follow my orders. I will do everything in my power to keep as many of you alive as possible."

Looking up at Asha, Hilla squeezed the younger woman's hand. "Do *you* trust him, Asha?"

The woman nodded. Hilla sensed fear and worry from her, but underneath that she did indeed seem to trust this man—whoever he was.

The hands on her shoulders pulsed with that icy energy again and he sighed. "I'm sorry, we've run out of time here, Nama is searching for you and it isn't safe for him to meet me yet." He lifted his hands from her shoulders. "I'll give you until midnight to think about it. Asha, let me know when a decision is made."

"Yes, Sir."

* 10 *

Taelin looked a lot like Asha remembered. Even at sixteen he had been strong and mature, so much like their father. But now he looked old—old and world-weary. She wondered what his life had been like while she was in the Agency. His messy black hair was peppered with gray, and there was an unusual crease in his forehead just above his eyebrows as if he concentrated too much all the time. At twenty-seven, surely, he wasn't old enough to start getting wrinkles?

He just looks so tired.

A little pained smile crossed her face, she wanted so much to touch his cheek and stroke his hair, to wake him up so she could talk to him and introduce him to his little niece, Tempa. They had been so close as children and it was wonderful to see him again, despite the circumstances.

Taelin lay on his side near the windows. Old Ren sat behind him showing the girl how to stitch up the gunshot wound in Tae's back. Asha stood at a distance watching her brother's sleeping face.

The second floor of the old Rebel building was quiet. The children were playing downstairs, others were out collecting food from the various gardens they tended, and Krena's cot had been moved closer to the heating vent across the room to ease her breathing while she slept. It was oddly comforting to be back in Rebel company.

"Asha?"

She turned, and behind her at the top of the stairs stood Hilla, who fiddled with something in her hands.

"Tell Hawk that I'll do it." She swallowed tensely. "I'll hand over the leadership of the Rebels to him."

"OK." Asha nodded. "The first thing he wants is for me to bring Jerna Ree's notebook to him."

Hilla's faced dropped into an expression of horror, as if she had asked for one of the moons or even one of the children.

Asha smiled and put a hand on Hilla's arm. "I promise, he'll keep it safe and I'll see if we can return it as soon possible. Can I ask what changed your mind?"

"This." Hilla handed her a sealed envelope that was faded and yellow with age. On the front, written in an older-style handwriting was one word: *"Hawk."*

Asha gaped at it. "How old is this? Where did it come from?"

"Krena told me it was written fifty years ago by Ren's mother, Isa, before her and her husband left the Rebels."

Asha was gripped for a moment by a deep shaft of terror. *Fifty years ago? But that's a good thirty before he was even born!*

She swallowed. "How? How could she know?"

Hilla shrugged. "She was a Time Speaker—a channeler of the Great Fates. What the Agency calls a Time Psi Prophet," amusement lifted into Hilla's bright blue eyes. "I'm not exactly going to argue against the forces of Time itself."

Asha kept herself still so she didn't tremble or otherwise make a nut of herself in her sudden confused terror. Hawk was a brilliant and sometimes frightening man, but he was just a man.

He's just a man... He's just a man... She repeated the mantra to herself in an effort to calm the rising tide of panic.

A shiver ran down her spine. It was so strong that her thoughts and fears dissipated like smoke. Something was wrong and she wasn't sure what it was.

Ren and the girl looked up across the room where Krena Ree slept, and Asha realized what was happening.

The four of them ran across the room to the cot. Hilla got to her first and immediately cried out. "No! Krena!"

When he got there Ren lifted his hands to Krena's neck and diaphragm. His voice was pained and sad. "There's nothing more I can do for her. She's gone."

Hilla dropped to her knees and started to wail.

The other Rebels in the building seemed to sense what had happened or hear Hilla's wails. One by one they came upstairs and gathered around Krena's body.

Krena's young boys approached their mother's side from the back stairwell and were immediately embraced by Hilla and the other Rebels as they grieved together.

Standing a little back from the group and watching their grief, Asha remembered Krena from her childhood. Krena had been snarky and grumpy, but an incredibly loving and loyal woman. Asha swallowed.

With all the empathic pain around her that she couldn't quite block, Asha started to cry. The grief bubbled out of her, not only for the loss of a childhood figure, but the other losses in her life of her parents, the separation from her brother, friends who hadn't survived the Desert Training base she'd been sent to, and recently her dear husband Tesh.

The Rebels wept and wailed for a long time. Unable to help ease their suffering once her own tears had dried up, Asha led the girl and the two newest escapees into the kitchen. The four women did their best to cook what food they could find for everyone else, and together they created a sparse meal of fried vegetables and homemade flat bread.

It wasn't much but it was warm and filled empty tummies. They dished up the meal onto plates and made sure everyone in the room ate, even through their tears.

After eating her own and helping to clear and wash the used plates, it was time to feed Tempa again.

She sat in a corner, the carrying-sling covering her for modesty as the baby fed.

"Asha," Hawk's mental voice was quiet, perhaps even gentle, and she wondered if he knew that Krena had died. *"Are you ready to come back yet?"*

"I was hoping to stay long enough to be here when Taelin woke up."

"I'm sorry, Asha. We need to leave Arām tonight."

Her face tightened into a conflicted frown. *"Why?"*

"The first escape in Marakan is tomorrow morning. To get there in time to help, we have to leave just after midnight."

"When do we come back?"

"Once we have a cell in every major city we'll come back to set up a master cell here," he paused as he changed the subject. *"So, what else needs to be done there before you can leave?"*

She sighed. *"Not much, I've got his book, I just have to hand over your instructions, but, you'll never believe what changed her mind."*

"The envelope."

"How did you know?" she asked, mildly annoyed.

"I saw a vision of you opening it. Have you yet?"

She shook her head slightly. *"No, it's addressed to you, and quite frankly it freaks me out."*

There was a mental laugh. *"If you understood Time a little better it wouldn't worry you so much. Time doesn't flow in straight lines, it swirls and branches out in a huge network. I can only see what is already in my path. So, sometimes messages have to come from other high rating Time Psi to bring new threads onto my path for changing. The source of the envelope was Time Psi, correct?"*

"Yes, a Time Psi Prophet." She sighed, feeling a little resentful of his condescending tone and pitched her mental voice with a touch of mocking sarcasm. *"So, what now, oh great one?"*

She felt the empathic equivalent of an amused snort. *"Well, now you get to open it for me, so we can see if it needs our attention immediately."*

Balancing the baby with one hand, she shuffled in a pants pocket for the envelope. She was trying to figure out how to open it with one hand when Ren approached and sat down next to her against the wall.

Tears stained his wrinkled face, but his expression was kind. "I heard you were given my mother's envelope."

"Yes." She smiled. "Could you help me open it?"

He took it from her hands, ripped open the envelope and unfolded it for them both to read.

"Dear Hawk,
I have had dreams of your hawk mask and what paths you will weave with the threads of time. Everything else you need will come to you as you expect it. From me I have only one instruction: protect and trust my granddaughter because without her help and wisdom you will fail.
- Isa Zuru-Yen"

Asha stared at the note feeling mildly dumbstruck. "But, Ren, you never had any children, how could there be a granddaughter?"

The old man smiled. "She wasn't talking about any child of mine. I suspect she was referring to my sister Anita's child." Lifting one arm, he pointed across the candle-lit room to the girl, who stood watching over Taelin as he slept.

"The girl?"

"Yes, her name is Nalana Yen." Asha sensed a flare of very strong joy from him. "I have a niece and she's here with the Rebels where she belongs. It's good to have more family around."

She stared across the room at her brother. "Yes, it is good."

"Asha," Hawk's voice was almost a whisper in her mind. *"I don't see any immediate danger to this girl. She should be safe with the Rebels for now. We can investigate it later. For the moment, I need you to get here as soon as you can."*

She sighed and nodded slightly. *"Of course, I'll see you soon."*

Asha shuffled her free hand around the baby and into her front pocket. Pulling out pages of notes, she handed them to Ren. "All of Hawk's instructions are in there. Included are some instructions on how to avoid a couple of potential attacks, as well as the location and timing of some escapes. Could you give it to Hilla once it's—" she swallowed and glanced sadly across the level at Hilla's grieving form in the candle light. "Once it's the appropriate time. I think the first event is in a couple of weeks so there's no huge rush."

He took the collection of pages from her with a nod.

Tears rose into Asha's eyes and her voice broke slightly. "I have to go soon. Could you tell my brother that I'm sorry I couldn't stay. I really wanted to be here when he woke up but Hawk needs me tonight."

Ren nodded. "Of course I can, Asha." He leaned over to give her a broad comforting hug.

Wrapping her free arm around him, she rested her head on his shoulder and sighed. "I promise I'll be back as soon as I can."

Part Two

Three Years Later

* 1 *
Day One—Misdirection
3003 (Three years later),
Arām Church of the Founder

Father Andrew reached into the dim closet and pulled out a new set of priest robes. A sad little smile lifted into his face and he stroked the red embroidered four-petal symbol of the Founder that ran along the lapel of the garment. It was the symbol of everything he held dear in his life—the Church, his appointment as Head Priest, the priests under him and those innocent souls the Church protected. He sighed. The young man in the other room risked the destruction of it all by mixing the Agency with the Rebels by working directly though the Church.

Andrew swallowed tensely. *This isn't going to end well, I'm sure of it.*

Every bone and muscle in his old body screamed at him to somehow put a stop to what was happening even as he told that instinct there was nothing to be done, it was out of his hands. What could he do? The young man seemed far too focused on his intentions to think about the risks involved. Despite his claim of having no wish to harm the Church, the young man was still an Agent, which meant they had no choice but to do as he asked.

The old priest sighed again and turned out of the narrow closet. He made his way back down a stone hallway to the open door, where he stopped at the sight of those vivid blue eyes. The man watched him impassively for a few seconds, and then one side of his mouth twitched upwards.

"Well?" His eyes looked down at the robes in Andrew's hands.

"Oh! Sorry." Andrew laughed and stepped into the room, handing him the new robe over-shirt.

He took it from Andrew and shuffled the stiff material over broad shoulders.

Andrew cleared his throat. "Are you sure they won't get suspicious?"

That one sided smile lifted again. "It'll be fine, Father Andrew."

"But—"

"The Rebels trust you, don't they?"

Andrew nodded. "Yes, but—"

"And they know you wouldn't send someone to do the deliveries if *you* didn't trust them. Correct?"

That feeling of doom rose up in Andrew again and he swallowed. "This is a dangerous game you're playing."

The man's chin lifted and revealed a brash confidence. "I'm good at playing dangerous games, Father Andrew. I've played them all my life." His expression softened. "Don't worry so much, I won't get caught by the Rebels, I promise."

"Best not or they *will* kill you, son." Andrew stepped closer and straightened the man's collar for him. "And after that, if the Rebels don't turn around and come after us, *your* people just might."

Stepping back again to check the man's appearance, Andrew brushed nervously at some lint on the firm black cloth. He hoped for the sake of the Cathedral Monastery—and his own neck—that the man's bravado wasn't all the cocky ignorance of youth.

"Trust me, Father." A broad hand dropped onto his shoulder. "No matter what happens, the Agency won't shut down the Monastery. You're helping us after all now, aren't you?" The young man lifted his hand. "Now, you mentioned you had a name I could use?"

"Yes," he replied. "How does Father Owen sound?"

That odd one-sided smile twitched again. "Perfect. Thank you, Father."

* 2 *

Taelin Kān's Rebel Cell building
Early evening

The old abandoned building was dank and drafty. Cheetah wondered how anyone, even Rebels, could live in such an environment. The air was suppressively damp, even in the warmer areas of the building where the small group of Rebels squatted. Nothing was clean or dry, and some sections of the building were overrun with nests of rodents and other small disgusting creatures. Crouched in front of the first floor stairwell door, she shivered, as much from the cold and damp as from the thought of all those rodents. Creatures who would likely nibble on her corpse if she was captured or killed by the Rebels.

Her target list instructed her to take out all of the adult Traitors in the Rebel cell. That meant she had to take out the parents of the three children, the two women who were a couple and the old man. But it also left three children, twin teenage boys, a girl her age and the leader of the cell, Taelin, who were all Illegal Psis and not required marks for a completed mission.

Unfortunately, even though the twin boys weren't Traitors she would still have to take them out, and they'd have to be first. Being twins, they were able to magnify each other so that together they were the only telepaths strong enough to call for help. If they managed to call for help and their reinforcements came before the mission was done, it wouldn't matter how good she was, she would not escape this mission alive.

Cheetah got to her feet. Her onyx-handled gun was heavy with the silencer attached, but she'd trained a lot in the firing range so that the extra weight no longer affected her accuracy.

Through a gap in the door, she watched the first floor stairwell. The adults of Taelin's Rebel cell were climbing the stairs with boxes of food and supplies to their second-floor living space. She waited for the leader to pass her, the two parents of the youngest children, the old man and the two women. The twin boys would be last to pass where she hid, making her job easier. She heard their laughter echo up the stairwell.

"Haha! You lose!"

"Did not!"

The two boys were identical twins. They were tall and willowy with scruffy red-black hair, yellow-brown eyes, and mouths that lifted easily into a smile. As they came into sight, one of the boys took a large can from the box he was carrying and put it onto his brother's armful. The second boy let out a wordless cry of dismay and started to argue with his sibling about who had in fact lost the game.

Reaching with a telepathic hand, Cheetah brushed the surface of their minds. There was an immediate silence as they both stared at the door behind which she was hiding. They exchanged a glance and carefully put their boxes down on the top step.

Clicking her safety off and preparing her mind for what was to come, she opened the door wide. The weapon kicked as it fired and the shots, even muffled, were loud enough to echo through the stairwell. The two boys fell back dully on the landing. Their deaths should have been almost instant.

Above her in the stairwell she heard startled voices, and returning the weapon to its holster in the small of her back, she stepped over their bodies to escape downstairs.

* 3 *

Taelin stood with his back to the wall, gun raised and listening intently to the noises of the basement around him. There was the sound of water dripping somewhere, an uneven fan thrum from the old limping air-conditioning unit and random traffic noises from the street above him, but no discernible indication of whether this intruder might be with him in the basement.

~ "Tae, third floor cleared, over." Hiran's voice wobbled a little over the radio. They were all hurting over the twins.

Lifting his hand from his weapon, he pressed the earpiece with one finger. This sent a noise pulse over the radio letting Hiran and the others know that he'd received the message, but was currently unable to respond with audio.

Taking another step, careful of the rubbish, he made his way down the hall. If the assassin was in the basement, there weren't many places for him or her to hide. The stairwell stood at one end of the hall and the generator room door at the other. Of the six doors between those two extremes, only one could be opened. That room was filled with rotting trash and he'd just checked it, so if they were in the basement, they had to be in the generator room.

He sighed. The whole situation made no sense to him. Why would an assassin target their cell? They had no real resources or intel for the Agency to take. None of their seven adult members participated in Rebel raids on the Agency, and no one was rated above a three in any Psi ability. There was no logic to it.

Not that any of it matters to the twins now.

He suppressed a twinge of sadness—he would sorely miss the twin's mischief. The only comfort was that they'd died together and by the look of their wounds they'd also died quickly. It could have been much worse.

Taking a deep breath, Taelin pushed the generator door and leaned in to get a quick look over the barrel of his weapon.

There were boxes of tools and junk piled up against the far left wall, the huge rusting dripping pipes of the generator covered most of the back and centre of the room and in the far right the floor was covered in rubbish and debris. For a brief second, he saw something move behind the old generator and pulled himself back under cover.

Hai di'chena! The intruder's here!

Tae stood for a moment with his back against the door frame and wall. His eyes flitted left and right at the same pace as his nearly panicked thinking.

He only had two options: call them out or withdraw. Withdrawing would need him to call for back up so he could effectively secure the basement stairwell. But doing that would take time and let the intruder know that he'd spotted them. He sighed and checked his weapon was loaded. Swallowing the dry ball of fear in his throat, he opened his mouth.

"Come on out of there with your hands up. You've got about ten seconds before I come in firing. And don't think that generator will cover you—it's ninety percent rust."

There was no reply for three whole seconds.

"Please, sir, I'm not armed." The voice that came through the door sounded young and frightened. "Please don't shoot. I just fell asleep here."

Keeping as much of his body behind the cover of the door-frame, Taelin leaned around to look inside again.

A teenage girl stood in front of the generator with her hands up. Her long raven-black hair was tied-back loosely in a pony tail and vivid green eyes stared fearfully at him. She didn't look very old, maybe fifteen, but she was tall and skinny.

He raised his revolver and stepped out of the cover of the door frame. "What's your name? What are you doing in my basement?"

"I'm Abi." She stared wide eyed at the gun as her body started to shake. "I just needed somewhere warm to rest. There's a snow storm coming. I didn't know it was your basement, I'm sorry, I'll leave if you like."

She stepped closer to him as if to escape, but he backed up and put the gun in her face. "Not so quickly, Abi. How old are you?"

"I... I just turned seventeen last week. Please don't shoot me, I haven't stolen anything, I promise."

Everything about her seemed to match her story. Her body language, the tone of her voice, the fear in her eyes, but... but... there was a deep feeling of distrust in him. He wasn't about to make a mistake by not listening to that instinct and then find himself joining the twins in the afterlife.

Taelin lifted his other hand to the earpiece of his radio. ~ "Hiran, Ana, I've found a trespasser. Come down to the generator room, right now."

He only took his eyes off her for a moment, but in that moment the girl stepped in close. She disarmed him with a twist of his wrist and arm, and pushed him off balance. Before he could recover his footing, something hit him hard in the temple and he found himself falling backwards into a stunned grayness.

* * * * *

A sharp noise forced Tae's awareness out of the grey fuzz of his mind.

What does that noise mean? He thought dimly. *That noise is important. But why?*

He lay on his back somewhere. Cold seeped through his shirt into his shoulders, and one side of his face ached somewhat. A second gunshot fired nearby and he felt his body twitch in response.

Someone was yelling and he could hear running footsteps come towards him.

"Tae! Tae! Are you alright?" The voice sounded scared and he tried to answer them, but he couldn't yet.

A cool hand touched his cheek, and a string of painful jumbled thoughts and feelings flowed into him. Fear, confusion, adrenaline and a sense of desperate concern all filled the space inside his skull.

"Is he alive?" Hiran's thought cut sharply into his mind.

Groaning, he moved his head away from her hand.

"Tae! Wake up, come on."

His eyes opened slowly and a moan escaped his lips.

"Come on, get up, you lazy a'kenān! Get up!" Firm hands pulled at his arms, forcing him unsteadily to his feet.

He leaned against the wall and brought a hand to his face. His right temple and cheek-bone were very tender. The girl must have hit him pretty hard.

Sighing, he looked sideways at Hiran. "What happened?"

She gave him a sarcastic smirk. "You found the assassin, Tae, that's what happened. You're lucky you're not dead!"

"Probably—" his smile dropped as a sense of abject doom settled into his stomach. "Wait. Ana, where's Ana?"

Hiran indicated behind her with one thumb. "She followed the assassin upstairs."

Touching a finger to the radio, he headed back down the hall and Hiran followed. ~ "Ana, come in Ana. Do you read me?"

He moved up into the stairwell and ran two steps at a time to the ground floor. As he ran, he listened intently to his earpiece but no response came from Ana.

Tae paused on the stairs to sense for any trouble. It was quiet and he felt no immediate tension from his meager Danger Sense Talent. His eyes dropped and he found a trail of blood leading from where they stood, through under the door and into the ground floor level.

Glancing sideways at Hiran, he put his finger to his lips and pointed at the splatters of blood.

"Gun?" he whispered.

She passed him a small revolver with a handful of bullets from a jeans pocket.

He reloaded while he continued. "Tell Nalana to take the kids down the back fire-escape and run for Nama's. Once they're out, let me know and we can go from there."

She climbed her way around him onto the next set of stairs. Dropping the remaining bullets into a jacket pocket, he approached the ground floor entrance and waited for Hiran to get out of sight.

Once she was clear, he stepped through the door. On the other side, there was no sign of the girl and for the moment he sensed no sickening ill-ease, which usually meant he was in immediate peril. Further up the hall towards the front door, a body lay on the faded black and white checkered linoleum. Trying not to think about who it might be, Taelin approached.

The person lay in the center of the entrance hall on their stomach with their arms sprawled around them. A large full-length jacket covered the figure like a matted corduroy blanket. It looked like Ana's jacket, but he couldn't let his thoughts hold onto that resemblance. Surely it was the assassin and Ana was elsewhere?

He squatted down and reached amongst the folds of cloth to find a pulse in her neck, but she was dead. Pulling at her shoulder, he turned her over.

A flash of long golden hair and the side of a strongly boned face caused him to gasp and tighten his lips against the sudden shot of grief.

Ana's grey-blue eyes were wide with surprise—the assassin must have caught her unaware. The coat she wore had covered the puddle of blood underneath her from a single bullet to the heart.

Taelin covered his mouth and swallowed. Whoever this assassin was they were good—terrifyingly good.

* 4 *

When Hiran stepped into the damp third-floor sitting room, she found Nalana and the two eldest children were already standing outside on the fire escape. Ella was in front of them, inside the empty apartment with baby Heth in her arms.

Hiran smiled. "And who says you're not a telepath?"

"I'm not." Ella looked back and winked at her. "I'm a mother."

She watched Ella hand baby Heth through the open window to Nalana. Even with tears running down her cheeks, Nalana pulled a funny face at the baby as she took him into her arms. He giggled, wriggling his little legs up and down in his innocent happiness.

After waving at her children through the glass of the window, Ella turned back to walk past Hiran. "Bez and I are going down to protect the weapons store. Tell Tae?"

"Of course." Hiran nodded. "Be careful."

"Always." The radio crackled and she heard Tae's voice.

~ "Ana is dead, I repeat, Ana is dead."

No! Not Ana! The thoughts carved a burning line through the center of her heart. *It wasn't true!*

Swallowing back the agony, she stepped up to the window, and closer to Nalana and children. "Go now!"

Nalana nodded at her through the glass and stepped out of sight with the three children.

~ "Hiran?" Tae's voice broke slightly. ~ "Brān? Where are you?"

~ "I'm on the first floor, Tae." Brān's deep voice rumbled over the radio in her ear.

She touched the receiver. ~ "Third floor." Her voice trembled. ~ "The others are safely away. Bez and Ella are protecting our weapons."

~ "Good. Can you two get down to the ground floor?"

~ "On my way," answered Brān.

~ "Coming."

Pulling out her second weapon from the inside of her coat, she made sure it was loaded while she walked.

A noise sounded from somewhere in the building. It was too quiet for her to identify it specifically and she stopped in the doorway to listen. It sounded again and she realized it was a silenced shot.

~ "Tae, shots fired, I'm en-route." Closing the door behind her, she ran out into the dingy hallway towards the stairwell.

~ "Where?" Tae's voice was flat.

~ "I'm not sure, second floor?"

~ "On my way."

Hiran leaned on the heavy stairwell doors and jogged down to the second story. Her fingers gripped the door handle as another shot fired somewhere below her.

She touched her earpiece. ~ "Tae? Did you hear that one?"

~ "Yeah. Right above me. I'm checking it out."

~ "Copy," she answered as she pushed through into the corridor beyond.

Hiran looked down the grimy hall towards the one fairly dry and safe area of the building where they lived. A body lay in front of the apartment door, but in the dim light she couldn't see who it was. The person lay face down as if they'd been running when they fell.

Cautiously, she walked towards them. The figure on the floor was male, with dark unkempt hair and broad shoulders. She crouched down next to him to check his pulse, hoping it wasn't who it looked like. There was a very definite gunshot wound to the middle of his back and no heartbeat. She brushed his hair from his face.

~ "Tae." Hiran's bottom lip twitched. ~ "I've just found Bez."

~ "Ella?"

A tear dropped down her cheek and fell into Bez's dark hair. ~ "I don't know yet."

She crouched there for a moment so that she could control the rising panic and grief in her. It wasn't time to be grieving, and panicking certainly wouldn't help them survive either. She had to be cold and focused if they were going to get out of this alive.

She swallowed, wiped her face of tears and got to her feet.

The door was slightly ajar and through the gap she saw another body lying close. She put one hand on the door and took a deep breath before she pushed it open.

Her gun followed her eyes as she looked quickly around the large space that served as their living room. To her left stood the open-plan kitchen. The space in front of the kitchen was clear. Her eyes followed around from left to right over the couches, along the walls, past closed doors in front of her, more couches with children's toys scattered over the floor, and to the far right, the closed bathroom doors. It seemed clear.

Ella lay on her back with a surprised look on her pale face and a tidy round bullet wound in the exact center of her forehead. Hiran touched the radio.

~ "Tae—" her voice cracked and she swallowed. ~ "I found Ella." Grief swelled into her and she covered her mouth with one hand.

~ "Level one. Now. Be cautious." Tae's voice was whispered and he sounded very afraid. His fear was enough to trigger her own and she used it to suppress the grief for a little while longer.

Getting to her feet and wiping her face again, she turned out of their living quarters. Pacing quickly out of the apartment and down to the stairwell, she refused to look back even once. Any more grief or fear and she'd be useless to Tae in hunting this assassin.

Leaning on the first floor door, she opened it only just wide enough to look in. Taelin sat on the ground next to Brān's body. He looked up at her, a line of tears hovered in his dark blue eyes, and she knew without needing to be an empath that he was just as scared and grief-stricken as she. A little tense smile passed between them and she stepped through.

Old Brān lay on his back. He looked as if he was asleep, but at the same time as if he wasn't quite real. Her bottom lip twitched a little and she reached to brush the old man's pepper-gray hair from his face. Even dead he still looked mildly grumpy.

"I think the assassin is here on this level," Tae whispered. "She'll have to come through here to get out. We'll go one room at a time. Got it?"

She nodded.

They made their way past Brān to the nearest door. Counting silently down from three with his fingers, Tae got to one and opened the door wide. They stepped inside. Tae turned right and she turned left.

Vivid green eyes met hers over the barrel of a silenced weapon. There was a flash and something dove deep inside Hiran's chest, knocking the breath from her lungs. She let out a pained choking sound instead of the scream of agony waiting at the back of her throat. Then, she fell numbly back as everything faded into a sticky cold darkness.

* 5 *
Dusk
A few blocks south
Nama Ree's Rebel building

Nama dumped the last box onto the pile he'd made next to the building entrance. Outside, a backfire sounded through the open door. It faded into the familiar rumbling, temperamental engine of the monastery van.

He enjoyed the visits from Father Andrew. The old man had a dry wit and a gentle soul. He also had a soft spot for Nama's homemade rum that made the company profitable as well as enjoyable.

Stepping outside, the early evening sky was a mix of bloody cotton candy and shimmering stars against a cobalt blue. The orange-tinged light cast odd shadows on the street and painted the dark van an off-purple as it came to a jolting halt. The driver-side door opened and a figure with startlingly blue eyes looked around the metal framing at him.

The man was not Father Andrew. He was perhaps in his early twenties—younger than Nama, certainly— with short light brown hair. Half-obscured by an old leather jacket, the man wore the black and red robes of an apprentice priest.

A friendly smile softened the man's square features. "You must be Nama."

"And who are you?" Nama lifted his hands to his hips. "Where's Father Andrew?"

The smile widened. "I'm Father Owen. Father Andrew couldn't come so he asked me to do the deliveries for him."

Nama lifted an eyebrow at the priest. "Why didn't Andrew send up a red flag? You could be anyone. Nuth! You could be an Agent for all we know."

The man's smile dropped as he stepped back, and crossed his arms over his chest. "I'm sure if he had known it would be such a problem, he would have."

Nama stared suspiciously at the man for a few moments, unsure whether he should send him on his way just to be safe, or to shrug and get on with it. After a few breaths of thinking, he shrugged. Andrew wouldn't give the van keys to anyone but another priest, so it was probably safe. Besides, this man didn't have the look of an Agent. There was no darkness in his eyes, stiffness in his motion and no mental shield (artificial or otherwise) to hide the thoughts that mirrored his story.

Nama flicked his head towards the doorway. "Fine. Give me a hand with these boxes?"

Together they ferried the ten or so boxes of Cathedral supplies into the old van. A comfortable silence settled into the space between them. There was a sense of quiet peace about the young man that Nama couldn't help but like. And his surface thoughts were quiet—a rare quality in non-telepaths—which enabled Nama to just work without having to focus on blocking out the noise.

Nama set down the heavy wooden crate that held a dozen bottles of his homemade rum into the van, and pushed it up against the other boxes inside. The young priest, whose name he'd already forgotten, came up behind him with the last box, so Nama moved out of the way and leaned casually on the van.

"So, what kept Father Andrew from coming himself?"

The man pushed his own box into the van and shrugged. "I'm not sure, some meeting with another Head Priest. From Aramān, I think?"

"Well, next time—"

"Nama! Nama!"

He turned away and saw Nalana running down the street towards him, baby in her arms and Ella's two eldest children in tow.

Stepping away from the priest, he called out to her. "Nalana, what's happened?"

"We need help!" Tears ran down the young woman's face and in her arms little Heth was grizzling fearfully. "Someone attacked us. They killed the twins. I... I don't know who. We didn't see anything."

A breath of shock escaped him. "The twins?"

Her bottom lip trembled and she nodded.

Swallowing a suddenly rising ball of grief, he turned back to face the priest. "Tell Andrew the bottles with red lids are his." Swallowing again, he ignored the shake in his voice. "And tell him next time he sends someone new for deliveries to give us a head's up, if anyone else but me had been here, you would've been shot."

Not waiting for a response, Nama turned from the priest and collected Nalana by the elbow.

* 6 *

Emerald green eyes stared icily at Taelin over the extended barrel of her weapon. The assassin's shooting arm was wounded, but she held her gun steady. It was as if she didn't feel pain at all. Tae looked over his own gun barrel at the strange girl, feeling very unsure about how he could possibly survive this.

"My mission is complete." Her tone was icy cold. "Let me pass and you will live."

"You have killed everyone." His voice shook slightly in his fear. "How can I believe you?"

"You're not hearing me. My mission does not include you and neither does it include the girl who escaped down the south-west fire escape or the three children with her. Unless you make me, I will not kill you. I am simply giving you a chance to survive."

Tae was unsure if she was tricking him into lowering his guard or if she was genuine. He decided it was better to err on the side of caution.

"I... I don't believe you."

The moment he said it he felt a terrible pain in his head, as if someone had thrust a thick burning rod through his temples and into the center of his brain. He let out a yell of agony, the gun fell from his hands and he involuntarily dropped to his knees.

Reality warped around the edges of his vision from the abject strength of her invading mind. Unable to move, he watched the assassin come right up to him.

Her voice was almost a whisper. "At dawn the sweeper team will come to confirm my kills. Don't be here when they arrive."

An odd dizziness pulled him down and blessedly away from the agony in his head.

* * * * *

When Taelin came to it was dark in the room and he lay on his back. His brain cells throbbed in time with his heartbeat. He lifted his head to look around and the world spun nauseatingly as a sharp thrust of pain pushed through his temples. He grunted, resting his head back on the carpet, and closed his eyes again.

He faded in and out of a hazy pain-induced fog.

After an indefinable amount of time passing, something rumbled in his mind. He opened his eyes, staring up into the darkness of the ceiling. It rumbled again. The sensation felt almost as if his mind was a still pool of water and someone brushed the surface of it with their fingertips.

A third time it rumbled and, impossibly, it vibrated with words. *"Tae! Where are you?"*

It was a telepathic voice—something he'd never heard without direct physical touch. He tried to reach out to it, but failed.

"He's got to be here somewhere." The voice sounded like Nama.

Again Taelin reached and this time he felt like he touched something solid. The connection was rough and painful.

"Help!" he called out.

"He's here! Tae, we're coming!"

The mental voice was stronger, it cut a deep gouge into his mind and he called out wordlessly.

"This way!"

A flashing torch flooded through the doorway to his left, and half-blinded him. Sensations of fear and relief cut through the room and into him like a ripple made of sharpened steel.

Taelin whimpered in the agony of their presence.

"Thank Divinity, Taelin. I thought we'd never find you!"

His voice came out broken and pained. "Nala?"

"Yes, hun. I'm here, so is Nama. Are you shot?"

"No, my head. It... it hurts, so bad." He whimpered again and closed his eyes.

"Stay with me, Taelin."

Someone else came into the room, they spoke but he couldn't understand the words. Hot green flames of agonized grief came towards him, burning his mind and heart with just their presence. He cried out, begging the grief to get away from him. His mind reached a line of agony and unable to handle it any longer, he felt himself fade away into nothingness.

* 7 *

Asha's combat boots made echoed footsteps in the dusty wood floor as she paced. Taelin lay in the middle of the room on a cot. He was pale and gray, and seemed worse than he had three years ago when Asha last saw him.

Pacing down the cot towards his feet, she sighed angrily. "I swear, if I find the Agency spy in the Rebels who tipped them off and caused this, I'm going to slice them ass to nostril!"

"He's Quad-Psi, correct?"

Asha glanced down at the man sitting with his hands resting on Taelin's temples. Hawk had told her quite a bit about him and that he was an ex-Interrogator, but she'd already forgotten his name.

She nodded. "Yes."

"What were his ratings before this?" His calm gray-blue eyes met her gaze and she sensed a strong personality behind them.

She shrugged. "Zip; he's always been Psi locked. Touch-only telepath-empath and an instinct expression of his Time Psi genes, why?"

"I'm not sure about his other Psi abilities, but right now his mind has the reactivity of a 5/5 Telepath—even while unconscious."

"A five?" she gaped. "But, that kind of increase so quickly—"

"Yes, exactly, it's too much. He should already be dead."

Her shoulders lifted and her voice came out like that of a child's. "Can you help him?"

He brushed a thread of long blond hair off his face. "Yes, I think so, as long as he can hold on. I should be able to set up a temporary artificial mental shield for him. That is of course, as long as the assassin's damage isn't too extensive."

She swallowed. "Can I do anything?"

"Yes, for now we need a high rating empath to help shield him. Also, if you have the discipline to remain psychically silent, I'd appreciate you sitting in while I do what I can. He seems to be more stable with you in the room. But, we have to be quick."

"Of course, I'll talk to Nama and come back." She stepped towards the door, but looked back over her shoulder at him, "I'm Asha by the way."

"Kita Oran." A friendly smile flashed in his gray eyes for a moment, then it was gone again behind a focused frown.

She closed the door behind her and looked through the dimness into the concerned faces of Nama and Nalana.

"How is he?" said Nama.

Asha wrapped her arms around her middle and swallowed back her tense fear. "The attack seems to have unlocked Taelin's Psi genes. Kita thinks he's in severe psychic shock. We need Kala in there to help shield him empathically."

Nama mirrored her stance and wrapped his arms around his stomach. "How bad is it?"

"He said that Tae's telepath reactivity is at a 5/5 level."

"Mārā Nūthen! A five?"

Young Nalana frowned. "That's a lot, right?"

"Yes. It's usually fatal for any telepath to increase by three or more ratings in one go, and he went up by at least five. He should be dead from the telepath increase alone." She swallowed. "And he's Quad Psi, so it could be even worse, we just don't know yet."

The girl shook her head. "Quad-Psi?"

"Like me, he has active genes in all four Psi abilities—telepath, empath, kinetic and time sensitive. He's just not been able to access them until now."

Nama turned away into the dimness. "I'll go and get Kala."

"Can I help?" Nalana stepped closer to her. "I can shield empathically."

Asha grabbed the girl's hand. "I'll ask, come on."

Inside, Kita hadn't moved. He sat on the floor cross-legged, eyes closed with his palms resting on Tae's temples.

"Kita, Nala is a healer, but not a telepath, do you think—"

"Yes," he interrupted her without opening his eyes. "If she's fast and able to block empathically I can shield him. His concussion is making things difficult."

Nalana let go and knelt on the floor next to Tae. She put a hand on his forehead and another on the bruised side of his face. Asha sensed the pulse of something staticy that throbbed through the girl and started to wash away his physical pain.

Nalana stood up to leave and Asha smiled a gentle thank you at the girl.

On her way out, Nala passed a tall woman with a steely strength in her grey-blue eyes, who stood in the doorway. "You're Asha?"

Asha nodded. "Kala?"

"It's nice to finally meet you." She gave Asha a tense smile and sat down next to Taelin.

Asha walked to where Taelin's feet were and got into a comfortable meditative position on the floor with her legs folded under her. Taking in a deep breath, she let it out slowly through her nostrils. Her mind reacted instantly by shifting her consciousness slowly down into a half-trance state, where she could sense and watch what was happening without broadcasting and harming Taelin psychically.

Over many hours, Kala and Kita worked on building up Taelin's Psi shielding as Asha watched impassively. By the time dawn light filtered through a little grubby window into the room, Kala lay asleep on the floor to one side and, Asha and Kita still sat at the head and feet of Taelin's body.

There was a pained moan and Asha dropped out of her trance.

"Tae?" she said uncertainly, as she got to her feet.

A second groan developed into a word. "Ouch."

At Taelin's head, Kita opened his eyes. "Don't try to move yet, Taelin, you almost died."

"What happened? Where... Hiran!" Tae's body tensed, then his hand lifted to brush at his face. "Oh, my head. Hiran... did she...?"

Asha swallowed. "I'm sorry, Tae. Hiran is gone."

Perhaps sensing that it was a private moment, Kita got to his feet and left the room.

Taelin looked sideways at her from the cot, a weak smile lifting into his bruised face. "Asha? You're here?"

She knelt down next to him. "Yes. How are you feeling?"

"Odd." He sighed and closed his dark blue eyes for a moment, "migraine too. How about you?"

She laughed. "Fine, I'm just glad you're OK. Kita and Kala worked all night to save you."

A frown wrinkled his brow. "What happened?"

"The assassin's attack unlocked your Psi genes and put you into a coma. You should have died."

He put one broad hand over his eyes. "Awesome."

She touched his arm gently and got to her feet. "You rest."

"Asha?"

She looked down at him over one shoulder. "Yeah?"

"I'm glad you're back."

A chuckle escaped her. "I missed you too, you big dope. Now get some sleep."

* 8 *
Day Two—Timān
Around lunchtime
Hetera Beau's Rebel cell in the South East of Arām

Hetera brushed a thread of unruly dark hair from her eyes with an irritated flick of her wrist. Her project was almost done—frustrating thing as it was.

So'then, Nama and his so'then limoncello! She grumbled wordlessly and tried to make her fingers do as they were told with the defiant thread.

"They're here! You'd better hurry up!" Young Jeran chortled from the nearby doorway.

"Shuddup!" Whipping out a backhand, she smacked the twerp a good one to the base of his skull. He let out a child-like squeak and skittered out of the room again.

Gritting her teeth, she attempted one more focused twist with her fingers. Finally the thread and her fingers co-operated, knotting tightly the last of her slightly crooked stitching. She'd worked on the so'then thing for over a week. She'd stolen scraps of leather and PVC from a craft store, and even managed to score a metal clasp from some bag in the second-hand shop down the road. Now, finally, it was done.

She mentally rubbed her hands together. A bottle of Nama's special limoncello traded for a strong leather clip bag for his belt.

Victory. She grinned triumphantly.

Grabbing it off the workbench, she turned to her little son Timān who sat next to her in his car-seat cot. He babbled away at her contentedly and she touched his little face with one hand. She glanced sideways to double-check that young Jemma was still there knitting something in the corner in the sunlight. Jem would keep a physical eye on Timān while she dealt with their visitors.

As she headed back out of the room, she touched the baby's mind with a gentle connection so he knew she was still nearby.

The stock doors were wide open at the end of the main hall and people were already ferrying boxes inside from the delivery lane. Nama stood in the entrance smirking at her.

"Do you have it?" His deep baritone voice echoed down the hall.

Keeping the clip bag behind her as she approached him, she grinned. "Do you?"

"Of course!" His arms widened into a *gimme a hug* gesture. "How are you Hetty?"

Grinning, she stepped into his arms. "Don't call me Hetty."

"Why's that, Hetty?" He laughed and let go of her.

He was an attractive, tall, broad-shouldered man with the most remarkably golden brown eyes she'd ever seen. And he smelt good too. But she didn't think for one moment of trying it on with him because he only had eyes for Kala. That, and Kala would likely come after her with a butcher's knife or a four-by-two, if she tried anything.

Hetera gave him a mock-glare. "Gimme. The so'then. Cello!"

He laughed and flicked his head. "Come on, it's in the van."

She followed him outside into the winter sun and down the narrow lane. When she got to Nama's battered white van, she found Taelin sitting inside and pushing boxes towards the doors for people to grab.

"Hey, Hetera." His face was badly bruised around one eye, across the temple and down onto the same cheek. His smile was tense, but still friendly.

She lifted an eyebrow at him. "What in Nūthen happened to you?"

Taelin's dark blue eyes were red around the edges and the moment she saw a line of moisture build up in them, she regretted asking.

"Assassin," Nama said quietly. "Hit his base..." his voice lifted into a gently playful tone. "Taelin got beat up by a girl."

"A girl?" She stared back at Tae. "You got beat up by a girl?"

He gave her a sad smile. "Yeah. Knocked me clean out."

She glanced sideways at Nama and spoke telepathically. *"Who was lost?"*

"Everyone." Taelin answered her unvoiced question. "Everyone but me, Nala and the three kids."

"How did you—"

"Trauma triggered his Psi genes." Nama lifted a large bottle of creamy-yellow liquid from the van and winked at her. "His telepathic ear is longer than yours now, Hetty."

She handed the clip bag to Nama and tightly gripped the bottle of limoncello. It was bigger than they'd agreed upon, but that was all good. There was a sense that perhaps it was inappropriate to grip so strongly to a bottle of intoxication after hearing such news, loved ones of both of these men had been killed. She also knew once she started drinking, she'd remember that some of those who'd been killed were her friends too and she'd probably get all somber and sad as well. But for the moment she felt obliged to ignore such strong emotions.

"Well, I'm going back inside to get kitāsa-faced drunk. You're welcome to join me if you like!" She turned back towards the stock doors and Nama's laughter followed after her.

"Save some of that! We might come back after the deliveries are done!"

"Bring your own, I ain't sharing!" She stood at the stock doors and lifted one hand from the bottle to wave back at them. "Bye!"

Turning inside, she strode down the hall as Jeran came towards her. The boy was only barely eighteen, a gifted kinetic and an orphan. He had a bit of mouth on him, but she liked him, despite her gruffness.

Looking first at the bottle in her arms and then at her, Jeran winked. "Happy now?"

She gave him a broad grin. "Yep."

He laughed. "Well, stock's been put upstairs in the dry room. I'm on my way up now to help sort it all out, you coming?"

"Yeah, I'll just put this away and meet you up there."

A touch of mischief crossed through his face and she sensed he was thinking she'd have a taste test first. She gave him a knowing wink, just to encourage the idea.

An old remnant of the prosperous times before the Agency, the building in which they all lived had once been a small department store. The shop front was a vast empty space, cold and impractical to heat because of the high ceiling, so they couldn't really use the room for much, even storage. Instead they lived upstairs where it was mostly warm and dry in the winter. At the back of the building on the ground floor, with the only other back door, was the "sunroom". It had the right amount of windows and walls in fortunate places to capture and hold a lot of heat and light in the mornings. Consequently, at the times of the month when they ran low on heating supplies anyone sensitive to the cold hung out there, and often enough it was just her, Jemma who had arthritis and the baby.

Timān was still wiggling and babbling happily from his car seat-cot on the workshop table when she stepped into the room. Jemma looked up over her knitting and gave her a broad smile. Returning the smile, Hetera placed the bottle onto the table and touched Tim's warm face with her hand. He gave her an odd little baby smile, and tried to get his mouth around her fingers—he was teething and wanted to chew on everything.

"There, there, my little zombie baby, I'll get you something to gnaw on soon." Leaning forward, she kissed his soft hair and lifted the blankets higher around him.

She made her way back up the hall intent on going upstairs. Reaching that end of the corridor, she stopped mid-stride. At the base of the stairwell near their back door, someone lay on the ground as if they'd fallen.

He lay on his stomach, dark hair obscuring his face. There was no heartbeat, but his skin was still warm. Gently, she pushed at his shoulder to turn him onto his side. Her yell of surprise was half-choked. It was young Jeran. He was shot in the heart—she hadn't even heard a shot.

But, even a silenced weapon would make some kind of noise I would hear?

Her mind grappled with the impossibility of this event for several seconds, and then her practical side won out. It didn't matter how it happened, someone was inside the building and that someone was dangerous.

She had to call for help.

* 9 *

The world was very loud and Taelin's head still ached somewhat. It was like he had a million arms stretched out around him that touched people and absorbed into him a little of what each person was feeling. Kala had made some kind of barrier so that the sensations were duller, but there was apparently no way to fully block him empathically until he re-learned how to do it himself. He rubbed at the pain between his eyebrows with a knuckle.

"You've got to think like you speak," Nama continued telepathically as Tae tried to focus on the lesson. *"Has to be with words. You can be loud or quiet, short or long distance, open or private band and you've got to become aware of how strong you're pushing because you can hurt people. Right now you're so loud you're making my ears ring."*

He imagined himself whispering. *"How's this?"*

Nama's face twitched and Tae sensed a flare of irritated pain.

He sighed. "Sorry."

"You'll get it."

Tae turned in his seat to look behind him. A sensation came towards them of desperate fear, which transformed into the odd shimmering silver call of Hetera's mind energy.

"Nama!" Her mental voice was so loud it seemed to distort and echo in Taelin's ears and he flinched. *"We need help! Come back!"*

Nama pulled the wheel and the van spun around into a U-turn, nearly lifting two wheels off the road.

"We're coming. What's wrong, Hetera?"

"There's an assassin here. Abe Kashān, I can't find them, it's like they're invisible. I have to get to Timān—" her voice and mental presence cut off with a twitch of burning pain.

"Hai da! Tae, you got a weapon on you?"

Tae ducked into the pocket in his jeans and brought out his father's service weapon. "Yep."

Their van skidded around another corner, crossed the median line and dove up onto the footpath. They came to a stop in a screech of breaks and smoke at the front entrance of Hetera's building.

Without pausing, Nama got out of the van, went straight to the building entrance and kicked in the door. They entered what had once been the shop floor. Sunlight pushed through gaps in the mucky panes above them, and cut white lines in the dust and rubbish on the cracked linoleum floor.

They ran across the room to a man who lay on his back and was splayed out like a scarecrow. His gun lay next to one hand with the safety still on. There was a distinctly surprised expression on his face and a bullet hole through the middle of his forehead.

Staring at the surprised expression, Tae swallowed. *Just like Ana.*

Next to him, Nama swore under his breath.

Together they approached the open door leading into a hallway, which bisected the entire building. They stopped on the threshold to listen. It was far too quiet.

"I can't hear anyone," whispered Nama.

Taelin looked down at the floor and listened to his new senses. "I think I can."

Something niggled at him off to his left and he followed it down the hall away from Nama. He wasn't sure what he was sensing. There was pain and fear, but it was overlapped by an odd contentedness as well as a kind of icy tension.

Tae stepped in through a doorway and stopped. Hetty lay on the floor to his right—alive but terribly injured. Baby Tim sat in his car-seat cot on a table, and in front of the baby stood the assassin girl from last night. Her gun was aimed at the baby's head, but Timān gripped the barrel with his little hands and was trying to suck on it. She glanced over her shoulder.

For a second he and the assassin blinked at each other in surprise. Then she seemed to recover from her shock, and lifted the weapon from the baby to bare down on him. He dove for the floor as a muffled shot went off in the room, and Tae heard feet run outside through the other door.

Nama came into the room behind him and, getting up on one arm Taelin pointed to the back door. "That way. Same girl from last night!"

"*She's... got... Tim...*" Hetera lay on her back next to him, blood all over her.

"I'll get him back, Hetty." Gripping his weapon, Nama ran out after the assassin.

Taelin knelt down next to her. He was afraid to touch her because it might cause him pain, but she was bleeding badly and needed pressure on her wounds. Gritting his teeth, he put his hands firmly down on the bullet wound in her chest and they both cried out in pain. The magnifying feedback from her body through his touch-sense and his non-touch senses was agony, but he refused to let go of her.

"*She killed everyone... she'll kill Tim...*"

"Nama will get her. Just relax, stay with me."

"*The children...*" her mental voice was weakening. "*They're... hiding... in... in....*" The pain from her eased away and under his hands her breathing stopped. He sensed the silvery energy that was Hetera Beu blow away like sand in a storm.

"No!" Taelin closed his eyes. "No, Hetty!"

Footsteps came towards him. Lifting his gun with bloody hands, he looked into Nama's face over its barrel. They stared at each other for a moment.

"Timān?"

Nama shook his head. "She got away. Hetera?"

"Gone." He lowered his weapon.

Nama swallowed and Taelin sensed him suppress his grief. "Come on, we'll have to check for survivors. I'll call in reinforcements."

Taelin got to his feet again. "She said the other children were hiding somewhere, maybe we can find them." He tried to wipe his hands on his dark pant legs but Hetera's blood was already drying and clotted on his skin.

"I'll start upstairs," Nama turned off to the left. "You find anyone, practice your whispering and call me down."

"*Right,*" he whispered mentally.

He heard a sigh. *"Your* volume, *Tae. It's still yelling even if you use a husky voice."*

Tae stood in the doorway and watched Nama check a body at the base of the stairs, and then step over them.

He felt utterly heart-struck and defeated. The girl. It was the girl again and she'd taken out a second Rebel cell within twenty-four hours. They couldn't stop her. He couldn't stop her. This cell was a large one with nearly thirty adults and they could all be dead. He closed his eyes to push away the grief and helplessness.

From somewhere else in the building, a niggling, washed-out fear called out to him. It was so very dim, but it had direction. He turned to his right, walking slowly and listening to that quiet faded terror.

"Momma..." grizzled a little person.

"No, you have to stay here..." an older one replied.

They were voices of the children and they were really close, but at the same time faded and patchy. There were no doors nearby, but the left wall was closer to the faded voices than the right. He put a bloody hand to the wood and the children's fear pulsed into his mind. Through the wall-surface, he felt the lines of wood framing—where natural fibers met nails and metal bracing. The spaces between the wood and metal, however, were filled with something black that absorbed his senses. Through the dark fuzz, he saw that the lines of framing wrapped a box shape around the children, and on the other side of the box was a door that stood in the front of the building. The children's terror pulsed at him through the wood.

He had to tell Nama that he'd found them, but he didn't want to yell. He looked back up the hallway anxiously, then at the wall and his hand. Perhaps, the dimness of the children's voices was what Nama meant by volume? But if that was the case, it was more like *emphasis* than volume to Tae. Stretching out towards Nama, Taelin carefully made the emotion behind the words almost nothing.

"Nama?"

There was no sense of pain in his old friend.

"I found the children."

Through the mental contact he sensed that Nama's mind and heart were an ocean of barely contained, burning grief. *"Where?"*

"They're in a cupboard."

"They're OK?"

Taelin swallowed. *"Yeah, I think so."*

"That's good, everyone's dead up here."

* 10 *

Cheetah held it at arm's length and stared at it like it was an alien. The baby blinked sightlessly back at her. It was podgy and warm, and it had a giant head with eyes bigger than she thought possible for such a small creature. It lifted one little arm up and put most of its hand in its mouth to suck on. Drool spilled slowly down the strange creature's chin and arm.

Cheetah blinked at it. What was she supposed to do with this ball of flesh and bones and... and... fluids?

For a completed mission, I must kill the child. She thought firmly. *But I tried to shoot it before. The crazy little thing wanted to suck on the barrel!*

She frowned in her abject confusion. She wasn't sure why, but she knew suddenly that she could not kill this strange creature. It didn't matter that her orders were to kill everyone in the building, men, women and children. It didn't matter that if *they* found out she would be executed and there was the very real risk of putting her family in the cross-hairs as well, she simply could not kill the child.

But, now what should I do with it?

It was completely ridiculous to take it back to the Agency and her Supervisor. The baby would be killed immediately and there would be consequences. But she only had a few hours before her exit pass expired and if she wasn't back by that time to report in they would assume she was MIA or that she had defected. She did not want either of those outcomes on her flawless record, nor the potential risk to her family that both consequences might threaten. So, the only solution was to find someone to take the child with no questions asked.

But who would take on an orphaned baby?

A wind brushed through the nearby open door and coated them in a flash of icy air. She shivered. The baby; only clothed in a diaper, looked up at her with an odd little baby noise, and she sensed the distinct telepathic impression that it too was cold and wanted her, as the adult, to warm it. The assassin turned her head on the side and raised one eyebrow at it. The child wasn't even old enough to speak or walk, and yet it could communicate telepathically.

How strange.

Cheetah cautiously brought the child closer to her body. Tucking the small thing under her jacket, she transferred all of its weight onto one arm and her hip, and held it to her side under her jacket. She felt it curl up against her shirt and get comfortable in her body heat. With the child warmed and seemingly comfortable, she put her mind back to the task of finding it some kind of home.

She stared out through the door and down the long driveway towards the street. She couldn't be seen dumping the child at an orphanage or even at the front door of some private residence because if it got back to them that she couldn't kill it, and worst still that she had attempted to hide it from the Agency, she would be in even more danger. Assassins who did not kill on command were retired and at the young age of seventeen, retirement meant death.

However, once a home was found for it, she could lie to her supervisor about the child. She could just simply say it wasn't there like the other children. She frowned. But, where could she leave it without being seen?

* * * * *

The assassin stood uncertainly in an alley behind the old Cathedral. There were too many people at the front doors. Maybe there was some kind of afternoon service happening, maybe a wedding, whatever it was there were too many people at the front for her to go in unnoticed. But now she didn't know what to do. If she knocked on the back door and left the child on the threshold there was no guarantee that someone would answer, and she had no cover or time to simply watch to make sure.

Her arm had started to get tired from the bullet graze last night, but the baby was asleep and she was afraid to move it in case waking it would cause it to yell and attract unwanted attention.

In front of her the back door opened and she nearly jumped out of her skin.

A man stepped out of the door and looked up at her with mild surprise. He dropped a small plastic rubbish bag onto the concrete and stared at her. She didn't really notice his appearance except for his vivid blue eyes. She stared at the blueness and wondered if she should just turn and leave, maybe find some other solution.

A cool breeze floated down the alley towards her. On the wind were the evening smells of the city and foods from the many restaurants nearby. She was also dimly aware of the feeling of static laced into those various scents. The breeze and static flowed around her, brushing at the loose hair of her ponytail, and swirling towards the man who stood rigid in the doorway. The static meant something Time Psi related—perhaps he was the one to look after this child.

The priest looked kind and aside from his eyes, painfully normal. Surely, he would find a home for this baby sleeping under her jacket? With a deliberate control of her own body language, she allowed the shock on her face to fade into fear and uncertainty. She wanted to look like some girl who'd found a baby in a dumpster, but was scared and didn't know what to do with it.

The blue eyed man reacted immediately to her shift in body language with a welcoming smile. "Good evening, can I help you?"

She feigned fear and made her voice quiet and uncertain. "I... I don't know. I... I found a baby and I don't know what to do with it."

Shifting her weight, she opened a corner of her jacket and let the priest see the baby's sleeping face underneath. He stepped forward and she allowed herself to flinch a little. This body language would tell him that she was afraid and quite ready to run off, and that would produce slow and careful movements in him so she could predict his behavior, as well as get away quickly if need be.

He looked up from the child directly into her eyes. The slightest twitch of a frown creased his forehead and then he smiled carefully. His voice was calm and almost gentle. "The church can find a safe home for the baby. You don't have to worry about him any more."

He lifted his arms towards her, implying that he wanted her to hand over the baby. Brushing her long jacket aside, she lifted the baby from her hip. In the process, her elbow knocked the hidden gun holster under her left armpit and her onyx-handled gun fell out onto the concrete.

Quickly, she dropped the baby into the man's hands and retrieved her weapon from the ground. Dropping all pretense of a frightened teenager, she lifted the weapon to point it at him. He didn't seem afraid or react to her other than his eyes widening again.

Her voice was cold. "Tell no one where you got this baby."

"I wouldn't have told anyone official. You needn't threaten me." His voice was calmer than she expected and there was no trace of fear in his face. "I can imagine an assassin's job is difficult when it involves innocent children."

He smiled. A gentle confidence passed over his face and she frowned. He wasn't like any one she'd met before. He wasn't afraid of her weapon or her coldness, which usually terrified most ordinary people when they caught a glimpse of it.

"Remember for future reference that anyone can find private sanctuary in the Cathedral, we have no political ties here. That includes orphaned children and Agency assassins. If you ever need help again simply ask for me by name. I am Father Owen."

With the baby held tightly in his arms, he turned and walked towards the back door of the Cathedral. Cheetah took this opportunity to disappear silently into the shadows of the evening. By the time the priest reached the door and turned around to look out at the alley she was gone.

* 11 *

Nalana sat cross-legged on the floor of their kitchen. Young Jena sat opposite her on the concrete as they colored the pictures she and her brother had drawn in crayon last night. The girl leaned sideways and shuffled through an old cardboard box filled with used crayons.

"Here, Nala, I found a yellow!" Jena lifted the battered crayon to show her.

Nalana grinned. "Now I can color that wonderful flower your brother drew!"

The girl handed her the crayon.

She took it with a deliberately polite, "Thank you, Shan Jena."

Without batting an eyelid, Jena replied in kind. "You are most welcome, Mishāna."

Nala grinned approvingly. "That's good, Jena, you remembered—"

Down the hall came the sound of a double rap on wood, likely the front door. Nalana frowned. No one ever knocked at Nama and Kala's base because no one visited who wasn't expected.

"Stay here."

The little girl nodded and continued coloring the rough lines on the floor. Nalana got to her feet and headed towards the front entrance. She sensed no malice outside. In fact the two presences seemed calm, contented and friendly. She didn't have a gun and wouldn't know how to use it if she had, but she figured that few people could fake friendliness empathically, and few others would know where Nama's building was located so it should be fairly safe.

When she opened the door, a priest stood there in his black robes. He held a baby in his arms, and had the most startling blue eyes she'd ever seen.

"Uh, hi," she said uncertainly.

The man grinned and she immediately liked him. "Hello, is Nama around? I think this little one belongs with you guys."

The baby turned in his arms and immediately reached towards her with tiny clenching fists.

"Nananananananana," he babbled happily.

Smiling at him, she touched his dark hair. "You're friendly, aren't you?" The boy's empathic personality was a deep blue, not unlike another little boy about his age that she knew. Realising, Nala blinked at the priest.

"Timān? How did you get Timān Beu?"

There was sympathy in the man's eyes. "I suspect his parents were killed by an assassin. You might not have heard yet."

"I..." she couldn't handle any more loss, in fact she refused to. "Thank you, Father. Um, what was your name?"

He seemed to sense she wanted more information than simply his name and supplied it. "I'm Father Owen. I'm a friend of Father Andrew's. I did the monastery trade run yesterday and met Nama. Is he around?"

She shook her head.

"Nalana..." Jena stood in the open kitchen doorway staring down the hall at them. "How would I address him? He's not Misha or Mishān 'cause he's not family."

Nalana swallowed the ball of pain in her throat and turned to smile at Jena. "You would address him as Shān. Or Jān Kashān because he's an apprentice priest. But here and now, you'd call him Sir or Father."

The little girl wandered up to them and standing close to Nalana, she bowed formally. "Good afternoon, Father. I am Jena."

With a hand to the baby's back, he bowed just as formally. "Good day, Lady Jena, it is nice to meet you."

The girl giggled at being called Lady and skittered back towards the kitchen.

"Where did you learn the language of the Ancients, Nalana?"

Turning back to him, she shook her head. "I can't speak it, but my mother taught me little bits like the correct way of addressing people and greetings. You recognize it?"

One corner of his mouth lifted slightly. "Yes, I've been learning to read the early scriptures, and the oldest are in Ancient. I'm not fluent either—it's a very complicated language." He lifted the baby up and she took little Tim into her arms. "Please tell Nama—"

"Naaalaaaaaaa!" This time the interruption came from Jena's five year old brother, Nada. He ran down the hall from the stairs clutching his hand. When he got to her the little boy was crying.

"Oh dear, what did you do this time?"

"Door," he sniffled, "bit me." He showed her his red fist.

Shuffling Timān onto her hip, she placed one hand gently over the bruise. At the moment of contact with his stinging skin, a pulse of staticy healing energy pushed through her body. The energy washed away the underlying pain of damaged flesh, filling the spaces with a cooling sensation that would cover the pain and increase the boy's ability to heal, so that by the time the cover wore off there would be no underlying pain left. The energy shut off and she lifted her hand from his. The redness was gone and only a little bloodless graze remained.

"Thankee, Nala."

"No problem, now go help your sister with the kitchen drawings, I won't be long."

She watched the boy walk down the hall. From behind her, the priest's voice was gentle. "You're a healer?"

She looked back at him with a laugh. "Yes, but not as good as uncle Ren, he can heal so that bullets come out of... wounds." Her words trailed off as she realized that she was giving out information about someone else to a stranger, and changed the subject a little. "I wish I could learn how to be a better healer."

"Well," he said with a smile, "did you know that the Cathedral College is offering a free nursing program? As long as you're not on the Agency watch list, you should be able to study anonymously. If you're interested, induction starts tomorrow at 10am. Just come and find me before then and I'll get you in—if you want."

"Eee! That would be perfect! Thank you!" She put a hand over her mouth to suppress the string of joyous curses that wanted to come out.

He bowed formally as he had to Jena. "It was nice meeting you, Nalana. I hope to see you tomorrow."

She returned the formal bow—careful not to tip the baby out of her arms. "Thank you, I will do my best to be there. And I'll tell Nama that you came by when he returns."

* 12 *
Day Three—Madness
Mid morning of the next day

The morning was sunny, but cold enough to make the assistant shiver through her wool-lined blue suit jacket. Her new high heeled shoes click-clicked on the side walk at a nice ordered pace as she carried groceries back towards the Agency safe house.

She had his favorite coffee, some of those sweet maka rolls that he liked so much, a few snacks for later in the day and the makings of a curry and noodle dinner. Brushing at the lines of her suit, she mentally and physically preened herself.

Who is the best assistant ever? Me!

Behind her, there was a noise like that of a weapon safety coming off, and a hand dropped onto her shoulder. The nice comforting click-click pattern of her new shoes halted abruptly.

A harsh voice spoke. "You may be the best assistant, but you're not a very good Agent."

Trembling, she tried very hard not to drop the groceries.

"Turn around," he barked.

The man behind her was tall, fairly attractive and his eyes were so light brown that they bordered on yellow. He wore a ratty leather jacket over several of layers of rags and battered jeans. In one hand, he held a weapon that was aimed at her middle.

The assistant swallowed. "You're a Rebel aren't you?" Her voice quivered a little, but she got the words out without stammering.

"We're not after you. So, if you do exactly as you're told and don't make trouble, you'll be able to eat that curry noodle dinner you have there. Got it?"

The assistant nodded slowly.

"Come with me."

* * * * *

Lunchtime

Agent Gān, the Computer Talent, was tired and hungry. The pokey little granny unit he'd been given from which to do his work was out of coffee, and unless he liked hot-sauce on stale crackers it was out of food as well. But there wasn't time between tasks to go out for supplies and his so'then assistant had gone poof early that morning and never returned.

His fingers flittered over the keyboard and he sighed. *This job is for monkeys.*

The job was simple. The surveillance hub received messages from the Tower that were de-coded, stripped of their identifiers, encoded and sent off to their recipients, who were active Agents and spies under cover around Arām City. If he'd had a break, even just a day's break, he could have hacked out a small efficient program to do much of the hard work for him, but of course he hadn't had a day off in a long time. Unfortunately, his next day off would be a rest between job transfers, and because he never knew what he was going to do next, there was no way of taking the time to make his job easier and more efficient.

He sighed again. In his opinion, the Agency was too inefficient with its use of valuable resources—he, of course, being one of those valuable resources.

A priority message alarm jingled and another window opened up on top of the work he was doing. It was a message from the spy in the Primary Rebel cell.

"Main Hub, you've been made. Get out now."

Panic leapt through his body. "Nuth!" Tabbing through twenty or so backed up job windows, he got to the base communication hub command line.

What code is it? Nuth! What code? His fingers hovered over the keyboard for a moment, the panic blanking his normally brilliant mind for a second. *Code six!* His fingers shot across the keys.

"So'then nuth!" Launching from his chair, he searched around the room for his weapon and ID. They, with his suit jacket, were on the bed in the other corner of the sitting room. He scampered over, picked them up and threw the jacket over his shoulders.

In front of the wide north-facing windows, the laptop jingled with another message alert and he paced back to it. On the screen, blinking in big red lettering was: *"Asset A2.0248, Codename: Cheetah, inbound."*

Agent Gān sensed danger at that moment and stopped to listen. He wasn't a particularly gifted Psi, in fact at a 1/5 Telepath rating his Danger Sense and Computer Talents were far more useful resources for the Agency.

His Danger Sense was always spot on and it was burring loudly in his head. The danger came from all around him, the front and back doors as well as the large north-side windows in front of him. The south, however, felt a little less dangerous.

Running, he shot through the narrow central hall and zigged into a dinky little bathroom. The window was tiny and he wasn't sure if he'd fit through it, but he had to try because the sense of danger was intensifying.

He got up onto the edge of the converted bath and pushed his shoulders through the window. It was tight, but he could move a little bit by wiggling further and further out. But when he got to his ass it wouldn't budge. A crash sounded from inside, and he heard broken glass and yelling. Wiggling himself, he kept struggling. Footsteps sounded in the hall behind him. Then, finally his ass pushed through the gap and he slipped out of the window. He dropped for what felt like forever, before landing onto a heaped pile of grass clippings.

Gān lay there for a few moments listening for any nearby threats and calming the panic in him. Once calm enough to think again, he set about vaulting over the low back fence to safety.

Only as he ran down a narrow street on the other side of the fence, did he realize he'd left his laptop behind. A laptop that had all the codes and system access the Rebels would need if they wanted to take down the Agency's external communication network or the tools with which to find any of the spies in their ranks.

He swore obscenely.

* 13 *

Asha skimmed through the bookcase, which sat in one corner of the granny unit for any useful information. She found only coding manuals and a variety of trashy fiction. Such books were the unsurprising off-duty reading for a ditzy personal assistant and her computer analyst.

The spy in their ranks—the one responsible for the loss of Hetera and Taelin's cells—had given the Hub Agent a heads-up. The fact that the spy had known where they were going to attack with enough time to warn the Hub, worried Asha. It meant that he or she was definitely one of those in Nama's cell, and more specifically the half who were helping on this particular job. It was still ten or so suspects left to check out but she and Hawk were slowly closing in on them. The spy would eventually pay for the damage they'd done— Asha would personally see to it.

Making her way carefully through the shattered glass on the carpet, she glanced around her for any other useful information the Computer Talent might have left in his rush to escape.

They'd deliberately isolated the assistant and raided the place from all angles so they could take the Operator as well as the Hub. Now, without a high rating Computer Talent they would need to acquire another to hack into the Hub. She was sure another Computer Talent would become available soon enough. Hawk often unintentionally worked that way with the timing of his escapes, and as irritating as that was for her on a personal level, it was very helpful for the Rebels.

Reaching the desk in the middle of the room, Asha pulled out a wheeled office chair and sat down. When she cleared the screen saver with a mouse click, she saw one message window was on top of all the others. Big red flashing letters declared that an alarm had been tripped and Cheetah—the new and dangerous assassin—was headed their way.

"Hai di'chena!" she whispered as she lifted the radio from her belt.

~ "Evac. I repeat. Evac. Team One and Two drop everything and get to the periphery, over."

Unplugging the cables to the sounds of footsteps rushing outside, she shoved the laptop under one arm and turned to leave.

Two paces from the door, a distinctive sense of overbearing danger made her skip sideways for cover. A gunshot fired as she moved, and ducking behind a small couch, she landed on all fours. Bits of plaster and dust fluttered into her hair from a new bullet hole in the wall.

She needed back-up and went for the radio, but it wasn't on her belt. Searching around her, she looked out across the floor to see that it sat in the doorway— too far out of cover to grab. Being an Agency building, the unit was Psi shielded, which meant she had no way to call for help.

Hai da! she swore mentally.

Someone leapt through the smashed sitting-room windows and two feet landed in the mess inside with a thud. It had to be the girl. Asha knew she could probably take her out by herself—after all that's what she was trained for—but there had to be something for the others to find if she failed. Carefully, Asha tucked the laptop through a gap under the bookcase behind her.

The assassin girl was almost invisible, both empathically and telepathically, but her movement wasn't invisible telekinetically. Asha could sense the location of stationary and moving objects, as well as what things could be moved, so the girl's slow almost silent steps across the room created a bright shimmer in her telekinetic senses.

The girl walked towards the couch, and Asha, icy calm, simply waited for her to get close enough.

When a shoe crunched broken glass very close, Asha knew it was time to fight. She gripped the two-seater with her mind, kinetically picked it up, and threw it as hard as she could at the assassin's slim form. But the dark-haired girl flipped backwards out of the way, and missed being taken out by the couch and the wave of kinetic thrust by only a hair's breadth.

Asha let go of the couch, which continued to fly across the room and broke through the other wall into the kitchen beyond. She aimed her gun at the girl and ran sideways. As she fired, she kinetically gripped a bed in the corner and lifted it clean off the floor.

The girl landed from her back-flip low to the ground. She slid on her knees across the glass-covered floor and underneath the now flying bed, before sliding through the doorway into the hall out of sight. A line of bullet holes in the wall traced the girl's trajectory, but none hit their target. The bed smashed through one side of the door frame and out into the hall.

Asha ducked through the couch-shaped hole into the tiny kitchen and pulled open an old metal fridge door to use as cover. The girl stepped back into the sitting room towards her with a gun up, and for the first time Asha caught sight of the green eyes her brother had talked about.

In the millisecond they stared at each other over their weapons, Asha sensed a heart that had long ago completely disconnected and iced over.

So young and already broken by the Agency, she thought.

She felt a spark of pity for the girl. It must be a terrible thing to be forced to kill even before the Age of Consent. However, Asha's compassion was cut off abruptly by the sharp and forceful mental thrust of the girl trying to telepathically gain control. Asha called out defiantly against the attack. They both pulled their triggers at the same time. Asha felt the bullet impact her stomach and as she hit the linoleum, she heard the girl fall as well.

Ha! she thought defiantly.

The pain was pretty bad but she had to move. Panting, she got up from the kitchen floor. Putting one hand firmly to her stomach, she lifted her weapon with the other. Stepping through the mess of wrecked wall, she assessed the damage of the living room.

Blood was splattered on the floor, showing where the girl had fallen but there was no body. More specks of blood led towards the broken north windows and outside.

She's gone!

Asha was oddly relieved that it was over—even if she hadn't managed to kill the assassin. Shuffling through the lounge, into the wrecked hall, she forced her slowly numbing limbs to obey her. Just a little further and she'd be able to call for help.

The entrance door was open and she fell to her knees in front of it. Outside, Nama and her brother ran down the concrete path towards her and she reached for their minds.

"Get... Ren..."

* 14 *

"Asha!" Taelin yelled, as he ran up the steps towards her. Blood stained her hands and stomach, and she looked so pale. He got to her before Nama. The moment he touched her, a sharp spiking agony flowed into him and he cried out.

"Don't, Tae!" she said breathlessly.

He ignored her warning and grabbed her free arm to help her, gritting his teeth as he did so. "Lay back, Asha."

Coming up from behind him, Nama physically pushed Tae out of the way and forced him to let go of Asha again. Kneeling down next to her, Nama put his hands over her stomach wound and she gasped as he applied pressure.

Taelin leaned around Nama and grabbed for her fingers. Her skin was oddly cold. She gripped his hand tightly for a moment and let go of him again.

"Get back, Tae, please—"

"Don't speak, Asha." Nama interrupted her. "Just stay with me. Ren is almost here."

"Cheetah, she got away. Get the... laptop." She let out a terrible moan of agonized pain and Taelin put a hand to his face to suppress his fear and grief.

She opened a broad mental channel that any telepath in their vicinity could hear. *"Get the laptop, Hawk needs it for his plans. It's under the bookcase in the sitting room."*

Footsteps approached and Tae glanced at the doorway to see Ren running up towards them.

"Ren's here," Tae said. "Don't worry about the laptop, I'll get it."

He backed into the sitting room doorway to allow Ren inside, and turned to look around. The place was a total mess. He stepped over the remains of a bed that was half in the hallway and half in the sitting room. A hole in the west wall led into a battered kitchen beyond with a couch smashed against the line of a counter top and cupboards.

In the sitting room, the windows in front of him had been shattered inwards and opened the room to the midday air through shreds of net curtain. A line of blood led across the shard-covered carpet and out through the open window frame. To his right in the far corner, stood a waist-high bookcase filled with technical-looking manuals and the occasional intact pot-plant.

Approaching it, Taelin got on his hands and knees and shoved a finger into the narrow gap underneath. His finger hit a metal surface and he jimmied the modern-looking laptop out of the gap. Its cover was made of shiny metal, the size of a sheet of printer paper and only barely thicker than his finger. It was bizarre to think such a thin piece of metal could house a full digital communication hub with remote satellite access.

With it in his arms, Taelin stepped back out into the hall. Asha was unconscious but breathing steadily. A wrecked bullet sat on the ground next to her, covered in blood.

He handed the laptop to Nama and stared down at his sister. He couldn't have faced losing her too. She was all that was left of his old life and their parents. He knelt down and brushed some of her dark hair from her face.

Cheetah had nearly killed her. That girl had already killed so many people. Old Brān. The twins. Hiran. Strong, loving Hetera. He felt a flicker of rage come to life inside him.

That girl assassin. He gritted his teeth.

The rage flared up and pulled his mouth into a hateful grimace. He got to his feet again. There was a blood trail leading out of the sitting room—a trail that led to a girl who could kill without mercy.

"She's not going to get away with this again!" he snarled.

Nama frowned at him. "What?"

Tae turned away from him and into the sitting room. He pulled out his gun and approached the gaping space that had once been a large floor-to-ceiling window. Jumping out and landing in the grass below, he looked around the side-yard. The sun was warm despite being early winter. There was nothing in the yard other than well-tended grass and a white picket fence that seemed to surround the property on all sides. To his left was a garden gate. It was half-open and smudged with a blood-caked handprint. Glowering at the long-fingered print, he stepped towards it.

"Taelin! Come back!" Nama stood in the broken window above him. "What the Nuth are you doing?"

"Going after that so'then girl!" He snapped back.

"Your sister was Ao trained and she nearly didn't survive. What chance would you have?"

"She's injured," he growled over his shoulder. "Shouldn't be too hard to kill her now." Tae stepped through the gate and out into a narrow driveway that accessed the backs of surrounding houses.

"Wait, Taelin! This is madness! You're going to get yourself killed!" Nama called out behind him. "Hai da! At least wait for me!"

* 15 *

Church of the Founder

Nalana rather liked Father Owen. He was emotionally quiet, friendly to everyone, and loving with the orphanage kids. She sensed there was more to him than she saw, but couldn't believe for a second that whatever was hidden under that calm blanket inside was anything but good.

"I have a name you can use in class." He handed her an old wrinkled birth certificate for a woman her age. The name on the form was "Gabriella Sohl". She wasn't a Gabriella, not really, but she was happy to pretend if it meant she could learn to be a proper nurse and not just a walking talking pain-killer.

"But please, keep your involvement—" he paused as a fellow priest walked close by. "In things best kept secret, a secret. I have vouched for you—"

"And if I screw up you'll get into trouble." She finished his sentence for him. "I totally understand. I'm pretty good with secrets..." she looked away for a moment. "Well, most of the time. But I promise to be good with this one!"

When she looked back up into his face he was smiling, and again she sensed that quiet amusement in him that she'd triggered a number of times that morning. She wished for a moment that she was a telepath so she could find out why she seemed to amuse him so much, and either increase that behavior or stop it altogether.

They walked through a door and out into the main Cathedral area. Lines of pews filled up much of the huge empty space, and carvings of the twelve Church Patrons (and twelve months of the year), stood on the edges of the room at regular intervals. From over the length of the vaulted sanctuary, Nalana sensed a terrible agony. She stopped and stared across the space at the main entrance.

"What's wrong?" he asked.

"I... I don't know." She frowned. "Someone's hurting really bad."

As she frowned at them, the double doors opened and a dark-haired woman stumbled in. Even across the distance, Nalana knew immediately that the woman was shot and dying. Nalana took a step forward, intent on helping but Father Owen moved to stand in front of her.

"No," he whispered. "That is an Agent. Go to my office and stay there until I come for you."

She looked up at him. "But—"

Blue eyes were firm. "No! You need to keep hidden. There are plenty of people here to help her. Just go."

Nalana only paused for a moment before she turned around to do as he asked. She skittered out of sight back through the door and into the main hallways behind the Sanctuary. She knew it was important that no Rebel or free Psi were caught in the Cathedral. If caught, it wouldn't just be her in trouble. Father Owen, the other priests, priestesses and lovely old Father Andrew could all be arrested and executed for harboring fugitives. She couldn't do that to them—not ever.

Father Owen's office was next to a U-turn in the main hallway. Inside, his office was very sparse but fairly big. In the middle stood a broad wooden desk and a turn-of-the-century-style leather chair. In one corner to the right of the door was a bookcase that towered over the room. It was filled from floor to ceiling with ancient books, manuscripts and scrolls, many of which had symbols on them that she did not recognize. She walked from the doorway towards those beautiful books and ran her fingers over their aged leather spines. Her mother had been fluent in Ancient, so whenever she saw such books they reminded Nala of her. One brown leather spine had many letters she couldn't read on it, but she recognized one symbol, the Ancient letter for "Xa" and she touched it with her finger. The edge of a smile lifted into her lips.

"You really like my books, don't you?" There was a grin in his voice.

She laughed and turned to face him in the doorway. "Yes, very much. I wish I could read them all, but I can barely read and write in Common."

"We can look into that later, if you like. But, for now, I think it would be best if you leave, you shouldn't be here when her people arrive. Andrew will do the rest of your papers and finalize your enrolment for you."

Nalana lifted her fingers from the beautiful book spines and sighed. "OK."

They zigzagged through the stone hallways, but it was a different path to the one she knew. All of a sudden, she was in a broad kitchen made of clean shiny steel. There was a back door and he opened it for her.

"I hope you don't mind," he smiled, putting a nice sparkle in the bright blue of his eyes. "The Agency will arrive through the front, so, I figured that the back door is a better escape for you."

Nalana bowed formally. "Thank you, Father."

"Until next time, Alashāna."

She blushed, recognizing the Ancient title for Master Healer, and tried very hard not to giggle at the compliment as Jena had the day before.

* 16 *

Taelin strode in through the double door entrance of the Cathedral. The rage in him was so deep he almost didn't recognize Father Andrew when the old man approached him.

"Taelin, you must leave the Cathedral."

"No, not without that assassin!" he snarled.

"Tae." The older man grabbed him weakly by the elbows. "You have to go, the Agency is coming. Please, just leave."

He shook off Andrew's grip and glared down at the old man. "Where is she?"

Father Andrew pulled back from him in fear.

"Taelin Kān." A new voice, much younger than Father Andrew, echoed across the pews. "Leave this place."

Taelin walked around the old man and approached this younger one. He seemed more confident than any priest his age should be—the man couldn't even be twenty five.

"Give me the girl and I'll go."

"Father Owen, be careful—"

The new priest lifted a hand to stop Andrew finishing his sentence. Then the man glanced back at Taelin. His eyes were ice blue and Tae sensed something very strong behind them, like an unyielding wall.

"Taelin, whatever this girl has done to the Rebels will be nothing in comparison to what you will bring to this monastery if you stay. I am asking you calmly and quietly to leave."

Tae lifted his chin and re-gripped the handgun. "Or what?"

The priest moved into his personal space so fast, disarming him, then knocking his knees out from under him. Suddenly, Taelin found himself on the stone floor looking up at the priest over the barrel of his own weapon.

Ice blue eyes glared down at him coldly. "I said leave. Now."

The coldness in the priest's eyes was oddly terrifying to Taelin. He'd seen it before, but he wasn't quite sure where. The man standing over him clicked the safety and stepped back. Tae got to his feet again, as he stared fearfully at the priest. Behind him, footsteps came in through the entrance and stopped abruptly.

"Tae?" Nama's voice was afraid.

Outside, the sound of Agency sirens drew near.

"You hear those sirens?" the younger priest said angrily, as he handed Tae's gun back to him. "If you two aren't out of here by the time they arrive you will shut down this monastery and kill a lot of innocent people." His voice lowered menacingly. "Get. Out."

* * * * *

Nalana was good at being invisible. She'd learned how to do it at the Ace of Spades Casino. She would whip in and out between rich customers, pick-pocketing gambling chips and cash, or collecting the stray coins that sometimes bounced out of sight when the slot machines spat out large numbers of quarters. She and her mother had done pretty nicely from what she'd been able to steal and find, and all without Fritz ever finding out that they were earning more than the allotted wage of a debt-bound slave and her debt-bound child.

By the age of fifteen Nalana's ability to blend into a crowd and be invisible had become instinctual. So, when she came around to the front of the Cathedral to discover all of the Agency vehicles and lights, she managed quite well to meld into the crowd. Anyone who saw her would think she was just some poor shoeless street urchin made curious by all the pretty shiny lights and straight-laced Blue Suits.

She knew where the security camera was in front of the Cathedral, and knew which angle to stand or walk on so that it didn't see her face without looking like she was deliberately avoiding it.

A small crowd had formed in front of the Cathedral entrance. A white and blue Agency ambulance sat on the cobbled square near the front doors and a couple of blue Agency patrol vehicles were parked either side of it.

Pushed between two tall sightseers, who conveniently blocked the camera from seeing her, she watched the Agency EMTs bring out the woman who'd been shot. As the stretcher passed her, Nalana sensed that the unknown woman had been given a number of painkillers and was somehow less close to death than she had been when she came into the Cathedral. The stretcher was lifted into the ambulance and the back doors slammed closed. Flashing blue lights fired up with the motor, and crossing the cobbles of Cathedral Square, the ambulance drove back onto the main street and out in an easterly direction towards the Agency Tower building.

The crowd started to disperse and she was about to make her way safely out of camera range to head home, when two Blue Suits came out of the Cathedral dragging a third in handcuffs. When the handcuffed man looked up at the crowd, she had to fight her reaction of horror and fear, least someone noticed that she knew him.

Father Owen's face was red on one side and she figured that one of the arresting officers must have hit him. They'd taken his priest collar and over-garment so he looked more like an ordinary man in black clothing rather than a priest.

As they passed her in the crowd, Father Owen saw her and for a microsecond they locked eyes. He wasn't afraid but she sensed that he wanted her to keep quiet, to run and hide, not to risk herself. As she watched, he was pushed roughly into the back of one of the Agency cars, and a few minutes later it drove away after the ambulance.

* 17 *

"What do you think you were doing, Tae? That was so stupid!"

Glaring at his friend, Taelin dislodged his elbow from Nama's grip. "She killed the twins. The others. Hetera's cell. She would have killed little Tim if we hadn't interrupted her. And she nearly killed Asha. What the Nuth am I supposed to do, just sit there and let her kill more of us?"

"How exactly is bringing Father Andrew and the Monastery down to the gutter stopping her?"

"I didn't want that," he sighed and shook his head, "I didn't think—"

"No. You didn't think at all!" Nama smacked the back of Tae's head roughly. "Don't you think I want that girl dead too? But mindless vengeance is not a smart way of going about it! Especially at that cost. Those priests are the only legal friends the Rebels have!"

"I know, I'm sorry. I—" Taelin stopped walking and turned to look behind them. He could feel fear and a pained sensation that implored desperately for them to stop and wait. He frowned.

"What?" Nama asked.

"Not sure. Someone's following us?"

He saw a figure step into the narrow lane between buildings and run towards them.

"Nalana?" he called.

"Tae! Nama! Father Owen... he got took!"

When she got to them she practically fell over herself, but Tae caught and steadied her. "What? Nala, start from the beginning. What's happened?"

"I was at the... Cathedral." She panted. "Father Owen arranged... a fake ID so I can go to school... and learn to be a nurse. Some lady came in, she was shot, and Father Owen told me to hide. Then when it was clear he took me to the back door, 'cause Agents were coming. When I got onto the street again there were Blue Suits everywhere. I don't know why but they arrested him! The Agency has Father Owen! They're going to kill him!"

The breath in his lungs left Taelin and he stared at her in utter shock.

"Hai da! I told you it was stupid, Tae!" Nama turned and kicked at the alley wall. "Marana so'then dai'chena!"

Realizing what that meant Tae looked sideways at Nama. "But—"

"Yes," Nama interrupted him. "Father Owen knows where we live. He knows the faces of many Rebels—"

Tae swore. "They'll take what he knows and then they'll come after us!"

"Who cares about what he knows! The Rebels can just run!" Nalana was crying. "A nice, loving, innocent man is going to be killed and all you can think of is how it'll affect *you*!" Brushing at her tears with one hand, she ran away from them.

Nama sighed. "She's right, you know. And it's our fault."

"What can we do?"

Nama brushed one hand through his dark hair. "Well, unless they've changed their procedures since Kala and I got out, they'll take him to Gora Prison first. If he survives until tomorrow, he'll be transferred to the Tower and the Interrogators."

"Are you suggesting we break into a prison to rescue him?"

Nama lifted an eyebrow. "See any other choice?"

"But, aren't prisons secure? You know, hard to break out of let alone into?"

"Generally, but Gora Prison was my first posting, I think we can do it—the place is mostly abandoned now anyway. We just need some gear and a unified plan." Nama flicked his head. "Come on, let's get back home. We've got to initiate an evac and we might even have time to apologize to Nalana."

* * * * *

Agent Rasa pulled his prisoner down the long entry corridor of Gora Prison. The place had seen better days with peeling paint, water damage all over and rats skittering away from their footsteps. The building was certainly not up to code. However, the quality of the facilities didn't matter so much because the prison served only as a temporary holding cell. They didn't need to smarten the place up in line with "basic sentient rights", because tomorrow the prisoner would be transferred to the Telepath Interrogators to be stripped of all useful information and die of extreme psychic shock.

Walking dead, Rasa thought cynically. *They're all walking dead if they come in here.*

The prisoner had remained silent the entire drive there, which was unusual—they often begged for mercy or denied whatever charge they were given. He also didn't seem particularly frightened. Tense maybe, but not scared at all.

What kind of man trades his life for that of an old man and yet is not frightened of torture and death?

They got to the end of the hall, where a metal grating protected the front of the guard control-room. Rasa nodded to the uniformed man inside and a door in front of him unlocked. He pulled it open and stepped into the one area of the old prison still in use— what had once been solitary confinement. There were five sealed metal cells with no internal window and no furniture inside other than a chair. In its hey-day it must have been a truly unpleasant place to stay, but it all looked a bit rotten and muted now.

They walked to the end and the last cell, which was Psi shielded. Unlocking the metal bar, he guided the man inside to a chair that sat in the middle of the darkness. This was usually the time he was accustomed to the need of hitting a prisoner to stop their cowardly begging and weeping. It was strange not to have to do so.

He tied the man to the chair and frowning, Rasa went to stand in the light from the door directly in front of the priest. He looked down at the younger man, a deliberately hostile expression on his face. "I am Agent Rasa. What is your name?"

"Code In: A0.4.0177, Access 101826." The man's voice was very calm. Ice blue eyes looked firmly up at him and Rasa sensed empathically that this man would be difficult to break.

"That's very nice, you know the Code In sequence of some dead Ao Agent. But that's not what I asked for." Gripping his fist tight, he back-handed the young man hard across his broken cheekbone. "What is your name?"

The pain was obvious in his face, but his voice remained calm and clear. "You do not have clearance to know who—"

Rasa hit him again causing the man's lip to bleed. "What is your name?"

His answering voice was quieter, but no less defiant. "Code In: A0.4.0177, Access 101826."

The Agent lifted his handgun out from under his jacket and leaning over him threateningly, he put the barrel in the man's face. "You will tell me what I want to hear."

* 18 *

Gora Prison was a broad, one-storied concrete building rotting on an acre of land. The back-end of it was overgrown with large trees and an unkempt garden. It was from this end they approached and parked the van on the side of the road. He and Nama left the vehicle and jogged across tarmac into the overgrown greenery.

They pushed through long threads of jade-colored willow tree and a slimy gray wall quickly revealed itself. Tae couldn't help but grimace when he nearly touched the slimy water-stained surface.

Following the wall, Nama walked ahead. Taelin sensed that a great storm was building inside his friend. But he knew him well enough to just let Nama simmer without saying anything. His friend would work through it, he just needed the time and company to do so.

They stopped at a metal door. Taelin expected it to be locked, but Nama simply stepped inside. Following, Tae closed the door behind him and looked around. The whole place was utterly blackened and burnt like someone had come through with a flame thrower. Looking above him at the mangled roof, he wondered why the walls were still standing, despite their being brick.

"So you used to work here before you and Kala escaped the Agency?"

Ahead of him Nama snorted. "Not in this section, obviously, but yes, in the less run-down part of the building. My first post was as a guard here."

"So, how did you know about that unlocked door?"

"It was one of my planned exits. I figured no one would think to look here if I escaped this way."

Tae shuffled around a half-mangled door and into the next section of hallway. "Why didn't you escape then, instead of later with Kala?"

A few paces ahead of him Nama shrugged. "I was put on leave and planned to escape once I got back on shift again, but on my break I met Kala."

Laughing, Tae was about to call out something rude about sex being a poor excuse, but his foot caught on something and he nearly fell on his face. He caught himself with his hands and carefully stood upright again. His laces had caught in a collection of half-melted metal wires and he leaned down to start untangling them.

"Here we are... uh... where are you?" Nama called out to him through a doorway.

"I'm here." Taelin released his shoe from the metal and moved towards his friend's voice. He stepped into another space, which was wider than it was long and filled with charred bed frames and half melted springs. Across the room Nama stood in front of a closed wooden door.

Nama took off a long back pack and placed it on the ground in front of him. "Can you find a hole in these boards and tell me if the door across the yard is open?"

Taelin stepped forward. The walls behind Nama were actually glass-less windows, which were boarded up. As he searched, he caught glimpses of a square courtyard beyond. It was dusty outside and the concrete was broken up at various points by plants that had managed to push through to get at the sun. What windows he could see through the gaps were boarded as well. He went around Nama, who was shuffling in his bag for various supplies. One board, immediately behind him, had a large hole in it and Tae looked through it for a better view. Beyond, he saw an open door.

"Yep, it's open."

"Can you see the guard tower up to your right?"

He squatted down to get the correct angle and looked up above the roofline. There was a battered metal box, perhaps a couple of meters square that stood above the old crockery tiles.

"Yep. It's empty."

"That's good." Nama lifted a crowbar out of his bag and adeptly popped the door lock. Leaving his crowbar behind, Nama grabbed an automatic rifle and stood up. "In and out as quick as we can, got it?"

"Yes, Sir!" Taelin said with a slightly playful smile on his face.

Nama snorted and led them outside.

They crossed the dusty concrete yard and shot through into the doorway on the other side. A man sat eating some kind of pastry and reading a book, with an ocean of monitors in front of him. Nama fired his auto in a short burst. The man dropped his meal and slumped forwards in his chair.

The room was small and cramped by boxes of paper and many different screens with various views of the building. To one side of the monitors sat a control panel with a keyboard. Above the control panel was a metal grating that looked out onto a long plain hallway. Nama pushed the guard to the ground using his boot and took his place in the chair. He hit a big red button in front of him and an alarm sounded once.

"Shut down has started, that should block off some of the guards for a while. Father Owen's in the room at the end, Tae," Nama indicated a door behind them. "Go and get him, I'll hold down the fort here. But be careful, the interrogator might still be in there."

"OK." Tae stepped around behind Nama towards the door.

* 19 *

The hall beyond the control room gave Tae a distinctly uncomfortable feeling of being trapped. Rats skittered ahead of his footsteps. Broad windows to his left had been loosely boarded up, choking the sunlight into haphazard lines that cut across the dusty air. Five big rusted metal doors, like those on giant ovens, were stacked horizontally to his right. He jogged past four of them and found the door at the end was open a little. Through the gap he heard a low voice.

It was dark inside and he was certain it would be impossible to go in, find the bad guy and shoot him before he was shot himself. So Taelin kept his distance out of sight.

"Yes? What is it?" an impatient voice barked from inside the darkness.

For a moment Tae's mind was blank and then he lowered his voice an octave. "Um, there's a message for you, Sir... it's... it's urgent."

A sigh sounded through the gap. "Fine. Stay here and guard the prisoner."

A Blue Suit at least ten years older than him stepped out of the gap in front of him. The man had black hair and dark angry eyes.

The interrogator halted in surprise. He looked Tae up and down, likely noticing that he wasn't wearing a guard uniform, and went for his gun. Tae already had his weapon up and fired first. The man let out a cry of pain and fell back onto the floor.

Leaning over the Agent's prone form, Taelin searched his jacket and found the weapon. As he stood, he dropped the spare into his back pocket. He moved to the cell door and strained to pull it open.

It was very dim and damp inside. He couldn't see much despite the open door. A line of sunlight pushed through the gap, fighting against the pitch black and illuminated the outline of a figure tied to a chair with his back to the door. A face looked back over a shoulder at him. The person's eyes reflected the flecks of sunlight making them seem to glow a vivid ice-blue.

Taelin frowned. "Father Owen?"

"Taelin?" His voice was a gasped whisper. "What are you doing here?"

Pulses of pain on different levels emanated from the priest, so much so that Tae couldn't tell the extent of his injuries. Pulling out a knife from a pants pocket, he approached the chair to cut him free.

"Nama and I are here to break you out."

The ropes that tied the young priest to the chair were wet with something slimy, and only after touching his arm and sensing the distinctive shaft of agony from a bullet wound, did Taelin realize that it was blood on the rope.

"You're shot."

"Not as bad as it could have been." His voice was a little stronger. "How did you break into a prison?"

"Long story," Taelin's knife cut through the rope and freed Father Owen's hands. "But I think Lady Krena was fixing luck in your favor today." Taelin put his knife away and, focusing on making a psychic barrier between them, he helped lift the younger man to his feet.

"Well," he heard a smile in the priest's voice. "I'm relieved for such special treatment."

They stepped out into the hallway and the dust-choked sunlight. Taelin looked sideways. Father Owen's bruised face was pale and tense with pain but Tae was surprised to see that his eyes were clear and awake. He didn't seem to be in shock or about to faint even though blood dripped down his left arm to his fingertips and the floor. He must have only just been shot.

"Come on, we have to be quick."

"Yes, of course. Do you have a spare weapon?"

Tae smiled back at the priest. "You want to help?"

He nodded slowly. "If I can, yes."

Fetching the Agent's gun from his back pocket, Tae handed it to him. "Funny for a priest to know how to use a gun?"

A one-sided smile flashed in his direction. "I wasn't born a priest."

They made their way up the hall, and entered the guard control room to the thumping pulse of automatic weapons fire. Nama sat crouched on the floor in front of the metal grating with his auto pointed out at the hallway beyond. The weapon paused and Nama glanced sideways at them.

"Alarm's been tripped before I could stop it. There's guards in the tower above the yard. Reinforcements are on their way and I've only got a couple more clips for this auto. We're trapped. Either of you happen to have a brilliant escape plan?"

Taelin sensed a deep shaft of fear in Nama, despite the tone of cynicism in his voice.

Father Owen's voice was quiet. "Are you two telepaths?"

Tae frowned. "Yes, but—"

The priest lifted a slightly shaking and bloody hand to his weapon and cleared the chamber. "Taelin and I can take care of the guard tower. When we're done, he can signal the all-clear for you to withdraw."

Tae frowned at Nama.

The mirrored look of puzzlement in his friend's face shifted slowly into an apathetic shrug. It didn't matter how a priest knew how to help, what mattered immediately was that there might be an escape.

Nama turned back to the grating to fire out into the hall and they skirted around him to the yard door.

Taelin looked sideways at Father Owen. "So, what are we doing?"

"Simple. I'll draw their fire and you shoot them." There was no fear in the man and Tae wondered for a moment if he was just exceptionally cocky. "What direction is the guard tower?"

"To our left. What do you mean draw their fire?"

"Just be ready to shoot them, I can't do this for long while injured." Father Owen closed his eyes for a second and then he skittered out into the yard. Gunfire sounded almost immediately and bullets hit the concrete millimeters from the priest's feet. He ran zigzagging across the yard as if his feet knew where the next bullet was about to hit, and dodged out of the way.

He's a Dodge Talent. Thought Tae with surprise.

Stepping out of the doorway, Tae lifted his weapon and aimed at the guard tower. There were three figures in the metal box and he fired at them. One fell almost immediately, the second took two shots to drop out of sight, but the third returned fire. A bullet ricocheted off the concrete next to Tae's feet and he flinched.

As he re-aimed, another gunshot fired from across the yard and the third man fell away. Tae stared at Father Owen across the yard. Remembering Nama, he shook his head and reached back into the control room.

"Yard's clear, Nama."

"Right, I'll be there presently."

Dropping his gun, the priest stepped out of sight through the door across the yard. When Taelin passed back into the burned-out part of the prison, Father Owen sat on the floor panting.

"You can dodge bullets?" Tae stared at the younger man. "Are you a Talent? How come you can shoot? Are you an Agent?"

A tired smile met his questions. "Did you know there are only two professions from which the Agency can't conscript?"

Tae frowned. "No. How is this—"

"The armed forces, because they're already working for the government. And, the other," the man's smile widened and Tae sensed a flare of mischief, "is the Church, because a person's duty to the Founder is a higher calling than their duty to patriotism."

Taelin's frown deepened. "So you *are* a Talent?"

Nama dove through the doorway and landed on his side next to them. "Come on kids, let's get out of here. Talk later."

* 20 *

They jogged down a long hallway through many half-melted and barred doors towards the exit. Nama was in front and Tae in the rear. About three quarters of the way down the hall, Father Owen swayed unsteadily on his feet and swerved sideways to put his hand on a nearby wall. Careful to block and minimize the psychic pain, Tae ducked under the man's good arm, gripped the priest's waist to keep him upright while driving his unsteady steps forwards towards the door.

His voice was very tired. "I'm OK."

"No you're not. Now's not the time to faint and make a preta of yourself. Now come on."

Ahead of them Nama got to the door and turned to look back at them.

Tae answered his unspoken concern mind to mind. *"Worry about what's outside, I've got him."*

Nama nodded and lifting his auto, he slipped outside. Walking crookedly, he and Father Owen made their way to the exit. As they came outside, Nama's auto fire started again.

The greenery of the overgrown garden swallowed them and he struggled to keep both of them upright. As they stumbled, Taelin sensed a mumbled mental noise that slowly came out of the wary agony inside the priest's mind.

"Life is breath, breath is life..." a male voice, calm as if in prayer, faded into a second voice.

"I wanted to call you David..." the woman was whimpering and sobbing as if in pain. "I'm so sorry, I didn't... didn't see what he was doing... will you forgive me?"

"Life is breath, breath is life..."

The two voices, one chanting calmly, the other gasping and whimpering, overlapped and slipped back down into the dark gray shadows of the young man's mind. Neither voice hurt Taelin, but both were loud enough in his senses to make them stumble awkwardly to the edge of the wild greenery.

"Nama?" he reached telepathically.

The sound of Nama's auto fire paused a moment. *"Go now, I'll cover you."*

"Come on, Father Owen. We're almost there." Tae shuffled his arm into a stronger position around the young man. Together they stepped forward, pushing through the bushes and bursting out of the green onto the road. He pulled him towards the van on the other verge. As they got to it, the van door slid open in front of them and Nalana reached out to help Father Owen inside.

Nama stood in the middle of the street several meters away. Tae opened the driver's door and turned to watch his friend. Nama fired another quick burst and further up the road two guards dropped. Abandoning the auto, Nama turned to run towards them and Tae jumped into the back of the van.

Their doors slid and slammed closed, and for once Nama's old van started up on the first go with a jolting lurch. Father Owen lay on the metal in the back of the van with his eyes closed. He looked very pale and his breathing was rapid. Blood had run down the front of his black shirt and arm—it looked like a lot.

Nalana took off her battered jersey and placed it firmly over the wound. Father Owen was conscious enough to flinch in pain, but his eyes didn't open.

"Tae, keep pressure for me?"

He leaned over and put his hands firmly over the wound. He could sense the pain and wariness in the priest, as well as Nalana's tense fear, but it wasn't invading him any more. He wondered for an absent second when in all the madness had he learned how to shield.

Nalana put her hands either side of Tae's on Father Owen's shirt, and closed her eyes. He sensed the flow of warm buzzing static energy. It pulsed in his mind with a layer of warm white static that was Time Psi and overlapping it was a calm blue empathic peace. Combined, Nalana's healing energy felt like a warm, forceful and buzzing thing, almost with a life of its own. Father Owen's breathing deepened and the tension in his limbs released.

"Where's Uncle?" said Nala.

"He's at the new evac base." Nama called from the front seat. "We're going there now, once I make sure we're not followed. How is he?"

"It's a clean through-and-through. So, if we can get him to Uncle quickly, he should be OK."

Looking over the front seat at Nama, Taelin sensed that his old friend was fearful and a little rattled—he needed something to loosen the mood.

"New base? Don't you mean *my* new base?"

A snorted laugh sounded from the front. "Not yet it ain't. Remember you've no cell members other than you, Nalana and the children."

Tae smiled, Nama felt better already. "What about Asha?"

"What about Asha? She's Hawk's territory, likely she'll stay where ever he is."

Father Owen's eyes were still closed, but he spoke drowsily. "Asha?"

"Just rest, Father Owen. You're OK now." Nalana stroked the young man's face and Tae sensed that pulse of warm buzzing energy again. The priest's consciousness seemed to fall sideways into sleep.

* 21 *
Day Four—The Spy
The next morning
Outside the new Rebel base

Sitting on the roof of an abandoned apartment building, with a half-wall mostly hiding him from the view of the people below, Agent Bana Malar watched down the sights of his sniper rifle. His cross-hairs hovered over the face of a man standing in the entrance of the old building across the street. It was a face Bana knew from the most recent round of wanted posters: Nama Ree. He had ebony hair that was peppered with gray, amber-yellow eyes and a broad-shouldered body.

Nama Ree laughed soundlessly and swaggered out of the front doors of the building like he owned the place. He walked to the driver's side of a white van and started up the engine. Half a dozen others followed and got into the back of the van. When the sliding door was closed, the van moved off in a westerly direction towards the center of town.

Bana slowly pulled the sniper rifle back and automatically disassembled it into a carry case at his feet. Despite it being an obvious Rebel base below him, the signal tracker still insisted that there was an active Mobile Surveillance Hub inside.

How the Rebels had captured a hub intact and who was at fault, was a matter for some bureaucratic committee meeting sometime in the future. However, Bana and his wife Lii would recapture it and use the impromptu mission for their own political gain—perhaps a transfer for their little family to another city far, far away from his insane brother Hoyal and his "best buddy" Jaran Cowdy senior.

He and Lii had watched the Rebels since dawn. There'd been a lot of activity in and out of the old marble building, but no sign yet of another Agent or Task Force group having picked up on the signal. The Hub could be ripe for them to take.

Or, just the tracker circuit could be inside and it's a trap, he thought cynically.

Despite their being on opposite sides of this conflict, Bana had a respect for the intelligence of the Rebels. He was certain if they found a homing beacon in something as precious as an A3 Surveillance Hub, they would be devious enough to disable it quickly, or to plant it somewhere as a trap for any pursuing Agents. But, there was also the very real possibility that no one had discovered it yet and the hub was still inside and was available for them to take. His brother, had he known about it, would insist that they take out the entire Rebel cell just for good measure while they retrieved Agency property. But, hopefully it wouldn't come to that. Despite his position in the Agency and his family affiliations, Bana would prefer to get in and get out without much killing.

Lii's reddish mind reached out across the road and connected to him. *"You having fun, dear husband?"*

He grinned at the playful undertone in his wife's voice. *"Are you, Kitten?"*

"Yeees, this building is deliciously un-secure."

"So is it time?" he prompted.

"Yes. Yes, I think so. The Hub seems to be in storage on the second floor. No guards. South-west side door?"

He nodded slightly. *"Meet you there in a few minutes."*

Bana put his hand-held tracker into a backpack at his feet and zipped up the rifle bag. Leaving the gear, he got to his feet.

* * * * *

"Asha, wake up, but keep still. You don't want to pop your stitches." Hawk's voice burred with dark static and the flowing watery blue of his empathic energy. *"Besides,"* he added with an amused tone in his voice, *"you're being watched."*

She wanted to sigh, turn over and push him forcibly out of her mind so she could get some more sleep—she was so tired and sore—but she knew him well enough to recognize that tense undertone in his mental voice.

"Uh. How bad is it?"

"It's not good. I'm almost certain our spy is amongst those left in the building. But that's not the biggest problem. There are two Ao Agents in the building."

"The Hub? Already?"

"Yes, Bana Malar and Liina Meel."

She tensed. "Hai di'chena! We've got to get everyone out—"

"No. It's too late, but there's a way through with minimal damages. Get everyone and the Hub into the dining room. Call back Nama's crew and get Kita here. We'll orientate from that position using people and resources to resolve this quickly. Just don't panic."

"Don't panic?" she thought incredulously. "Do you know how good those two are? How dangerous?"

There was a mental chuckle. "Yes, Asha. But they also have weaknesses we can play on. There's a clear and simple way through this problem, just be as good as I know you are and it'll be fine."

* 22 *

It was deliciously warm in the new base building. The marble exterior seemed to absorb the heat of the day and distribute it evenly throughout every room. All of its windows were intact as were its floors and walls, it might even have insulation. It was perhaps the nicest Rebel building Nalana had ever visited, and that was including the lack of electricity and having only one set of toilets that worked.

She stood in a north-facing room on the first floor, bathed in sunlight. Grinning, she squidgied her toes into the soft faded carpet with an inner squeal of delight. It was such a luxury for her to stay in a warm dry place. She hoped they could stay there indefinitely.

The sacking cloth she'd recycled and washed an hour ago was already dry on the windowsill. It was still stained gray and black from its previous incarnation as a Rebel delivery bag, but it was all she could find for her purposes. She stood for another minute in the light and heat of such a perfect room, and turned back into the hallway that ran through the center of the building.

Two or three rooms down the corridor, she saw Father Owen standing in a doorway with his back to her. She sensed he was introspective, with a deep frown in his empathic energy as if he was worrying about something. She walked towards him and started folding the sacking cloth into a triangle. He seemed to sense her presence and turned.

She smiled. "I have a sling for you. I'm sorry it looks kind of bad, but it should ease the pressure on your shoulder."

"Thank you." He crouched a little, so she could tie the sling at his neck. When it was done, he glanced back into the room where Asha lay, still asleep. "Is it true she's connected to Hawk?"

Nalana's heart skipped a beat and she gave him a deliberately playful smile. "We're all connected to Hawk, even you."

His blue eyes sparkled a little in amusement. "Me? How am I connected to Hawk?"

She took him gently by the elbow and led him away as she continued to speak. "You're connected because you're here. He wouldn't allow you to be here if there wasn't a reason."

His voice was gentle, but ever so slightly correcting. "He's just a man, Nalana. Not a divine entity, he can't know everything."

"Yes, he is just a man, but he's also a Time Speaker. My grandmother once told me that the Great Fates; the Great Guardians of Time, are weavers. What they weave is a huge unfinished tapestry that is Time, and each thread is one person and their lives. A Time Speaker is a thread that the Fates have put into the weaving deliberately to moderate those threads around them, and keep the tapestry from breaking apart. Through the Time Speakers flows the intention and power of the Fates. So that if you weren't meant to be here, he would know and you wouldn't be."

One side of his mouth lifted up in amusement. "Well, please don't take offense, Nalana, but my faith lies in the Founder and His teachings, not in a veiled man who channels the intentions of the Old Gods."

Nalana guided him towards the stairs and the ground floor. She'd distracted her new friend from

Asha, which was good, both for Asha's continued recovery and because despite being fond of Father Owen, she hadn't known him very long. It was one thing to risk herself on someone she didn't know well, but something completely different to risk Asha and by association, Hawk.

She grinned, deliberately dropping any negative or fearful thoughts. "I bet you're hungry, Father. Whenever someone gets a bullet taken out by Uncle Ren they're usually ravenous for a few days after. Want to go down to the kitchen and see if there's anything to eat? I think Raen unblocked one of the fireplaces last night for cooking, so we might even be able to get something hot."

His smile was gentle again. "That would be nice, I am hungry."

* * * * *

Agent Rahan Aria sat at his desk, scrolling through lines of programming code on his laptop. His free hand fiddled with the yellow sticky he'd found on his bedside table that morning. The meaning of the sticky ate at the back of his mind and kept him from concentrating on any one thing at a time. His laptop sat in front of four flat screens, each of which were bisected into six camera views of different areas of the building. A Rebel group could attack the supply depot from any angle, and he was supposed to be on alert watching those screens at all times. But Raha couldn't concentrate and programming calmed his nerves.

From the outside, the building looked like an ordinary house. It had a white weatherboard exterior, two stories with bay windows, a broad front deck and a perfectly manicured flower garden. At first glance it looked like the house of an affluent family with an anal-retentive gardener. But, if someone was to stop to watch the place and document all the in and out activity, any person with half a brain would realize the place was a government-run facility.

It was constantly surprising to Raha that the place hadn't already been raided, but he still jumped when the nearby front door blew in with a cracking boom.

Six roughly dressed men and women piled in through the door and lifted their weapons towards him. Terrified, Raha stood and put his hands up.

A dark-haired man came towards him with a handgun. He wore a battered leather jacket over a navy rag-shirt, and holey brown pants that were a little too short in the leg for his above-average height.

"Come away from the screens." The man's dark blue eyes seemed to drill calmness into Raha and he couldn't help but do as he asked and stepped into the empty part of the room.

"Sit in the corner there. If you do as I say you'll be OK. We're just here to rob the place."

Raha nodded at him and lowered himself into the empty corner of the room across from his desk. The other Rebels moved through the internal door into the rest of the building and his guard paced slowly across to the desk.

Several minutes passed by in silence as one by one, Rebels came from the right hand door with armloads of supplies from the storage rooms, out through the front door; likely to some kind of vehicle, and then returned back past him to get more supplies.

The tall guard sat against one corner of Rahan's desk, watching him warily. There was a calming aspect to the Rebel that Rahan kind of felt drawn to. The man must have been in a fight recently because there were lines of bruising around his eye and temple that looked at least a couple of days old.

Raha sighed and looked down at the yellow sticky between his fingers. Perhaps it was a joke from the other guard who relieved him. Surely the Rebels would have been told if there was a real escape planned for him. He turned it over and over in his fingers. If it was a joke, it was a cruel one.

"What have you got there?"

Rahan looked up at the man, then back at the sticky. He shrugged. "It's probably just a practical joke from my workmates."

He frowned. "How so?"

"Well, you guys might know better than I, but there's a rumor in the Agency that when Hawk wants you to become a Rebel you'll find a yellow sticky-note with instructions on it for your escape. They say he only puts on the sticky exactly what you need, no more, no less."

"And, what's on yours?"

He sighed. "That's just it. There's nothing. Like I said, I think it's a cruel joke from one of my workmates."

"You're disappointed," he said it as a statement and not a question.

Rahan looked sideways at the man and nodded. The inside door opened and in stepped another man who looked down at him with the yellowiest eyes he'd ever seen.

"Show it to me." A large hand was thrust into his face and it took a few moments for him to realize that the man meant his note.

He handed it over.

"Where'd you find it?" The man barked.

"On my bed-stand this morning."

It was given back to him. "Would it be almost impossible for someone to have put it there when they did?"

He shrugged. "I hadn't really thought about it. I guess so."

"What do you do? Are you Talented or Psi? What are your ratings?"

A little smidgen of hope flickered in Raha. "Computer Talent. 9/10 rating. Base code specialist."

The two men's eyes widened and they looked at each other. "We do need a good Computer Talent right now," said his original guard.

There was silence for a long time and Raha expected that they were both telepaths discussing the situation. He waited tensely.

The yellow-eyed man looked sideways at him. "How would you like a crack at breaking into a mobile surveillance hub?"

Sudden excitement lifted Raha to his feet and he grinned. "Would I! Those things are fantastic machines! Multi-encryption systems, layered storage capacity, mobile satellite access... I've always wanted to play with one of those!"

They both laughed and the yellow-eyed man patted Rahan on the arm. "What was your name, kid?"

"Rahan Aria. But everyone calls me Raha."

"Well, I'm Nama, and this is Tael—" the yellow-eyed man trailed off and his broad easy smile faded. "Hai da! We gotta go, right now. If you're coming you do exactly what we say when we say it, no arguments, you got that?"

Raha nodded emphatically. "Yes, Sir."

* 23 *

Asha lifted her mouth into an obstinate expression. *"I'm doing this, I'm not taking any chance with the children's lives!"*

"It's not a chance because they'll be fine in the kitchen." Asha sensed a gentle amusement in Hawk. She hated it when he did that, it was so condescending.

Sighing slightly, she ignored him and focused her attention on the little girl in front of her. Jena's wide blue eyes looked out at her from the cramped dumb waiter.

Asha gave the girl an encouraging smile. "Jena, you're the grown up now. I want you to look after your brothers as well as Tempa and Timān." Behind her, Nalana handed the torch and a small bag of food to Asha, and she passed it to the eight year old girl. "Keep quiet and wait for one of us to find you. You got that?"

The girl nodded fearfully and looked past her. "Nala?"

"It's OK," Nalana stepped forward and reached to touch the girl's outstretched hand. "We'll find you when it's safe again. It'll be like you're camping out. Just don't let Tim eat anything yucky."

The girl laughed, relieving the tension in her. "No spiders today, I promise."

Asha pulled the dumbwaiter door down and wrapped the rope around one arm ready to lower the children to the basement.

Hawk's voice spoke firmly in her mind. *"Tell Nalana to take your back-up weapon to Tae—"*

"No! I put a gun in her hand and they'll shoot her for sure. We need to protect her, not put her in harm's way."

"Asha." His mental voice had a sudden undertone of unmistakable command. *"Do it. There's no risk in this because I know exactly what is going to happen if you do as I say. She will be protected by a new friend of hers."*

She sighed. "Nalana." Hand over hand, Asha started to manually lower the children to the basement. "Take my spare weapon. Under my shirt. Go give it to Tae."

Nalana did as she was told, lifting the back of her shirt up and taking the weapon out of its holster before turning to the side door. Asha watched the young woman step out of sight through the little cupboard that led out into the dining room.

"If that girl gets hurt—"

"Asha, after all you've seen in the last three years, why do you still doubt me?"

The rope in her hands loosened, which meant the dumbwaiter had gotten to the basement. She put the length of rope back into its slot in the side of the old-style dumbwaiter and turned around. She pulled out her primary weapon.

"Because you're just a man and a man makes mistakes. You treat the risks you take like they're a game of Strategy. People are not *pieces in your game to sacrifice at your whim."*

Walking around stone benches of the old kitchen, she reloaded her weapon and dropped the spent clip.

"It is not *a game to me, Asha. We're waging a very dangerous war, people will die and continue to die until it's finished. I'm not cold to that, but neither am I naive to its necessity. Now concentrate, it's almost time and you need to be sharp."*

* * * * *

The dining room was beautiful to Nalana. It had a high stone roof that was carved with flowers and geometric shapes, a polished wooden floor and varnished wall panels. There was a big old stone fireplace on one side that had also been carved with flowers and other shapes. It must have been a stunningly decadent house in its best days.

About fifteen people sat or stood on the dusty wood floor. Everyone was confused and afraid—no one knew what was going on, only that there was some kind of threat. Nalana looked around at all of the faces in the room and she couldn't find Taelin. Father Owen stood in the hall doorway, still in his black priest clothes and the sling she'd given him. He seemed wary of whatever danger was coming.

"Father, have you seen Taelin?"

He smiled at her and nodded. "Yes, he's across the hall putting something away in storage."

"Thank you."

As she stepped past him, there was a sense of something huge rushing in her direction. Nalana turned to look down the corridor. A woman in black with short blond hair ran towards her, a weapon up, aimed and ready to kill her within a heartbeat. Nalana barely had time to gasp before Father Owen stepped in close, grabbed Asha's weapon from her fingers, turned, with his body between her and the blond woman, and fired. The woman tripped and fell as Nala stared. Father Owen grabbed her roughly, pulling her back into the dining room. He pushed her down to the ground and covered her with his body.

* * * * *

Bana rushed after Lii only a moment behind her. He saw her drop and the agony in her stomach pulsed empathically through him as well, blinding him for a microsecond. He roared in sudden grief and pain, but it dropped almost immediately into an icy cold rage. Jumping over her prone body and into a room on his left, Bana fired three times. Those in the room yelled fearfully and clambered out of the way. He hit two people square on and they fell to the floor dead, a third was only clipped. No one seemed to be armed. To his right in another room he sensed someone else.

"I see you there!" He bellowed as he strode out of the first room, back into the hall towards the hidden person. Reaching, he gripped a mind that was very strong but completely undisciplined. The man yelled out.

This one hurt Lii, Bana thought and roared, pushing psychically at him. The figure screamed and fell to his knees, coming into physical sight as he collapsed on the floor.

Something cold touched the back of Bana's neck and he froze. The empathic energy signature of a female materialized behind him. This person with a gun to his neck was a trained assassin, trained above at least A2.

"Let go of him." The mind behind the gun was iron tight, so he couldn't launch telepathically into her before she shot him. The cold rage he'd felt dissipated quickly into an aching pain. Defeated, he psychically let go, and the dark-haired man on the floor whimpered in relief.

"Tae? You alright?" said the icy voice behind him.

The man groaned from the floor and Bana glanced at him, surprised that such a sensitive mind was still conscious enough to respond after his attack.

Behind Bana and his captor, Lii called out to him wordlessly. He sensed her terror and reached back to her mind.

"I'm here my love. We'll be together soon."

She grasped desperately at his mental touch for a few moments, and then death pulled her away. Bana lowered his chin and closed his eyes. Tears ran freely down his face.

"Drop your weapon and get on your knees."

Lowering down to the floor, he put his weapon on the ground and pushed it back towards her.

A hand touched his shoulder. "Let me knock you out, Bana."

It was then he recognized her voice. "Asha? Asha Kān?"

"Yes, let me in."

He looked sideways over his shoulder. "Aren't you going to kill me now?"

"No. For the moment Hawk wants you alive."

* 24 *

Taelin's head throbbed horrifically. Dragging himself up onto his hands and knees, he rested his forehead on the dusty wood.

"Taelin," his sister called out again. "You OK?"

"Not really," he groaned.

Holding onto the door frame, he pulled himself to his feet and looked around. Two bodies lay on the polished floor, the man made of rage and a blond woman. He was breathing, she was not.

"Did you shoot her?" asked Asha, who stood between the two bodies.

He shook his head. "No, I didn't even see her."

Asha stepped over the woman's body and into the dining room. Tae; leaning on walls and door frames, followed her dizzily. Through a haze of pain, he saw the dining room beyond was a mess. Blood pooled around two bodies that lay haphazardly in the middle of the room. The fifteen or so survivors, plus one injured man were all crowded against the far end of the dining room. Fear and surprise were still on their faces.

Tae leaned his shoulder against a wall and slipped down to the floor in an effort to stabilize the world. He couldn't seem to sense anything psychic through the pain, which was both a worry and a relief on his sensitive nerve endings. Whatever the man had done, he hoped it wasn't permanent.

"Who shot the female assassin?" Asha's voice was quiet.

"That would be me," said a male voice. Tae looked up and through the pain, he saw Father Owen on the floor near the doorway, with Nalana underneath him as if he'd protected her.

His sister sounded unimpressed. "And who are you again?"

"That's Father Owen," Tae spoke up, his voice uneven. "You were unconscious, Asha. He was arrested 'cause of me. Nama and I broke him out."

"Where did you learn to shoot, Father?" There was a dark undertone to Asha's voice. "And move that quickly?"

The man got up off of Nalana, and stood with his hands behind his back in a respectful semi-military stance. Nalana immediately came over to sit next to Taelin. Her warm pain-easing hands lifted to touch his temples and Tae closed his eyes.

Echoing in the broad room, Father Owen's voice was tense. "That's a long story, ma'am."

"Short version. Now." Asha snapped.

"My parents were Army. I went to military school and planned to join when I was eighteen. But my parents died before then and I had to run. Father Andrew offered me somewhere safe. He said if I became a priest I couldn't be conscripted."

"Of course," Asha agreed, "the military and the priesthood are the only places the Agency can't take people. Is your name Owen?"

"No. It's Naethan."

"Last name," she barked.

"Amon."

Impatience underlined her words. "Psi? Talent?"

"I was never tested," the priest's voice was almost a whisper. "But I can dodge bullets."

"Bullets?" Asha sounded surprised.

Tae spoke up again, his eyes opening to look at Asha's back. "Saw it yesterday. He's definitely a Dodge Talent. Fairly high rated too."

"Well, Naethan Amon, you're on a short leash until Hawk clears you. For now help Raen and Brea carry the man outside, up to the second floor."

There was a pause as no one moved.

"Now people!" Asha barked and the three she'd named, moved to do as she said. "New guy," she turned to address someone directly in front of her that Tae couldn't see.

"Raha," the person replied.

"Whatever, you get to earn your keep by finding the tracker in that so'then hub, if you haven't found it in thirty minutes the hub will be destroyed." Asha turned and glanced behind her. "Nala once you finish with Tae, get some people to help you with our injured." She moved to address the room again. "We'll also need some volunteers to bury our bodies and dump that woman out there somewhere far away. Everyone else, I want you to pack up this building ready for an evac in one hour. And for Founder's sakes, someone send Kita Oran upstairs when he gets here."

His sister sounded angry, but as she turned around to face him again, Taelin saw in her eyes that she was more afraid and pained than particularly angry.

She looked down at him, her voice very gentle. "Are you OK?"

"Yeah, I think so." Nalana's hands lifted from his temples as he nodded. "Thanks, Nala."

The girl smiled, got to her feet and headed across the room.

Asha gave him a tired smile. "You have the most remarkable Psi flexibility, brother dear. Everyone else I've seen attacked like that by Bana is dead." She offered a hand to help him stand up. "Come, walk with me upstairs and tell me what you know about this priest guy."

"Nama knows more, I only met him yesterday." He took her hand and stood, still feeling a little wobbly, but not as bad as he probably should be.

They turned towards the door. "Well—"

In front of them Father Owen was helping the others to lift the assassin's body with his good arm. Taelin sensed a very gentle mental touch from Asha and her voice sounded with little to no pain in his mind.

"What are your first impressions of him?"

Walking behind the three struggling with the assassin, they headed towards the stairwell. *"He's more than he seems. Quietly cocky and he doesn't seem to be afraid of much, even death. I don't sense any hostility towards us, but there is something..."* he frowned and let his words fade into a feeling of uncertainty.

"Does your gut think he's a threat?"

Taelin shook his head. *"My gut doesn't know. There's something about him that's hidden, but I can't see if it's hostile or not."*

They started up the stairs and she continued verbally. "Listen, when Kita gets here I'm going to need you to go away for a while."

He frowned. "Why's that?"

"We need to Interrogate the prisoner. You're too sensitive, it'll hurt you."

They reached the top of the stairs and as they turned into the hall, he looked sideways at her. "That bad, huh?"

She nodded. "It's agony, especially for someone as sensitive as Bana."

"What about you? You're an empath."

They reached the north end of the second floor hall. Waiting behind the others, they watched while the prisoner was dragged through the doorway into a warm sunny room and dumped on the carpet.

"Yes, but I'm only a 2/5 Empath, more than half as sensitive as you but with ten times the training, I can handle it. I've sent Nama outside. Can you go and help him with his errand?"

He frowned. "What errand?"

"Ask him to explain, I don't have time." She stepped forward into the room, again the commanding leader that she had been downstairs.

"Naethan and Raen, stay in here. Brea, guard the door." She turned to look back at Taelin. "Go now, please."

He took one last look at Asha and turned to head back downstairs.

* 25 *

Warily touching her aching stomach wound with one hand, Asha glanced at the two people in the room with her. Silver-haired Raen was a telepath and not an empath, so he would be able to keep a physical guard while they did this thing.

And this 'Naethan', she thought in frustration. *As if we really need any more complications.* She cleared her throat. "Naethan, are you an empath?"

He shook his head. "No, Ma'am."

"You and Raen are here in case Bana tries to fight physically. Otherwise, no one must interfere with either Kita or myself. Understand?"

The two men nodded and Asha sighed heavily. The pain still throbbed through her abdomen—final remnants of the previous day's gunshot wound. She could really do with more sleep before doing this Interrogation, but they couldn't wait. If Bana had reported their location to the Agency, reinforcements would be sent very soon.

Nearby, the door opened and closed quietly. She looked sideways to see Kita there. He looked calm, but she empathically sensed a deep shaft of dread from him.

She gave him a sympathetic smile. "I'm sorry to ask this of you, Kita. But it needs to be done."

Kita looked down at Bana's unconscious body. "I do understand. But, just so you know, Bana is my cousin."

Surprised, Asha stepped back. "Your cousin?"

He brushed a stray lock of blond from his eyes. "Yes, maternal cousins."

"Do you have—"

"No," he interrupted, "no problem getting answers from him. I have never been close to my family."

She smiled. "That explains why you weren't in the same graduating class."

Those calm gray-blue eyes of Kita's looked into her for a moment, and then he frowned. "You were Ao?"

"Not technically. My husband was, we can talk about it later. We need to get this done before the evac is complete."

"Of course. Do you know how to do a hand-off?"

"Yes."

She linked momentarily with Kita's mind and then Bana's. Undoing the sleep program, she handed the rest of the telepathic process over to Kita, who expertly took it and anchored firmly in Bana's mind ready for the Interrogation. Careful to fully disconnect from Bana and Kita, and as subtly as she could so the others wouldn't sense her, Asha stretched her mental touch to Hawk on a tight private telepathic band.

Bana woke quickly and was immediately confused about his surroundings. The confusion lifted with a grunt of pain, as Kita tightened his mental grip.

"Name, Rank and Code In," she said coldly.

There was a moment of quiet, and she sensed Kita apply pressure to Bana's mind.

"Bana Malar," he gasped. "Ao. Rank fourteen... Specialist Assassin. Elite Class. Code in: Ao.4.0180, uh, Access 4059."

"Immediate superior," she barked.

The pain increased and Bana started to pant. "Heth Pallen."

"Have you reported your location to the Agency?"

His square face screwed up and he gasped. "No... Open book assignment... only way we work."

She nodded slowly. "No reports broadcast until mission accomplished, correct?"

"Yes."

"Ask him about the spy." Hawk's voice rang in her mind.

"The spy within the Rebels, what do you know about them?"

"I... can't..."

Kita tightened his grip around Bana's mind and he cried out in agony. She closed her eyes in an effort to suppress the pain spiraling out from him.

She let her voice sound a little gentle. "Please, Bana, answer the question."

"Hoyal will find me and kill me, please—" he screamed again and curled up into a ball with his hands grasping at his head. "Spy... is... male..."

Kita seemed to loosen his grip on Bana, easing some of the pain and allowing him to speak clearer.

"Spy isn't... one of the Originals. But... he wasn't very high rank in the Agency... Heth is always complaining how... how... undisciplined he is." He gasped again as Kita tightened his mental grip. "Un... until recently... the information from him was too general and useless."

He paused for a moment rolling onto his side and swallowing repeatedly. Asha sensed he was suppressing the urge to vomit.

"I... I don't know much. I don't have a name."

She nodded. "How long has the spy been working for the Agency?"

He lay on his side curled up from the agony in his mind. "Two years... I think."

"How did Heth recruit him?"

His voice was getting quieter. "Spy approached us."

"How does he pass on information?"

"Not sure." Bana stretched his body out again, hands flat on the carpet with his eyes closed and tears running down the sides of his face. "Hub... he contacts one of the hubs."

"The spy must have a satellite device," injected Hawk.

"Yes, and if our new recruit can get the tracker off the hub we can use it to trace the device. What else do we need? He won't last much longer."

"Ask about me. About their investigation."

The others of the room, including Kita were looking at her expectantly. She wished for a second that she could multi-task better and cleared her throat.

"What does the Agency know about Hawk?"

"Not much." Bana lifted one arm and rested the crook of his elbow over his eyes. "All sounds like mamon to me."

"Mamon or not, what do you know?"

Kita tightened his mental grip again and Bana groaned. "Y... yellow sticky-notes. Perfect timing to help Traitors escape. He's like a ghost. Gets in and out of places no one can get to. Does the impossible. That first escape in 3000... they used Jaran's login codes." He laughed weakly. "He was so mad."

"Jaran?"

"Jaran Cowdy senior. Head of the Ao Council. He's a psycho like my brother Hoyal. Worse... he's going to kill every single one of you... or die trying..." Bana closed his eyes. He seemed to be half conscious, almost delirious. "Hope it's the latter..."

"Bana," her voice was quiet and almost gentle. "Do they have any idea who Hawk is?"

"No, he's a ghost." He lifted his arm from his face and looked up at her with dark pleading eyes. "Please, Asha. Put our bodies somewhere the Agency can find us. Save my daughter... she's only four."

Asha swallowed. "Already being done, Bana." She glanced sideways at Kita, whose ordinarily handsome face was so ice cold, he looked like some kind of alien. "Put him back under."

* 26 *

Raen's heart beat thunderously in his ears. Asha, Hawk's second, was getting too close to discovering him and he was terrified. As Asha, the priest and the Interrogator descended the broad stone stairwell down to the ground floor, Raen deliberately lagged behind them. He had to slip away, shut down his remote device, free the prisoner and get them out of there before Asha found out and killed him. He hadn't known that Asha was ex-Ao and the thought terrified him. He knew with every cell in his body that if she got hold of him she would make him suffer before he died.

Downstairs in the ground floor hall, people ran around with boxes and bags in their hands piling supplies up along the wall for evacuation. The female assassin's body was gone and as they stepped into the dining room, he saw that the bodies of the two dead Rebels were covered by stained cloth.

Asha approached the new guy, obviously a Computer Talent of some description, who sat in the middle of the dining room with pieces of the hub laptop spread out in front of him. The under-casing of the computer, screws and plating were all placed in tidy ordered piles on the hard-wood floor. The young man still wore his Agency issue blue suit pants and cream shirt, although the uniform jacket was nowhere to be found.

Behind them, Raen slowly crept backwards towards the door as he watched.

"New guy—" Asha barked.

"It's Raha and I found it." The man handed a small piece of computer chip to her.

"Good."

Raen stepped back again as he watched her take the computer chip from the young man, drop it on the ground and stamp the heel of her boot down onto it.

"How long do you think it would take to put that computer back together and re-program the uplink to find the nearest signal?"

"Not long, a few minutes." The gray-eyed Computer Talent started to put the pieces back onto the laptop base. "You want to attack another hub?"

"No, maybe later," hate flickered into Asha's voice. "Right now I'm after a spy."

Her words echoed out into the hall and in the doorway, Raen nearly stumbled from the shaft of terror that shot through him. Stepping out of sight, finally, he ran down the corridor and up the stairwell again, two steps at a time.

At the door to the north-side room, Raen grabbed his weapon out from its holster, pulled the sliding lock, and stepped inside. He lifted his gun and fired at young dark-haired Brea, who had been left in the room as a guard. The bullet hit her square, splattering blood onto the wall behind her. She didn't even let out a sound before she fell, dead.

He got down on the floor next to the Agent and touched the man's face. Raen wasn't nearly as strong or adept telepathically as the Interrogator, but he knew enough to undo much of the sleep program.

It didn't take long for Bana to regain consciousness, and when he did, Raen sensed through their physical touch that his mental shielding had been quite badly shredded by the Interrogator.

"Can you walk, Sir? You need to get up, there isn't time."

"What? Who are you?" said a tired voice.

"I'm Raen, I'm here to help you, come on we have to go before Asha gets back."

Dark eyes opened and stared up at him. "You're the spy."

"Yes! We can escape, but we have to go now." Raen pushed at the man's shoulders. "Come on! Get up!"

"No." Bana's voice was strong.

* * * * *

Enigma watched Bana and Raen silently from the doorway. His shielding and natural Talent for being psychically invisible kept even the high-rated Bana from sensing his presence unless he was physically seen.

"What?" The young man, Raen, sounded incredulous.

On the carpeted floor, Bana's voice was strained. "At least I know Asha will kill me quickly. Not so with my brother. If you want to escape, go. Even if I could stand I'm not coming with you."

One corner of Enigma's mouth lifted in dark amusement. This was a new development. Bana, a seemingly dedicated and loyal Agent deciding he'd rather stay a prisoner of the Rebels than go home to the Agency. He could certainly use this to his advantage.

Raen got to his feet and Enigma stepped back into the shadows of another room out of sight. The young man was terrified, so much so he was obviously not thinking straight. Enigma watched Raen try to go up the hall to the stairwell, but he seemed to decide, against it, instead he ducked into another first-floor room.

Enigma silently followed Raen. In the other room the young man stepped through some broad windows, onto a fire escape and down a metal ladder out of sight. Enigma stepped into the room as the sounds of Asha and a number of others came ran the stairwell and past him.

Pacing slowly towards the rusting floor-to-ceiling windows, but remaining out of sight of both the incoming rabble and Raen, Enigma looked outside. Below, Raen pushed through the overgrown garden, opened the side-fence and jogged out onto the street.

From his vantage point above Raen, Enigma saw Taelin and Nama standing guard further up the road. The corner of his mouth lifted again. The spy's escape route had been anticipated and very soon Raen would be dead.

Asha had done a very good job at putting the fear into Raen and flushing him outside without even knowing his identity.

Enigma suppressed an amused chuckle. *Undisciplined fool.*

With the spy identified and dead, everyone would now relax a bit. It would be easier to integrate into the Rebel Cell without all of their anger and suspicion darting around looking for targets. He almost couldn't have planned the situation better, he just had to preemptively control their new prisoner's behavior so he wouldn't tell them his real name, and he was set.

Asha's rabble were talking to Bana in the next room, and returning to his Naethan persona, Enigma moved back towards the noise before he was missed.

* * * * *

Bana sensed the spy stand up and turn away from him, but he'd already closed his eyes again in an effort to slow the painful throbbing in his head. He wasn't permanently damaged—his cousin was very good at what he did. But it didn't matter if he was damaged or not. His daughter would live and that was all he cared about. The rest was simply waiting for Mecra to come.

Nearby, the door bashed hard against a wall and Bana flinched. Asha stood in the doorway with his cousin Kita. Several others stepped into the room and surrounded him. Their weapon barrels lifted.

"Why are you awake? Where's the spy?" Asha demanded.

He sighed. "Said his name was Raen. He was trying to free me."

"Why didn't you go with him, Bana?"

He leaned his head back on the carpet and closed his eyes again. "Here or there I'm dead anyway."

A gunshot echoed from outside on the street. There was an extended pause of silence, and Asha's voice was cold. "Raen's dead now." Her tone dropped into a grumpy bark. "You others, come with me. Naethan, guard him until I can send someone up to relieve you."

"Yes, ma'am."

A number of sets of feet left the room again and the door shut. It was quiet. Bana couldn't feel the man who was supposed be in there with him, they were probably an ex-assassin and deliberately hiding. He wondered if they'd play a game with him that ended with his death, it would be almost welcome.

There was a long moment of silence, and he wished they would just get it over with or put him back to sleep so he could escape the throbbing pulse in his head. Near the door, a male presence stepped out of his psychic invisibility.

"How are you holding up, Bana?" The voice was cold, calm and oddly familiar to him.

Bana opened his eyes and looked up. His eyes widened and he stared in absolute terrified surprise. He knew the man standing nearby, wearing black, his left arm in a stained sling and his square face bruised and beaten. Bana knew the ice-blue eyes—the youngest son of Jaran Cowdy senior.

His voice came out as a whisper. "What's going on, Sir?"

"I'm surprised you didn't take the spy's offer and leave with him."

Bana sensed an icy hostility underneath the man's words and he swallowed. Even injured and unarmed Enigma was a formidable enemy.

"Perhaps you want to become a Rebel like your traitorous parents?"

Bana swallowed and tried to defend himself. "I—"

"Understand this, Bana." There was venom in his voice. "I am after Hawk and Hawk alone. Live or die here with the Rebels, I don't care."

The man leaned over him and Bana fearfully pulled away.

"I can even keep silent to my father about your survival if you like, to protect your precious daughter, but in exchange for this freedom I expect your silence." He stood upright again, glaring coldly. "I have plans for this cover identity. And if you ruin those plans in any way, no matter where you go or what you do I will hunt you down and kill you. Do you understand me?"

Bana swallowed. "Yes, Sir."

"Good."

* 27 *

That evening

The cold at Nama's new building permeated right to Nalana's core, making her shiver almost constantly. They'd only been at that pretty building one night and she already missed it. She and Taelin worked for over an hour to get the fire going in the central room of the new building, from bits of damp wood and rubbish they'd found in the basement. Finally, after discovering an old newspaper, they got the fire lit and roaring away.

Nalana sat on the dusty wood floor, with her back to the fire. She let the heat push back the shivering ice in her limbs. Their new Common Room was fairly large, but had no natural light because it sat in the very middle of the building. The hallways that came off the central space were like a crazy dungeon maze of dim corridors and confusing offshoots all over the place. But, on the positive side, there didn't seem to be any holes in the wooden floors and walls, the ceilings seemed intact and what windows it had, were all sealed with double-glazed glass, so that once the place got warm and dry it would probably stay that way. It wasn't her idea of a nice place to live—not enough sunlight and no floor coverings—but with the fire it would be tolerable.

After an hour, the heat had permeated her body so that she was finally warm all over with no cold spots. She sighed happily.

Candles burned in little crockery trays at random intervals, adding to the flickering amber light that pushed against the shadows. Others of Nama's cell were pacing through the dimness doing their nightly chores and those Rebels who had managed to swap duties, or perhaps finished theirs, were collecting in a wide circle in anticipation of Nama's evening card game.

"Come on, Naethan, I ain't read the Holy book from cover to cover, but surely a little card game ain't against the Founder's teachings?"

Nalana looked up across the room to where Nama and Father Owen—*Naethan,* she corrected herself— stood in a doorway.

One side of the priest's mouth lifted up in that familiar expression of amusement. "It's not specifically mentioned, no, but I have many chores to do. Maybe some other night, Nama."

Naethan seemed so mysterious to Nalana. A man, who had been a soldier, then became a priest just to stay out of the Agency. It was an odd combination, more so because until she'd seen him shoot the assassin woman, she wouldn't have pegged him to be the kind of man who could kill people. She was usually such a good judge of character.

Naethan turned away into the shadows as Nama come towards the circle of people collected together in the fire light.

"Y'all ready, I take it?" he addressed the room with a broad playful grin on his face, and then he saw Nalana. "You in too, Nala?"

She lifted the watch and rings she'd pick-pocketed from some business man in the street the day before. "Yep."

Nama's laugh was good-natured. "Never ceases to amaze me, your pick-pocketing. How could such a nice girl be so good at thieving?"

"Survival!" she retorted.

He sat down and put a bottle of his rum into the middle for the first round of cards. Nalana wasn't as familiar or good at the Aranan card game as she would have liked, but she enjoyed the jovial company, and when she bet the things she stole it didn't feel so much like a loss.

The rules were that telepaths and empaths weren't allowed to cheat (this wasn't really enforced, but very few people cheated anyway). Other than that one rule, the game was the same as one of those at the casino. It involved certain combinations of cards having more value than others and betting against other players that your cards were a more valuable combination than theirs. The winner was either the person with the best cards or the best bluff, and Nama was very good at bluffing, so he usually won.

The game went on for many hours, and rounds. Slowly over that time the numbers of players dropped from nearly twenty to a small handful. Surprisingly, by the last round Nalana had won enough hands to still be playing.

She grinned happily at Nama across the considerably smaller circle of people and he grinned back. "Well, Nalana, are you going to bet or fold?"

She pushed the bottle of rum she'd won in the first round into the center. "Bet."

The other three Rebels dropped their cards immediately and folded almost in unison, including Taelin.

Nama laughed and winked at her. "On three?"

Looking down at her cards, she couldn't help but grin even broader. "Yes."

"One, two, three!"

Together they dumped their cards face-up. Upon seeing her perfect hand, Nama swore in amongst the gasps of surprise of those still watching the game. "You had Lady Krena on your side tonight, young Nala."

A happy, bubbly laugh came out of her and she reached to pull in her winnings. Bits of jewelry, small and large bottles of alcohol, Taelin's father's necklace and a lone twenty dollar bill were now hers. She grinned, knowing that she was not likely to be that lucky again.

Lifting the silver four-petaled flower that used to belong to Seda Kān by its rough metal chain, she handed it back to Taelin.

He gave her a bashful but relieved smile. "Thanks."

She lifted an eyebrow at him. "You shouldn't bet stuff that precious."

A gentle smile lessened the blush in his cheeks. "I know. Won't happen again."

"Better not, 'cause next time I'm keepin' it."

Still laughing, Nama collected his cards, which had once belonged to his grandfather, and put them into an ornate leather box. "OK, bed time, kids."

* * * * *

Nalana woke to a dark but warm room. Deep breathing and the occasional snort told her that it was very late and everyone else was asleep. She wasn't exactly sure what had awoken her, but now that she was conscious she sensed some kind of tension in the air. It was something nearing anxiety or perhaps frustration, but it was not her own. The blankets next to her on the wood floor were empty and she sat up to look around.

Naethan's figure dodged adeptly through the ocean of sleeping forms towards a nearby exit.

"Father?" she whispered. "What are you doing?"

He tensed and froze like a thief who'd been caught. There was a moment of silence and he turned to look back at her. The firelight reflected off his ice blue eyes making them seem to almost glow.

"I can't sleep. I thought a brisk walk would help. Go back to sleep, Nalana, don't worry about me."

"I can help you sleep," she said a little louder.

There was a quiet laugh. "Oh really, and how is that?"

"I can take the ache out of that shoulder for you and tell you a story. My nan used to tell me all sorts of stories when I was little. In fact, it's the fastest way to get *me* to sleep."

"What kind of stories?" There was a gentle amusement in him.

"The Old Gods, Time Speakers, the first Rebels... I could tell you a story about Hawk if you like."

There was a shift from amusement to peaked interest and she knew she had him. "About Hawk? What do you know about him?"

"Just what Nan used to say. Come back to bed and I'll tell you one."

The shadow with glowing blue eyes looked away for a moment, making the blue flicker off like an electrical light.

"OK."

He managed to cross back through the crowded room over tightly packed sleeping bodies without making a sound or waking anyone. Slipping into the loaned sleeping blankets, he rested an elbow on the pillow and looked at her. She couldn't see the details of his face except for the occasional flicker of glowing blue from reflected firelight, but she sensed a man who was expecting to be right about something.

"Lie back," she said, smiling at his inherent cockiness.

He did as he was told and she placed her hands over the pulsing pain in his shoulder. It had been mostly healed by Ren, but there was still a surface injury that had to heal in the normal way. It also took at least a few days for the body to catch up with the fact that it was suddenly not injured, so there was usually an odd ache associated with healed bullet wounds.

The buzzing warm energy flowed through her body and out of her hands into his shoulder. It wiped away the tight throbbing ache, and lifted out the underlying muscle pain of still injured surface flesh. He let out an unconscious sigh of relief.

The healing energy shut off, but she did not lift her hands from him.

She took a breath. "Not too long ago, there was a man. He was just a man with all the same flaws and weaknesses as everyone else. He lived a comfortable, happy life. But one day, Mecra came to his house and rose up a great winter's storm, destroying and killing as it blew through the man's house." She paused, adeptly channeling a sense of deep fatigue into the unconscious parts of his body in a way that would ease almost anyone into sleep. "When the Storms of Mecra faded away, the man was left badly injured and the only one alive in the rubble. As he lay waiting for help to come, one of the Old Gods, one of the Guardians of Time, reached down to him in his agony and offered him a wooden Hawk mask. He asked the figure, what was he to do with such a mask?

"The Guardian answered: 'Put the mask on and become the one to save everyone from the coming darkness.'

"The man was confused and asked, 'What darkness?'

"The Guardian bent over his prone form in the rubble and touched his forehead with a single finger, giving him the gift of True Vision—the Vision of a Time Speaker. The Guardian continued and said, 'And because I charge you with this mission you can not die until it is fulfilled.' So, the man also found himself healed from his wounds."

Nalana watched Naethan's eyes close drowsily. His breath slowed as he floated sideways towards sleep under her empathic manipulations. She lowered her voice to the tone her mother had used in doing the same trick with her.

"The man agreed to take on this mission and from that day on he became Hawk; the one man charged by the Old Gods themselves to save the Rebels from the Agency, but also as an Agent himself."

Naethan's face twitched for a moment and she sensed what was left of his conscious mind fight to remain conscious before dropping away into sleep.

Getting back into her own sleeping blankets, Nalana grinned with an uncharacteristic sense of cocky victory. Very few people could fight that empathic trick of her mother's, and she was proud to be able to do it to help her friend sleep.

* 28 *
Day Five—Nalana

Nalana smiled. It was a warm sunny day. In the heavens above her their biggest moon, Taena, sat in her full moon glory against that perfect sapphire sky. Nalana was unboundedly happy on such a beautiful winter's day. She loved the sunlight, more specifically, she needed sunlight and the winters in Arana were particularly difficult for her.

The flea market south of the Docks was crowded with people and stalls. Bright colored materials flickered in the breeze above her and the smells of cooking meats permeated the air. Haggling voices called loudly over top of each other, and underneath the rabble, someone played a soulful melody on a flute.

She pushed some of her loose brown hair behind one ear, and gleefully looked over the assortment of pretty jewelry in front of her. She only had the twenty dollar bill she'd won last night, but she wanted to buy something small, something that wouldn't be eaten or broken, lost or even stolen. She wanted something that was just for her to hold onto and treasure as a permanent reminder of the life she would like to lead one day.

Reaching one hand out, she touched a pretty blue gem that was set into a silver pendant. It was beautiful. But, it was also thirty dollars and therefore too much. For a moment, though, she allowed herself to imagine that she would buy it and wear it, keeping it safe next to her heart.

"If I had any money I'd chip in for it, Nala, that'd look lovely on you."

Nalana lifted her fingers from the cool gem and chuckled as she glanced sideways at Taelin. "It's OK. Someone'd pro'bly mug me if I had a rock like that 'round m'neck."

He laughed. "Probably true." Looking around him at the people and noise, he frowned. "Well, I don't know where Naethan went, but will you be OK shopping while I go trade with Diggs? I won't be long."

She nodded. "Sure."

As he melted into the crowds of noise and motion she heard his voice call out. "Hope you get something good!"

"I will!" she yelled.

Turning away from the expensive jewelry stall, she entered the flow of people down the middle of the street. Ahead, a line of children chased each other between the crowds. They were laughing playfully and making a good show of being a bunch of innocent children playing in the street. But she knew better and turned away from them as they passed, so that the pickpocket at the end of the line couldn't take her precious twenty dollar bill from her.

Further along the narrow street were food stalls. Beyond, through the smoke and sounds of cooking, she saw another table with jewelry and headed straight for it. The food smelt amazing as she walked past. On one stall, flat breads were cooked on hotplates, folded up into a parcel and filled with various meats and salad. Another stall owner was cooking some kind of mince meat into patties and making burgers. On the other side of the street there was also a huge display of different fruits and vegetables. Her stomach grumbled as she walked, and she told it that she would buy food once she'd found something special.

The second jewelry stall was filled with all sorts of junk jewelry made from plastic and painted up to look like metal. But in the center of the table, locked in a small case were some nice pendants on chains and a few plain metal rings. The rings held no interest for her because they could be stolen or lost far too easily. Most of the pendants were too expensive, except for one that hung on a plaited leather cord. It was silver and cast into the shape of a Sea Mern jumping out of the water. Having being born on a coast where the Sea Mern frequented, Nalana was very drawn to the pendant. It was a lovely subtle reminder of home and only ten bucks! She smiled excitedly at it through the glass.

"Please, can I have the Mern pendant?" She handed the bill over to the burly stall owner. He looked at her in confusion, and she remembered that in Arana they weren't called Mern. "Oh, sorry, the whale pendant."

"Sure, sweetheart." He handed her back some change and lifted up the metal case to unlock it. "You want a bag?"

Nalana smiled politely and shook her head. "No, thank you."

As she moved away from the stall, she stared at it sitting in her hands. Tracing the shape of it with her thumb, she felt stupidly happy to have something of her own that wasn't clothes or cutlery. Lifting the leather cord over her neck, she let the pendant fall under her shirt out of sight. She walked back towards the food stalls with the intention of getting one of the stuffed flat bread meals, but didn't notice the tall darkly dressed man step out of the crowd towards her.

Only after handing over the last of her money and turning away, as she took a bite of the hot yummy food, did she see the man and stop in her tracks. She knew his face and he knew hers, but it wasn't a positive kind of knowing. Nalana yelled, dropping her food and turned tail.

Her heart beat loudly in her chest as she ran. She could not allow him to get her. She had to somehow find Naethan or get out to the far edge of the markets to Taelin. There were so many people to dodge around at the flea market and the street was narrow. It made running at any speed dangerous but she had to keep going, had to get away from Fritz.

Dodging around a group of children and a large clothes stall, she caught her foot on something and found herself falling down to the grubby street. The nearby children chortled and ran away. She tried to get up quickly but it was too late. Fritz had caught up with her. He pushed her down to the ground and towered menacingly over her. She scrambled back, fearfully trying to get away from him, but her shoulders met wall and she was trapped.

"Nalana Yen, I don't suppose you have the money you owe me?" His deep rough voice mirrored the danger inherent in him.

She tried to gather her strength and glared at him defiantly. "I don't owe you anything, Fritz."

"I'm afraid that you do, and with an attitude like that you're not going to like the payment terms." The broad-shouldered man grabbed her arm and roughly yanked her up to her feet.

* 29 *

"Nala!" Taelin called out, pushing his way through the oddly incompliant crowd of people. "Nalana!" he called louder.

A sudden hand on his chest stopped him. "Don't."

He turned and Naethan stood close as if he'd come out of nowhere. "Why? We've got to get her back!"

"Did you see who has her?"

Tae shrugged. "A Spades, I know. If we take him by surprise we can get her back."

"No. Look, there to the right." The younger man pointed across the crowd to an alley entrance near the gangster, where a man stood in a dark tailored suit and hat. "And there." The alley on the other side of the street also had a dark-suited gangster standing in it. "That's not just an ordinary Spades gangster, that's Ayala Spades; Fritz. A head-on conflict with him and his goons would be suicide."

Taelin's heart rate increased at the name of the well-known slaver and he swallowed. "Well, then, what do we do? We have to get her back, we can't let them..."

His voice trailed off and he looked away. It was unbearable to think about what happened to young eighteen year old girls once Fritz got a hold of them.

Naethan's voice was oddly calm. "We know where they're taking her. That means we can sneak in and get her back in more strategically desirable surroundings."

Tae lifted an eyebrow. "How is the inside of the Ace of Spades in any way strategically desirable?"

One corner of Naethan's mouth lifted, bringing that disconcerting amusement into the priest's face. "Better a casino filled with gangsters, than a public street crowded with collateral damage, surely."

Taelin sighed. "Indeed. I'll call Nama to meet us there with the van."

* * * * *

Marius' wrists bled almost constantly from the rough rope that tied him to a broken wall heater. He sighed and let his legs drop him to the chipped linoleum floor. They'd held him for days, perhaps even weeks in this tiny windowless room and all because he'd stopped them from taking a young woman. Now, he was thousands of miles from his homeland and a prisoner of gangsters. He closed his light-purple eyes, trying to block out the agony in his wrists.

Above him the neon buzzed on and off in time with the light. The noise and flickering invaded his focus, making it impossible to block it out. He sighed again.

At the other end of the long room, the door opened. He flinched, eyes opening and staring fearfully. Two gangsters came through the door, dragging a limp figure into the room.

"Rizz, untie the scum."

One of them let go of the figure and walked towards Marius.

"Hands!" demanded the grizzled gangster.

Standing, Marius pushed his arms forward, while at the same time trying to push his back further into the corner to get away from the gangster. Rizz brought out a flick knife and Marius shrank from it. His arm was grabbed and the man proceeded to cut the ropes. His wrists were suddenly free and he had the bizarre urge to dance on the spot, but suppressed it.

"Scum, you gonna patch up this girl. You try to escape again, we hang you by your neck this time."

"Yus, Sir," he mumbled. Marius kept his gaze on the floor—he'd learned the first day not to look them in the eyes.

He waited until the gangsters had left and the door locked behind them. Slowly, he approached the bloodied figure on the floor.

Long light brown hair covered her face in messy ringlets, one arm was bent oddly underneath her and her rag-clothes were ripped and bloody as if they'd cut her with a very small knife many times. A whimper sounded from under the mess of hair.

"I'm not going to hurt you," he said gently. "I'm Marius—"

"No..." a quiet but strong voice answered. "Leave me 'lone. I ain't sleeping with y—anyone!"

He got down low on his hands and knees to be as unthreatening as possible. "No, I'm a prisoner too. I won't hurt you."

"No!" she said, her voice still quiet but stronger. "Don't touch me!"

Sitting back on his bum, about a meter from her, he rested his aching wrists in his lap. She had obviously been badly beaten and yet her spirit wasn't broken. A little smile etched around his lips.

"They can't break you, can they?" His voice was very gentle. "What's your name?"

"My friends are coming." Defiance flared into her voice. "They'll kill you... and anyone else who gets in their way."

Marius leaned his back against the wall and pulled his knees into himself. "Are they gods? Because only gods could get in here. Perhaps they're friends of Mecra." His voice dropped into an introspective tone. "He could get in here. Imagine that, a storm of death and ice and madness blowing through this building and clearing a path out of here. Then maybe both of us could get out." He rested his chin on his knees. "I've tried three times to get out. They only don't kill me because I can fix their electronic things. Stupid gangsters, so stupid they can't fix their own machines..." his voice had degraded into a grumbling mumble and he stared blankly at the flaking wall paper in front him. "If I had a weapon I'd show them. Evil a'kenān make slaves out of free men and young girls! Mecra will come for them!" He looked at his bleeding wrists and sighed. "One day."

The girl made an odd noise and it took him a moment to realize she was weeping.

"What's wrong?" He wanted to comfort her, but didn't want to scare her by getting any closer.

"My arm," she wailed. "He broke it... it hurts so bad... I can't think through it to stop the pain."

He frowned. "Stop it? How do you stop pain?"

"My hands... I'm a healer... but I need... I can't..." she sobbed.

He lifted his chin from his knees and looked at the mess of hair that covered her face. "Can I help?"

"You touch me wrong, I'll kick you in the crotch!" The defiance in her voice, even under the sobbing, reassured him that she would indeed fight back no matter how injured she was.

"I won't touch you wrong," he said quietly. "Let me help you." Shuffling towards her, he reached and brushed back her light brown hair. When he saw the state of her face, he had to suppress a cry of outraged grief. The one who had beaten her had hit her so badly that nothing was recognizable under bruises, cuts and swelling.

Intelligent purple-brown eyes looked up at him through the mess.

He smiled tensely and quickly wiped at an errant tear on his cheek. "Hihi."

"My... right arm... it's under me... I can't move it..."

He shook his head. "If it's broken, it'll hurt."

A puffy bottom lip twitched. "I know. But you gotta anyway. Don't move it too much... just... out."

Swallowing, he put one hand under her shoulder and readied himself to lift her body off of her arm. When he did, he tried not to hurt her but she screamed anyway. He moved her arm out from under her, put her shoulder back on the ground and skittered off as far away from her as he could get.

Her yell degraded into a weeping sob and he crouched in the corner covering his head with his arms. "I'm sorry! I'm sorry!"

"It's OK." Her voice was very small. "It's OK. Jus'... gonna... sleep..."

* 30 *

The ground floor of the casino was huge and virtually heaving with celebrating drunken people. Lights flashed from winning and losing slot machines, and the smoke-filled air obscured the vivid reds and golds of the décor. Taelin constantly fought to keep his footing, as people pushed past him in their inebriated revelry.

The purely physical side of the casino was intensely overpowering on its own, but psychically it was even worse. The telepathic noise stabbed like shards of glass into his brain from all of the unshielded minds of patrons. Another person bumped into him, placing their hand on his shoulder as they passed. He flinched from the stab of voices and drunken nausea of their physical contact.

The pulse of empathic force in the room was like a wave that ebbed and flowed across the space. It was a flowing mountain etched with patterns of drunkenness, random flares of the emotive peaks and troughs of winning and losing, and smattered chaotically with an underlying tension. It pitched towards different corners of the room back and forth like great ocean swells, and the motion added to his already upset stomach.

Naethan had disappeared into the crowd again, but as clear as each of the minds in the room were if he concentrated on one at a time, he couldn't sense Naethan at all. A hand touched his arm and he turned to see Naethan right next to him. Taelin frowned, wondering how he managed to do that so well.

"I've found a way through to her." Naethan yelled over the noise. "This way."

Tae followed him through the sea of faces and jingling, blinking gambling machines to the far side, where an open door led to a corridor and public toilets. It was significantly quieter in the hall and he almost sighed in abject relief. Naethan walked to one end of the space, but instead of turning around, he leaned against the gold-patterned wall paper and pushed hard. There was an audible click and the entire wall moved inwards like a door.

Taelin frowned. "How'd you know about that?"

"Lucky guess?" That familiar half smile and vivid blue eyes flickered at Taelin for a moment.

Sensing the lie, Taelin slipped past the surface of the priest's mind and saw that he'd worked at the casino for a short time. He saw flashes of things he really didn't want to see, and sensed that Nae hadn't wanted to see it either. Tae understood immediately why he was being coy and nodded.

The hall on the other side was fairly wide and quite long. It ended at another gold-patterned wall. The space looked a bit like a hotel corridor, with many doors along one side and plastic pot plants sitting on the off-blue carpet at randomly spaced intervals. There was another click at the other end of the corridor, and a rough-looking man barged in through the gap, glaring as he strode towards them.

"You'd better be here for the whores!" the dark-haired man bellowed. He was all shoulders, broad and tall, quite strong looking and his blue eyes were so light they were almost white.

Tae stepped forward. "We're looking for a girl, Nalana—"

Mine. His thought was practically a bellow. The man's eyes gained a touch of menace and Tae dived off to the side as the gangster pulled out a weapon. Looking up from the floor, Tae watched as Naethan moved towards the gun and dodged expertly as the gangster fired. He got in close, pulled the weapon from his fingers and swung him into a head-lock in a matter of seconds.

As Taelin watched, Ayala Spades found himself at the end of his own gun barrel.

"Nalana Yen. Where is she?" Naethan's voice was ice cold and Tae swallowed. The young man was very surprising when he wanted to be. Tae got to his feet and approached them.

The gangster was scared, but not so scared he was going to immediately give away the location of his newest acquisition. Taelin put a hand on the gangster's arm and dove into his unprotected mind. Fritz called out in pain.

"Where is she?" he demanded telepathically.

A location flashed through the man's mind even as he tried to fight it. Fritz knew about telepaths, but he wasn't in as much control of his own mind as he thought. Taelin saw a door. They'd passed it in their short conflict with him. Nalana was behind that door, beaten but still intact in a Psi-shielded room. Fritz had the door key in the breast pocket of his black suit jacket. Tae pulled the jacket open and grabbed it.

"Can you hold him, Naethan?"

"Of course, go and get her."

* * * * *

Fritz struggled under the firm grip of a man at least twenty years his junior. The older of the two intruders, the telepath, paced immediately to the right door and using his key, unlocked it. When the door closed, the grip on Fritz tightened and he felt an increasing tension in his shoulders and neck.

"We are going to take this girl and walk away. You are going to cease hunting her." The boy's voice was commanding and utterly fearless.

Fritz grunted in pained amusement. "No. We are going to hunt you two down like rats—"

"No, Ayala Spades."

"Why's that?" he snorted. "You got super powers too?"

"Of a sort." His voice was too calm and Ayala sensed the snippet of danger in the young man's voice. "I'm sure you remember Jaran Mehan, my father, he worked here before he became the Head of the Agency."

Ayala stiffened at the name.

"If you go anywhere near that girl again, or attempt to take me out, the Agency will come down and wipe you all off the face of this planet, and I will personally make your death as slow as humanly possible."

"Why do you care about one stupid girl?" he barked. The pain in his shoulder was getting intolerable, but he wouldn't let Jaran's whelp see any weakness.

"The same reason you do: she is a resource. *My* resource. You will let us leave. You will hunt her no more." The boy's voice deepened into a gruff intimidating whisper as his arm tightened around Fritz's neck. "Do you understand me?"

* **31** *

Taelin pushed the door open and stepped inside. The room was dim and dirty. The neon overhead flickered and didn't do near enough of a job to bring light to the corners of the room. The off-green wallpaper was faded and peeling at odd places, and there was no furniture, just the stained faded-grey linoleum floor and a chipped wall heater on the far side.

Nalana lay on her back in the middle of the room. One arm was splayed out next to her and a man in dark clothes sat crouched over her tying something around her wrist.

Tae lifted his weapon. "Get away from her!"

The man flinched back against a nearby wall in surprise. He was obviously Tolān, with dark red-brown skin, shaved black hair and vivid purple eyes. Small piercing rings looped around both edges of his lips, one nostril and an eyebrow. He looked rough, perhaps another gangster.

"What are you doing to her?" Taelin demanded.

Dark purple eyes widened and immediately Taelin sensed that the Tolān man was not a threat.

"Tae," Nalana's voice cracked painfully. "Mar was helping."

He dropped to her side. "We've come to get you out. Can you stand?"

Her face was so terribly swollen, he barely recognized her. Deep brown eyes looked up at him. She radiated agony and he knew her answer before she spoke.

"I don't think so."

Taelin knew he couldn't carry Nalana for very long with the agony she was in, and he got to his feet with the intension of getting Naethan to help him.

"I..." the Tolān man in the corner stepped forward uncertainly. "I can help... please... take me with you."

Tae looked down at Nala, then back at the man. "You think you can carry her?"

"Yes!" The Tolān moved towards her and gently lifted Nala into his arms. She moaned in pain, but didn't fight him. Taelin sensed that she wasn't afraid of the young man, and turned back towards the door. "Come on, we have to be quick."

Outside in the corridor, Naethan was on his knees with a limp, unconscious gangster still in his headlock.

Taelin stared. "What are you doing?"

"He's not dead." Naethan released the man onto the floor. "He's unconscious. But we've only got a few minutes."

"Right. Fastest way out of here?"

"This way." Naethan took point, leading them back into the hall adjacent to the casino floor, and then left through a door marked as staff only. At the door, Taelin held it open for the man carrying Nalana, and looked around for any sign of threats, but it seemed clear for the moment.

The corridor beyond was narrow and cluttered with boxes and housekeeping trolleys filled with linen. He heard the repetitive throb of dryers and washing machines off to one side, and as he passed a doorway, he saw a snippet of faded green metal and stark white neon lights.

At the end of the corridor was a fire exit, which opened out onto the street behind the casino. Running past cars and across the one-way delivery lane, they entered an alley between two old stone apartment buildings.

Taelin mentally reached back across the width of the Ace of Spades Casino to the front entrance, where Nama sat in his van waiting for them.

"Nama, come get us." He showed Nama where they were in relation to him.

His mental voice was tense. *"On my way. How is she?"*

"She's bad, but she's alive."

They came out of the alley to the next street over. Tall stone buildings towered over the narrow road, cutting off most of the morning light and casting jagged shadows on them as they stopped to rest on the side-walk.

"Nama's coming in the van," he panted. Leaning his back against the wall, he looked sideways at the Tolan man. "Mar, was it?"

The man crouched on the concrete and rested Nalana on his knee. "Marius."

"OK, Marius. Look, we're Psi Rebels, so you might want to leave us here and—"

"I've got no home to go back to," he interrupted. "I can help you, I'm a Tech Talent. And..." purple eyes dropped to look at Nalana still in his arms. "I want to stay with her."

Taelin smiled. "OK."

A white van screeched chaotically around a nearby corner and had he not been able to sense Nama's flare of green and blue, he would have thought the driver was drunk or mad (or both).

The van screamed to a halt immediately in front of them, and the driver-side door opened.

"Get in kids!"

* 32 *
That evening

Taelin sat next to the fire, with his back up against the unpainted wall, watching over Nalana as she slept fitfully. Pain pulsed around her in a sickening spiral, but he refused to leave her despite the uncomfortable psychic sensations. Ren had pulled the broken bone back into place and strapped her arm to two pieces of an old broom handle to keep the bones in place. Unfortunately, the last of the medical plaster had been used up several months ago by young accident-prone Jena, so they had to just make do until they found more plaster to steal.

The fire pushed back the shadows and coldness of their new Common Room with a flickering orange warmth. Flames illuminated the moving shadows of the others as they came and went with their evening chores.

Marius, despite his own injuries, sat on the other side of Nalana holding her little hand in his as she slept. Taelin admired his quiet dedication to her.

"I got it." Nama's voice arrived in the room before his feet brought him through the doorway. Dangling from his hand was Nalana's necklace on a new metal chain.

"Rana swapped it for the last bottle of my whiskey."

Taelin gave his old friend a sad but gentle smile. "Rana's a thief then."

"I know," Nama looked tense and kind of lost. "But it's the only thing she owns, she deserves to wake up with it. Help me get it on her?"

Tae got to his feet. He brushed her hair away from her neck so that Nama could get the chain around.

A silver whale leapt up towards the line of metal chain with its back arched. It was lovely and suited her well. She must have bought the pendant in the market because he'd never seen it before. But, knowing her he probably would never have seen it had the leather cord not broken when they'd moved her from the van. It was odd, she always seemed to keep the truly special things close to her heart and hidden even from them.

Nama's grubby fingers fiddled with the clip. "If she's got any totem at all, she's whale totem. She's joyous like they are and she sings the most beautiful songs."

Nodding in agreement, Taelin swallowed back the tight ball of emotion in his throat.

"Nama?"

Taelin heard his sister's mental voice even though he was almost certain he wasn't supposed to.

"Yeah, Asha?" Nama fastened the clip around Nalana's neck and stood upright. *"Did you get confirmation from Hawk about Naethan?"*

Taelin returned to the floor and sat with his back to the wall as he stared into space. He wasn't sure how to block their conversation, or even whether he wanted to if he knew how.

His sister sounded tired. *"Sort of. He said he can't see a threat, but he can't confirm him either. He said he's probably a Time Psi-based Dodge Talent and that's mucking up the picture."*

Nama's mental voice growled. *"Like that blasted assassin girl?"*

"Yeah, like Cheetah." There was a sense that she shook her head. *"Anyway, he said to just keep an eye*

on him, there's no immediate threat, but we don't involve him in anything important just in case." Asha's voice shifted. *"How is Nalana?"*

Tae sensed a shaft of hot grief slice through Nama.

"Ren said she'll be OK, just in a lot of pain right now. Aside from her arm there's no serious injuries. But we do need to get some medical-grade plaster."

"Sure, I'll see what we can do." There was a deep wariness in Asha's mental voice. *"I've sent Naethan downstairs to you, can you bring our new recruit up?"*

"Of course."

Nama turned to look down at Marius and broke the physical silence. "The boss wants to see you, come on, I'll take you upstairs."

Marius nodded and let go of Nalana's hand as he got to his feet. At the doorway, he took a long last look at her, and then Marius and Nama were gone.

Taelin felt so tired. It had been a very bad week and he was exhausted. He put his head back against the wall and closed his eyes. The wariness pulled him down and away from the room. He fell into a light doze, hovering in and out of an exhausted unconsciousness.

Colored blob-people and the patterns of emotions attached to them flitted backwards and forwards around him. Time passed slowly, or perhaps quickly, as he hovered in the empathic buzz of other people's movements. Amongst the colored blobs that were the other Rebels, an icy gray blob floated into the room and came to a stop next to Nalana's vibrant green and rich blue.

"Naethan..." a pained voice spoke both in Taelin's ears and in his head.

"Go to sleep, young Nalana. You need to rest." The voice in his ears was gentle and almost loving, but very little emotional color mirrored it in the gray blob.

A pulse of red itchy pain flared around Nalana. *"I can't sleep... it hurts too much... tell me a story, Naethan."*

Tension rippled through the gray-blue. "I'm not good with stories, Nalana."

"Please... I can't sleep without one..."

A sigh met his ears. "OK, just for you... I'll tell you my favorite."

"A thousand years ago, at the time of the Reformation there lived two friends, Mecra and Nera. Both priests and both Patrons of the new Church of the Founder. Nera was a gentle and loving soul who believed in absolute compassion and unconditional love. Mecra was a warrior who only understood life through the eyes of war and destruction. He believed that anything that remained of the Old Gods and the Old Temple would always threaten to destroy the new Church of the Founder.

"With this belief in mind, he started a campaign to hunt down and kill all of the priests of the Old Temple. Appalled that her friend could be so heartless, Nera tried to save as many of the Old Temple Priests as possible, but eventually Mecra found her. He was so enraged by her betrayal that he killed her.

"Afterwards, for his loyalty to the new Church of the Founder, Mecra became High Priest. But the guilt for killing his friend Nera ate away at his sanity, and eventually Mecra went mad. On the first snowstorm of that winter, he put on his long coat and walked into the storm hoping that Death would take him and he would finally be free of his guilt. But they say, Death utterly refused to take him into the Afterlife because of the great crime of killing a soul as pure and loving as Nera. Instead, Mecra became Death himself, forever cursed to walk within the winter storms collecting the dead and fighting with his own unending madness."

It was quiet for a moment and Taelin sensed a flare of gentle affection shift around the gray blob that was Naethan. "Go to sleep, young Nalana. Taelin and I will watch over you."

Day Six—Heth
* 33 *

Agent Heth Pallen sat at his broad wooden desk with a pen in hand and a litter of paper spread across his desk. He hated desk work, but as a Project Head it was simply part of the job and there was a lot of work associated with the search for Hawk. They had a massive network of Resources, through every echelon of the Agency as well as out in the public—all collecting information and rumor in the hope of finding something, *anything*, about this strange Rebel leader.

His office door opened and someone stepped in without even knocking—a sign of someone undisciplined or simply disrespectful. He glanced up at the man who stood in his doorway and sighed.

Disrespectful, spoilt and egotistical are more accurate descriptions.

"What do you want?" He deliberately put some respect in his tone so that he couldn't be accused of hostility, but enough anger to show he was not impressed with such blatant and deliberate disrespect.

"I hear condolences are in order." Ice blue eyes, like mirror images of the young man's father, shone darkly at him.

Heth frowned. "What do you mean?"

"Your spy, he's dead." One corner of his mouth lifted mockingly. "And you were so patient with him."

Heth got to his feet. "What? What are you talking about?"

"Oh, you haven't heard? Well, I'm sure your underlings will find him eventually. Meanwhile, the Rebels keep causing trouble."

Heth suppressed an impatient sigh. "What is it you want?" Jaran Cowdy's youngest son got on his nerves far quicker than any of the others of his age and rank.

"I want Hawk."

Heth crossed his arms over his chest. "Don't we all?"

"No, I want the prestige of bringing him in myself."

"So?"

"You need a new spy and I can do that for you. But I want everything you have on Hawk, and I want to be kept in the loop of all other operations."

Heth laughed. "And what makes you think you're in a position to make such a deal?"

"For one thing, I'm alive. Here," he handed him a scrap of paper with an address scrawled roughly on it. "That's where they dumped your spy's body. For another, I'm in with the Rebels—Nama Ree's cell. I've had contact with Hawk's second in command and I have a source that seems to think that Hawk is an Agent and not a Rebel."

Heth reached across his desk for a notepad. "Tell me more."

"No, that's not how it works. The deal is I give you free-flowing information on the Rebels themselves, if you give me free-flowing information about all aspects of the search for Hawk."

Heth lifted an eyebrow at the man. "Does your father know you're making unreasonable offers?"

"I can go and get his authority if you like, but do you really want him to know you lied about your spy? An ex-A2, really! Such a fibber. Raen Malderān was barely an A4! He was an undisciplined fool. Do you want Father to find that out?"

Heth swallowed and forcing himself to remain calm, lest he appeared weak, he looked down at the scrawled address in his hand.

"Give me a few days. We'll check this out and I'll collate what information we have on file about Hawk. Come back with some good information that we can pass on to one of the external assassins, and we'll negotiate. For now I have a great deal of work to do." Heth indicated his office door with one upturned palm. "Good day."

Part Three

A Year Later

17 Aracan 3004
(Nearly a year later)
Early morning
In the Great Northern Desert
Just south of Epa City

Standing in front of Xak was a man wearing a wooden mask. It was colorful with thick lines of black, red, white and orange painted on it to accent its avian features. The mask was oddly terrifying to look at. But it was also something hopeful to Xak because it was the Hawk mask. The man under the mask wore all black, and floating in the palm of one hand was a flame, which flickered red and green as it burned.

The cry of a hawk bird sounded from above Xak, and he turned from the man to look up at the sky. He was standing on the road and staring up at the Agency Tower. The city around him was utterly silent as if it was holding its breath. A loud boom vibrated through the structure and down into the concrete under his feet. Fire blew out of the building many stories above, exploding glass and debris into the air.

Xak stared up at the fire and watched the debris fall towards him. He wasn't surprised, nor afraid, he simply watched it fall towards him and the road.

He closed his eyes, hearing the sounds of broken glass as it hit the tarmac around him. He knew any moment that a large piece would cut through him and he'd be dead.

"Bwah!" Xak woke suddenly, a squeak of fear escaping him as his whole body tensed up.

He groaned and closed his eyes again. He knew it was useless to try and go back to sleep, he never could after the Hawk dream, but he tried to anyway.

Xak didn't mind having dreams or visions because he'd had them for as long as he could remember, but what he disliked was when they were about things he couldn't change or interpret.

He understood the Hawk dream a little. He knew the mask was simply the symbol of Hawk, and the fire was the explosion in the Tower building that would happen in the future—when, he didn't know. He even sometimes dreamed of the location where Hawk would get the explosives. What he didn't understand was exactly how he, Xakarii Kane, stuck in an Agency desert "training" base until he was eighteen, was going to do anything with that information, other than not telling the Agency.

He wiped his face and sat up on the narrow cot. His feet ached and he pulled them around to rest his scorched soles on the cool concrete floor. He sighed and looked down at his reddened toes. Three days in a row the weather had been scorching hot outside, so hot it cooked the black sand of their exercise yard to a point where it burnt skin. And three days in a row the guards refused to let anyone over the age of fourteen wear their sandals outside. The kinetic kids could protect their feet by virtue of their Psi ability, but, as one of the few older non-kinetics left in the base, he had to simply suffer through the exercise.

Roughly cut black and red-speckled hair fell over his gray eyes, covering but not hiding the helpless fear in his face. What was the point in having the Hawk dream—or any Time Psi dream of the outside world—if he was only going to die there in the desert like all the other non-kinetic kids in the training base? If the guards didn't get him, one of these days Rega, the biggest bully, would and his friends wouldn't be able to help.

Closing his eyes as he felt it, a deep wave of static pushed out of his stomach and flowed up and down his body in an oddly tickling sensation.

The static wave brushed aside all sensations of pain and fear, replacing them with an odd feeling of disorientation that quickly turned into vertigo.

Images flickered through his mind, one after the other in quick succession, like an old-fashioned movie. The guard, the one with the nearly silver gray eyes that always picked on Xak, stood over him. The guard lifted a metal rod and started to beat him. Over and over the rod came down, and under the barrage, he watched himself slowly die in an ever increasing puddle of blood and broken bones. Along with the disturbing images, he also sensed how very little time he had left.

I'm going to die in a week. Xak swallowed. *I have to get out of here.*

The images continued until he reached his own death, but then the vision did something that had never happened before. The process reversed, unwinding the video of his own death, back through the days to the time that he was currently living.

The vision hovered over the present moment for a few seconds, echoing oddly with reality as he watched himself watch himself. Shifting again, the images sped up a little and went forwards a few minutes.

Knowledge poured through his mind and with his eyes still closed, he reached to the shelf in front of him for a drawing pad and pencil. Without looking, he scrawled a sequence of numbers across the page.

When the sensation eased away, Xakarii Kane was very calm. He put the paper down on the gray blanket next to him. Leaning forwards again, he looked down at his feet and smiled at his scorched toes. It would be OK, because dawn would reveal a massive rain front coming across from the east towards them, so there would be no more burning sand.

He waited.

A sense of blue calm spread through the narrow concrete room. The blue came from a point directly in front of Xak and sparked at the edges with a deep dark static. Xak knew who it was. He lifted his face to look at the point in front of him where he knew the invisible presence of Hawk hovered.

"Hawk," he whispered. "My name is Xakarii Kane. I've seen you there in the threads of time. I know how to get the fire you need for your attack on the Agency." He swallowed tensely. "I can help you, but you have to get me out of here. If I stay, I'll be dead by the 1st of Mecra." The boy lifted his drawing pad from next to him and held it up for Hawk to see. He didn't know exactly what the numbers meant, but he knew that they would help Hawk find him.

A line of cool static flowed towards the paper and touched it for a moment. The formless touch withdrew and a sparking blue voice spoke from the air in front of him.

"The Rebels will come."

* 2 *

Same day, mid morning
Church of the Founder, Arām City

Father Andrew stood in front of the dark-wood door, his knuckle centimeters from the wood. He wasn't sure if he should interrupt whatever the young man was doing, because it was probably something important and something to do with the Agency. But he had asked to be told, so after pausing, Andrew knocked carefully.

"Come in, Andrew," a voice spoke through the wood.

Andrew took a deep breath to ease the anxious tension in him and pushed the old door inwards. The room was warm from the late morning sunlight, which filtered through stained glass windows on the far wall. The light flickered color across the nearly empty room, painting the dark stone walls, white painted ceiling and the old hard-wood desk in the center with flares of colored shapes and shafts of white sunlight. Andrew smiled slightly, he'd always loved this room.

"Yes, correct." The young man stood at the desk, an old phone receiver to his ear and a serious look on his face. "There should be a large shipment of illegal arms in the east-facing bedroom, as well as a small number of Illegals protecting the cache... an hour? Confirmed."

The young man put the phone down and looked at Andrew across the room with those vivid blue eyes of his. It continually baffled Andrew how a man in his position could remain so utterly calm. He would easily have had a heart attack in the first week, let alone nearly a year under cover.

The young man gave him a reassuring smile. "What's wrong, Andrew?"

"Um... yes... um, the girl—her exam has nearly finished. You asked me to tell you."

"Oh, thank you." One corner of his mouth twitched up. "Father Andrew, you shouldn't be so tense. You look anxious enough that you'd risk a heart attack at any moment."

"Well... well..." Andrew fussed for a moment, mildly uncomfortable that his anxiety was so obvious. "I wasn't made for a life of intrigue and deception. I'm not very good at lying, especially so to a young innocent girl."

A patient look crossed the man's face. "Father, you lie to protect. I've ensured that the Cathedral is safe from the Agency, they wouldn't dare come here again looking for trouble, and the Rebels won't come if they have no reason to do so. All you have to do is be calm, play your part and you'll be just fine. So relax. I've got it all under control."

Andrew sighed again, still afraid but pretending not to be. So far the young man had kept every one of his promises. All he could really do was trust that the Founder had a plan and have faith.

Pulling a battered leather jacket on over his tattered brown rags, the young man bowed his head slightly. "Thank you again. I should leave before Nalana comes out of her nursing exam."

Andrew lifted a small leather-bound book out of a pocket in his robes. "I've got another apocryphal text for you—"

"Would you give it to Nalana, please? It'll help towards my cover."

"Of course. What about *your* exams?"

The man seemed impatient. "We'll have to postpone them. For now, I must go."

* 3 *

Nalana left the Cathedral floating on a cloud of excited joy. Her first ever exam! Nine months worth of hard study condensed into one three hour exam and she'd done it! Her mother would be so proud.

Laughing in her joy, she skipped across the black cobbles of Cathedral Square and into the relative safety of a dim lane between buildings. It was safer for her in the alleys instead of out on the street, where someone could spot her without her spotting them. Sure, in the alleys you occasionally met up with dangerous folks, but she was always careful that there was nothing obviously worth mugging her for and for the times when someone might want to take something else from her, she had the nasty looking flick-knife Marius had given her to dissuade them.

As she walked down the narrow lane between buildings, she sensed Naethan cross the edge of her empathic range from behind. He was physically invisible, but she was almost certain he let her sense him because they both knew he could do that empathic invisible man thing and completely hide from her senses.

Stopping, she laughed and looked behind her. "You know full well I can feel you, Naethan. Come on out."

A trashcan behind her chuckled and he stepped out of the shadows next to it. "It was worth a try."

"So," she re-started her swift pace down the long alley. "What's going on today?"

"Not much," he said, as he matched step with her. "How was your exam?"

She grinned. "I should get an 'A'—well, 'Gabriella' will."

His normally stoic face had small signs of happiness. Shining blue eyes and the edge of a smile twitched at the sides of his mouth. She sensed that he was excited about something.

Nala lifted an eyebrow at her friend. "So, come on, what is it? What's going on? I can feel something itching at you—spill!"

The edge of a boyish excitement flashed in those amazing blue eyes of his. "We're going to attack a Desert Training base."

She blinked at him. "Really? How're we gonna to do that? Aren't those places really secure?"

Mischief lifted one corner of his mouth into a smirk. "And?"

"You!" Laughing, she brushed playfully at the back of his unruly sandy-colored hair. "You have a death wish, don't you?"

He straightened the mess she'd made with his fingers and chuckled. "No, not a death wish." His voice softened. "And how is Father Andrew today?"

"He's good." Pushing her hand under the flap of her bag, she lifted out an old book. "He sends his love and your homework."

He took it from her and opened the old leather-bound text. "Thank you."

"So, what's this one about?"

"This is an apocryphal text," he answered, but didn't look up from the book. "It pertains to the Nera and Mecra mythos, but more about their historical counterparts than the modern myth." He lowered the page to show her the vertical script where a rough pen line had boxed in a passage. "Look here, Nera, despite her absolute goodness, is said to be jealous and petulant about Mecra's attainment of mid-priest before her." He flicked the page to another boxed passage. "And here, Mecra—embodiment of all evil—lets a thief live due to his compassion." Excitement was in his eyes as he glanced at her. "Some of the historical facts of the Patrons contradict with doctrinal stories. It's part of my training to explore both sides. How can I be expected to have faith in the Patrons if I do not know what they were really like?" He closed the book. "Like Hawk. I want to know the man not this ridiculous story that so many people tell of him. He's just a man, not an infallible supernatural being..."

His voice trailed off and she smiled. "You want to hear more about Hawk, don't you?"

A playful half-smile twitched at one edge of his mouth. "Maybe."

Laughing, she shook her head. "Fine. Where did we leave off last night?"

"How different Time Speakers are."

"Ah, yes." She turned off to the left into an adjoining lane and he followed. "Time Speakers are not in possession of powers greater than anyone else. What makes them extraordinary is that they experience time differently from other people. Nan talked of Time like threads that flowed in branching lines or spirals, sometimes even coming upon themselves in perpetual loops. She spoke of certain moments in her life where it felt as if she was *many things at once*. She said it was as if she was somehow many people all living their lives at different points in time, but that she was experiencing them all in the now. As if she was living all of her past and future lives at the same moment."

"That is the strangest idea." His voice was quiet, almost introspective, and then it shifted. "So, you said your grandmother felt Hawk was different from other Time Speakers?"

She shuffled the strap of her bag to a better position over her shoulder. "Yes, but she never really explained why he was different. Just that—" she caught herself. *That information could be dangerous to Hawk.* Giving a little shrug and a frown, she looked sideways at her friend. "You know I can't really remember, just that he was different."

Naethan was quiet for a long time as they walked through alleys and lanes. She couldn't sense anything in him other than a sort of muted introspection, and for the millionth time she wished she was a telepath, so she could see what he was thinking. Two whole blocks went by in an easy silence between them, and then his voice was quiet.

"Do you think the Agency *could* take him down? I mean, he *is* just a man."

She smiled. "Well, for everyone's sakes, I hope not. But I guess that's why only one person knows who he is—to protect that secret."

"What would *you* do if you found out?"

She shrugged. "I don't know. It would depend what he wanted me to do with that secret. But if I knew and I was about to be captured I'd probably kill myself."

He seemed surprised. "Why is his life more important than yours?"

"It's not. But without his skills to see the future, and the symbol of hope that he represents, the Rebels will die. So in protecting him, I'm protecting the Rebels."

Irritation flared in his blue eyes. "But, he's just a man. It's wrong that so many of the Rebels deify him. It's also a blatant lie."

"It's not a lie," she corrected. "It's just not the complete truth. People need hope to survive, and to keep that hope alive they need heroes and silly stories. This story is Hawk's mask. It keeps himself and the Rebels safe. As long as *he* knows that it's not who he really is, I don't think he's lying by letting the Rebels tell those stories."

Naethan grinned at her, bringing a genuine affection and amusement into a face that was too often stoic. "You're very wise for someone so young."

She laughed and in an attempt to hide the blush that was rising into her cheeks, she skipped ahead of him around a corner onto the street beyond.

There was a frown in his voice. "Where are we going, anyway?"

"Risa's safe house," she said over her shoulder. "They found some crayons and stationary in their last raid. She offered them for the kids if I came and got them."

She sensed a flare of surprise behind her. "Risa? Didn't they also get a large stack of weapons?"

She laughed. "Yeah, but I'm not visiting for the weapons."

His voice shifted into tension. "We've got to get back to base for chores. Why not come back later?"

She pointed across the road at the one-storied house. "Her building is just here, it won't take a moment. I'm sure Nama won't bring out the whip if we're a little late."

"I'm not so sure about that. I swear he doesn't like me."

Nalana laughed. "Nama's just like that." She glanced back at him and her smile dropped—he seemed to be genuinely tense about something. "What is it?"

"Please, let's just go back. I've got a bad feeling. Something's wrong."

She frowned. Perhaps, she could go back. Everyone knew a Dodge Talent came from either kinetic or clairvoyant genes (or both), and if his Talent came from a clairvoyant parent, he might be able to sense when something was wrong before it happened.

"Nala!" someone called from across the road. "What y'doin' standin' on the street lookin' daft?"

Risa's voice broke the tension in Nalana and she turned, laughing at the older woman standing on the porch. "You got those crayons?"

"Yep, feel like some lunch?"

She glanced sideways at Naethan. "Naw, we don't have time, maybe next visit?"

"Sure, chickie-babe," Risa gestured with a wave for Nala to come inside. "Come on in and I'll get them for you."

* 4 *

The young man with Nalana was tense and Risa eyed him warily. He wasn't much to look at, plain square face, scruffy brown hair and barely taller than she was, even his bright blue eyes seemed painfully normal and non-threatening. But her Instinct for people never steered her wrong, and it knew that something was off about this man and it was the kind of off that was usually dangerous.

In the entrance of their old wooden house, Risa put an arm around Nala's shoulders, steering her away from this "Naethan" and towards the sitting room.

"So, was it today you had your exam?"

"Yes!" Nalana exclaimed enthusiastically. "I'm hoping for an A!"

Risa chuckled. "Smart girl like you, 'course y'are!"

Looking around the cluttered sitting room, she tried to remember where in all the mess Nalana's stuff had been put. The whole house was full, almost as if they'd moved from a ten bedroomed mansion into a small apartment. Stacks of boxes were piled high, up to the ceiling at some points and scattered all around, making movement throughout the house, and especially their sitting room, really rather hazardous. She let go of Nala's shoulders and leaning over a nearby crate, Risa shuffled through a bunch of kitchen odds and ends.

"I'm sure they're in here." She frowned. "Somewhere. Hey, Rob? Where'd ya put that stuff for Nala?"

"In the corner," a voice called through the open doorway that led into their tiny kitchen. "On top of those clothes. Are they staying for lunch?"

"Nope!"

She pushed her feet carefully through the miasma of boxes as she made her way to the far corner of the room near the kitchen, Nalana followed.

They'd done a number of raids recently and had everything from canned food, to clothes and even weapons, but the weapons had been put in the east bedroom, where they could be locked up. The two-bedroomed house really was far too small for such a large haul of supplies, but soon enough it would be cleared out as Rebel groups came to collect their share.

Bending over the haphazard lines of crates, Risa noticed in the corner of her eye that Naethan inched steadily closer to where Nala stood in the doorway. Something was wrong, she could sense it. Glancing sideways, she eyed him warily.

Naethan launched towards Nala while grabbing Risa's elbow, and pulled the three of them down to the floor in a heap. As they landed, gunfire sounded, and above their heads bullets ripped holes in the walls and shredded the head-high boxes all around them.

When the gunfire ceased, Naethan dragged everyone to their feet and pulled them towards the kitchen.

Dislodging her elbow, she glared at him. "How did you know?"

"Dodge Talent. Danger Sense," he said curtly. "Back door?"

"Yes." She gestured across the kitchen to the other side with a flick of her hand. "But we can't not fight."

"If you stay here, you'll die."

Ice blue eyes stared into her and for a moment, Risa recognized something deeper in this young man. It was something cold and veiled, something that acted without emotion and was therefore capable of anything. Risa swallowed.

"Nalana," his eyes dropped from Risa to take in the young woman. "You trust me?"

"Of course, Nae, but what—"

"Do exactly as I say and we'll get out of this. Understand?"

A loud bang from the direction of the front door shook their rickety walls, and echoed through the floor.

Again gunfire sounded, but this time from inside the house.

Pulling her weapon out of its holster, Risa glanced sideways at her second in command, Rob, who stood behind them at the kitchen bench.

"The others?" she asked him. He was a telepath and would know if the other two were savable.

Rob's bottom lip lifted and he shook his head.

"OK, let's get out of—"

"Down!" Naethan ordered and in front of him Nalana ducked. He pulled a weapon out of his jacket and fired through the doorway, over the girl's head. In the sitting room, a black suit Agent stepped into the line of fire and dropped dully to the floor like a rag doll.

"Come on." Naethan grabbed Nalana's hand and pulled the girl past Risa, towards the back door. With one tense glance at her friend, Risa decided to follow this man and retreat.

Outside, Naethan led them hurriedly down the steps and across gravel towards the old garage at the back of the property.

"Down!" he commanded again and this time all three of them ducked. He fired one shot over their heads at the backdoor.

As Risa got to her feet again, she looked behind her and a second man in black fatigues lay motionless on the gravel. She blinked at the body. He was a very good shot, too good to be just an Illegal Psi like herself.

"Run!" Naethan yelled and they followed him into the old garage.

A hundred years ago houses were either made out of wood or brick. The rich could afford to buy the expensive dark bricks from the Marakan quarries to build their houses. The poorer working-class were forced to build with wood, which tended to rot or succumb to termites over time. Their old garage was a perfect example of the finite life of wood buildings, but perhaps this time it was fortunate, because there was a large rotted hole in the back wall from which they could escape. How Nala's friend knew this, was another matter entirely.

The four of them scrambled through the gap, out onto a street beyond, and over the tarmac for the cover of a narrow path between buildings. Running for several blocks in a southerly direction, they dipped in and out of lanes and alleys to brush off the Agency pursuit. When they could run no more, they slowed their pace and slipped into another cobbled gray driveway behind buildings.

"Looks like..." Nalana gasped between words. "You saved me again, Nae. Someone might think you...you want to get into my knickers!"

The young man laughed. "I'll leave that to Marius. Besides, how would I get any sleep without your stories?"

They both laughed at each other and Risa lifted an eyebrow. "This's happened before?" Lifting one hand she shook her head dismissively. "No, don't tell me, let's focus on gettin' out of here. Either o'you know how to get back to Nama's?"

* 5 *

Nama grumbled wordlessly. Naethan had disappeared again when he wasn't supposed to and Nalana was overdue from her exam at the Cathedral. He turned around at the entrance to their building and paced back down the hall towards Taelin.

"One of us should have gone with her!" he barked.

Taelin sighed. "For Founder's sakes, relax. Naethan will look after her, it'll be fine."

A spark of anger stopped Nama's pacing, and he glared at Taelin. "You're assuming they're together, what if they're not? What if Nala's alone and in trouble? What if those gangsters found her again?"

Taelin shrugged. "She's not completely helpless, have you seen the size of the flick-knife she carries with her now? Besides, where else does Nae usually go? When they're not here they're always together. I'm sure they'll be fine."

Nama grunted, brushing off Taelin's logic with a dismissive hand gesture and continued to pace.

Footsteps walked towards them on the street, and Nalana stepped in through the open doorway of their building.

"Hey, Nama." She put a tiny hand on his arm as she walked past.

His worry dissipated into a smile. "Hey, how was your exam, kiddo?"

She grinned back at him. "I want an A!"

He laughed as she kept walking.

"Is Marius back from doing deliveries yet, Tae?"

"Yeah, yeah," Taelin smiled. "He's in front of the fire I think. So, was your exam really that good?"

Sensing Naethan's mind outside, Nama pushed through the grimy doorway, stepped onto the street and glared down at Naethan as he walked towards him.

"What did I ask you to do this morning, Naethan?"

The young man was forced to step back. "I did all of those chores before I left."

"Well there's more to do!" he roared. "Now get inside!"

"Aren't I allowed a break?" Naethan sighed.

Nama put a broad hand on his back and pushed the young man through the doorway. "Maybe when you're dead, son."

Nama's flash of anger blew away as he saw that Naethan wasn't alone on the street. "Risa. Rob." He grinned at the two ex-desert dwellers walking towards him. "What brings you to our fine establishment?"

The answering tension in Risa's nearly black eyes loosened the smile on Nama's face. "Our safe-house was taken out. I need to talk with you in private."

"Of course." He indicated the door with an up-facing palm. "Come on in."

He led them through a maze of dark passages and hallways, to the center of their building where a large windowless space served as their main Common Room. A fire burned in the hearth, warming the rooms around it and keeping much of the building dry from the inside out. In the flickering glow of the hearth and leaning back in Marius' arms, Nalana was talking about her exam. Next to them sat Naethan and Tae listening to her exploits.

Nama led Risa and Rob through to the other side of the common room where a door led off into Asha's office. It was a glorified cupboard, with desks and bookcases on every wall and very little standing space.

However, it was also mostly Psi shielded, so they could talk in relative privacy. When they entered the room, Asha was sitting at one of the desks writing with pen and paper.

Tired, angry blue eyes looked up at him over her work. "What is it?" she barked.

"Asha, this is Risa and Rob from the central supply cell. They've got something to discuss with us."

Not knowing who Asha was, Risa stepped confidently towards her. "Yes, your Naethan, is he trustworthy?"

Asha straightened in her chair. "Why do you ask?"

"Our safe-house was taken out by the Agency. I lost two men and he seemed to know there was danger before it happened."

The tension in Asha flowed into boredom and she shrugged. "He's a Dodge Talent, it's normal for them to sense danger before—"

"Do you know what my specialty is?" Risa didn't pause long enough to let Asha reply. "I know people. Never steered me wrong before, and that boy's dangerous. Mark my words."

Asha sighed. "Do you have anything other than instinct to give me? I can't lock him up for that."

Risa shook her head. "Not really. He was tense when they came 'round. Knew when to duck. He's a crack shot too, took out two Black Suits one bang each, dead. And calm as a statue all the while. No fear. If the boy's not an Agent, he's dead crazy."

Asha got to her feet. "Yes, we're all well aware of his odd personality traits. But he's been with us for nearly a year, and he has shown no sign of hostility towards us. If he was an Agent, surely he would have attacked by now?" She sat back again in her chair with a sigh. "Look, thank you for bringing this to us, we appreciate your concern. But, now that you're here, I actually have a request for you from Hawk. We need your help for a mission we're going to start the day after tomorrow."

Risa frowned, putting her hands on her hips. "Us? What use can we be?"

"We're going to raid a desert training base."

"Hai di'chena! Are you mad?" retorted Rob in his oddly East-Ronan accent.

"No, not mad, if Hawk says it can be done, it can be," she said firmly. "What we need is for you to go north to Epa, and using your local contacts, set up the groundwork to get us safely in and out of the desert." Asha handed over an envelope. "Here are Hawk's instructions and enough resources to get you up there immediately."

Risa looked confused as she took the envelope. "What? You want us to go now?"

"As soon as possible, yes."

The confusion on Risa's face deepened. "What about this 'Naethan'? I still sense he's trouble."

"We'll keep an eye on him, don't worry about that." Asha looked down at her work. "Good day."

Nama moved to let the others leave and when they were alone in the room, he crossed his arms over his chest. "What's wrong? You're not normally that brisk with people."

She sighed. The anger had lifted from her features, revealing a deep wariness in her dark blue eyes. "I'm sorry, Nama, I haven't slept much with all of this work. Hawk forgets sometimes that I'm only one woman."

"Can I help?"

"No," she sighed again. "You would need to meet him, and it's not safe yet."

Nama lifted an eyebrow. "Yet?"

"Yes. After certain events, you and a few of the others will be allowed to meet him. For now, it's barely safe for *me* to know let alone anyone else. Could you go check on our prisoner down in the basement for me?" She leaned over the desk and put her forehead on her arms. "I'm going to rest my eyes for half an hour and keep going."

He smiled. "Yes, ma'am."

* 6 *
The same day
Agency Tower
Approximately midday

Triian Rena stood in the hallway of the level nine Agency accommodation block. Several months ago her grand-nephew Bana and his wife had been killed by the Rebels on-mission. Their little daughter Gusa had spent all that time being handed from unwilling relative to unwilling relative. She sighed and crossed her arms over her chest as she waited.

Triian's mother had given birth, fed her newborn, and then killed herself for no reason. Everyone said it was because her mother had been a high rated Time Psi—and everyone knew that high-rated Time Psi were always mentally unstable. But whatever the cause of her mother's death, it had left little Triian alone in the world. Her father had totally rejected her in his grief and passed her on to other relatives. She'd spent her childhood being handed from one family to another, alone and unloved.

As an adult she'd made it her mission to change the Agency from the inside and to help every orphan child she was able. A lifetime of work in the Ao Council had only amounted to the constant danger of being in opposition to Jaran Cowdy senior, and adopting a series of abandoned and orphaned children over the years, including bringing up her own four children.

She swallowed. And now, in the last few years before her retirement, she was about to take on the responsibility of Gusa, the second generation of her adopted waifs.

The door opened and the little blond-haired girl looked up at her with massive gray-blue eyes. She looked so much like her mother. Triian swallowed back her grief and tried to smile. The little girl's mouth was formed into a pout and Trii sensed an unyielding anger in her.

"Come, Gusa." Trii lifted the massive faded pink backpack from the girl's grip and led her down a carpeted hallway towards the main elevator.

They made their way through the bustling central lounge of level nine in silence. People rushed about, some wore the uniform blue suits of on-duty Agents and others were wearing the muted colors of allocated off-duty clothes. No one dawdled or milled around doing nothing, everyone had something that had to be done urgently somewhere else in the building.

As the elevator doors opened, she lifted the little five year old girl into her arms and stepped inside. Gusa rested her head on her shoulder and Trii sensed that the girl's suppressed grief and anger was exhausting her.

"Where are we going, Aunty?" Her voice was quiet.

Trii tucked the child's head under her chin. "We're going to my apartment, dear one."

"Oh."

When the elevator doors opened on level twenty, Trii gently put Gusa back on the ground. The carpet on level twenty was a faded red color—a deviation from the rest of the building's blue or green—but Trii appreciated the difference.

Young Gusa ran ahead of her as she strode down the hall towards a frosted window at the end.

"Aunty Triian," the girl turned in front of the window, muted sunlight shimmering in her straw-yellow hair. "Are Mommy and Daddy in your apartment? Is that why we're going there?"

Triian's lips tightened together for a moment as she suppressed her grief. "No, dear. You're coming to live with me like your daddy did when he was young. We'll make a really nice lunch. How do rainbow sprinkle sandwiches sound?"

The little girl covered her mouth and giggled. "Silly! Sprinkles don't go on sandwiches, they go on cake!"

"Of course they go on sandwiches! How could your father forget such a thing?" She turned left and putting her hand to the black security plate next to her door, Triian released the security lock. "Come on, Gusa, I'll show you."

The girl walked around her and into the large apartment. Sunlight shone through the broad windows of her sitting room, spilling into the parlor in long golden puddles. Still running, the little girl shot through the parlor and into the sitting room, only to stop abruptly. Triian sensed confused tension in the little girl and dropping her bag to the floor, she followed.

"Hello," said the little girl shyly. "My name's Gusa, what's yours?"

A voice answered but was so quiet Triian didn't hear the words.

She stepped into the sitting room and, behind her robin's egg blue couch sat Triian's daughter Gwen. She was in the corner all curled up with her own daughter Cassandra in her arms. Trii sensed fear and pain in Gwen and forgetting her ailing knees and hip, she dropped down next to Gwen on the cream-colored carpet.

"Abe Kashān! What's wrong?" She rested one hand on her daughter's aching body. Blond hair covered Gwen's face but there were dark finger-shaped bruises on her bare arms. "What's happened? Gwen?"

"Mother..." Gwen lifted her chin to look at her. Tears filled her daughter's dark-blue eyes and a dark welt sat across her cheekbone.

Triian's jaw tightened. "Did Morna do this?"

She nodded.

"I'm going to rip that boy's face off!" Triian nearly roared.

"No, Mother. You know you can't. Jaran will make you suffer if you go near his precious son." The look in her daughter's eyes was one of pained anger, but not of defeat. "There's a way out of this." She unfolded the arms that were wrapped tightly around little Cassandra's shoulders and held up a yellow sticky-note.

Triian gasped. "Is that what I think it is?"

"Yes. It says for us to come here."

"Come, sit on the couch and I'll get you an ice-pack. Are you hungry?" She glanced at little Cassandra who gripped her mother tightly and wouldn't meet Triian's eyes. "Did he hurt her?"

"No, as far as I can tell she's OK. Aren't you my love?" Gwen affectionately kissed the six year old's white-blond hair, but there was still no response from the little girl.

The doorbell jingle sounded from the ceiling with a little artificial bird twitter and Triian tensed.

"Gusa," she touched the girl's arm gently. "Let's play a game. I want you to hide with Gwen and Cass here. You need to be as quiet as a mouse—quieter. Do you understand?"

The girl nodded and sat down on the carpet up against the wall. Gwen opened her arms and pulled Gusa into her embrace with Cassandra. Blond and blue eyed, the two girls were only second or third cousins, but they were so similar in coloring and shape that together they looked like sisters, close enough even at the age of five and six to look like twins. Triian gave the threesome a tight little smile and dragged herself to her feet.

With a well practiced calm, she made her way to the security panel and swiped a finger across it. The door unlocked and opened sideways to reveal another of her many relations.

Brushing nervously at his dark hair with one hand, Tiras gave her a tense smile. "Great aunt Triian." He said in an overly formal voice. "May I come in?"

The man was not normally a tense or a nervous person, which meant something was up. She nodded and indicated he was welcome with a sweep of one arm. "Of course, Tiras, please come in. Would you like a hot drink?"

He stepped inside, shaking his head as she closed the door. "No, thank you, aunty. I've..." he paused and she sensed that he really was very tense. "I was... I don't..." he sighed and lifted one hand out of his suit jacket pocket. Between two fingers he held a yellow sticky-note.

"You're here for Gwen, aren't you?"

He frowned, bringing black brows together over his gray-blue eyes. "Gwen?"

"She has one as well. What does yours say?"

"To come here, why? Do you know what's going on?"

She shook her head. "No, I don't. But if *he* wants to help my daughter escape I'm willing to give it a go. Can I see it?"

Tiras handed the scrap of paper over. The handwriting on the note was curved and ever so slightly sloped, but there was no more information other than to come and visit her.

"If this is from—*you know who*—we'll have to be very careful about disposing of these. Please, go into the sitting room and say hello to Gwen, Cass and Gusa, I'll be there in a moment."

She turned towards her kitchen. It was a nice room, long and fairly wide with wood cupboards on either wall, and a nice creamy stone-top island that ran through the middle. She went to her fridge and opened the freezer door. An ice pack sat on the bottom shelf with two small yellow sticky-notes attached to it. She blinked at it in surprise—not even Jaran Cowdy senior should have clearance to get into her apartment without her permission. However, Hawk was known to get his notes to places that seemed impossible, so she shouldn't be too surprised.

Grabbing the sticky-notes and the ice pack, she closed the freezer door and walked back into her sunny sitting room. One note started with "For Triian" The other "For Tiras".

"There's more, Tiras." He sat on the floor, his back against her couch, facing Gwen and the two girls. "Here Gwen." She handed the icepack to her daughter and his note to Tiras.

Pulling a low chair around next to them. Triian Rena sat down and put on her reading glasses:

"Book a day-trip for two adults and three children for tomorrow. 11.30am. Be cautious, he will trace it. Keep them with you."

Triian knew what Jaran would do to them if he discovered those yellow notes in their hands. She'd been there on the Council when Jaran took over from Ara as Head and she'd seen the danger in the young man's eyes even then. Twenty years later, Jaran was now probably the most dangerous man in Arana, more-so even than the most powerful Spades Boss.

"I've got to go." Tiras' voice was quiet and he looked first at Gwen, with an icepack to her cheek and then at Triian. "Be careful, Aunty. Here." He handed her his sticky notes. "Burn them all. We'll probably only get

one shot at this. I'll let you know when I know more."
Tiras got to his feet and walked towards her parlor. She
heard the door click closed and looked down at his
second note.

"*Meeting. Second floor. In the blue room. Five
minutes.*"

Triian folded the notes in half and collected her
daughter's one as well. "Come, dear daughter, I'll burn
these in the kitchen and we can show young Gusa and
Cassandra how nice rainbow sprinkle sandwiches are."

Her daughter smiled at her over the icepack.
"You're still making sprinkle sandwiches, Mother?"

"The day I stop making sprinkle sandwiches is the
day I die!"

* 7 *

Hawk stood utterly still in the darkest corner of the
Blue Room. The shadows from gaps in the blinds cast
oddly around him, making him practically invisible at
first glance. He waited impassively for Tiras Malar to
arrive. Asha would say such a move was too much of a
risk—to reveal himself to someone whose alliances
weren't known was very dangerous. But she didn't
completely understand their situation nor what was
really at stake with Gwen and Cassandra escaping. If
Asha knew what he knew, she would probably come for
them herself and tear up the Tower.

A wave of dark static energy triggered from his
center, and moved slowly out from him, like a solar
flare.

Tiras must be close, he thought dimly.

The echoes of what will be would very soon meld
with what is, and then what was. It was important that
all three were the same or Tiras would turn away and
innocent lives would be lost.

The door handle moved and someone stepped
through into the room while barely making a sound.
Even in the darkness, Hawk recognized the tall lean
form of Tiras Malar—cousin of both Bana and Kita.
Tiras looked around the dim room but, as many people
were apt to do with a "ghost", he didn't see Hawk
standing in the shadows even though he looked right at

him. Tiras closed the door and stood in the shadows for a few moments. His fearful breathing and tense shoulders betrayed how afraid he was. Then, as expected, he turned to the enviro-panel on the wall and lifted the light level with the flick of one finger over the touch pad. The lights came on, brushing away all of the shadows and illuminating Hawk's figure. Tiras turned back to look at the room again and called out in surprise. Hawk stepped out of the corner towards him, still not saying anything, waiting for the right *time* to say the right words.

Tiras' surprise lifted into fear, then, just as quickly, his shoulders dropped into defeat. His voice was quiet and very sad. "I knew you were cold, but I didn't know you were so heartless that you could set up two little girls for execution, simply to get three Traitors."

A smile played at the edges of Hawk's mouth. "Is my cover really that good?"

Tiras frowned. "Cover? What, now you want to trick me into thinking that *you* are *Him*?"

"But, I am."

"Y... you can't be. You're not even Time Psi."

"I am now. How do you want me to prove it to you?"

There was a pause and the two men stared at each other. One absolutely calm, the other with a little tense frown on his face.

"Dog," they said in unison.

"Red wine, carbon copy, Bluetooth, Beretta," again said in unison. Tiras was too strong a telepath and Hawk not strong enough, for that particular trick to work in any way other than with a high rating Time Psi ability and they both knew it.

Tiras leaned on the wall next to him, seeming to suddenly realize what it could all mean. "But if you're Hawk—"

"Yes, I'm taking a great risk meeting you. I'm showing you a depth of trust that exceeds our current social and professional situation."

"Why did you then? Why take such a risk? You know as well as I what he'd do if he got hold of this information."

Hawk nodded slowly. "I did it because what I am about to ask you to do is insane. I'm revealing myself to show you how important it is that they escape."

"Gwen and Cassandra?"

"Gwen, Cassandra, Gusa, Araian and Boe." He paused and gave the older man a slight smile. "And you, if you survive."

Tiras frowned. "Why Gusa? She would be safer with Aunt Triian, surely?"

"Bana is alive."

"He is?" Tiras seemed genuinely surprised. "But he went MIA months ago, is he a Rebel?"

Hawk shook his head. "No, not yet, he's a prisoner. But the only way to convince him to join us is by freeing Gusa. And we need *him* to help *you* escape."

"Why Bana?"

Hawk smiled. "He can fly a helicopter."

Tiras stepped back, a tense smile crossing his face. "Exactly how insane is this escape going to be?"

"Fairly, but not impossible. However, I think you have some understanding of the seriousness of this situation and that if you agree to do this—"

"I understand. It's all or nothing, right? Because if I get captured you're dead as well as the hundred or so Rebels."

"Two and a half thousand Rebels." Hawk corrected. "And yes."

"Two and a half *thousand*?" Tiras laughed. "You're not half putting on the pressure are you?"

Hawk grinned. "As I said, there's a lot at stake here. But you're perfectly capable of pulling it off."

"OK." Tiras nodded slowly. "So, what exactly am I going to have to do?"

Hawk lifted out a small PDA computer from his jacket and flicked the lid of it up and around to reveal a video recorder.

"You are going to offer a full interview to the news station, which comes to the roof of the Tower with a helicopter at midday tomorrow. This recording will be broadcast on all channels thirty minutes before midday. If you make it to the roof by that time, Bana and my second, Asha, will be there with a helicopter to get you out."

Tiras laughed. "You're right, that is insane."

"But, will you do it?"

He frowned. "How do I know you're not setting me up?"

"You don't," Hawk smiled confidently. "Not for certain. The fact that I'm standing here in front of you should be enough for you to trust that I'm not setting you up for execution."

"Good point," he said quietly. "So, if this succeeds, what do you want me to do on the outside?"

"We can talk about that when you're out. Will you do it?"

Mischief lifted into Tiras' square face. "A chance to thumb my nose at Jaran Cowdy senior, get *Gwen* out and jump off a building into a helicopter? How could I refuse?" The mischief lifted away and he looked off to the side. "What about Alaha and the children? Will they be safe?"

"They're all out of the city, and there is no link between them and your escape. Your ex-wife may not ever forgive you but they will be safe. The only person left behind with any risk will be Triian, and I'll do my best to help her."

"OK then," Tiras rubbed his hands together. "Let's start."

* 8 *

Desert Training Base
Just south of Epa
3pm

Xak sat in an uncovered corner of the exercise yard with the rain pouring down around him. Everyone else; the forty or so students between the ages of eleven and seventeen, were huddled under what few roof covers there were, trying to avoid getting wet. Xak wasn't worried about the rain. He figured he was going to get wet anyway, so why fight it? It was easier just to sit there and enjoy not being hot for a while.

His frown deepened. Hawk had come to him. To him—Xakarii Kane—sixteen years old and seemingly a nobody. Hawk wanted him and his friends to become Rebels, and he was going to send people to break them out. He would become a Rebel and he would finally be able to tell Hawk about the dreams. It was all he'd ever wanted to do and be since he was twelve years old and realized that his dreams were connected to a real person.

A little smile etched back the edges of his frown. He was *actually* going to meet Hawk.

All morning, even at that very moment, the lines and threads of Time seemed to quiver around him. It made the air and the rain that pelted down seem charged with an itchy excited static. The effect on Time itself from their one interaction was massive—World-changing, even. Nothing else he'd ever experienced with his Time Psi ability made the world shake and shimmer like that. So he had no doubt that it had actually happened and wasn't some kind of trick. The problem was that he couldn't prove it to anyone else.

He sighed and looked down at the black sand covering his feet. How was he going to bring up what had happened that morning with the others? How could he even start to explain it?

Oh, by the way I talked to Hawk this morning. He said the Rebels are coming to get me, and you guys can come too!

He snorted at how ridiculous his own thoughts sounded. The other four didn't really understand his visions to begin with, let alone something like this. Would they believe him? Would they come with him? Could they pull it off and not get killed?

He sighed again and lifted his feet out of the sand. If he kept thinking like that, he was going to make himself crazy. Xak stood and looked around for his friend Levi, who was one of the few other non-kinetics left of his age. He was also the one who'd invited Xak into their little group to be protected. Xak knew he could probably tell Levi about what had happened and then Lii could help him tell the others. Looking around, he caught sight of his friend on the other side of the yard near the main door. Levi was tall and thin with mousy hair and an easy smile. They made eye contact across the yard, and he stepped towards him.

Xak sensed danger, ducked, rolled out of the way and was up on his feet again before his conscious mind figured out that someone had tried to attack him. There was a roar of frustration to one side of him and Rega, the worst bully, lunged for him.

The dark-haired boy was bigger and stronger than Xak, and they both knew if Rega hit him, even once, he would go down and stay down. Being smaller and quicker made him a target, but it also helped him to stay out of the bully's reach.

"Xak!" someone called out from behind him. He ducked down under huge lunging arms and skittered towards the voice. Levi stood with his hand pressed hard on the metal of the exit door. The lock was magnetic, which meant that with a little time Levi and his EM Talent could reverse the polarity and open the lock but it wasn't open yet. Reaching his friend, Xak put his back to the door and turned to face Rega.

Tall, blond-haired Liz stepped out of the crowd on one side and put herself between him and Rega.

"Rega," she said with an ominous tone to her voice. "What did I tell you about Xak?"

"If I can get to him first he's mine!" growled the older boy from the middle of the yard.

"No, you dumb a'kenān," she said with an angry growl. "Let's try this again."

The bully lifted up into the air with a whimpered squeal. Liz juggled the boy up and down in the falling rain above them like a rag doll. She was the strongest kinetic of all the kids, but even that wasn't enough to dissuade Rega from still going for those kids she protected. Xak wasn't the kind of person to get enjoyment from the suffering of others, but the squeal of fear in Rega's voice as he was tossed in the air was oddly satisfying.

Behind Xak, the metal wall shifted and, stumbling, he nearly fell backwards into the corridor beyond. Levi, grinning with victory, played silently on an invisible electric guitar.

Xak skittered through the gap and looked behind him.

"Don't get caught, Xak." He saw the outline of a smiling face and the door slid closed again.

He stood alone in the dark concrete corridor. It was against the rules for a student to be in the halls when they were supposed to be in the yard. So he had to hide. But there was only one place without a camera—the unisex bathroom.

As he ran down towards the doors, he made the decision. He had to tell the others what had happened. They probably wouldn't believe him, but they deserved the choice.

* 9 *

18 Aracan 3004
The next morning
Arām City

"Naethan!" Turning from a dingy hallway into the sunlit sleeping room Nama called out again. "Nae! C'mon! Wake up!" He bent over Naethan's cot and shook him by the arms. The young man flinched and grabbing the base of Nama's thumbs, he dislodged his grip with surprisingly strong fingers.

Vivid blue eyes opened and Naethan blinked at him. "What? What's wrong?"

"You slept in, numb-nuts." Nama grinned. "Come on, we've got a mountain of mamon to sort before today's festivities begin."

"Right." Naethan let go of his thumbs and got out of bed. "Any breakfast today?"

Nama turned towards the door as Naethan put his sneakers on. "Naw, the kids got first dibs, wasn't much left. Dana's team should arrive with more before we head out though. C'mon on."

They made their way through a maze of dark corridors to their central common room. It was dry and warm from the fire that roared in one corner. In the middle of the space, one group of people cluttered around an old pool table animatedly discussing some strategy involving the maps and papers that littered the faded green surface. Kala and Nalana sat on blankets near the fire giving the ten or so Rebel children of their cell lessons in reading and writing. On the far side of the room furthest from the fire, Asha stood in the middle of another group giving out orders.

"Naethan!" she called from across the room. "Can you drive stick?"

"Yes, ma'am, I can."

"Good, you're our new driver, go get geared up."

Nama walked towards Asha, as Nae turned away. He waited for the young man to be out of ear shot before giving Asha a tense look. "What happened to Marius and to keeping an eye on Naethan?"

"I need Marius in the first car so you and Tae can still do the rounds in the van," she snapped. "But, if you know someone who can drive stick and doesn't already have a job, point them out to me."

Nama lifted an eyebrow at her. "What's got your knickers in a twist?"

"What?!" Her deep blue eyes were angry for a moment before she sighed and shook her head. "Oh, sorry. Big day."

"Tomorrow will be bigger." He gave her a wink. "What's left to do?"

She brushed at an errant thread of curly black hair across her face, and looked thoughtful for a moment. "Only waiting on Dana, we really need to eat before we go."

"OK." He turned away in the direction of the old kitchen and basement access. "I'll get Tae and Bana from the basement."

"Thanks. And keep an eye on Bana until he's in the van. He's not trustworthy until he's done his part."

"Yes, ma'am," he called over his shoulder.

* 10 *

"But Mother! He'll kill you!" Much of one side of Gwen's face had come out nearly black overnight and it hurt Triian to see such damage on her daughter.

"No, my dear," Triian shook her head as she glanced at the large flat-screen hanging nearby on her sitting-room wall. Adverts flickered over the screen and she looked back into her daughter's ocean blue eyes. "Suspicion of treason is not justifiable grounds for execution. I'm on the Ao Council and only two ranks below him. He can not touch me without proof."

"He will suspect you." Gwen's eyes pleaded with her to see reason. "Please, come with us."

"No." She shook her head. "I'm staying here. Yes, he will suspect me, but if he could kill everyone whom he suspects of treason there would be only he and Hoyal on the Council, and the rest of Arana would be empty. Trust me, daughter, I've been dealing with him for over twenty years. I know what I'm doing. He can't hurt me." She glanced back up at the muted screen to see Tiras' face mouthing words. "Sound!" she ordered and the TV un-muted itself.

"And I will offer an exclusive interview about the Agency to any news station that comes to pick me up at midday from the top of the Arām Agency Tower building."

Staring at the TV, Gwen covered her mouth in shock. "Holy Founder, messenger of Divinity!"

"Mute!" commanded Triian. "That's the signal, Gwen, we're just waiting for two more people to arrive and we go."

Her daughter was distressed and didn't seem to hear her. "What is Tiras doing? He's going to get himself killed!"

She rested a comforting hand on her daughter's arm, making sure her voice was gentle and loving to counter her daughter's fear. "Yes, that may well happen, but he's doing it to get you out, so let's not make that sacrifice in vain—" her bird-call door bell sounded from the ceiling and she turned. "Go and get Cassandra and Gusa."

Triian waited for Gwen to step out of sight before swiping her system panel to open the door. She looked down into two ice-blue eyes framed by short white-blond hair. Triian's heart lifted into her throat.

Araian Cowdy, she thought fearfully, *Jaran's only daughter.*

The woman held her little boy, Boe, and both of them were dressed for cold weather in expensive wool-lined brown suede jackets and hoods.

The young woman respectfully bowed her head. "Good day, matron. I'm here for a day trip to the Museum of Natural History." She lifted a yellow sticky-note from out of her cream faux-fur jacket sleeve for a moment, and then slipped it back under cover again.

Triian swallowed the fear in her throat and stepped out of the doorway. She closed the door and turned to look at the woman who was only a year younger than Gwen.

"I must say, I am a little surprised to see *you* here."

The well-practiced ice dropped away and a flare of mischief lifted into the young woman's face. It was the sort of mischief that Trii hadn't seen since Araian's mother died. "Don't take offense, Matron, but that's a good sign. If you wouldn't suspect me, my father wouldn't either."

Triian nodded slowly. "It's good to know that some of your mother lives on in you, perhaps there's hope for your siblings."

Araian laughed. "That's very doubtful. Junior and Morna are vicious like Father, Krenān is steadily catching up, and David..." she seemed sad for a moment, letting her words fade into silence.

Trii gave the woman a sympathetic smile and nodded. "Yes, dear. I know. I mourn his corruption as well."

"Mother?" Gwen called out uncertainly from the next room.

"Come out, it's time for you to go now."

"Who's coming with—" Gwen stepped through a doorway and halted stock-still when she saw Araian. Both little girls sensed Gwen's terror and gripped her legs tightly.

Triian put a hand up to stall her daughter's fear. "It's OK, Araian is coming with you."

"You're not coming, Matron?"

She shook her head, looking back at the young woman. "No, Araian, someone has to stay and oppose your father on the Council, without my vote he'd be unstoppable. May I have your sticky-note, please?"

The note was handed over and Triian went to the kitchen sink where she lit it on fire. When it was fully aflame she dumped it into the metal basin and faced the two women again.

"I will take you to the checkpoint on level eight, from there you'll have to go alone down to the bus bay. Gwen has your official papers but still be careful inside the building. Tiras said that once you're out on the streets *they* will find you and get you to safety."

By the time she finished speaking, the note had all but turned to ash in the sink. She ran the faucet for a few moments to wash the remains down the drain and stepped back into her parlor.

"Come, it's time."

Triian lifted young Gusa into her arms. She led the others out of her apartment and down the hall to the elevator. The main doors opened to greet them with the astringent chemical smell of carpet cleaner. She stepped inside the broad elevator and pressed the button. The doors opened and she stepped out, leading the group in a zig-zag pattern through the halls.

Trii neared the security station and as if on an unsaid cue all three of them, trained well in the art of deception, manipulation and acting for the precepts of their jobs, animated into a group of excited women.

Turning into the main security hall, she led the others towards an intersection. It was filled with armed guards, a single barred door and a very bored looking security man who sat in front of a flickering computer screen.

"What are you going to see first?" she said excitedly to her daughter.

Gwen laughed "The first thing I'm going to do is find a cafe and have a proper espresso coffee."

"Oh, yes, real coffee and some chocolate cake!" Araian joined in with an empathically genuine flare of want.

Triian put her hand on her daughter's shoulder, giving her a gentle smile. "I wish I could come with you, but there's just so much work to be done in the lab. We also have another Council meeting at three." She rolled her eyes. "The paper work has been unending for weeks on this new initiative of Jaran's. Do bring some cake back for me, if you can manage it?"

"Of course, Mother." Turning to face the security guard, Gwen took out their papers from her jacket pocket and handed them over to the man behind the desk.

"A day trip to the museum?" His voice dripped with sarcasm. "Aren't we lucky ladies?"

Triian sensed the tension in the two young women, but she didn't bat an eyelid at the man's obvious disrespect. "It's not for them but the children. They're doing an art history module in their Year One class and I suggested that their learning would be augmented appropriately if they could experience it first hand. Is there a problem?"

"Where is your second counter-sign?" the man barked, still with an undertone of disrespect in his voice.

She hadn't been able to get a second signature in time but it shouldn't stop them. She lifted her voice into an imperious tone and looked down her nose at the guard.

"Excuse me, young man, but do you know who I am? Surely a Council member and Head of Psi Research doesn't require a supervisor's countersign? Considering there are only two others of higher rank than me in this entire building, the procedure is rather moot, don't you think?"

"Procedure is proce—" the radio strapped to his bullet-proof vest blared incomprehensibly. The man lifted the radio to speak into it. ~ "This is Hub-Eight, please repeat, Ra-two?"

What replied over the radio the second time sounded just as incomprehensible to Triian as the first lot of noise, but the guard seemed to understand the static-distorted voice.

~ "Copy, Ra-two. This is Hub-Eight, sending extra troops now." He handed the papers back to Gwen and waved them through the check-point.

Triian put Gusa down and wrapped her arms quickly around her daughter's shoulders. "You have a good time, dear daughter. I love you."

"Love you too, Mom."

Jonah, the guard who worked full time in the level ten security room of the Agency Tower, liked being a "nobody".

People who are invisible in the Agency, thought Jonah. *Didn't get shot by moody superiors, and they—*

"Where is he, you incompetent preta?" A nearby screen and the back of Jonah's neck were peppered with little drops of spittle from the screaming crazy man looming over the back of his chair.

"I... I don't know. How can I?" Jonah scanned the ocean of screens in the security hub room. "Sir, there are over a thousand cameras—"

Jaran Cowdy junior angrily smacked the control panel with the palm of his hand. "I don't want to hear excuses! What I want is a competent worker! Where is your supervisor?"

Jonah swallowed. "I... I think he's on a lunch break, Sir. I've paged him, he... he should be here soon."

"Where is that?" The man pointed to a screen in the middle of the wall. A dark-haired man stood on camera in a hallway. A smile lifted into the man's oval face and he waved at them.

Jonah felt it prudent not to point out the labels below each screen, he simply answered the question.

"Level fifteen, sir. North side of the Research Labs."

"Where's your radio! Send troops to that location. Now!"

He glanced sideways at the Ao Agent and lifted the radio receiver to his lips. ~ "This is Ra-Two, we need all available troops to level fifteen, over."

The radio buzzed with numerous copy signals from security teams all over the building.

~ "This is Hub-Eight, please repeat, Ra-Two?" came a muffled response over the radio.

Above them, the man on the screen stepped out of sight again. Keeping his eyes on the screens above him, Jonah lifted the radio again.

~ "Copy, Hub-Eight, this is Ra-Two. All available troops to level fifteen, over."

~ "Copy, Ra-Two. This is Hub-Eight, sending extra troops now."

Jonah's eyes flickered tensely over the screens, the longer this traitor was out of shot the further away he could get from the incoming security teams. The older man stepped back from him, still pulsing with rage and indignation, but currently focused more on the screens than unfairly abusing him for incompetence.

"Where is he... where is he? If Tiras escapes—"

A face flickered over a screen, long enough to catch Jonah's eye before moving off again. "There!" He pointed. "That's level twenty! He must have found an elevator or stairwell without a camera."

Blue eyes glared at him. "How many of them are there?"

Jonah tried not to tremble. This man was the son of the Head. He could probably kill him for no justifiable reason and get away with it.

He swallowed, thinking hard. "Accessible stairwells, uh, maybe two or three but there's only one without cameras covering the doors. There's only one elevator without a camera and it's on the north side of the Tower. But it's supposed to be closed for maintenance."

Again the dark-haired man flickered into camera view with a wave and a smile for them, this time it was level twenty-six.

The older man swore. "That so'then akenān is trying to play with us. Shut out all elevator use from above level ten. Shut the whole so'then building down if you have to! Send Teams up the stairwells from level twenty, and for Founder's sakes send a few to the roof as well!"

Jonah glanced sideways at the man, confused. "Sir?"

"Just do it! I want that man in the morgue or with the Interrogators within the hour!"

* * * * *

Tiras tapped his foot impatiently on the carpeted floor of the elevator. He had one arm resting on the metal rail that lined the walls and his other hand was slipped into the side pocket of his pants with his fingers touching the handle of his secondary weapon.

The elevator was taking forever to get to the top level. He didn't want to be killed in a crowded little elevator by security just because the thing was so slow. Nobody used the elevator most of the time—it was on the wrong side of the building and far too small for most purposes. But it was the only elevator without a camera, and it wouldn't take long for Jaran Cowdy junior to realize that he wasn't about to climb forty stories of stairs because elevators weren't tactically healthy places from which to make a last stand.

His impatience became acute to the point of torture. He couldn't stay in one place, he had to keep moving. He smacked the button of a level above him so he could get out sooner. It was a good five levels below where he wanted to be, but there were a number of other options he could take that were less like a potential ambush than the little service elevator.

The doors opened to reveal a narrow hallway and a security guard standing directly in front of him. Instinct kicked in and he stepped into the man's personal space, took his weapon and gripping the man's throat he gained entrance to his lightly shielded mind to trigger a telepathic sleep program.

When the man was unconscious, Tiras pulled his body to the side and opening the nearest door, dumped him out of sight in a cupboard.

So, they were onto him. There were five levels to cover and cameras everywhere, it was likely that Junior had already ordered Teams to the roof to head him off. He'd probably also figured out by now that Tiras knew where all the cameras were, so he'll be expecting him to be in the camera black areas. This was going to be difficult, but it was all or nothing now, he could not be captured and taken to the Interrogators.

The sounds of running combat boots on carpet came towards him from up the hall somewhere. He ducked into a door on his left. A chemical smell met his nostrils and he knew, even in the darkness, that he must be in some kind of lab-room.

Reaching out his hands in the pitch blackness, he searched for something to guide him. His fingers brushed the line of a high table. Using touch alone, he followed the length of the wood to a wall on the other side of the room.

He knew there wouldn't be a door to his left because that should be the north wall of the building so, shuffling quietly in the dark he followed the wall to his right. Edges and blurred lines hovered in the darkness around him, and he wished that he'd risked turning on the lights. One hand on the wall, one stretched out in front of him, he shuffled a careful step forwards. His fingertips met a second wall perpendicular to the first. An insert in the surface revealed another door. His fingers found the handle and pushed down as he heard someone knock on the entry behind him in the dark.

Light met him on the other side. With his fingers groping to turn the lock, he spun around and at the click of metal on metal, he realized he was trapped. The room was a little adjoining storage area. There was shelving on three walls, which were cluttered with glass bottles and jars. From the different chemical scents, he knew not to knock over any of them by accident or risk some kind of chemical reaction or poisoning. Next to the door on the fourth wall was a single clear table.

There was no exit. He sighed.

Voices sounded from outside and the handle moved as someone tried to open the door. He stepped away from it in case the person on the other side was touch-sensitive and they could feel him through the wood and metal. More voices sounded and he knew it wouldn't be long before they broke through.

It was freedom or death for him, because he knew who Hawk was and that information could not reach Jaran. He glanced around the room, either for possible escape or a possibly quick death. Something above the door caught his attention. A yellow sticky-note protruded out of a fairly large air vent in the ceiling. Tiras leaped onto the bench and pulled the sticky out.

"Go up!" it said.

Of course, he thought, *they wouldn't think to check the air vents.*

He would have to buy Hawk a drink once he got out, the man certainly thought of everything!

* 12 *

Pedestrians flitted around Asha on the sidewalk like hundreds of bees, all too busy with whatever they were doing to notice her. She waited quietly in amongst the moving world, wary and attentive. Not really nervous but tense.

The Agency transport vehicle should reach the intersection to her left in the next few moments, and turn right towards the Museum. Less than a minute after turning, it would pass by where she stood.

She felt the odd static-encapsulated mental touch of Hawk shimmer for a moment, the itchy black wave flowed from him and over the surface of her mind, making her face tingle oddly. She suppressed the urge to shiver as the hairs on the back of her neck lifted. The fact that he lived with this odd sensation as a "Time Speaker" every day still confounded her—she would find it so utterly distracting. But, at least it was a helpful sensation because the static shimmer meant it was *Time* to move.

Careful to remain calm, she expertly dodged the perpendicular flow of pedestrians across the pavement and into a gap between two parked cars. With her back to the flow of people she lifted a silenced handgun from her dark wool jacket and flicked the safety off.

She counted her calm breaths before the vehicle arrived at the nearby intersection.

One. Two. Three.

She sensed the distinctive deep-red of her old friend Araian and the frightened minds of three young children. The driver and the other adult in the van were both ice-cold calm—probably telepaths.

Four. Five. Six.

The vehicle pulled through the intersection as the lights changed, and they drove towards her.

Asha aimed her weapon, waiting for the next signal from Hawk—the flicker of static across her energy. When it came, she fired two shots in quick succession and took out the tires on one side of the vehicle. The driver tried to keep control but it shifted into a sideways spin. There was a high-pitched screech of overtaxed breaks before the Agency vehicle came to an abrupt halt in the middle of the road. The car stopped exactly perpendicular to the traffic with its nose and tail facing their respective sidewalks.

Other cars braked hard to avoid them but no one hit the downed Agency vehicle. When all traffic was still, shock washed through the street and filled the area with an odd silence. Asha stepped out onto the tarmac.

The driver was checking that their passengers were OK and didn't see her approach. She reached an angle where any through-bullets would not hit the passengers, aimed low and fired. The side window cracked and the driver slumped over the wheel, dead.

She returned her weapon to its holster under her jacket and pulled the back door open. Immediately inside, three little faces looked up at her fearfully. All three children were blond and blue eyed.

Another face ducked down to look at her. "Asha? You're alive!"

She hadn't seen her friend Araian for six years but she looked almost the same. Arai's ice blue eyes were lit with that mischief they shared, and a little sideways smirk added to the familiar personality.

She grinned at her across the width of the vehicle. "You had doubts?"

"Not doubt," Arai laughed. "Only suspicions. How did you survive four years on the run? Krena's magic pixie dust?"

She chuckled. "It's a long story. And I hope one day I can tell you the whole thing."

Sitting next to Araian was a beautiful woman. Her long elven face was partially covered by shoulder-length blond hair. Her thin waif-like body made even the short lithe figure of Araian look a little plump. Asha focused her smile on this woman.

"You must be Gwen. I'm Asha, Hawk's Second. You guys need to get out now, the crash alert has probably already gone off. We don't want to be here when they arrive."

Gwen nodded and shuffled out of the car with a young girl who would not let go of her. The girl looked up at Asha with big bright blue eyes and she sensed a flicker of black static behind that blue. She knew then that the girl was important to Hawk's plans somehow, more so even than Arai or this Tiras fellow.

She gave the young girl a gentle smile to reassure her obvious fear. Glancing back up at the girl's mother, she pulled a sealed parcel from out of an internal jacket pocket. "Hawk gave this to me himself. You can trust its contents."

Gwen took the parcel with a quiet nod. But she still seemed anxious even with that reassurance. Asha noticed, then, as the woman's hair moved out of the way for a moment, that one side of her face was badly bruised as if someone had beaten her.

Asha's mouth tightened into a tense frown and she said a silent prayer to the Old Gods that Mecra would find whoever had beaten this graceful woman.

"Gwen, you and your daughter will be going in that green car just in front of you." Asha indicated the vehicle parked on the side of the street with one hand.

"Thank you," she said, and mother and child walked away.

Another little girl shuffled out onto the street and called out. "Aunty Gwen! Aunty Gwen!"

Putting a hand on the girl's shoulder to stop her, Asha bent over to get eye-level. "You must be Gusa. You're coming with us."

A little heart-shaped face stared at her defiantly with an expression not unlike her father's. "But, I want to go with Aunty Gwen and Cass!"

"I'm sorry, sweetheart, they're going somewhere different. Besides, don't you want to see your dad?"

The light went on in her blue eyes. "Daddy's here? Is Mommy here too?"

Asha shook her head. "No, I'm sorry, just Daddy. Come with me." She offered the girl her hand to hold and young Gusa took it trustingly.

"Hawk's Second?" Arai stepped out of the car herself and lifted a small boy into her arms. "How did you manage that?"

She laughed at the incredulity in her friend's voice. "As I said, it's a long story. Now, we've got to hurry."

* 13 *
The Arām Great River Bridge

Asha stared out through the front windscreen at the grid-lock traffic on the bridge. All six lanes of traffic were at a complete standstill. Cars, busses, transport trucks, all shoved in close together. They weren't going to move any time soon. She sighed and looked sideways at Marius who was driving. He glanced back at her, his vivid purple eyes were tense. They didn't have time for this. The longer it took them, the closer Tiras was to death.

The blue tickling static of Hawk's mind called out to her. *"Asha, are you across the bridge yet?"*

"No," she answered, with a twitch of aggravation. *"Gridlock."*

"Ah. Is everyone else in position for the next stage?"

"Yes. Do you have any suggestions on how to get off the bridge?"

A trace of playfulness underlined his mental tone. *"I'm sure you and Araian can find a way through."*

She snorted. *"Of course, why didn't I think of that?"*

"Sleep helps. Do you have the rest of the plan straight?"

"Yes. Leave it with me."

"Good luck to both of us." She sensed a flare of tension in him as he mentally disconnected. Unbuckling her seat-belt, she turned around in the front seat to look at Araian.

A playful mischief lifted into her face. "Feel like playing a little stack?"

One of Arai's light eyebrows lifted. "Stack? Stack what?"

"Cars." She winked. "Tag-team?"

Araian's laugh bordered on a maniacal cackle. "You're on."

Asha put a gentle hand on Marius's shoulder. "Mar, follow us when we clear a space for the car, and keep the kids inside. Got that?"

The tall, lean Tolān man nodded firmly. "Yes, ma'am." Doors opened and closed, then the central locking flicked on with an audible thunk.

Asha and Araian stood at the front of the car, next to each other in the small gap between bumpers. She glanced sideways at her friend. She'd missed her so much. Arai was the only other friend of hers aside from Hawk who was there with her in the desert training base, and survived. She would trust Araian with her life even more so than she trusted Hawk. Asha wished for a moment that she could tell Arai about Hawk, but the less she knew the safer she'd be, not just from the Agency but from Hawk himself. What Arai did not know could not be taken from her by Interrogators.

Asha smiled. "Ready?"

"When am I not?" Her friend gave her a cocky grin.

Asha sensed the weight of Arai's kinetic energy build up around the black hatchback in front of them. The car groaned slightly and lifted into the air. Reaching up mentally, Asha concentrated on keeping the doors of the car closed, so that the panicked man inside didn't hurt himself by getting out and falling. Side by side, the two women walked into the gap the flying car had left in traffic. Behind them, Marius drove their white vehicle slowly forwards. When they were in position, Araian lowered the flying car and put it down gently in the space behind them.

They made slow but steady progress across the bridge to the shocked terror of other commuters. By the time they got to the source of the traffic jam, they were both laughing maniacally.

There had been an accident on the bridge. The lines of black rubber on concrete told the story of a large eighteen-wheel transport truck losing control and skidding, breaks screeching, across an entire line of traffic, taking out some cars and re-bounding others into the median barrier as it slid sideways. After leaving a trail of destruction behind it, the truck had crashed through two safety rails and lodged itself in the outer rail of the bridge, where it now teetered over the water. A fire engine with a long ladder was trying to evacuate the driver of the truck. Around them the rescue crews were cutting people out of variously damaged vehicles down a hundred meters of debris.

"You want to help?" she asked.

Araian grinned sideways at her. "Try and stop me."

Laughing, Asha turned to signal Marius to stay where he was with one hand. Together, she and Arai jogged across the carnage. Each of them knowing their strength levels, Araian walked towards the truck and Asha towards the nearest wrecked car.

An unconscious young woman was trapped behind the wheel after smashing into the median barrier. Her dark-colored car was a mess of crushed and warped metal. A child wailed, frightened but uninjured, from the back seat as rescue crews were struggling with the Jaws of Life to get them both out.

She put a hand on the shoulder of one of the rescue workers, who was dressed in bright yellow overalls.

"I'm a kinetic, let me help."

The man gave her a look of absolute confusion but stepped out of her way.

Focusing hard on the top of the car, she gripped the edges of the roof and pulled. Metal groaned and graunched under her kinetic pressure. The entire roof came away from her grip and flew up into the air. With a mental flick, she caught it and put it carefully down on the concrete nearby. Reaching with her mind she lifted the child, still in his car seat, out of the back and put him gently on the ground. With the child safe and being checked by paramedics, she got to work on the framing around the trapped woman. She pulled the door apart, piece by piece, and started to bend the metal bar that had collapsed and trapped her inside.

The rescue worker put a hand up to stop her. "We don't know the extent of her injuries, we need to wait for the ambulance before we fully free her." The man swallowed, she sensed his fear of her but that he wasn't letting it control him. He smiled tensely. "Thank you, whoever you are."

She returned the smile with a nod, and looked out across the bridge to where Araian was standing. She'd already freed the driver who was on the fire truck ladder and she was waiting for them to get clear.

A deep pained moan of stressed metal sounded in the air like a beached Giant Whale. Asha watched as the entire truck pulled back onto the bridge. The front wheels spun slightly as they finally touched road surface again.

When the truck settled down with all of its wheels on the tarmac surface, the silence on the bridge became palpable. Such a public exhibition of high rating kinetic abilities was almost unheard of. She knew their faces would be all over the internet very soon and the Agency would arrive not long after. She walked towards Araian.

Bana's deep red mental energy reached out towards her. *"Where are you, Asha?"*

"We got into a little trouble on the bridge. We're coming."

"You'd better hurry, it's nearly midday. How... how's Gusa?"

Asha grinned at the hopeful tone in the man's voice. *"She's fine, looking forward to seeing you again."*

"E.T.A.?"

"Don't know, nearly across the bridge so it shouldn't be long. Would you contemplate going without seeing Gusa?"

"No, Asha, it's her or I don't go up. But hurry, my cousin doesn't have long."

An ambulance siren sped towards them, very near. It meant that help was coming for some of the injured and that the way out on the other side of the bridge was clear enough for them to continue.

She put a hand to Araian's arm. "We gotta go, Arai. If we don't get young Gusa to her father, Tiras is going to die on that roof."

"Yes, of course."

* 14 *

The car smelt of leather polish and the musky remnants of cigarette smoke. Gweneth Rena wondered absently if the car had been stolen by the Rebels or if they owned it somehow, but she guessed it didn't really matter either way. There were no seat belts in the back of the green car. It made Gwen feel a little insecure, sitting unsupported against the cracked leather of the back seat. Little Cassandra sat on her lap—she hadn't spoken for two days, but Gwen knew if she just kept giving the girl as much love as she could, she'd get over her fear and start speaking again.

The package Hawk's Second had given her was a self-sealing postage bag. She ripped it open to find that inside were work papers and IDs for a new identity, a non-Psi certified work permit and a lot of money tied up in little blue bricks. At the bottom of the bag, giving the package the bulk of its weight, was a small black handgun. She lifted the weapon out and checked it. It was fully loaded, safety on. She frowned at it in her hands. Why would Hawk give her a gun?

The car slowed and parked on the side of the road. She looked up through the water-stained side windows to see they were parked on the wrong side of the road.

"Have we arrived?" she asked, frowning at the back of the driver's head. Gwen glanced at him through the mirrors and a shot of fear blew through her: ice blue eyes.

The driver turned around in the front seat, lifting a weapon to bear on her. Dobid's sandy hair had grown long and scruffy, and he looked like he hadn't eaten or slept properly for a long time but he was still recognizable under all the mess.

"Hello, Gwen." His voice was icy calm. "Long time no see."

Her arms tightened protectively around her daughter. "Let Cassandra go. I won't fight if you just let her go."

He shook his head slowly. "You know I can't do that."

Her bottom lip trembled with her second wave of fear. His training was far superior to hers, if she fought him, she would almost certainly lose.

Her eyes narrowed. *Unless I fight dirty.*

Reaching out empathically and telepathically, she searched for some chink in his armor. To her surprise, his mental surface was unshielded in the first few levels of his mind. She pushed and sensed a Buried Mind Shield—good for appearing to be a non-Psi to most people, but it also had one weakness. She gripped the parts of his mind that were unshielded as tightly as she could. He cried out in the sudden pain and his body stiffened.

Opening the car door, she lifted Cassandra out to stand on the pavement. She approached his door and pulled it open. Because of how tightly she gripped the unshielded parts of his mind, he was completely unable to move and therefore helpless.

Holding Cassandra so that she faced away from what she was about to do, Gwen lifted her new weapon towards him and fired.

No one was going to bully her any more.

* * * * *

From the corner of Cathedral Square, Nalana stepped off the curb and crossed the road towards the center of town. She was in a state of shock—surprised and delighted but absolute shock. Her nursing exam had been graded and she was rated at the top of her class with a 98% mark!

Stepping back up onto the sidewalk again, she turned south down the street towards home. Sky scrapers towered above her, blocking out what little sunlight there was in the overcast day. Busy pedestrians ambled past on both sides, all wrapped up warm against the chilly day, but she barely noticed the cold in her excitement. A proud grin slowly lifted into her lips and filled her entire heart-shaped face.

"Top of the *class!*" she yelled. Laughing and not caring who saw her, she spun around on the spot in her joy.

She hadn't dared to even dream before she met Naethan and Marius. Now she could, now she knew that she was capable of so much more. On the day when the Agency fell, the first thing she wanted to do was sign up to a bigger college and become a doctor. Perhaps a doctor for kids. She tried to remember the name for that kind of doctor... pediatrician? She shrugged. Whatever the right word was, that would be something to work towards.

The sound of a nearby gunshot stilled her joy. Her protective instinct took over and she fading empathically into the background. She maneuvered herself around pedestrians to a corner and listened. Footsteps came towards her. A lovely looking woman with long blond hair walked past. She carried a little girl in her arms. They shuffled past Nalana and into the crowds on the street. The woman's energy was angry and afraid, but also kind of powerful, as if she'd just stood up to something that terrified her and she'd won.

Nalana looked up the side street where the two had come from, which was also the same direction as the gunshot. For a moment Nalana turned, thinking it was best to walk away in case of danger, but up over the slight curve in the road she sensed someone in a lot of pain. She couldn't easily turn from someone in pain. It had gotten her into trouble in the past but even being fully aware of this, she still moved towards it.

She jogged up the slight hill, and followed the flaring pain to a car that was parked on the wrong side of the road. Both the driver's and the back door were wide open. She ducked around to the driver's side and looked inside.

A man was slumped over the steering wheel. There was the scent of gunshot residue and blood. Nalana leaned inside and brushed scruffy light brown hair from his neck to check his pulse. At her touch the man flinched and suddenly she was looking down the barrel of a weapon at cold blue eyes. The ice was so present and so familiar she cried out in absolute fear.

By the Gods it's an Agent! she whimpered in terror.

"Nala?" said the Agent drowsily. "How is it... you... you're so good at finding trouble?" His gun did not lower but the ice lifted from his face.

"Naethan? What... what's going on—" it was then all the pieces in her mind connected together and she realized what she should have already seen. Her good friend was a spy. She lifted her hands up submissively and tried to back away from him. "I won't tell anyone. I promise, just don't—"

His voice was very quiet. "You and I... both know how bad you are at... at keeping secrets. There's only one option left now. Get in the car, Nalana."

* 15 *

Tiras sat in the stifling humidity of an air-vent and listened. Above him, the vent lifted into what should be the roof. There would be Taskforce Teams out there, but how close they were was unknown. There were no sounds of voices or weapons being loaded, only the deep thrum of air-conditioning fans.

His wristwatch told him it was five minutes until midday. He'd have to take out as many of the Teams on the roof as he could before Bana arrived to pick him up. The helicopter wouldn't take much weapons fire and he certainly wasn't wearing a vest. So he had to be at his very best—and incredibly lucky.

Careful to keep the noise as minimal as possible, Tiras stood up inside the air vent and peered out at the roof. Looking all the world like a periscope, the vent surrounded him on all sides except at the round opening. Someone had unscrewed the vent cover from the outside and left it resting on the roof surface, but still covering much of the opening. Hawk must have some kind of ally to do all of these little tasks to help and Hawk himself must be a very highly rated Time Psi to know all of these little details. Surely, Jaran didn't stand a chance in the long run against such preemptive knowledge?

The metal around him hadn't been painted with Psi suppressant material, but there were other things out on the roof making his empathic senses patchy at best for locating the nearest target.

As he pulled himself onto the roof surface his foot bumped the vent cover and it thudded down onto the slate. The noise wasn't particularly loud but he froze and listened.

"What's that?" said a voice too near to him.

"Don't know," said a second.

Crouched, Tiras lifted his primary weapon from the small of his back and his secondary from a pocket. They were both loaded. Flicking off the safeties of both weapons, he stood upright.

Moving sideways around the edge of a wall, he caught sight of a four-man Team and started firing. Two of the four went down immediately with bullets through their foreheads. A stray bullet ricocheted off another air vent and the third dropped to the ground screaming and grasping at an injured leg. Weaving back undercover, he moved around the wall to the other side and took out the fourth man from behind. Another shot finally silenced the screaming man.

Withdrawing away from the decimation, Tiras looked around for cover. The roof was a miasma of periscope-shaped air vents, walled boxes for elevator maintenance, aerials and stairwell entrances—there was a lot of cover. Ducking behind an elevator box, he put his back against the metal Psi suppressant surface and reloaded his primary from the stash of clips in one pocket.

Yelling came towards him from his left. He waited until they were close enough, before stepping back into sight and taking out two of the next team before they were even aware of him. Automatic fire sounded from the two remaining Agents and he dropped behind cover again. He skirted the back of the elevator box to get around to a better firing angle.

As he walked, the vibrating alarm of his wristwatch went off. It meant it was midday, and that Bana should be there soon.

Pulling out of cover again he fired, taking out the two remaining members of the second Team.

Flicking on the safety of his handguns, he shoved them into the small of his back and a jacket pocket. The auto lay on the ground next to its dead owner and grabbing it, he found five auto clips in the dead man's jacket.

More gunfire came towards him—figures running with their weapon barrels flashing. There were two more Teams but so far only one auto. He dropped the old clip and reloaded the auto with practiced ease. Stepping behind the cover of another elevator box, he opened fire on the Agents running towards him. Some fell, others jumped for cover.

Above him the air began to hum with the sound of helicopter blades. Three 'copters came into view at a distance from the tower, close enough for their cameras to be rolling but not so close that a stray bullet would easily take them out. Turning, he saw two more coming towards him from the south. Five helicopters in the air and none were getting close to the roof. Bana was late.

Well, at least my death will put on a show for their cameras, thought Tiras with a cynical snort.

Returning weapons fire made him duck and run near the edge of the building. Crouching over a vent, he aimed and fired a short burst at one man who was out in the open. He ran again to the next cover. He had to keep moving; being still for too long meant death. Weaving between vents and broad aerial bases, he took out two more Agents as they came into view.

He reloaded the auto and skirted around the back of a stairwell entrance. Yelling and the sounds of running came out of the open doorway towards him. It sounded like a lot of Agents were coming up to the roof.

He laughed. *Junior really wants to stop me.*

The Agents came out onto the roof firing their autos. He took out a few before their numbers overwhelmed his ability to get all of them and keep from being shot. He pulled left, running for better cover further away as bullets ricocheted off the metal behind him.

There were too many of them now. He was running out of time. *Hai di'chena! Where the nuth is Bana!*

Diving behind a broad black power dish, he rolled back up to his feet and got into position over the dish edge. A deep thrumming pulse vibrated the air and it was so close his eardrums started to echo the noise into his skull.

A gunshot fired behind him and he spun around, lifting the auto. The helicopter was huge and shiny black as if it had never been flown before. The markings on the side claimed it was a television network 'copter, although he knew it had to have been stolen or loaned for Bana to be sitting in the pilot seat. The back door was open and a dark-haired woman sat with a long barreled sniper rifle aimed out at the roof. The rifle fired again.

"Tiras, get in the so'then helicopter." The woman's mental voice was cool and crisp, a deep dark blue with a flare of orange mischief waiting under the surface. He knew immediately he'd like this woman. Dropping

the auto, he ran towards the edge of the building and jumped, landing on the deck, side on.

"Go!" someone yelled on a broad telepathic range, and the floor dipped sideways and down.

"Tiras Malar, I presume?" The tall leggy woman grinned down at him.

It was too noisy to speak so he answered mind-to-mind. "At your service. You're Asha?"

"I am. It'll be a while before we have time alone to talk. But we will. For now we'll be landing in a nearby airport then taking the others to a secure safe house." He sensed her switch to a narrow telepathic band, so tight a 10/5 telepath would struggle to pick it up. "As far as anyone else knows you haven't met Him. Do you understand?"

Tiras nodded slowly. "Of course."

* 16 *

Bana stood in the blue and green tones of the broad central sitting room of a Rebel safe house. He held his daughter in his arms. He was distantly thankful that the safe house Asha had taken them to was clean and dry, and not the normal Rebel fare of being an abandoned building. He tightened his grip around Gusa's shoulders and suppressed the ridiculous urge to cry for the joy of having her back again.

Gusa's little giggle penetrated the high roofed space. "Daddy! I can't breathe!"

He lifted her higher into his arms and just laughed for the joy of it all. "I'm sorry, honey. I just missed you so much."

"I missed you too, Daddy." She wrapped her little arms around his neck for a moment. He sensed a flow of love and comfort from her. She was only five and yet she understood that he needed comfort too.

Gusa let go of his neck and frowned at him. "Did you know Nanny Triian puts cake sprinkles on sandwiches?"

He laughed again. "Yes, I did. What do you think of them?"

"Yummy! They were crunchy and tasted just like bubble gum!"

He lifted an eyebrow at her. "And how do you know what bubble gum tastes like?"

"Aunty Dela gave us some! Me and Mana and Wolf! It was yummy, but I got in trouble for swallowing it. Why chew something if you're not going to eat it?"

Bana leaned forward and kissed his precocious daughter's light hair. "I don't know, my love. Adults can be silly sometimes."

Asha brushed past them, going through the sitting room into the nearby kitchen. He glanced in her direction, feeling a little spark of guilt. The Rebels had given him back his life, his freedom and his daughter. Well, Asha and Hawk had. And he had information which would put them in danger.

He lowered Gusa to her feet and gave her a loving smile. "Honey, Daddy needs to talk with Asha alone, would you go into the other room and play with Boe and Tempa?"

"OK, Daddy."

As her little form went out of view down the hall, he felt an irrational stab of fear that he might never see her again. He sighed and turned to look sideways at Asha as she finished pouring herself a coffee in the kitchen.

"Asha, I have something to tell you. But I need a promise from you and Hawk first."

Lifting a mug to her lips, she leaned back against the kitchen bench. "OK, what do you need?"

"Protection. I need you two to guarantee protection for me and Gusa."

She smiled, an edge of mischief lifting into her dark blue eyes. "You're in our most secure safe house, how much more protection would you need?"

He shook his head. "Yes or no, Asha?"

She shrugged. "Of course, you wouldn't be here otherwise."

He knew it might not be enough to keep him alive against Enigma's rage, but he also knew he couldn't keep silent any more. The Rebels he had met were good people and didn't deserve whatever Enigma was planning.

He sighed. "You have a spy in your midst. The one you call Naethan."

She stood upright. "What?"

"His real name is Dobid Cowdy, he's Araian's brother and he's extremely dangerous. I'm sorry, I knew from the day I was captured, but he threatened Gusa if I told anyone who he was."

"Hai da!" she whispered.

He didn't sense any anger in her, though she was very tense.

She put her mug down on the bench behind her. "You stay here with Araian and the three children. And for Founder's sakes don't tell Araian or she'll run and we won't be able to protect her."

"Of course." Bana nodded.

Asha walked towards him and as she passed by, she put a hand on his arm. "I would have done the same in your position, Bana." Her hand dropped and she continued walking. "Tiras!" She yelled. "There's trouble, I need your help!"

* 17 *

The motor was still running when Nama and Tae found it—a green car parked haphazardly on the side of the road. It sat barely ten meters from their building entrance. Nama swallowed. It was not a good sign, not at all. He lifted his weapon and checked the back seat, but it was empty.

"Nama!" Taelin called from the driver's side door. "It's Naethan! He's been shot!"

He moved around the car towards Taelin. As he walked, Nama mentally reached through their building to the nearest telepath. *Bring a stretcher outside! Now! Get Ren too!*

Naethan must have driven himself from where he'd been shot because there was blood all over the steering wheel and his clothes. He was very pale and his breathing was shallow. It looked bad.

Behind them, one of their non-combatant Rebels shot out through the front doors of the building towards them with an old canvas stretcher in her arms. She put the stretcher down on the sidewalk next to them. He and Taelin pulled Naethan out of the car and together, they carefully lowered him.

Once Naethan was properly laid down, he and Taelin lifted the stretcher. The other Rebel ran ahead of them, and opened the door to their building.

As he walked, Nama felt Asha's mind connect to him. *"Nama, have you seen Naethan?"*

"We've just found him on the street, he's been shot."

"How bad is he?"

"Not good, but Ren's inside, should be fine if he holds on."

"We're nearly back, keep him at the entrance?"

"Yes, ma'am."

They carried Naethan into the dim entrance hall. Old Ren came towards them out of the darkness and they put the stretcher down on the ground. It was colder in the lobby and it took a moment for Nama's eyes to adjust to the gloom.

Old Ren lifted away Naethan's battered jacket and started clearing the rags away from the bullet wound in his stomach.

Behind Nama, footsteps entered from outside and he turned to look. Asha stood in the doorway, she and the tall dark-haired man behind her were very tense.

"Nama, this is Tiras, he's come to help."

He lifted one eyebrow at the man. "What do we need help—"

"Nama!" Marius interrupted him.

He turned to see the young man come towards them from inside the building.

Marius came around Taelin and the stretcher, but looked down at the ground with a frown. "Is that Naethan?"

"Yes, he should be fine." He shook his head dismissively. "What did you need?"

The light reflection from outside made Marius' purple eyes almost glow when he looked up from the ground. "Have you seen Nala?"

Asha interrupted. "She's not back yet?"

"No. She's nearly an hour late."

"Right!" Asha used her commanding voice to bark orders. "Mar and Tae, go and look for her."

"Marius." Nama pulled the van keys from his jeans pocket and threw them. "Take the van and let us know when you find her."

Marius caught the keys and nodded. "Yus, sir." The two of them passed the group and disappeared outside.

The narrow entrance hall was quiet for some time as those who were left watched Ren healing Naethan's stomach wound. When the bullet pushed out through the rags Nae wore and Ren stepped back, the new arrival with Asha moved around the stretcher and lifted a weapon to bear on Naethan.

Nama frowned at him. "What's going on?"

"This man's name is not Naethan." The new guy's voice was cold and almost hostile.

"What?"

"He's an Agent."

Nama glanced at Asha for confirmation. Her eyes were tense but she nodded. "We need to move him down to the basement. And I want this kept under wraps. Got it? If the others find out they'll kill him before we can get any information."

Nodding slowly, Nama was too speechless to answer.

Asha put a hand on Ren's arm. Her voice was softer but no less commanding. "Ren, would you go find the sedatives?"

She stepped around the stretcher to grab one end and looked up at Nama, her dark-blue eyes betrayed a sense of tension that her body otherwise hid. "Ready?"

He nodded and together they lifted Naethan and made their way through the maze of narrow corridors towards the basement stairwell.

While they walked, Nama struggled with his surprise and shock. He knew Naethan had some peculiar behaviors and tended to disappear at inopportune moments. He was also oddly stoic most of the time. But a spy? Wouldn't a spy have killed everyone, already?

They started to descend the stairs into the dank basement air. At the foot of the stairs they angled across the room to another door. The place had once been used as some kind of workshop, with an old wooden bench in one corner, and empty shelving and nails for hanging tools scattered around the walls. The adjacent room must have been used for storage, but it was lockable and mostly Psi shielded, so they'd used it to hold Bana when he was a prisoner.

Nama finally got his voice back. "Are you sure?"

"Yes." The newcomer was very serious. "He's Ao, very high ranking and extremely dangerous. I can't imagine what he was here for. What was he doing?"

"Chores mostly. Nothing big. Why?"

Tiras shook his head. "He would have been here for a specific reason. His specialty is killing not recon or spying. What else did he do?"

He and Asha stepped through into the dingy side room and placed the stretcher down onto a low table in the center of the room.

Nama shrugged. "I don't know. Nothing. When he wasn't doing chores he hung out with..." he swore under his breath. "Nalana."

"And she's missing?"

Nama swallowed and nodded. "Yes."

"Well, I hope for her sake that she's found soon. He's not the type to leave loose ends." The look in the man's dark eyes forced a shaft of icy fear down Nama's spine.

* * * * *

Nama stood with his back against a grimy wall. He swallowed. *I really don't want to be here.*

Naethan lay unconscious, tied to a cot in the middle of the basement room. Nama had never witnessed a Telepathic Interrogation, and he'd kind of hoped he wouldn't ever have to.

Asha glanced at him across the room. "You OK with this?"

"Not really."

She gave him a sympathetic smile. "It's the only way w—"

"Yeah, I know." He interrupted her. "Is Kita here yet?"

"No, if he's not here soon, Tiras will have to—"

A groan of pain came from the cot and they both stiffened. Naethan's arms and legs tightened against the ropes that held him down.

"What's happening?" a broken voice asked the air.

"Why did you come back to base, Naethan?" she demanded. "Is Gwen dead?"

"What are you talking about?" His drowsy voice was quiet. "She shot me."

Naethan's square face was pale, but his eyes were calm. He didn't seem to be afraid, even though anyone with half a brain would be.

Nama cleared his throat. "What about Nalana?"

Ice blue eyes glanced at him. "She's at the Cathedral, isn't she? Will someone tell me what's going on?"

Asha's voice was cold. "You're a spy."

"What?" He made another noise of pain. "That's ridiculous—"

"No," Tiras stepped in through the open door with Kita in tow. "It's not ridiculous, Dobid Cowdy."

Seeing Tiras, Naethan's jaw clenched and he sighed. "Tiras Malar."

"What did you do with Gwen and Cass?"

"She shot me." His tone became almost imperious. "Do the math."

"So, the great Enigma got taken down by a lowly A2?" Tiras laughed. "Never thought I'd see that!"

Asha stepped forwards with her hand up. "Enough. Taunting will not get the information we need. Kita?"

"Yes, ma'am." Kita stepped forwards out of the doorway. His voice was quiet and although Nama wasn't an empath, he could sense in his manner that he disliked doing this job—a lot.

There was a pause before Naethan grunted. The young man's whole body tightened under Kita's enforced mental pain.

"Name, rank and Code In," demanded Tiras. His voice was ice cold, harsh and utterly dripping with hostility. Nama swallowed back the shaft of instinctive terror that shot though him. Tiras had transformed into something emotionless and alien. He hoped for an absurd second that it was Tiras who was the spy and not Naethan.

"Dobid Cowdy, A0, Rank six." Naethan's voice had the same alien hostility under the crackle of pain. "Elite Operative, First Class. Code In: A0.4.0177. Access 101826."

Nama sighed. The fear and uncertainty in him dropped away, and in its place flared a spark of rage. His jaw tightened. *Betrayed again.*

"What is your mission?" Tiras barked.

Naethan's face lifted into a smirk and he did not reply. Something was wrong. Nama frowned and looked sideways at Kita. Sweat had formed on the man's forehead, darkening his blond hair. The muscles throughout his face were tight and strained. Kita let out a gasped breath and shuddered.

"Asha, Tiras... he has a buried mind shield."

"So?" said Nama, lifting one eyebrow at him.

Kita leveled him with calm gray eyes. "You don't understand. Because of the shield I can not fully anchor in his mind. If I pierce the shield to anchor, I'll almost certainly kill him."

Nama let his rage underline his voice. "So kill him."

"No, Nama," Asha's tone was low but commanding. "We need information from him before he's killed." She sighed tensely. "Kita, can you at least knock him out?"

"No, ma'am."

"Then will you go upstairs, find Ren and get the sedatives from him? We have too much to do right now. When we get back from the desert, we'll sort out what we're going to do with him. Nama, I need you to stay in Arām on guard duty."

He crossed his arms over his chest and growled. "Why me?"

"Because I trust you to keep him alive." She turned out of the room with Tiras in tow. "Twenty-four hours. That's all."

* 18 *
Late afternoon
Great Northern Desert

Xak sat in the corner of the exercise yard with a chewed pencil in one hand and a small sketch pad in his lap. He leaned back on the rusting wall and glanced around at those others in the yard with him. Fellow "students" milled around the edges of the yard, avoiding the center where the three oldest bullies stood glaring and looking for an excuse to cause trouble. Xak made sure his eyes never met theirs as he skipped his gaze past them. In the far corner, all huddled fearfully in a little group, sat the youngest kids—the eleven and twelve year olds. Usually the bullies left the youngest ones alone as long as they kept quiet. No such luck for the older ones.

With no immediate threats in the yard, Xak's eyes drifted back down to his sketch book and he adjusted the nose on his caricature of Rega, the most violent of the bullies. He needed a bigger nose to make him look as ugly as he was on the inside.

Motion nearby told Xak someone was approaching and he looked sideways. Liz gave him a little smile of acknowledgment and sat down next to him with her back against the wall.

She pulled her knees into her chest and looked over his shoulder. "Whatcha drawing today?"

"Bullies." A mischievous grin lifted into his face, as he turned the pad a little so she could see. "Just about finished Rega."

She laughed. "Love his nose."

"Why thank you."

"Xak..." her ordinarily strong face became uncertain for a moment. "Did Hawk really come visit you?" The strength returned to her blue eyes and demanded the truth from him. "I mean, did he really?"

"Yes. Really." He smiled sadly. Even if they didn't believe him, he wasn't going to back down. The Rebels *were* coming and he *was* going to escape.

"And it's tomorrow?"

He nodded as he added long nose hair to the enormous nostrils he'd given Rega.

"Can... can we come too?"

He was so surprised he stopped drawing mid stroke and looked up at her. "But you guys said you didn't believe me."

"I know." She looked at her hands. "I'm sorry."

He flipped the page of his art pad and quickly sketched a cartoon girl with long straight hair and big eyes that looked very apologetic. "That sorry?"

She laughed. "More."

He added tears onto the cheeks and a little wiggly sad-mouth. An amused smile passed between them and he leaned in to push her gently with his shoulder. "Of course you guys can come. He told me that you were. He's got a job for all of us out there."

"He does?" She sat up. "What's mine?"

He shrugged. "I don't know. But surely someone who can juggle tanker trucks with her mind would have some use."

She snorted and started to laugh.

The sound of her laughter dimmed away from him as if he was suddenly underwater. A deep pulse of ebony static flowed over him and he closed his eyes. The images flickered across his mind very quickly. It was a short sequence with many lines of possible actions that could or could not occur if he chose, all centering on whether their friend Nick would live or die. The static dropped out of his body and he opened his eyes again. Liz couldn't help her, only he could.

Nick was in the middle of the yard, reading a book as she made her way towards them. Behind her, Rega watched her with dark eyes.

"Hai da! Hold this!" Dropping his pencil and pad onto Liz's lap, he got to his feet and sprinted across the sand towards Nick.

There were two options to save her, either step in the way and get beaten himself or make someone else get beaten with a distraction. He slowed as he approached Nick and touched her elbow to get her attention.

"Walk, quickly. Head for Liz. Don't look back."

Dark eyes came up from the book she was reading. On her face the puzzlement lifted away into fear, and she nodded.

He skirted around her and back behind another of the bullies. Counting down in his mind, he waited for Rega to step towards her.

Three, two, one.

Pretending to trip, Xak pushed the second bully hard across the back. The older guy lost his balance, falling into Rega with a cry of surprise. Crawling out of sight so neither of them saw him, Xak listened for Rega's customary roar of rage. It came barely seconds after and, as expected Rega threw the first punch. Xak got to his feet and zigzagged his way back to Nick.

He was out of breath when he got to her. "Abe Kashān, that was close! Nick! You don't walk near the bullies with your nose in a book!"

"Sorry." She looked bashful and a little afraid. "Hey did Liz—"

"Yeah, yeah, apology accepted; you can come. We'll all talk after dinner." His eyes shifted onto and immediately away from one of the many cameras around the yard. "It's not safe out here."

* 19 *
Back in Arām City

Marius gripped the gun nervously as he watched Nama untie Naethan from the cot. He still couldn't quite believe that someone who seemed so calm and harmless most of the time could really be an Agency spy. Marius swallowed. He'd actually considered Naethan a friend, and now this friend might be responsible for Nalana's disappearance.

The deception had been very convincing, so much so he felt really conflicted. A part of him couldn't believe that Naethan was the enemy and so, Nalana would be coming home any minute. But another part of him was terrified that such a complete deception could only mean the man was a definite and immediate threat. Which also meant Nalana was probably dead.

Marius forced his attention away from his raging thoughts. He didn't want to think about life without Nalana. He had to simply assume she was coming back and do his best to hold on. Otherwise, his grief would overcome him and he might do something stupid like try to beat the information from Naethan.

Still untying the ropes, Nama glanced sideways at him. His yellow eyes were wary and Marius remembered that he was in the company of a telepath. With a tense smile at his friend, Marius re-gripped the gun and focused his mind on the task at hand, that of helping Nama guard the prisoner.

Pulling the loose ropes away, Nama stepped back from the cot. "You've got a minute," he barked. "Use the bucket in the other room."

Naethan moved very slowly, lifting his legs off the cot before carefully getting to his feet with a grunt of pain. One hand tracing the wall, he stepped out of sight into the tiny side room.

"Mar, will you get another dose of sedative? And give me the gun."

Nodding, he did as he was asked.

Their supplies sat nearby in the main basement room on a dusty wooden work table. There were enough supplies to keep them fairly comfortable for two days. Everything else had been cleared out of the building with the evacuation to their next base. Marius pulled out a metal box from one of the backpacks and opened it to retrieve a single dose sedative shot.

It was dark and humid in the basement and Marius felt a little like he was trapped underground. He knew that feeling would only worsen when they had to sleep down there, but it couldn't be helped, he just had to ignore it and do what was required of him.

I wonder where Nalana is sleeping tonight? With his uncontrolled thought, a deep pang of grieving agony shot through him. He sighed and turned back towards Nama and their prisoner.

Naethan had returned from his bathroom break and lay on the cot again. Nama, tight lipped and angry stood with the weapon trained on him.

"Mar, give me the needle and tie him up."

Marius handed him the needle and stepped around Naethan. He tied one hand and then the other to the metal frame of the cot. Both were tight and non-slipping knots. Moving again, he went to the end of the cot and as he knelt down to tie one foot, Nama approached Naethan with the sedative dose.

Naethan's hand, which had been tied down only a moment earlier, whipped up, grabbed the sedative and dug it into Nama's arm. As Nama fell sideways, Naethan grabbed his gun and brought it around to bear on Marius, who blinked down the barrel in surprise.

Ice blue eyes watched him emotionlessly. "Untie my other arm, Marius."

He swallowed, and with shaking hands, untied the knots holding Naethan's left arm to the cot frame.

"Now, up against that wall."

He backed away. As Naethan got to his feet, this time without any sign of pain, the gun and his eyes remained level and aimed. Marius expected their prisoner to leave the room, but instead he came in closer. One long-fingered hand wrapped around Marius' throat and pushed him firmly against the wall.

"You have a choice, Marius. Either fight this and die, or surrender and live to see Nalana again."

Marius frowned at him. "She's alive?"

"Yes. Make your choice."

A pressure tightened in his temples and he screwed up his face in pain. There was a deep sense of being invaded, but at the same time as if he was the intruder not Naethan. For a moment, he tried to fight it but Naethan's words echoed in his mind. Even in his fear, Marius made the decision to close his eyes and surrender to whatever was happening. If Naethan was telling the truth Marius would see Nalana, if he wasn't he'd be dead and he wouldn't have to live without her.

There was a sensation almost like a click. Something had shifted, and only when the floor came up to meet him did Marius realize that he was falling unconscious.

* * * * *

Neither the hundred Rebels crammed in a delivery plane with no seats or air conditioning, nor the so'then engine pulsing through the length of the cabin with a consistent roaring throb, were good for Asha's already horrific headache. She grumbled again, rubbing at the piercing pain between her eyebrows.

Other Rebels slept against the curved metal sides of the plane, or in the flat center of the cabin curled up together like a pack of wolves for warmth. Araian and her little blond-haired son Boe were slumped on the metal curve opposite her, both asleep. Everyone else except for her and Tiras, were out to it and she envied them.

Tiras stood near the cockpit door watching everyone with calm attentive eyes as if he never slept.

She sensed a tight telepathic connection and Tiras's orange-brown mental voice sounded in her head. *"So, Miss Hawk's Amazing Messenger woman—"*

"That's enough of that!" She snorted and looked back at Tiras. *"I'm just Asha. If I hear any more of that other stuff, I'll throw you out!"*

A playful smile flashed on his face for a moment. *"Yes, ma'am, so what's the plan? The pilots seem to think we're just about to descend to land, is there anything more I need to know, before we get off this tin can?"*

She shook her head. *"No. Just keep an eye on everyone and be ready to act if you need to. Hawk said this event is in flux—it's too fuzzy for him to see and prepare for all eventualities. We just have to go on the fly and hope for the best. But it should work."*

"It is a pretty good plan. Who is this kid anyway?"

"A powerful Time Psi. Hawk thinks the boy knows how we can win a sizable victory against the Agency. Maybe even take down the Ao Council."

"Right," he snorted. *"The Ao Council, because they're all so evil, right?"* His skepticism came though not only in his mental tone, but in the empathic energy that flowed between them. The energy shifted into a sense of barely contained boredom. *"So, did he tell you what I'll be doing after this?"*

She gave him a mischievous smile. *"How does being 'Hawk's Messenger' in Aramān City sound?"*

He laughed so loudly that she heard him over the engine roar. *"Sounds like my kind of mission."*

Below them a new sound whined loudly like ailing hydraulics and there was the resounding metallic clunk, which could only be the landing gear.

"Would you help me wake everyone?"

* * * * *

It felt as if Nama's head had been crushed between two boots; two boots with spikes. He groaned and lifted his hand to rub his face. He wondered absently who had managed to drink him under the table.

Something itched in his arm. He reached to scratch it but his fingers found something metallic. Opening his grainy eyes, he took whatever it was out of his skin and squinted at it: a hypodermic needle.

"What the—" tensing, he looked up. A bare light bulb glowed dimly above him in the middle of a moldy ceiling. An empty cot sat not far from him with cut ropes still hanging from it. The memory of Naethan somehow getting a hand free flashed through his mind. Nae had been quick, getting the needle from his hands, sticking him with it and getting his weapon from him without the time for Nama to react before he'd dropped unconscious.

Marius!

He sat up further and searched around for his friend. Marius lay on his side against the far wall, his eyes were closed but he couldn't see any blood or obvious injury. Crawling and shuffling towards him, Nama reached out and touched the young man's face. He was alive and breathing, and on a second check, Nama sensed that he was under a telepathic sleep program. That meant that Naethan was a telepath. However, Naethan couldn't have been a particularly powerful telepath because the program was very loosely weaved in the young man's mind—Marius would have come out of it himself.

Mar's long oval face twitched and vivid purple eyes fluttered opened to look up at him. "Nalana." He sounded drowsy. "He said Nalana is alive."

Nama smiled at his friend. "I hope so."

"How late is it?"

Nama had been given a full dose of the sedative, which lasted eight hours. He sighed and shook his head. "Has to be way after dawn and too late to warn the others that he's escaped. We should pack up and get to the new building."

Marius looked at him with pleading purple eyes. "But she won't know where to find us."

Nama patted his friend on the shoulder. "She'll go to Hilla's cell if we're not here. Don't worry."

He wasn't sure if Nalana was still alive, Naethan could have told him that so he could get away. But he didn't want to mention that possibility because that would just be cruel, especially when they didn't know either way.

He sighed. "Come on, Mar, let's get out of here."

20
The next morning
19 Aracan 3004
(4 years since Hawk emerged)
Great Northern Desert
Just south of Epa City

Asha shuffled through the various weapons and ammo in the back of their big camouflaged truck. The morning was clear and sunny, and in the Northern Desert that meant their rescue had to be finished by midday. Most of the desert was made of black iron sand, which heated up pretty quickly in the sun. So, unless the weather changed, by midday the dunes would be hot enough to burn skin, and make the journey back to Epa over land far too difficult.

Asha lifted their only sniper rifle out of the camouflaged truck and continued searching for the cartridge of bullets that went with it.

She and Araian had dreamed of doing this sort of thing; breaking kids out of a desert training base, but the logistics of such a mission quite honestly scared the nuth out of her. Hawk said if everyone did as they were told no one would get killed, and they had a good chance of getting the kids out despite the fluxing nature of this event in time.

After searching for ages, Asha finally found the remaining shell cartridge for Nama's rifle and turned away. She wished she could have left Taelin back in Arām. There was an underlying sense of ill-ease about this mission and his presence there only made it worse. Unfortunately, she couldn't change it now, so she had to just get on with it and hope for the best.

She headed towards Tiras and Bana who stood at the base of a large black sand dune that blocked their line of sight to the A6 facility.

As she approached the two men, Tiras spoke. "What are you going to do after this, cousin?"

"I'm not sure, Tiras. It depends," answered Bana.

Bana was less jovial than his older cousin but as she neared them, she smiled warmly at him. "You could join us? I know Hawk would appreciate another high ranking gun hand."

Dark eyes looked away from her and she sensed a spark of guilty sadness. "I'm not sure it's safe for Gusa and she has to come first."

"Of course." Asha nodded as she handed him the rifle and cartridge. "So, I hear you're the best person to give this to."

Next to him, Tiras laughed good-naturedly. "That's an understatement." He put a hand on Bana's arm. "My cousin Bana is a gifted marksman."

"You're far too kind, Tiras." Bana chuckled and his dark eyes glanced back at her. "Has it been maintained?"

She nodded. "It's Nama's, he's very careful with his weapons. Unfortunately, that's all the ammo we have for it."

"That's fine." He smiled.

Checking her watch, she realized it was nearly time to start. She glanced back at the camouflaged truck. "I've got to check on Raha and then the second group. We're about ready to move out, you two want to corral the others into their positions? They're probably going to need to find their cover soon."

Tiras winked at her. "Yes, boss."

Walking back to the truck, she ducked under the sheet of desert camo. Young Raha sat with his back to her. A rough blanket formed a barrier between the black sands and the Hub they'd stolen a year ago.

"About done?" she asked.

Silver gray eyes looked sideways at her. "Yep, nearly, gimme another two minutes and I can shut off their coms on your orders."

She patted him on the shoulder. "Good work, Raha. I'll send a static signal over the radio when it's time to cut them off."

He nodded and hooked the cell radio headset over one ear. "Yes, ma'am."

* * * * *

Through the binoculars, the front gate of the massive stone facility was all chain link and barbed wire. The place looked impenetrable to Taelin and he wondered how they would get these kids out, despite having about a hundred Rebels to help. More importantly, why would any sane person put young adults and children in such a facility? It looked like a prison.

On the subject of innocence, his thoughts drifted back to Nalana, and he wondered where she was or if she was even alive. He and Marius had combed the city for hours before they left. She wasn't in the Ace of Spades, or if she was no one knew she was there. He was sure she hadn't been at the Cathedral either, even with the black stones mucking up his ability. And worse, with Naethan her constant companion shot for no apparent reason, it couldn't be good that she was missing.

"Tae!" Asha called out from behind him.

He shuffled back out of sight of the facility and slid down the sand to where she stood at the base. Brushing off the black grains from his ratty clothes, he looked sideways at her. "Yeah?"

"We're about ready to go. Just waiting on Raha to get control of their hard-line coms. We need to get into position." She looked tense and worried, more so than normal.

"Yeah, sure." He nodded, and followed her as she started towards their second group.

She led him along the base of the massive dune and met up with Araian and two more Rebels from Nama's cell. "Is everyone clear on the plan?"

The four of them nodded.

"Good. Arai, I know you want to help, but the moment those doors are open you have to run. Got it?"

The younger woman rolled her piercing blue eyes. "Yes, yes. I do know how to follow orders, Ash. I'll do what I'm told."

Asha started to laugh, a wonderful sound after so many days of seeing her exhausted and grumpy. It lasted for only a few moments and mid laugh, she stopped and swore.

"Hurry! We have to get out of sight!" She scampered up the nearby dune and over the other side. Taelin and the others followed her, and only when they got over the top of the dune to the other side, did Taelin hear the pulse of helicopter blades coming towards them.

The 'copter shot low over the dune and he looked up at its white underside as it passed. The sudden throbbing wind ripped at everyone's hair and faces, throwing dark sand into the air and making it nearly impossible for Taelin to keep his eyes open.

When the wind died down enough to open his eyes again, he watched over the next rise as the helicopter flew up over the fence to land on the roof of the two-storied facility.

"We don't have much time. Come on!" Asha yelled.

* 21 *

Xak felt a tickle of dark static twirl around his arms in a loop-de-loop, and rise up over the skin of his face towards the ceiling. The static behaved a little like some playful tickling flying insect, and he would have laughed at the sensation if he had been free to do so. The tickle meant that it was time for him to leave. He put his pencil down on the old wooden desk in front of him and glanced around the sparse classroom. The teacher stood at the front of the class with her stick, black hawk-eyes watching everyone and making sure they did their work in perfect silence.

He lifted up his hand. "Miss, may I go to the bathroom?" He tried to sound as apologetic as possible.

Her eyes narrowed at him suspiciously, and he sensed her mind tap inquiringly at his meager mental shields.

"Don't be long," she barked.

Getting to his feet, he stared at the floor and kept his face straight, as he made his way between the lines of desks towards the exit. The excitement tried very hard to burst out of him, and he only managed to keep it under control until the door was closed behind him. At the door click, he grinned from ear to ear and sprinted down the dim corridor to their meeting place at the unisex bathrooms.

As he ran, he heard the thrumming pulse of a helicopter above the building—that was the second signal and it was early.

"Nuth!" he swore and skittered in through the bathroom door.

The two cousins, Jai and Nick were playing thumb wars near the sinks to his right, Liz stood against a wall with her arms crossed over her chest and Levi sat on the baby blue floor tiles with his back against a stall looking rather bored.

"We gotta go now!" Xak panted.

Liz stood upright. "Go where?"

"The camera gap near the exercise yard. Hurry!"

* * * * *

Agent Hedān heard the helicopter land on the roof above him. Sighing, he got up from his paper-littered desk. An uninvited visitor was never a good thing. It was usually an inspector or someone from the city telling him how he should run his facility. This time, like any other, he wouldn't give an inch.

Coming out onto the roof and the artificial wind, Hedān pulled his mouth into a firm unyielding expression and crossed his arms over his chest.

The landing helicopter had once been white, but after years of ferrying folks across the black sands of the Great Desert from Epa City it was faded and scratched, so much so that it could have once been painted lime green and it wouldn't look any different.

The throbbing pulse of spinning blades lessened, and a door opened in the back of the 'copter. A light-haired man in an Agency suit stepped out onto the roof with an air of great authority. Their eyes met across the roof and Hedān knew instantly that this young man was trouble, not because of his manner or even the harsh expression on his face, but because of his ice blue eyes. Eyes of that color and intensity meant that the young man was probably some close relation to the Agency Head, Jaran Cowdy senior, and anyone related to him was trouble.

The man approached him and Hedān signaled with a wave that they could talk inside away from the noise and wind. They walked down a narrow stairwell and into the white stone corridors of the second floor.

The man thrust a broad square hand at him in greeting. "I apologize for the breach in procedure," he said briskly. "This facility is about to be attacked by the Rebels and I've come to take over command until the attack is over."

Hedān snorted. "Excuse me?"

"Lock down the facility, and send all guards to defensive external positions," the young man ordered with an authority Hedān found rather offensive.

"I'm going to need your authority before I submit control to you. Who—"

The man took something out of his dark jacket and threw it at him to catch. It was a leather-bound Agency ID. He flicked it open. There was no name, simply rank and the authority codes that said this man could do just about anything on his facility. As an A3 Agent (and ranking Agent on base), Hedān could do naught to stop him, because the young A0 out-ranked him by twenty five levels and three entire divisions.

"Oh," he said, staring at the badge.

The man seemed to know the layout of the building because he turned confidently down a hall from the stairwell, and went straight to the nearest lock-down button on the wall. Lifting the cover off, he punched the big red button underneath. The alarm sounded and lights flashed, signaling to all of the students to stop what they were doing and go directly to their sleeping cells.

With the same air of arrogant confidence, the new arrival strode into Hedān's control room. "Initialize a full lock-down of the facility, and send all guards to external defensive positions!"

Hedān stepped into the room behind him and the five or so computer controllers looked tensely over the young man's shoulder at him.

"Do as he says," he said quietly.

His people reanimated, turning back to their various computer terminals and camera screens. Approaching the young man from behind, Hedān attempted to sound respectful.

"Sir, don't you think we need a few guards inside to keep the children in their place?"

Ice blue eyes glared sideways at him. "My priority is to hold this facility. How many guards do you have?"

"A little under a hundred—"

"That's not enough, there is nearly double that waiting in the desert. Send all available staff to defend the perimeter." The boy's voice was utterly condescending.

Hedān spoke through clenched teeth. "Yes, Sir."

* 22 *

There were three cameras covering the hall that ran from their cells to the exercise yard. Close to the exercise yard, was a narrow blind spot in the camera range where a corner cut off the view of one camera and the angle was wrong for the other. Xak stood with his four friends huddled up close, so that all of them could fit in the small unseen gap.

If they were caught by a guard or seen on the cameras before everything started, all of them would be executed for attempting an escape. He sensed this thought flicker across some of the other's minds through their shared touch. He knew then that if they had to wait much longer they'd all panic and run.

"How much longer?" whispered Jai close to his ear.

"Almost—"

A siren echoed through the building, sounding the general alarm. According to procedure, on that siren all students were required to return to their sleeping cells. That was the signal for them to move.

"Go!" he whispered.

They skittered back into camera range and through the doorway into the exercise yard. Behind them, the yard door slammed down, blocking their exit. Now there was no way out for them.

Four sets of fearful eyes looked from the closed door and back at him.

"They'll be here," he said, unsure if he completely believed himself either. "Just start looking for the—"

There was a loud banging. It sounded again and he turned to see the far wall shaking.

"That's the doors!" Liz yelled and ran towards rusting surface.

It was odd to watch what he had previously thought was a wall, shake and rock. Even though he knew it had to be the Rebels on the other side, he couldn't quite shake the image of some hungry monster trying to break in—perhaps something with teeth.

Liz interrupted his thoughts. "There must be some kind of mag-lock keeping the door closed so they can't get in."

Xak looked sideways at Levi. "Do you think you can crack it?"

"Maybe." Levi nodded. "I'll give it a go."

"How's about we have a plan B too." Liz stepped back and collected Jai and Nick with wide open arms. "Let's push from this end."

Jai and Nick held hands and stood next to the much taller Liz. Through physical touch, the two cousins were able to magnify their kinetic ability to be nearly as strong as Liz, so that together, the three of them were fairly unstoppable.

Gunfire sounded from elsewhere. It wasn't close enough to be a threat to them, but Xak still flinched. Hawk had said the Rebels would be causing a diversion by attacking the building to help their escape.

Xak glanced anxiously at a nearby camera lens. He hoped that their attack was keeping the people in the control room distracted, because there was nowhere to hide from the cameras in the exercise yard.

* * * * *

Hedān watched the external cameras tensely. The Rebels were attacking the front of the building from two different sides. There were a lot of them and they had cover with the dunes and some old vehicles in the front yard. He frowned sideways at the young Ao. How he knew that the attack was imminent was something Hedān would have liked to know, and perhaps the more pressing question was why he hadn't brought reinforcements with him?

"Because," the young man glanced sideways at him. "To deploy the needed reinforcements would have taken more than two hours." His voice was clipped and emotionless, his tone bordered on hostile.

Hedān swallowed. The young man must be a telepath. He very deliberately, and with much discipline, redirected his thoughts away from questions that might get him shot for insubordination.

The radio wasn't working and neither was the back-up hard-line com-cable that ran under the desert. It was obvious that these Rebels had planned the attack for some time. Hedān wondered what their purpose was in attacking. So far, there had been no attempt to break down the front door—no chance of that without a tank—and there had been no demands.

"Sir!"

Both he and the Ao turned to look at one of his newer operators.

The controller cleared his throat awkwardly under the double gaze. "Uh, *Sirs*. There seems to be some kids in the exercise yard."

"What?" The Ao growled.

Hedān followed the young man and looked over their shoulders at the security screens. Five of the older kids stood in front of the yard gates. One had his hand to the wall, three young women were back from it and a fifth boy with dark hair, glanced nervously at them through the screen.

Next to Hedān, the young man swore obscenely, glaring back him. "I thought a lock-down forced the students into their cells? What are they doing in the exercise yard?"

"Don't shout at me," a twitch of nerves reminded him that this man was Ao. He adjusted his tie. "Uh, Sir. We can't control—"

"Sirs?"

The Ao snarled. "What?"

"Someone's hacking into the mag lock of those doors—"

Hedān tensed as the young man smacked the control panel with his fist. "They're trying to free the kids." A pair of ice-blue eyes glared at him. "How many of the staff are stuck in the lock-down between here and that exercise yard?"

Hedān frowned. "A handful, why?"

"Manually override each door as I get to it and tell the trapped guards to meet me at each section." The man lifted back his jacket and grabbed a weapon from a holster under one armpit. Hedān noticed a small pool of blood on the white of his shirt before the jacket covered it again, and it took all of his focus to not think about this observation.

The young man strode towards the control-room door, but turned at the entrance. "I want captives for Interrogation. Not bodies." His voice degraded into a hostile growl. "Tell them if they kill *any* of my captives I'll have their *heads* on *pikes!*"

* 23 *

Bana stared down the telescopic sights at the large gray stone building below him. Between his position at the top of the sand dune, and the building walls were the Rebels. They were scattered behind various kinds of cover and taking fire from the building above them.

Bana cleared the chamber of his sniper rifle and reloaded. Down the sights he saw a window; the glass was already shattered from combat. A uniformed guard stood inside trying to hide behind the line of the metal framing while he fired out at the Rebels below him.

Bana aimed, tightening his finger on the trigger, breathed in and with the out breath he fired. The figure in his sights hit the wall next to him, a bullet hole through his temple, and fell from view.

Below Bana the Rebels fired up at the building. They were giving the guards along the fence-lines and in the top floor windows a lot of trouble. No one seemed to have been killed yet in the Rebel numbers, but plenty of guards lay dead in the yard, and inside. They seemed to be winning. Hawk certainly knew how to arrange for an efficient distraction, Bana thought appreciatively.

He only had a few more bullets left and he wondered absently if the second team might need back-up. Carefully, he shuffled back down the dune out of sight and lifted the rifle across his shoulders.

* * * * *

Taelin stood behind Araian and Asha as they struggled with the massive metal doors in front of them. He watched, dumbstruck that any kinetic could be so strong to be able to bend two massive metal doors like they were heated Plexiglas.

There was a lot of swearing and Tae had picked up enough to know that there some kind of lock on the doors that neither of them could trigger. He sensed the fear of five young adults on the other side, but he also sensed that they were trying to help from their end. However, they didn't have all day to get the kids. At some point if they couldn't get the doors open, they'd have to evacuate and leave the kids behind to save themselves.

Something popped loudly and sparks shot out from the top of one wall. Metal groaned under the kinetic pressure. Two giant metal doors pulled off their hinges and flew up into the air. Taelin flinched as they both landed with a dull thud in the dunes behind them.

There was a moment of silence, without any gun fire and five young adults ran out towards them from the prison. Tae ran to meet them as Asha and Araian withdrew back towards their escape point.

The first one to reach him was a young woman. She was tall with long blond hair and very dark blue eyes. Tae sensed a strength to her and guessed that she was probably a high rating kinetic.

"Hurry! Follow them!" He gestured behind him with one arm.

Barely glancing at him, she nodded and continued running. The other four followed her but the last of them, a young dark-haired man slowed as he approached.

"Are you Hawk?" he asked.

Taelin laughed. "No! Keep running!"

The dark-haired boy grinned at him and continued past. Gunfire sounded behind them and Tae looked back at the prison. A man ran out of the building towards him with a number of guards in tow.

Unable to believe what he saw, Taelin stared in utter disbelief. "Naethan?"

His face was far too harsh and angry to be the Naethan he knew, and besides that, Naethan was still in Arām healing up from being shot, right? Perhaps he had a twin brother?

"Tae! Run!" His sister's voice ring loudly in his mind. Glancing back, he saw her standing on the top of a sand dune staring back at him.

Taelin's shock lifted just as a roar erupted from the guards behind him. He ran towards his sister but a weapon fired. Just one shot. Something sharp bit him in the calf and he tripped, falling unceremoniously into the hot dark sand. He tried to get up again, but one leg just wouldn't take any weight. By the time he figured out that he had been shot the uniformed guards were upon him, kicking and punching.

"Stand down!" someone roared from far away.

Either a knee or an elbow hit him hard in the face. Stars filled his vision and the light of the sun seemed to darken and fade away.

* * * * *

Bana watched the guards beating Taelin. He quickly reloaded and shimmied down onto his stomach in the sand. But by the time he was ready to shoot, the guards were dragging Taelin, unconscious, back inside the building. The leader of the guards stepped aside to watch them and Bana recognized the face.

Bana wouldn't have considered Taelin a friend. It was hard to consider a man who helped to guard him as a prisoner, a friend. However, he knew the man well enough after a year of captivity to know that Taelin didn't deserve to be taken prisoner by the Agency, and certainly not by Enigma. The youngest Cowdy would make Taelin suffer significantly before he was taken to the Interrogators.

He framed Enigma's face in his rifle sights. Dobid Cowdy. The youngest son of Jaran Cowdy senior. He hadn't been so bad in his youth. Dobid had been one of those defying his father for a long time and trying to bring a positive change into the Agency. That was until first his mother killed herself, and then not even three months later a serial killer took his wife and unborn child, and nearly killed him. After that, Dobid Cowdy became Enigma. Vicious, cold-hearted and the more serious heir to his father's "throne" than his older siblings. Jaran's new "favorite".

The fact that he was there in the desert meant that he'd escaped the Rebels. It also meant that the Agency probably knew now that Bana wasn't dead. He lined up the sights between Enigma's bright blue eyes and took a breath. If he killed him now there would be less trouble later when he became the next Head of the Agency.

Bana breathed out and rested his finger on the trigger. He breathed in, and on the out-breath— someone kicked the rifle from his arms and the shot fired off-target. Instinct drove Bana to grab his handgun from its holster. Rolling onto his back, he aimed it at the person before he'd even seen who it was.

Tiras stood above him. Dark blue eyes stared tensely as his hands lifted into the air.

"Why?" Bana growled. "Why did you stop me?"

"What do you think Jaran would do to the Rebels if you shot his precious son? You think he wouldn't want his revenge on every single Rebel in Arana?"

"He already wants that!" Bana snarled.

"Yes, but with his son's death it would become personal and not just duty. You know Jaran just as well as any high ranking Agent does. He's dangerous, more so when he thinks he's being personally attacked, and he has three other sons of similar disposition. Killing Dobid would only make it impossible for the Rebels instead of just extremely difficult. Do you want the deaths of two and a half thousand women, men and children on your heart?"

Shock forced the air from his lungs. Bana lowered his weapon. "Two and a half thousand Rebels?"

A laugh escaped Tiras. "Yeah, isn't it amazing? Hawk may only be a man, but he's damn impressive."

Bana put away his weapon and grabbed his rifle from the sand, as he stood up.

He sensed a deep relief in his cousin, which slowly shifted into sadness. "Now, this rabble sees Asha as an extension of Hawk. Enigma's taken Taelin, so she's going to need some support. Wanna help?"

Bana smiled at his older cousin. "Yes, I'll help. But not forever. With Dobid free I have to go underground with Gusa."

"Of course, cousin! Of course."

* 24 *
An hour later

They sat in the battered seats of a very dirty old propeller plane. It was better than the transport the ga on the way in, but not by much. Turbulence shook the cabin at odd times, things that shouldn't, rattled, and many of the Rebels sat or lay in the aisles because there wasn't enough room. However, it was certainly better than walking back to Arām.

Everyone had gotten out and evacuated on schedule. A number of those who had been fighting at the front of the building were injured but no one had been lost.

Except for Taelin. Asha swallowed.

Her brother hadn't run away like she'd instructed him. He stood there in harm's way staring at "Naethan" like an idiot. He got arrested; taken into custody. Not even Hawk could get him out now, at least not without revealing himself to the Agency.

Worse than that, Hawk would have to make sure Taelin died before he left the initial interview process. Taelin knew too much about the core Rebel cell to be stripped by the Interrogators. He knew that she was Hawk's Second, that Nalana was important to Hawk, that the Cathedral helped and traded with the Rebels, and the locations of every Rebel cell on Nama's supply run. Too many people would die if what he knew got to the Agency. Hawk would have to do what was necessary, and sacrifice her brother to protect everyone else.

Her bottom lip lifted and she closed her eyes. Rubbing them with her thumb and forefinger, she pushed back the tears. It would not do for the representative of Hawk to curl up in a ball and wail like a distraught child in front of all these Rebels.

Arai sat silently next to her, obviously involved in her own running thoughts. The woman hadn't said anything since they'd watched Taelin get arrested. Asha sensed her friend's terror and shock at seeing her youngest brother at that base. Hawk had told her that Arai would run if given any reason to do so. Seeing her brother—a man for all she knew was a clear and present threat to her—standing where he shouldn't be standing, was probably enough of a reason for her to flee.

Arai sighed and ice blue eyes looked sideways at her. "There has to be a spy in the Rebels." Her voice was quiet. "I can't stay with you, Ash. I have to make sure my son is safe."

Asha's bottom lip twitched. "I know." She swallowed. "At least let Hawk and I give you some resources to help you on your way. We have money put aside in one of the safe houses in Arām."

She nodded once. "Of course, Ash. Excuse me, I need the bathroom."

Asha watched her get to her feet and walk down the aisle towards the back of the plane. She wondered if she'd ever see her friend again after this. It wasn't safe on the run without help from Hawk, especially not for the Head's daughter. It would only be a matter of time before her best friend was caught and killed by the Agency.

Asha rubbed at her eyes again—those tears just wouldn't stay down!

* * * * *

Xak hated flying. He always had, even before the Agency came to take him away. There was something unnatural to him about not having his feet planted on the earth. However, being on the plane meant he had escaped and he was now a Rebel. He grinned.

At the front of the cabin sat the leader woman, whose name he'd already forgotten. She had long curly black hair and calm blue eyes. He sensed a strength to her that was similar to Liz, whether that was because she was kinetic or a leader he wasn't sure.

A shorter blond woman was sitting next to her, but got up and made her way to the back of the cabin.

Shuffling out of his seat, Xak headed towards the leader. When she turned to look at him, he promptly forgot what he wanted to say. Instead he gave her a goofy grin. "Hi."

"Hello." Her dark blue eyes were bloodshot and she looked tired, but she returned the smile. "Xak, was it?"

"Yeah." He nodded and sat down next to her, pulling one leg under him so he could sit sideways in the seat.

"I'm Asha. Hawk said you're a fairly high rating Time Psi?"

He shrugged. "I wouldn't know, never been rated."

She smile and looked away from him. The sadness and worry came into her face again and he remembered his question.

"That man who was captured, who is he?"

Her voice was very quiet. "My brother, Taelin."

"Oh," he said awkwardly, realizing why she looked so cut up. "But, surely Hawk could help him? He got us out didn't he?"

"No, it's different." She shook her head. "There isn't time to get to him before he goes to the Interrogators. You have to remember Hawk is just a man, he can do the improbable but not the impossible." She swallowed and looked at her hands. "My brother is dead, Xak. That's all there is to it."

* 25 *

The pain in Taelin's right cheekbone was so intense that as he came to a moan escaped from his lips. Someone was pacing nearby and he felt flares of agitation and frustration prickle the air around him. Only one eye opened and as he tried to look up, the pain in his face and bound arms made him grunt. The other person in the room stepped towards him and a face sat in his vision.

Vivid blue eyes glared angrily at him. "Why didn't you run, Taelin?"

He swallowed back the taste of blood in his mouth. "I... I don't know, maybe I thought you were in trouble."

"As you can see, I wasn't." Naethan stepped away and paced to the other side of the dim room, where he stopped. His voice was quiet, like the Naethan Tae knew. "I'm faced with a very difficult situation, Taelin. Once you leave this room you will go directly to the Telepath Interrogators." Tae sensed a flare of grief in the younger man. "I cannot let you leave here alive. You know too much."

Taelin glared. "Too much about the Rebels, or too much about our Agency spy?"

Naethan turned, and that odd one-sided smile of his brushed at the anger. "Both."

"Then kill me. If that's what you're hinting at. No conflict there."

Naethan strode up to him and crouched down to get eye contact "Why are you so eager to die?"

"We both know I'm already dead." He swallowed. "You kill me to protect yourself and I will die protecting the Rebels and Hawk from the Agency."

Ice blue eyes glanced down and there was a long silence in the room. Taelin didn't sense anything other than Naethan's normal stoic calm, but the frown in the man's face suggested he was thinking deeply about something.

The man sighed, stood upright, and turned his back to Taelin as he paced to the corner again. "You die to protect the Rebels from the Agency and I would kill you to protect myself. Fair point, Taelin, fair point. If only you knew the entire truth."

Tae grunted. "Then tell me."

Naethan turned and strode swiftly towards him. His voice shifted to sound angry and harsh, but Tae didn't sense anything empathically.

"No."

A fist came towards Tae and he was unable to avoid it. Agony shot through his cheekbone and jaw, amongst a galaxy of stars.

His last thought was of his sister, ten years old and weeping in his arms the day the Agency came for them—the last day either of them had been free.

* 26 *

Asha wiped at a tear that had escaped her eyes, and put down the last of the supplies they'd taken to Epa. The new building Nama's cell had moved to was the stone building where they captured Bana. Hawk said there was no record of it being logged as a Rebel building so it was safe for the moment. At least it was warm and sunny, and if they were there long enough the garden at the back of the building could be used to produce food.

She sighed and trudged from the dining room, which had beautiful wood floors and wall paneling. Turning in at the doorway, she made her way down the hall and started upstairs. Her old shoes made squeaking flop noises on the stairs as she went up. Her whole body and soul felt dead.

Her best friend was gone, possibly even forever. Her brother was gone. If he wasn't dead already, he would be soon. She put a grubby hand to her mouth to suppress the grief again. She would cry when she was alone. It would not do to let the Rebels see the woman they'd put up on the pedestal of "Hawk's Messenger", bare her soul to the grief for all to see like any normal person would on the loss of their family.

At the top of the stairs, she made her way down the hall to the north facing room where Nama was apparently sleeping. The upstairs area felt full, unusually full, but also very quiet. She heard weeping from one room as she passed it, but continued to the far end.

It was dark outside, and when she got to the room the only light came from candles. People lay on the carpet, with bags and supplies piled around them. Others lay in cots, and she sensed pain and injury. Nama stood in the middle of it all.

It was then she realized that something must have happened here in Arām while they were away. She stood in the doorway and stared across the shadows at him. To her meager senses, he seemed like a sharp green flame of utter grief that filled the entire space. His grief was even overshadowing the physical pain present in the room. He looked up. Grief and fear filled his face, he looked like she felt: as if the world was about to end.

"What happened?" Her voice was a whisper.

"Cheetah." He swallowed. "Hilla..." Tears ran down his cheeks and he didn't need to finish his sentence for her to understand what had happened.

She skittered from the doorway, around the cots and wrapped her arms around Nama. His grief triggered hers and they wept into each other's arms.

"Naethan escaped." Nama's mental voice was just as distraught as his spoken voice.

"I know. He came to us." She tightened her shields. They were touching and even though Nama's telepath rating was only a three, his range was a four and she couldn't have him knowing everything yet; even through her own grief she had to protect Hawk.

"Taelin..." she couldn't even think the rest of the sentence.

In her arms, Nama made a choking sound, and impossibly, the green flames multiplied.

They grieved in each other's arms for what felt like hours, and they only stopped because there didn't seem to be any more tears left.

They sat together on the carpet between cots, both of them resting their heads on the other's shoulder.

"I—" Nama tried to speak but his voice broke. He cleared his throat and sat up to look at her. "I need you to tell Hawk something."

"Of course, what is it?"

"I'm sorry, Asha. I can't keep following Hawk unless he takes out Cheetah. I won't stand by and let her kill any more of my family."

She nodded again. "I understand. I'll pass that along when I next hear from him."

"How long will that be?"

"A couple of weeks I would think." She wiped her face and swallowed. "Arai and Bana have gone. Tiras will be gone early in the morning. We have so much to do."

He sighed and gave her a brotherly pat on the back. "We can do it together."

* **27** *

The next day

A van arrived at their new base a little after midday. It was a nondescript white van with its windows tinted black. Asha, from an upstairs window, watched the woman who got out and knocked on their front door. She was short and stocky, but even from one level up Asha sensed a strength about her—this woman was not to be argued with.

Asha went downstairs. Few others but Rebels knew where they were, and as far as she knew none of the Rebels had a van as new as that. Perhaps the woman was lost.

She opened the front door and lifted one black eyebrow at the visitor. "Yes?"

The woman was unafraid despite Asha's deliberate hostility. "My name is Karen. I have a delivery for Asha."

Asha frowned. "From whom?"

"He said you'd figure it out. Come, let me show you."

Brushing the surface of the woman's mind, Asha looked for any sign of deception or a trap, but found none. The delivery wasn't supplies but two people the woman didn't know. This "Karen" was not an Agent, nor even Psi, though Asha sensed a smattering of static at the edges of her mind. However, she did have a fairly disciplined personality—a doctor, in fact.

Cautiously, she followed the woman, Karen, to the back of her van. The door lifted up to reveal a well upholstered cabin. One person lay on the deck of the van on a stretcher and another sat next to them. The face of the seated person was heart-shaped and framed with lovely golden brown curls. Deep brown eyes looked up at her.

"Nalana!" Asha ran to the door and helped her get out. "You're OK!" She wrapped her arms around the girl's slight form.

Nalana returned her hug tightly. "Yes, I'm OK." She let go and the girl's bottom lip twitched up. "But Tae needs help."

"Tae?" It was then Asha looked down at the figure lying next to them.

Her brother's face was very badly bruised and swollen. Dried blood caked his black hair and stained the old checkered shirt he wore, but his chest rose and fell in long even breaths.

Asha's voice was barely a squeak. "He's alive."

"Only just." Karen replied. "The drug I used to make him seem dead brought him too close to the edge a couple of times. But, once it's out of his system and if his broken bones mend properly, he should make a full recovery."

Asha touched his shoulder and closed her eyes to fight off her sudden tears. He was alive. Her brother was alive and she wasn't alone in the world. She swallowed. Hawk had managed to do the impossible for her, just this once.

"Asha," Nalana's dark brown eyes were wide. "Naethan's a spy."

She smiled at the girl's innocent fear. "I know, Nala, I know. Help me get Taelin inside. Marius is here, he's been out of his mind with worry for you." Asha grabbed the ends of the stretcher and pulled Taelin mostly out of the van. When Nalana had her end secure they walked back towards their building.

She glanced at Karen woman as they passed. "Thank you. Tell him, thank you."

* **28** *
19th of Mecra
(Three weeks later)

Cheetah stood in the doorway of an abandoned factory. The empty building wrapped its broad shadows around her like a cloak, and hid her from the Rebels she was watching outside. She hadn't yet traced them back to their primary building, but the Tolān man was not shielded telepathically, so it was only a matter of listening in before she could find reference to their building location and complete her mission.

The Rebels used a neighboring building tucked behind the others as a storage facility for non-spoiling supplies. She'd already looked around before their van turned up. A single room upstairs was dry enough to house boxes of clothes, tinned food, a couple of large metal stills and many sealed storage containers with medical supplies inside. The room wasn't even locked, but on the outside the building looked as if it had been abandoned for fifty-odd years, so very few raiders would think it worth the effort to check out.

The four or so Rebels outside were slowly unloading supplies from a battered white van, into the building and then returning with other supplies to be loaded up. The van looked as if the only thing keeping it running was love and duct-tape. The paint was chipped and metal siding dented. There were some bullet holes in the body of it, and a massive crack ran across the front windscreen obscuring the view of the front passenger.

Cheetah's jaw tightened and she sighed. Her mission was to hunt down Nama Ree. He was the last "free" descendant of the original Rebel leader, Jerna Ree. She was not happy about this mission. She'd found out in her research that Nama was her Nani Jean's baby brother—he was her father's uncle. He was family. She swallowed. She didn't want to do it. She wasn't even sure if she could. But she would have to attempt it because that's what she had to do to keep herself and her father alive.

Sighing, she dipped back into the Tolān man's mind. The faster she got this over and done with, the less painful it would be.

"But you've only been together for a year, how do you know she's forever?" Nama walked next the Tolān man, Marius, as they made their way from the warehouse to the van with their supplies.

"How did you know about Kala?" Marius said defensively.

Nama shrugged. *"I just knew. But we didn't get married for two or three years. It's best to take these things slowly. You're both young, you've got plenty of time."*

She sensed Marius pull his mouth into a pout. *"Well, I'm going to ask her anyway."*

Nama laughed and she sensed Marius's embarrassment.

"We can have a long engagement. I love Nalana, so there's nothing more to think about!" They pushed their boxes into the van and turned back towards the warehouse.

She sensed something behind her that she couldn't define and withdrew from the Tolān man's mind. Too late to react, she felt the cold metal of a gun barrel touch the small of her back and she stiffened.

The person inside the building with her had tight mental shields, so tight she couldn't even sense their gender, and certainly couldn't break their shield before they pulled the trigger. If they were a Rebel, they were definitely at least an A2-trained ex-Agent.

"Cheetah." The voice was low and graveled. Male. "You are treading on my territory. Get yourself reassigned to internal assassin, or the next time I find you watching these Rebels, I will kill you."

Snorting at the man's absolute bravado, she turned to address him. "Listen, whoever you—"

The weapon went off and a sharp agony pushed through her chest, making breathing impossible. She let out a wheezed moan and fell to the grubby concrete floor.

The last thing she saw before unconsciousness took her, were the black shiny shoes of a suited Agent; whoever had shot her was no Rebel.

* 29 *

Xak was lying back on the thick carpet, with his hands behind his head and his eyes closed. It was warm and comfortable in the north-facing room. He hovered there in a sleepy haze of contentedness as the voices of Nalana and Taelin flowed incomprehensibly over his head.

It had been three weeks since they'd escaped the desert and become Rebels. He'd never felt more at home in his entire life. Granted, he'd never been as cold, hungry or tired in his life either, but the contentedness made up for most of the difficult stuff.

Nalana's sudden bubbling laugh brushed away the doze from his mind.

"Tae! I'm *not* telling Mar I know he's to going ask me! That would ruin his surprise!"

Sitting up on his elbows, Xak grinned sideways at her. "So, you'll be saying yes, then?"

She flashed a little half-grin at him. "That's for me to know and you to find out!" Her bubbling laugh sounded again and Xak laughed along with her.

The three of them had finished their chores and sneaked upstairs to enjoy the rarity of a sunny winter's day inside. Xak's laugh faded and he sighed happily. He was where he should be and doing what he was meant to be doing—he knew this with every inch of his being.

On the other side of Nalana, sitting closest to the door, Taelin sat upright.

"Asha's calling me," he said as he carefully got to his feet, favoring his still-healing leg. "I'll go see what she wants."

"Alright." Xak watched Taelin hobble out into the hallway and called out after him. "Ask her when I'll get to meet Hawk!"

With a laugh, Taelin yelled back. "But she always says the same thing!"

Xak rolled his eyes. "Yeah, yeah, I know, 'when it's the right time!' But ask her anyway!"

Next to him Nalana chuckled. "Well, at least you're persistent."

"Yes, I am." He grinned.

"You do know you'll eventually meet him, right?"

He nodded. "Yeah, I do, and I know it's not going to happen until it's safe. I just like to remind Asha so she doesn't forget."

Xak sighed and lay back on the carpet again. A comfortable silence descended on them and hovered there for a few minutes. It was broken when Nalana started to hum a song she had regaled them with the night before. It was a lovely song with a story embedded into it about heroes triumphing over evil. She seemed to have three passions in life—aside from Marius of course—healing, looking after the children and telling stories in their many forms.

A thought struck Xak and he sat up again. "Hey Nalana, what's your thing with Hawk? I mean, why do you tell stories about him that you know aren't true?"

An expression of veiled mischief crossed through her face. "Promise you won't tell anyone but Hawk?"

He leaned in to listen. "Of course!"

"Well, my nan was a Time Speaker—kind of like you and Hawk. When I was born, she said that I would help Hawk succeed in his mission to free all Psi. Nan used to tell me stories of Hawk for me to memorize. She said the stories were important to tell to the Rebels because they helped Hawk."

He tipped his head on the side. "How do stories help Hawk?"

She smiled. "They're like a disguise. The Agency will hear the stories and be misdirected. The Rebels will hear the stories and feel comforted and hopeful. All the while, he can be free to keep doing what he needs to do, to win. They're like a mask for him to hide behind."

Surprised, Xak laughed. "I've seen your mask, Nala! It's part of my dreams and visions, and you know what? That's brilliant!"

She looked confused. "What's brilliant?"

"You give him the mask, and I give him the fire that he uses to fight the Agency! Don't you see? In the place of All-Time our threads both run along his; we echo him. Like Asha. It means we're a piece in the larger puzzle for what he's fighting." He grinned at Nalana. "That's totally awesome!

* 30 *

Taelin listened to the laughter of Nalana and Xak as he slowly hobbled his way down the hall to the stairs. It was nice to have laughter around him after all they had lost in the last year. The bullet wound in his leg still caused him a bit of pain to walk on, but he wasn't going to let it stop him. Somehow, Hawk had freed him from Naethan and the Agency, and he wasn't going to waste a day of whining about the pain. Instead, he was going to enjoy every second of free life he had.

Their building was very quiet. Only he, his sister, Xak, and Nalana had stayed behind to do chores. Everyone else was on deliveries, collecting food or selling crafts at the South Docks market—it was a normal weekend day.

His broken shoes slapped on the dusty wood floor at the base of the stairs. He put his hand on the railing and stopped to listen. The hallway was empty. They'd moved back to the beautiful stone mansion. The same building they'd moved to when he and Nama rescued Naethan from Gora Prison, and where Bana had been captured. It was odd now he thought about it. They captured an Agent who turned into a Rebel, and got a new Rebel who turned out to be an Agent.

He heard voices from the kitchen and walked towards them. The kitchen door in the main hall was one of those push doors—without a handle or a lock. It was beautifully carved from oiled hardwood, framed in polished brass and made almost no sound when it opened or closed. He put his hand on the wood and pushed.

"Nama's going to shoot you when he sees you, you know that don't you?" Asha's voice was cynical and amused.

"Yes, I know, but I'm sure we can figure out some—"

Taelin stepped around a large steel oven into the main area of the kitchen. He saw the recognizable vivid blue eyes, light brown hair, and that amused half-smile he'd gotten so used to seeing.

"Tae, calm down and listen to me." His sister stepped towards him with her hands up. But it was too late. Taelin's fear made him dive for his weapon and it was aimed with the safety off before she finished her sentence.

He stared down the barrel of his gun at Naethan. Naethan the traitor. Naethan, the Agent.

"Taelin. Look at me!"

His sister's voice was so strong with command he did as he was told.

"Taelin, put the gun down and let me explain."

"It's Naethan. He's... he's—"

"He's Hawk," she interrupted, her voice was very quiet.

His shock was so acute that his weapon hand dropped with his jaw. "What? I don't understand."

Asha approached him and took the gun from his fingers. "I wanted to tell you as soon as I saw you'd rescued him from Gora Prison but it wasn't safe. I'm sorry I had to lie to you, Taelin."

His mind struggled to get around this new information. "But... he's an Agent. He nearly killed me. He—"

"Yes." Naethan stepped towards them, hands up at head height. "I am an Agent. But I'm also Hawk." He smiled. "You can call me David."

Naethan's broad hand extended towards him in greeting, and Taelin took it before he realized he probably shouldn't show such trust immediately.

The man gripped Taelin's hand with both of his and spoke with a very gentle voice. "Let me show you the truth."

Naethan closed his eyes and let out a long calm breath. The empathic ice around him lifted away as if he'd taken off a dark cloak, and revealed a flowing vibrant blue energy that sparked and burred with dark Time Psi static. Naethan's energy filled the entire room and its edges flowed into the other spaces of their building.

Taelin gaped. He'd never sensed anyone quite so vibrant in empathic color, nor with such a radius of black static.

"Hai di'chena!" Taelin whispered.

The man had taken down all of his shielding, empathically and telepathically. For the first time Taelin could see the truth. This man was capable of anything, disciplined and compartmentalized. But most importantly, he sensed that this man was no threat to him. He wasn't sure how he could sense that fact, but he knew deep within him that whoever and whatever else this man was, he was Hawk and he was an ally.

Still in shock, Taelin barely felt Naethan let go of his hand. He stood there for a good minute gaping and wondering what he should do or ask.

Someone yelled from outside in the hall and the kitchen door opened. "It's Hawk! Didn't I tell you he was—"

Xak and Nalana ran through into the kitchen next to him but upon seeing Naethan, Nala yelled fearfully and tried to run away.

"Nala!" Taelin grabbed her gently by the arms and was overwhelmed for a second by a powerful wave of absolute terror. "It's OK. Calm down, he's not here to hurt you."

She blinked at him for several seconds as she started to tremble. "But it's Naethan."

Xak frowned at them. "No, Nala, it's Hawk."

Taelin wrapped his arms around her shoulders, bringing her closer to him in an effort to comfort her.

"It's OK, Nalana. It's OK. Xak's right. Naethan is Hawk. You don't need to be afraid of him anymore." He shared a calm feeling of safety through their touch and she physically relaxed into his arms.

When she stopped shaking, she looked uncertainly over her shoulder.

Hawk gave her a sad apologetic smile. "I'm sorry for frightening so much, Nalana."

"You knew."

Her voice was tiny but edged with anger, and sensing she'd fight him if he held her, Taelin let go. She strode up to Hawk, the anger building and filling the room. Taelin stepped forward hoping to stop her but before he could, she slapped Hawk hard across the face.

"I trusted you!" she bellowed. "You knew my loyalty to you. You knew you could have told me who you were, but instead you chose to do that!" She slapped him a second time. "I was prepared to die protecting you!"

She went to slap him a third time, but Hawk caught her wrist.

"Yes and that's exactly why I didn't tell you." His voice was very gentle. "I'm not worthy of your dedication. I'm just a man, Nalana. You know me. I may have lied about my name and my history, but you know me. I'm just a man who makes mistakes and is not worthy of your sacrifice. I didn't keep that secret to hurt you but to protect you. I am very sorry for scaring you so much, but I would make that decision again in a heartbeat to keep you or anyone else I care about alive." Hawk let go of her wrist and took a breath. "Now I need your help and you too, Taelin."

Vivid blue eyes glanced up at Tae and he swallowed back his instinctive fear of the man. It was going to be difficult to get used to thinking of him as Hawk, and not Naethan their betrayer.

"Nama is about to return home and I'm going to need all of you to help me talk to him. Nalana, I'm sorry but you can't tell Marius. I hate to require you to lie to someone you love, but the less he knows the safer he'll be."

"Have you dealt with Cheetah?" Asha spoke up.

Hawk glanced at her and nodded. "Yes, she's out of the way."

"Did you kill her?"

"No, Asha." His voice was gently correcting with a confidence Taelin hadn't seen before. "She echoes me, I'm not killing someone who may be important later. She's being transferred to internal assassin duty. It'll make escapes harder but she won't be bothering the Rebels again."

She put her hands on her hips. "I don't think that'll be enough for Nama."

Naethan chuckled, his half-smile lifting one corner of his mouth. "Well, he's going to have to learn there are more important things in my life than exacting *his* vengeance."

Taelin sensed a flickering pulse of black static flow out from Hawk into the room. The man sighed. "Nala, they're nearly here, can you go outside and distract Marius when he arrives?"

She nodded slowly. "OK."

* 31 *

Nama parked the van in an alley off the street. He and Marius walked around a brick wall towards the road and their building. When they got to the street, Nalana stood waiting on the sidewalk out front. When he saw her, Marius ran ahead to pick her up and swing her around in his embrace. She laughed and hugged him tightly.

"We're going for a walk," said Nalana quietly.

"Yes, a walk. Won't be too long." Marius gave him a wink and they turned away down the street.

Nama chuckled and pushed through the entrance door of their stone building. Inside, he dropped the box in his arms on the floor and turned to look around for the others. Asha stood in the hall. Her arms were crossed over her chest and her lips were thin with worry.

He raised an eyebrow at her. "What's up?"

"First, I need to have your weapons, Nama."

He laughed. "Pull on the other one. Where are the others?" He pushed past her.

"I'm not joking, Nama. I need you to hand over your weapons."

He shook his head at her and walked towards their dining room. "Where's Taelin?"

Behind him, she sighed. "In there, but don't say I didn't warn you, Nama."

He glanced back over his shoulder at her and frowned. It wasn't like her to act so strangely.

The dining room was finally empty of boxes or furniture, so their three technical people could set up their project of making a replica of his grandfather's electricity generator. Sunlight filtered through tall mucky panes of glass onto the dusty amber floor boards. Taelin stood to Nama's left in front of the cupboard door, which led back into the kitchen.

Taelin lifted a hand up. "Nama, wait before you—"

Nama sensed a second person and turned. A man stood in the other end of the empty room in a shaft of sunlight. In his abject surprise, Nama pulled out his primary weapon and was firing before he consciously realized it was Naethan at which he was shooting. The man moved so quickly towards him. Nama barely got two shots off before the magazine dropped to the floor and Naethan was close, twisting and pulling the weapon from his hands.

Stepping back, Nama went for his secondary, but the man dodged around his side and dislocated bones in his wrist and shoulder with surprising speed. The sudden pain made him drop his weapon with a roar.

"Stop, Nama!" called Taelin again.

In the fuzz of pain, he tried to punch out at Naethan, but he was pulled into a headlock. Naethan tightened his grip in such a way that he yanked painfully on Nama's dislocated joints. He cried out again, and his knees gave way. Naethan's grip was too tight on his neck, stars came into his vision and the room started to darken. Nama realized then that he was going to pass out.

* * * * *

When Nama came to, his wrists and ankles were tied and he lay in the dust of the dining room floor. His dislocated shoulder and wrist ached somewhat, but he could feel that the joints were back in place again.

"I warned you, Nama." Asha sat next to him on the floor with her legs crossed under her. "Don't ever claim I didn't warn you."

"Asking for my weapons is not a warning in any language!" he growled.

Behind him, Naethan sighed. "You didn't give us time to explain, Nama. Will you just listen?"

"Not like you've given me a choice," he grumbled.

Asha took a breath and said something impossible. "Naethan is Hawk."

He snorted. "Yeah, and I'm the Founder's long lost thousand greats grandson. Now untie me, so I can wring that little a'kenān's neck!"

Naethan's laughter sounded behind him. "She's not lying, Nama. I am Hawk. Actually, you can call me David."

"I think I'll stick with little a'kenān for now, thanks. Hawk would never betray us. You betrayed us.

Therefore, you are not Hawk. Now untie me and give us a fair fight!"

"Nama." Asha sounded angry. "If you fight him for real he'll kill you. Please, just listen. Stop being such a stubborn preta and listen."

"No," he growled as he struggled against the ropes. "You listen to me. That man nearly killed us. He nearly killed Taelin and scared the living Darkness out of Nalana. He's a spy for the Agency. When I get out of this I'm going to wring his so'then neck!"

The cold surface of a weapon barrel touched his temple and he suppressed the cry of surprise that wanted out of him.

"If I wanted Taelin dead I wouldn't have risked everything to free him again. I would have just killed him."

Naethan's voice dipped into an icy hostility and Nama tightened his jaw against his instinctive fear.

"If I was a real Agency spy you would all be dead. I would not have bothered to sedate you nor knock-out Marius so that I could escape. I would have simply shot you both in the head. And when Nalana discovered I was an Agent, I wouldn't have paused to capture her. I would have left her body on the street. I have risked everything to keep you and the other Rebels alive, including getting shot by Gwen, and I will not allow you to ruin that effort because you are undisciplined in your lust for revenge." The weapon lifted from his temple and the man's voice softened slightly. "I understand how much you've lost, Nama, and I'm sorry I couldn't stop it. But I need you to put your pain aside and join me. We're going to untie you now. If you wish, you can still attempt to attack me again. I don't want to kill you but I will if you force me."

With a tense expression on her face, Asha leaned forward with a knife and cut the ropes at his hands. Naethan cut his feet free.

As soon as he was able, Nama stood up and backed away from both of them. A part of him really wanted to kill Naethan, and that part whined and screamed at the back of his head. But now he was calmer, he understood that there had to be some truth to what they said. He also knew Asha and Taelin well enough to understand that they had to believe this man was Hawk, otherwise they would be attacking him too.

Nama looked at Taelin, who stood uncertainly in the cupboard doorway where he had been before. His old friend looked at him with wide eyes and his mouth slightly open. Taelin was very afraid. Probably afraid that Nama was about to be killed because of his temper.

Nama sighed. It was true, then, Naethan was Hawk. He rubbed at the swelling in his wrist and hand.

"So, which is it?" He glared at Naethan. "Owen, Naethan, Dobid or David?"

"Depends on who you ask." That familiar little half smile lifted one side of Naethan's face, but it was somehow an expression of sadness and not his more frequent mischief. "When it's just us, David or Hawk, will do."

"And how come Hawk is the son of the Ao Head?"

His smirk lifted slightly and Nama saw the mischief again. "What better cover is there than to hide in plain sight?"

"Well, this is a so'then crazy situation." Trying to regain some sense of confidence, Nama crossed his arms over his chest. "So, what now?"

"You told Asha that you wouldn't follow me any more unless I dealt with Cheetah. She's not dead, but she won't disturb the Rebels again. If you still want to stick to that statement, I have a place for you in my personal Rebel cell. We're going after the Ao Council. Want to help?"

The young man raised an eyebrow at him. Nama had the odd sense that he knew full well he'd say yes, and was just being polite in asking. The truth was, to go after the Ao Council like his grandfather once had, and with Hawk, filled Nama with an excitement he hadn't felt since he and Kala escaped the Agency almost fifteen years ago.

"The Ao Council?" He snorted, dropping his arms from his chest. "You know me well enough. Do I really need to answer you?"

"No, I guess not." Naethan smiled and glanced away. "Asha, can you bring them to Rose Road once the evening meal is finished?"

"Yes, Sir." She responded like Nama had often responded to her—as a second to her general.

Hawk moved to the doorway and turned to look back at him. "We can talk more tonight. I have to leave before the others return." After a slightly formal nod of the head, Naethan left the room.

Nama stared at the empty doorway for some time. His shoulder and hand were aching quite badly. He needed to get a cold cloth on them to stem the swelling.

Sighing, he nodded his head a couple of times. "Right." He turned towards Taelin, who stepped out of his way as he strode through towards the odd little cupboard and the kitchen.

"Nama!" Taelin and Asha called out in unison.

"Don't," he snarled over his shoulder. "Just leave me alone for a while."

* 32 *

The dingy Rose Road safe house was David's personal "cave". The entrance to the building was off the street down a little side alley, and the apartment itself was right at the back of the building, so getting to it from the main road sometimes felt like walking into an actual cave. Inside the apartment, everything was painted bright green—not his favorite color but better than the flaking rotting walls of Rebel buildings or the uniform cream of the Tower. Every room was just a touch too small, even the bathrooms felt as if he was moving around in a house made for a child, but the sensation lead to a sense of snug safety for him. Similar to when he was a child and upset, he'd crawl into one of Triian's lab cupboards (these she kept empty especially for him), and just sat in the peaceful darkness until the pain eased. But with five additional bodies in the apartment, the "snug" had bordered on and fallen into "crowded".

His sitting room was only just big enough for a couple of two-seat couches with a small square coffee table in the middle, and enough space between furniture, walls and doors to walk around. Nama sat with Taelin against the wall on one couch, Asha and Xak were on the second couch, opposite them, and he had brought his comfortable recliner from his bedroom for Nalana, which left him perched on the tiny wooden kitchen stool. He watched them all talking and eating their ice-cream, and a smile lifted into his mouth.

"So," Taelin leaned forwards to look at him. "Where did you meet Asha?"

"Desert training base," answered Asha for him. Playfully she crowed out their old saying. "Arai, Ash and David, us three against the world!"

David chuckled and pointed his spoon at her. "Sometimes it was you two against me, remember."

"Of course!" She grinned. "But only when you got cocky and deserved it."

To his left, Nama nearly snorted up his ice-cream. "Cocky then too?" he retorted. "Did he shirk his chores as well?"

David dropped his spoon into his empty bowl. "Hey, I did every single chore you gave me, Nama." His half-smile lifted. "I just wasn't around long enough for you to give me any more than that."

Nama snorted again. "I would have, too, just for the principle of the thing."

"What principle is that?" David laughed. "Pick on the new guy?"

"No. Pick on the guy who never volunteers to do his share without being asked."

David nodded. "Passive aggressive discrimination, OK, I'll look out for that next time."

Everyone but Nalana had finished their ice-cream and placed the bowls haphazardly on the tiny black coffee table. David got to his feet, and started gathering bowls and cutlery.

"Does Hawk do dishes?" The surprise in Taelin's voice wasn't matched in his face when David glanced up at him.

"Yes, he does indeed. I have an elite class rating for dishes."

He lifted the pile of bowls up and looked sideways at Nalana, who hadn't even eaten half of her ice-cream. He made sure his voice and emotions were as gentle as possible—she'd been very easy to surprise since they'd arrived. "Don't you like ice-cream, Nala?"

"No," she pulled the bowl in closer to herself, still with that look of a startled deer in her eyes. "I'm savoring it."

He turned away and walked to the nearby kitchen door with the bowls in hand. It would take time for her to learn to trust him again. In fact, it would take time for all of them—an unavoidable consequence of his situation. He placed the dishes on his green Formica bench, and stepped back through the door into the sitting room. They didn't seem to sense his return.

"This is weird." Nama sighed.

"Is a little," said Taelin. "But it's been a weird year."

David smiled at them. He adored how simple their lives were, how they could trust each other like family should. One day, he would be able to join them in earnest and be free of the Agency himself. For now, it was nice to live vicariously through them.

Still tense and a little frightened the others looked at Asha.

"What do we do now?" said Nama.

She smiled knowingly and glanced back at David in the doorway. She was one of the few people who seemed able to sense him when he wasn't deliberately thinking about being present in a room. The others were very suddenly embarrassed and David tried not to laugh.

He lifted one hand to stem their apologies. "It's OK, it's a fair question. What you do now is that you get to ask me questions. If I can, I'll answer them." One side of his mouth lifted playfully. "It's a one time offer, though, so get in some good ones."

Nama banged the palm of his hand on the wood coffee table. "I got a question. Something that's bothered me all day—why?"

David sat down again on the little stool, frowning slightly. "Why what?"

"Why didn't you get yourself out of trouble at Gora Prison? Why'd you let yourself get shot by Gwen? Nuth, why'd you let us capture you?"

He was forever explaining the functionality of Time Psi vision, but he took a deep patient breath and started again. "Being Time Psi doesn't mean I see everything. It's not straightforward at all, especially where White Static's are involved. When things get complicated I have to follow through with a situation to get out of it. Gora Prison happened mostly because of a poorly disciplined arresting Agent and Taelin being White Static, so I couldn't stop it before it happened. Getting shot and captured three weeks ago was simple, it saved lives."

"Who?"

"Well, Gwen needed to feel as though she had taken control of the situation. With her new-found confidence she will be able to survive longer with little Cass on the run. Getting captured saved your life, Nama—"

"And how's that?" Nama sat upright.

David grinned. "Well, if you weren't guarding me you would have gone to the Desert, and you would have died. Bana wouldn't have had your rifle to use and others in the attacking group would have been killed, including Amana. Beyond that, I also needed a cover from which to go and control the situation in the desert from the inside."

"That was you on the helicopter?" Xak, who hadn't spoken a peep the whole evening sat up in his chair.

"Yes."

"You let yourself get shot, captured, and then went into that horrible place just to get me out and stop others from getting killed?"

David lifted his eyebrows. "Yes."

The young man seemed shocked. "But, couldn't you have died?"

He shrugged. "Perhaps. But I could control the rogue elements sufficiently to make the gamble a fairly predictable one."

Nama crossed his arms. "You know I think Risa had it right, you're dead crazy!"

"Tell me about it!" Asha snorted. "But it works. Every time it looks like he's about to meet his maker, something changes and he lives. Against all odds. It's creepy." She pointed at David. "You know it's creepy too."

He suppressed a gleeful grin. "Maybe."

The room descended into an introspective silence. Knowing them fairly well, David waited patiently for the next person to speak.

"I have a question." Taelin's dark eyes were serious. "There's got to be some consequences to us knowing who you are. And considering the scale of this thing, they've got to be big too."

David had expected a few more questions before they got to this subject, but it did need to be addressed. "Well, the crux of the matter is that you can never make it alive to the Telepath Interrogators."

Nama rolled his eyes. "Yeah, that's a given."

"In the event you *are* captured there are only two outcomes. Hopefully, I'll be able to get to you in time and then I'll have to kill you. If I can't get to you in time, you'll need to have a mental shield constructed, which will kill you when the Interrogator anchors in your mind."

The room was silent for a moment. Nama looked at everyone and then back up at David. "That's not a very nice way to die, Nae."

David shook his head slowly. "No, no it's not. And that's why if you're captured I will do everything in my power to get to you in time."

"But..." Xak fiddled nervously with his fingers. "But... couldn't you just... get us out?" he stammered. "You, you got Taelin out." Young wide eyes looked up at him and David wondered if the boy was going to try and run.

He deliberately softened his voice. "No, I'm sorry Xak. It's not possible. It was only by incredible luck that we got Taelin out. The installation of the mental shield is only a precaution. We'll all do what we can to stop anyone getting captured. But I won't lie to you, being a part of this cell is going to be dangerous and I will require a lot from you. The consolation prize, however, is that the primary role of this cell is to protect the Rebels—so it's for a good cause."

There was silence again. He let the fear and questions simmer in their minds. He knew it was a lot to ask of them and they needed time to absorb all of the information.

The first one to speak was the last person he expected. "I'm scared," said Nalana. "But I'll do whatever it takes to protect the Rebels."

Taelin, Nama and Xak nodded in agreement and David let out the breath he had been holding.

"So, who else is joining us?" Nama lifted an eyebrow at him. "Pretty ineffective cell if it's just us six."

* 33 *

Xak stood at the kitchen bench quietly drying bowls and spoons from their evening supper. He took a deep breath and let it out slowly. It had been a big day. He had no idea what he'd expected of the real man behind the Hawk mask, but David had not been it. Also, the others had all of this history with Hawk that he didn't understand or share. The whole situation made him feel oddly disorientated and disconnected from the events of the day.

Next to him, Hawk washed the last bowl and put it on his counter-top. "How are you handling all this? You haven't said much tonight."

Xak picked up the last bowl and started drying it. "I don't really know. It's not what I expected."

Hawk grinned at him. "Life seems to enjoy keeping us on our toes doesn't it?"

"It does." He put the dry bowl with the others on the bench and dumped the wash towel on top of them.

"Here," Hawk patted Xak on the shoulder and indicated the chairs and table behind them. "Sit, let's talk now. It's a bit overdue."

Xak smiled warily and sat. "It is, isn't it?"

Hawk sat down opposite him, his smile was gentle. "First, I have to apologize. I'm sorry things came out as they did. I asked you to come tonight because I wanted you to feel like a part of the group, but I think I was too blunt. You looked about ready to do a runner on me earlier."

Nodding, Xak chuckled. "I sure was close. Then I remembered that I've dreamed about you my whole life. I'm meant to be here with you, Nalana and the others. It's like the entire world is being affected by what we're doing here and now. That's scary but it feels right."

"I'm glad you sense it too." Hawk nodded slowly. "This is bigger than just the Rebels. How much bigger even I can't see, I only know it's world-changing and you're a part of that change." His tone softened and he lifted his chin a little. "So, you have my fire?"

Xak grinned. "Yes. It's in Rona."

Hawk sat back, surprised. "Rona? Why Rona?"

"You're going after the Ao Council. You're going to plant a bomb in the Council chambers. The Rona-Abān have the explosives you want."

"Of course," he said quietly. "The only place we could get tactical explosives in Arana would be the Armed Forces, and that would be almost impossible. But will the Rona-Abān trade with us? Nuth, could we even find them to start a dialogue?"

"No, not yet. But the time will come."

"Do you see *when* we can start trading with them?"

Xak shook his head. "No, but I know it'll start with a little boy about eight or nine years old. I've seen his face in my dreams since the night the Agency took me."

Xak opened his mind so Hawk could see the boy. His eyes were so gray they were nearly silver. Light brown hair, with flecks of blond. Wearing the clothes of a normal boy but the clothes refused to look comfortable on his skinny form. Xak remembered the boy walking towards him, only little but moving like an adult, speaking like an adult. Those large beautiful silver eyes staring up at him, and there was a little fear in those eyes but they were mostly filled with determination.

"My name is Wolf Malar."

Part Four

Five and a half years later

* 1 *

Mid 3010
Five and a half years later
Arām Agency Tower building

"All parents share genetic traits with their offspring." Triian smiled down at the young boy sitting in her lap, and tapped the glass cage in front of them. Two six-legged lizards scurried over their rocks and into a tiny pool of water, but the third, the smallest, came right up to the glass behind her finger and stared at them with wide yellow slit-eyes.

"Look at this green horn-tail. He has red bands on his body and a red dot on his forehead. The other two are his parents. You can see that one parent has the red bands, the other the dot, but neither parent has both. Through a process called meiosis, the genetic traits of the parents get mixed together to form a new genetic profile of traits that the offspring inherits. So, this lizard is a mix of the traits of both of his parents."

Large silver gray eyes stared up at her and she sensed that young Wolf Malar understood what she was saying, even though he was only nine years old.

"So," he frowned. "I should share traits with my parents?"

She nodded. "Yes, Little Ghost. That is correct."

"What kind of traits? We don't have spots or bands."

"Or tails." Trii laughed and gave the boy a wink. "Well, traits can be anything. Hair color, eye color, the tone of your skin, birth marks, the shape of your face, your hands, even aspects of your personality such as how you deal with stress, your emotional stability, and any tendencies towards developing certain diseases and disorders. And of course our Psi genes."

He nodded. "Yes, and Time Psi genes can skip generations because they are triple recessive and can be locked, which is why neither of my parents are Time Psi like me. Correct?"

"Exactly," she said quietly. "Come, let's learn about the difference between mitosis and meiosis. I have a video on the computer."

"OK." He shuffled off her lap and she got to her feet. His little hand snaked into hers, and she suppressed a shot of sadness. Wolf was so very much like his real father had once been; calm on the outside but a wash of emotions underneath.

They crossed the room, past stark metal lab benches and mazes of glass apparatus, to the other side where her computer sat on its broad wooden desk. The computer was very new; considered the "best" you could buy. But the so'then thing was too smart for its own good and she'd spent nearly a month turning off all of the "helpful" programs so she could actually use it.

Sitting down in her chair, she placed her wrinkled hand on the desk-pad. Her identity was digitally confirmed and the computer unlocked itself. She flicked her fingers over the desk-pad, and loaded up the virtual keyboard on its smooth plastic surface. She inputted the relevant commands to bring up her genetics teaching module for her senior class, and loaded the meiosis/mitosis video sequence.

The boy's oval face was calm and attentive, but she sensed an underlying concentration in him, which meant he had a question and was thinking over how best to word it. She waited patiently as she pretended there were other things to check before playing the video sequence. He was not a boy to be rushed or he would shut down and never ask his question. But, being as smart as he was—as smart as both of his real parents—he needed someone to answer his questions or he would never reach his intellectual potential.

"Triian," he said in a very small voice. "If I'm made up only of parts of my mother and father, how come I'm so different to them?"

"Well," she said, lifting him up onto her lap. "You are different to them because you are you. It's like those connecting construction blocks you play with sometimes. There are a finite amount of blocks, but you can make many different things with them. You are made up of blocks from your parents, but from those blocks, you were made into something different to them." She wrapped her arms around his skinny frame and hugged him tightly. "Now, do you want to learn about meiosis and mitosis, or would you like to go back to class?"

"No!" He laughed. "Class is boring!"

She rumpled his light brown hair with one hand. "OK then, sit quiet and listen."

* 2 *

Wolf's mother, Dela, had pitch-black hair which was straight as an arrow and cut squarely around her oval face. Her dark brown eyes sparkled with her smile and small delicate fingers tickled his brother Mana in the ribs. His father, Kanān, picked up his son Mana by the ankles. Kanān's curly dark hair bounced around his face as he lifted the boy clean off the cream-colored carpet of their sitting room. Wolf's brother Mana looked like them. He had his mother's face and eyes, and his father's hair and hands. Mana was growing into a strong, broad-shouldered boy, just like his father.

Wolf was fair-haired, not quite blond, and not quite brown. He had grey eyes that were nearly silver. His hands were long-fingered with a square palm and he was strong but not broad, with fairly long limbs.

He wasn't like them at all.

For two days, Wolf had watched his family and he couldn't find even one thing that he physically had in common with Mana and his parents. Wolf had lived with the Malar family his whole life, but based on Triian's lesson on meiosis, he could not be their real son.

Dela saw him standing quietly in the doorway and she smiled. "Come and join us, Wolf."

The young boy shook his head and stepped out of view. His question burned in the back of his mind, and it wouldn't go away—he absolutely had to know the answer. His mother was a gentle soul (most of the time), and he knew that he couldn't ask her this question without upsetting her. There was only one person he could safely ask without a negative reaction.

* * * * *

Triian sat typing up a report on her computer. An hour ago, she sent out all of her lab assistants and students so she could actually get some work done. But the room was cold and the only light was a small yellow halo around her computer from the desk lamp. She brushed at her forehead and sighed. Two more reports and she would break for lunch.

Little feet skittered on the floor behind her, and she turned in her chair. Wolf had a face so much like his mother's. Oval and gentle, her silver eyes, her easy-to-smile lips, but his body was so much like his father had been at his age. Not tall, but lean and strong. With David's sandy brown hair as well.

She grinned at the boy. "Hello, Little Ghost, how are you today?"

"Who are my real parents?" The question burst out of him and she sensed it had been burning in the back of his brain for some time.

She laughed. "Straight to the point today aren't we?" She pulled her chair out from the desk. "What makes you think your parents aren't your real parents?"

The boy climbed adeptly onto her lap. She wrapped her arms around his shoulders as he leaned back against her, and she kissed his hair.

"You told me that children inherit traits from both parents. I don't have anything in common with mother and father—there are no shared traits. Therefore, they're not my real parents. So who are my biological parents?"

Triian brushed affectionately at the boy's light hair with one hand. She let his question sit in the air as she thought about how best to answer it without getting herself into trouble.

"Well, even if that were true, why would it matter who your genetic parents are? Don't you like living with Dela? Is she mean to you?"

He laughed. "No, she's fine. Mana is mean, but I'm told that's normal for brothers."

"Then what does it matter?"

"I'm not like them." His voice was quiet and she sensed a pang of loneliness. "I have to pretend to be like them or I get into trouble. If they are not my parents maybe I could find my real ones, and then I wouldn't have to pretend any more."

In her shock at his innocent honesty, Triian failed to suppress her very deep sadness for his situation. The boy, being a rather sensitive empath, turned around in her lap and looked up at her with those huge silver eyes of his.

"What's wrong? Did I say something bad?"

A tear dropped down one of her cheeks and she gave him a sad smile. "I understand how you feel, Wolf. I don't really fit in either. But, I want you to *listen-in* carefully..."

This was their code word for the boy to listen to her thoughts and not her words to circumvent any bugs or spies that may be in her lab-room. As she verbally said what she was supposed to say, telling the boy that of course Dela was her mother and to not ask such silly questions again, Triian Rena dropped her artificial mental shield to admit him. His telepathic touch was very gentle and she barely sensed the pressure in her mind. Being only an empath she couldn't hear his thoughts, making it an imperfect form of communication, but it was sufficient for her to tell him things that she couldn't verbally.

"Little Ghost, you know if I lie to you it's for a reason?" She asked a verbal yes/no question, so he could answer.

He nodded.

"Jaran would kill me if he knew I told you this, so whatever you do with this information, please be careful. Very careful."

She saw the fear rise up in his eyes, and she knew he would do all that was needed to keep her safe.

"The names of your real parents are Sarah and David Aenan. Your mother was killed while she was still pregnant and we barely managed save you. Your father was told that you died. No one but me and your grandfather knows who your real parents are, not even Dela. Now, if you wish to approach your father, be careful. He was like you before your mother died,

but since then he's changed for the worse. He may not welcome you if you go to him and if he finds out I told you, he may try to kill me."

She'd finished her verbal correction and gently pushed against the boy's mental touch so he knew it was time to leave. He withdrew and she lifted her shielding again.

"Do you understand?" Her tone was still "correcting", but he knew that it was part of the pretend game they needed to do to keep up appearances, even in the empty lab.

He mimicked a very chastised expression and lowered his head. "Yes, ma'am."

"Good," she lifted him off her lap. "Now, I need to continue with my work. How about you go up to the library and work on that assignment I set yesterday? I'll come upstairs and take you for lunch when I'm done."

* 3 *
Two days later

Wolf left the Tower at eight in the morning fully intending on doing the recon for his mission before he went looking for his father, but he found himself standing in front of the Cathedral an hour after leaving base.

The Cathedral loomed over him. Lines of black stone cut the edges of the building into towering angular sections. Broad tiered steps led up to a pair of ancient wooden doors. Ignoring the sense of being utterly swallowed by the great building, Wolf made his way up the stairs and stepped inside.

The sense of being eaten intensified as he stared up at a mouth-like vaulted ceiling. He swallowed down his fear and forced his eyes to look down again. All this internal space was disorienting. He made his way across to the far side of the room, around long pews and the figures of robed adults, to a door in the opposite corner.

Through the door, was a small square parlor that led out to two different hallways, one to his right and one straight ahead. He had memorized the Cathedral floor plan and knew generally where he was supposed to go, but he still paused to think. Rechecking his memory, he stepped forward into the central office area of the Cathedral.

The hallway beyond was framed at regular intervals by high stone support columns that curved inwards and met in the middle of the ceiling like the pointed end of a tear-drop. To either side of him were huge wooden doors with black iron trappings, each leading off to the offices of working priests and priestesses. Ahead, the hall turned right in a "U" shape and around the corner. After the bend, he knew there was one door on the left and the next was his real father's office.

Pausing at his door, Wolf consciously slowed his anxious breathing. He'd made it and there was no point in being nervous now. The little boy took a breath and knocked firmly on the wood.

He heard a dim voice from inside. "Come."

Leaning up, he turned the brass handle and pushed. The room beyond was large and mostly empty, a tall bookcase stood against the stone wall to his right and there was a big old wooden desk in the center with a man sitting at it writing with pen and paper.

He turned to look at Wolf with a kindly smile. "Aren't you a bit young to be walking around the monastery, little one?"

The man had sandy brown hair like his; not quite brown but not quite blond. Wolf looked at the hand that rested on the side of the desk. He had a square palm with long strong fingers; they had the same shaped hands. The man's eyes were a very bright blue like Jaran's and his face much squarer than Wolf's, but there was enough similarity in his features for Wolf to see himself in him. The boy carefully turned around and closed the door. He approached the desk, thinking deeply about what he wanted to say.

"My name is Wolf Malar."

As the words left his lips, the Threads of Time pulsed and quivered around them like water when it's disturbed. He blinked in surprise. He didn't know the right words, but he knew that whatever that ripple was he was meant to be there, and that it was a pivotal moment in Time.

He swallowed. This only made it more important for him to speak. Focusing on his words and not the flowing bouncing ripples in time and space around him, he continued.

"I am an A1 undergraduate. And I know you are an Ao Operative." He pulled out his underage Agent ID and placed it on the desk in front of him. "Your married name is David Aenan, born Dobid Cowdy."

The man didn't confirm or deny he just calmly listened.

"Nearly ten years ago your wife Sarah Aenan was murdered. And you were told that her unborn baby died as well."

Wolf sensed the slightest flare of sadness and the man swallowed.

"They lied to you about the baby. He did survive... I survived."

His father's man's mouth opened slightly and Wolf sensed a flare of absolute surprise. His calm face broke into a grin and tears rose up in his eyes.

His voice was unsteady. "You have her eyes."

Wolf turned his head on the side. "I do? What was she like?"

His father turned his chair completely around to face Wolf and leaned over to rest his hands on his knees. Wolf sensed an awkward uncertainty in his father.

"Well, um, she was happy and laughed often. She loved you from the very moment we found out she was pregnant. She would have loved you fiercely had she lived."

Wolf smiled at the thought of being loved even before he was born. "Tell me about you, Dad?"

He straightened in his chair. "Well, what do you want to know?"

"Everything?"

His father laughed. "Where do I start? I have no idea. Hey, do you want to go for a walk down to the City Park? We could spend the day and get to know each other."

For the first time in many months, Wolf smiled genuinely. "I haven't been to the City Park before. But, I am on a recon mission today. I need some things for my report at the end of the day or I'll get into trouble with my supervisor. I'm not even supposed to be here."

"I'm sure I can help you with that, I know the city pretty well. Do you have a favorite food, Wolf?"

"I don't know, isn't all food the same?"

His father chuckled. "Let's go to the Park first and you can tell me about the things you're interested in."

As his father got to his feet and approached, Wolf looked sideways up at him with a frown on his face.

"Are you like a ghost? People get upset with me because they don't notice me. Even Triian has nicknamed me Little Ghost."

"In fact I am a bit like a ghost, people don't notice me unless I want them to. They call me the Enigma because of that very same quality." His father's eyes sparkled. "It's fun though, sometimes, isn't it?"

Wolf laughed as they walked out of the office. "Yes, I like to sneak up on Triian Rena, but she's tricky and I don't always succeed."

"Do you see Triian often?"

"Yes. She's the only one who answers my questions, so I see her almost every day." Wolf paused, unsure if he should continue.

They stepped out of the hallways and into the vaulted Sanctuary. He forced his mind to focus on what he should tell his father, and not the sensation of being swallowed by some great beast made of gray stone.

Wolf sensed in his father, and in the deep ripples of time which they made together, that it was safe to tell him anything. But, perhaps it was better if he was overly careful as well. Wolf gently reached for his father's mind and switched to speaking without words.

"Triian told me that you're my father and she helped me find you." He swallowed. *"I don't want her to get into trouble because of me."*

They walked out into the vast cobbled Cathedral Square and as they approached the road, his father carefully lifted him up into his arms.

"I promise I won't tell anyone that Triian helped you, and I'll do what I can to help her." His father's mental voice was a crisp cool blue. It was very calm and vibrated with an underlying black static pulse.

Wolf frowned. *"Do you know about Time too, Dad? I can feel your static. But your file says that your Time Psi genes are inert."*

His father gave him a mischievous half-smile. *"Don't tell anyone, son, but my genes are no longer inert."*

"I won't tell, especially not Jaran."

"That is very wise, son. Your grandfather might kill me if he knew."

Wolf grinned wryly. *"Jaran doesn't see any real truth, only what he wants to see, and that's creating his own end. Hawk will kill him one day soon, and you and I will be free. I've seen him die in my dreams."*

There was a sense of tension in his father's mental voice. *"Do you see who Hawk is in your dreams?"*

He shook his head. *"No, Dad, I only see a wooden hawk mask holding fire. But I know Hawk will free us all eventually, I just have to wait long enough."*

They crossed a busy street and he saw a line of green ahead of them. It was a large block of lush green field edged on one side by a line of gnarled trees. Wolf stared at the expanse of grass and had the ridiculous urge to run across it as fast as he possibly could, just for the joy of it.

"Do you tell anyone of these dreams? Can they get inside your head and see them?"

Wolf smiled. His dad was asking if other people knew he wasn't loyal to the Agency. *"No, Dad. It's safe, I'm a 6/5 Telepath; they can't get in."*

Wolf sensed surprise in his father. *"But you've let me in? I'm only a 3."*

"That's because I can trust you, Dad. I can show you everything of who I am and what I've seen because you're..." he struggled to find the right words. *"You're like me, I'm like you. We're the same in the most important way possible."*

"And what way is that?"

"I don't know the proper words. But we fit. We match. In the place where Time exists absolutely, our threads run along each other. Our futures and our pasts are linked. Our threads run along the same path and make the same ripples in the world."

Wolf sensed understanding. His father smiled sideways at him. *"I believe the term is that we 'echo' each other, son."* His father gently lifted him down from his arms onto the grass he'd seen before. Blue eyes looked down at him. *"What if I told you that I know who Hawk is? Do you think it would be safe for me to tell you?"*

Wolf frowned and closed his eyes for a moment. He projected his mind through Time to see the effects of his knowing or not knowing on the future. Static tingled over his face and flowed lazily down his spine. He saw that there were no disasters caused directly by his knowing who Hawk was, in fact there seemed to be a more positive thread along that path.

"I see no negative effects in the future with me knowing, so it's probably safe, Dad. I certainly won't tell."

His father paused for a moment and then his mental voice was very gentle. *"I am Hawk."*

* 4 *

David took the colorful ice-cream cones from the vendor's hand and turned around, giving one cone to young Wolf. The boy looked at it as if it were some kind of strange alien insect and David grinned.

With a gentle hand on Wolf's back, he led his son away from the dessert truck. They walked up the short rise of a grassy hill, and sat down on one of the many park benches that overlooked the field and the playground to the south.

The boy hadn't touched his dessert. "What is it called again, Dad?"

"A triple scoop ice-cream cone. The top scoop is citrus, the green is sour drops, and the last one is plain with diced sunkiss fruit. Take a lick, see which one you like." David tried his own ice-cream as a model for the boy.

Wolf cautiously licked at the orange scoop on top. He made an appreciative noise and took a bite of the ice cream. "It's yum!" he said with his mouth full.

David grinned.

A static shiver started deep inside David. He frowned, his back straightening as he rode the sensation as best he could. A second later Wolf's body language mirrored his own. The black static wave bounced between them like a loud yell inside a cave, magnifying and warping oddly with each reflection.

The first piece of knowledge came through to him and David instinctively sensed that Jaran had just discovered Wolf's deviation in behavior.

He whispered an offensive string of curses.

The full force of the static wave hit them both at the same time. It was so strong that young Wolf's hands jolted and the dessert fell from his fingers.

In his mind's eye, David saw a familiar place. It was made of gray brick and rusting metal. A place of torture and fear deep in the desert; the place David and his sister had been sent when they were young. The vision switched and showed his newly discovered son entering that same terrible building. Wolf's little face was terrified in that place.

"No!" David's voice was barely a whisper.

He saw his son being beaten by guards and older kids alike. He saw him weeping in the dark. Tears dropped down David's face, as he gritted his teeth against the pulsing pushing waves of static and visions. The paths and consequences of the situation branched out in his mind, and blessedly, the energy started to fade away again.

When the wave had completely dissipated, young Wolf was trembling. David wrapped his arms around the boy's slight shoulders. He shifted his own sadness and fear behind his shielding, leaving only a calm strength for the boy to sense. Wolf climbed up onto his lap. Not crying or showing his distress in any other way, he simply closed his eyes and curled up in David's arms.

David sensed an innate vulnerability in the boy, which was so intense that he tightened his grip and tucked Wolf's little head under his chin. They sat like that for a long time. David, having learned a little about kids from the Rebel children, let Wolf decide how long he needed the hug.

Once his trembling stopped, the boy sighed and sat back to look at him. David loosened his hug but didn't drop his arms. The boy's face was white, his silver eyes were scared but determined.

"We have to go back now," he said matter-of-factly.

Another tear dropped down David's cheek. "I know."

"If I stay with you Jaran will find us. None of what must happen will happen if we're both dead."

David nodded. The boy had seen the same things.

Getting to his feet, David lifted his son gently into his arms and spoke mind to mind. *"You find a high rating PK kid to be-friend, or find a group of kids to join for protection. Keep your head down, don't fight unless you have no choice, and keep safe. I'll come for you."* Opening completely to the boy, empathically and telepathically, so he would see the truth in his words, David continued. *"It will take me a little while to come and get you, but I will. I promise on your mother and grandmother's graves, I will come for you as soon as I possibly can."* He paused, swallowing back his grief, and added quietly. *"And I'm so sorry."*

* 5 *

Taelin stood in the doorway staring at David across his Cathedral office. The man was slumped over his lap with his forearms resting on his knees. The colored light from the stained glass windows behind him played in the man's light brown hair and across the desk in front of him.

Tae sensed sorrow. "What's wrong?"

The vivid blue eyes that looked up at him were filled with tears. "I have a son." His voice wavered and a single tear dropped down his cheek. "A nine year old son. I was told he died with his mother." David wiped his face with one hand. "He came here. He found me. We had a perfect morning together. And then someone came to take him away. My nine year old son is being sent right now to a desert base because he came looking and found me." Another tear dropped. "And I can't go and get him without risking everything and everyone."

Tae sensed a flicker of rage him that turned very suddenly into an inferno. David stood up, lifted a domed paper-weight from the desk and threw it against the wall. It shattered on the stone, spreading water and shards of glass everywhere.

"Must I sacrifice everything?"

The roar was a little frightening to Tae, because he'd never seen him lose control over anything. But even in his fear Taelin stepped into the room towards him and tried to help.

"We can find him. The Rebels can get him out."

David's square jaw muscle tensed, and he looked sideways at Tae. The rage and sorrow fought for prime position in his ice blue eyes.

"The Rebels can not reach the base he's being sent to. It is an Ao level facility. Even if we could get close to the place, which we can't, it would be too much of a risk to get him out. Logic dictates I can not sacrifice my cover in the Agency or risk sacrificing every single Rebel if I got caught just for one person." Sorrow overwhelmed the rage and he sat back down on his chair. His voice was nearly a whisper. "Even if that one person is my son."

Tae didn't know what he could say to comfort such a terrible loss. He stepped closer to Hawk and gently put one hand on his back.

David wiped his face and sighed. "With time I can get him out through the normal processes of the Agency. But he's going to have to survive until then." Taelin sensed a flare of absolute despair. "He's only nine years old."

"Don't you have rights as his father? Can't you insist he's released?"

He sighed. "I do have rights. But, I can't cross my father right now. If I publicly defy him on this I'll lose my position. Then I'll almost certainly be discovered by his... spies..." his voice trailed off.

David stood up so quickly that Taelin flinched.

He stared at Tae but his eyes were unseeing. "He must have a spy here, otherwise how would he know about Wolf?"

Taelin frowned at the younger man. "Your son's name is Wolf?"

"Yes," he waved one hand absently. "In the Old Religion it was believed that the universe was created by a wolf's howl, it was Sarah's favorite name and she wanted it for her first son." David grabbed an old brown jacket from the back of his chair and shuffled it onto his shoulders over the black priest robes. "There's an envelope for Asha in my top draw. I need you to leave through the back way and not return until I send a message that it's safe. It's a small mercy that the spy hasn't noticed you yet, but if he does we'll both be dead."

"Y... yes, Sir." Taelin stammered, still confused, as David stalked towards the door. "What are *you* going to do?"

David glanced back at him and Taelin sensed a dangerous rage behind his ice blue eyes. The man's voice was low and hostile. "I'm going hunting."

* 6 *

David crouched in the rafters of the old warehouse waiting for his father's spy. His thoughts kept going around in torturous circles, distracting him away from the present moment. He kept seeing Wolf's silver eyes staring up at him. The boy had been so intensely vulnerable and helpless. It had taken more discipline than he'd ever needed to not rush forwards and defend that helplessness.

David's jaw tightened in his rage. He'd been forced to betray that protective instinct, forced to be "Enigma" for his father, and forced to watch without emotion as they took his son from him. But David had done what he always did—what was needed no matter the cost. He knew that if the boy hadn't gone or if either of them had fought against it, both of their lives would be forfeit. As much as it tortured him, he knew that if he died the Rebels would be lost, and without the Rebels to protect the important people their planet would be ashes. One billion sentient lives lost if he didn't do what was necessary. He couldn't sacrifice that, even for his son.

Wolf would survive. He'd checked the boy's files. Jaran had started Wolf in the Ao martial arts program at the age of five (instead of the customary age of eleven). It was ridiculous for his father to put such a young boy through that level of combat training, but the reality of it was that it meant the boy would be able look after himself long enough for David to get him out of there.

He closed his eyes for a moment and took a deep breath to release the tension in his body and mind. It was an emotionally taxing situation to be in, but he would get the boy out when it was safe to do so.

David could easily be killed in the coming conflict if he didn't get a hold of his emotions and his mind. He was too disciplined to let even this affect what must be done. He had to play the part, the game, and be the cold-hearted killer again. Not only to keep up the Enigma persona, but to continue to play his father in the direction he needed him to go. He forced his mind to comply to his will and clear all thoughts of Wolf out of the way so he could focus on what was happening in the Now.

When he opened his eyes again, he was utterly calm and focused.

It was sunset outside. Vivid threads of orange light filtered through the windows underneath him and cut fiery lines in the air. Below him, the brick warehouse was empty except for a single table and chair with a Hub laptop and retinal ID scanner. It was the nearest Agency info drop site to the Cathedral.

David had "accidentally" given the spy something else to report back to his father. It was something juicy that needed to be reported immediately—the youngest son of the Agency Head might be a double spy for the Rebels. The corner of David's mouth lifted cynically. It was a shame his father would never know who was going to betray him. David would have loved to see his father's face after such a revelation.

There was a wooden creak of a door opening and a foot crunched on the dust and debris-covered floor. David soundlessly secured his footing on the roof beams and aimed his silenced weapon. He fired twice, obliterating the spy's kneecaps and the tender tissue behind them. The man screamed in agony and fell to the dusty concrete. Jumping, David landed lightly while still keeping his weapon aimed at the man's head. He lifted his chin to feign arrogance and lowered his voice to an intimidating gruffness.

"You made a grave mistake, Agent Garen."

The man was whimpering and grasping at his shredded knees, too afraid and in agony to respond.

"What mistake was that, you might ask?" He added Enigma's condescending tone to the gruff hostility in his voice. "It wasn't taking the mission, because it was an order and a good Agent does as he or she is ordered. Your mistake was that you didn't come to me first so I could manage what information you gave to my father. If you had done that, you may have survived this mission."

He stepped closer, near enough for the man to see him through his agony, but not so close that an errant sweep of a desperate man's arms would knock him to his feet.

"You are going to die, I promise you that much. But first you will give me all of the information you passed on to my father. And only when I am satisfied will your suffering cease."

He aimed his weapon and two more silenced shots took out the man's ability to use his arms. Garen screamed again, but did not speak.

David knelt over him on the floor, gun pressed against Garen's neck as he dropped his voice back into his own natural icy cadence. "When they find your body everyone will think you are dead because you crossed Enigma. But I want you to know that you are going to suffer and die horribly, not because you upset *me*, but because you and you alone sent an innocent nine year old boy to a desert training base."

Getting to his feet again, David paced around the man, controlling his own personal rage by channeling it into what he was about to do. "Now, Garen, you are going to tell me exactly what you have told my father from the moment you arrived at the Cathedral two months ago. The faster you give me the information the less pain you will experience before you die."

The man's dark brown eyes were wide and terrified, but David sensed he was still conscious enough to understand his words and to respond. Garen was choosing not to speak. David put his weapon on the desk next to the immobilized hub and pulled out a knife from one sleeve. "You get one warning and that was it."

He stepped over the man and went straight for his left ear.

As the blade parted skin, Garen screamed. "No! Please, no! I'll tell! What do you want to know?"

* 7 *

Jaran Cowdy senior sat back in the desk chair with his coffee, and admired the awards and merits that littered the walls of his office. It was his lunch break and even though his useless assistant hadn't come yet with his food, he was going to enjoy what little free-time he had.

His grandson had disappointed him. *Ungrateful whelp.* Ice-blue eyes narrowed. *Well, you'll learn your lesson and you'd better come back suitably chaste.*

A knock sounded on his door and it was too confident to be his dumb-ass assistant. He sighed, lifted his feet from the desk and put his coffee down.

"Come," he barked.

The broad dark-wood door opened fast and banged against the wall as his youngest son strode through. Jaran didn't need to be an empath to realize his son was mad with him.

He suppressed a smirk. *He'll demand I release his son and I'll finally know if the boy is loyal to me or has been playing me for all of these years.*

The boy strode up to his desk and dumped something on its broad surface. Blood splattered papers and his suit shirt, and Jaran swore at the sudden mess.

"Your spy's ear. *Father.*" The boy spoke between gritted teeth.

Jaran snorted and looked at the roughly cut piece of flesh sitting on his desk. "*My* spy? Really? Which one?"

"Agent Garen."

"You're angry about the child aren't you?" He kept his voice deceptively nonchalant. "Why take it out on

Agent Garen? Is he alive or am I going to have to sign *another* MIA form because of you?"

"I don't care about some so'then child with delusions of grandeur. I care about *you* micromanaging *my* operation from your so'then desk chair."

Jaran lifted an eyebrow at the boy. "Delusions of grandeur?"

The boy scoffed. "Thinking he was my son? My son is dead."

He suppressed a little internal squeal of glee. Even with that woman's eyes and face, his son didn't recognize his own flesh. "No, actually. My grandson lived. And today he broke a number of laws to find you."

The shock on his son's face was worth the possible tantrum of admitting he'd lied to him for nine years.

"That child was telling the truth?" Dobid's voice was cautious.

"Yes." Jaran silently dared his son to react badly.

The young man's face hovered in a state of shock for a number of moments and Jaran waited for him to lose control.

"Well, I appreciate the lies for all this time." There was a spark of anger underneath the sarcasm. "But I'm not here to discuss the child. If I find another spy in *my* territory," his voice lowered into his familiar hostile growl. "I will bring their head to you next time. Stop treating me like some jackass kid. I am thirty-one years old, I do not need you micromanaging my operations, nor do I need you tipping off the Rebels to the Agency presence in the Cathedral with your unfounded paranoia." Dobid turned around and stalked back towards the door.

His son had recovered from the surprise well—too well.

"Wolf is going to the same desert training base you did." He couldn't suppress the smirk. "I wonder if he'll break as many bones."

The face that turned back to him was ice cold, but neither hostile nor angry.

Jaran lifted a challenging eyebrow.

"The child went against procedure. He did so knowingly. Whether or not he is my son, he needs to learn the consequences of his actions. He's lucky you didn't decide to execute him as a traitor. Perhaps, once he's learned his lesson he'll grow up to become a better Agent."

"If he survives," Jaran added, barely able to suppress the glee in his voice. He loved poking the old wounds of his sons and watching them squirm weakly under his thumb.

There was an almost imperceptible jaw clench and Dobid's voice was utterly calm. "My operation is more important than your paranoia, Father. If you do not take the threats to my cover out of my territory, I will." His voice dropped into an almost correcting tone. "And for Nera's sake, go and play with Junior's insecurities, I'm too busy to play your mind games today."

When the door closed, Jaran waited until he no longer sensed the mental shield of his son, and let out a bellowed laughter. If his youngest son was deceiving him, he was almost flawless in his deception. But no one was as good as him, so Jaran knew it was more than likely that Dobid wasn't deceiving him. However, it was still fun to try and rankle him. He chuckled again and lifted his feet back up onto the desk.

* **8** *

Asha watched her old friend pace backwards and forwards across the empty space. David was agitated, more so than she'd seen him for a long time.

She gave him a smirk. "You digging a hole there, David?"

Glancing sideways at her, his frown of stressed confusion took far too long to lift. His smile was forced and it was then, when he looked directly at her, that she saw the agony he was in.

"What happened?" she said quietly.

He swallowed. "I found out who Wolf Malar is."

She shook her head. "And?"

"My son." Tears lifted into his eyes and she realized why he was so upset.

"They took him didn't they?"

He nodded. "He's going to the desert." His voice broke. "Same place as us."

The mother in her flared up. "Well, don't just stand here like a wet blanket, go and get him!"

"I can't."

"That is a whole heap of mamon!" She pointed at him. "You're the Head's son—you're the scary one. You can do almost anything in the Agency."

He put his hands on his hips. "I could, yes. But if I defy Father on anything this big it'll be over. I can not sacrifice three thousand Rebels for my son."

"Well..." she sighed. "Well, to be fair, Jaran couldn't get all of us."

He brushed at his light hair with one hand and smirked. "He'd sure try."

The sounds of shoes on wood floorboards broke the spell in the room. Both of them straightened and put on their respective social masks—one of a confident, all-knowing general and the other his strong, loyal second.

Their Primary Cell had expanded to nearly twenty people over the six years since that night, when there was only six of them and they ate ice-cream in the sitting room of Rose Road. Most of the time, the Primary Cell wasn't actually its own entity. There was no building where they all lived, and they weren't on the supply trade-roster. It became something separate only in the times when Hawk called a meeting to orientate the actions of the other Arām cells, or if there was a special mission that needed their discretion.

The door opened, and eighteen tired, cold and probably hungry Rebels wandered into the empty room. Asha smiled at her brother and Nama as they entered. Stepping through after the two men was Amana, from the Original cell, who leaned in for a quick hug.

The group sat down haphazardly on the sun-faded carpet. The room didn't have a fireplace, nor did it have curtains, so it got cold fairly quickly as the sun left its windows. Many of them already knew this and brought their own warmth in the form of blankets. The space wasn't particularly special, just another empty part of Nama's cell building, but it was a decent size, and the walls were filled with Psi suppressant insulation.

David did not pace under their scrutiny. He was utterly calm—in that spooky way he was so good at. Some days she envied his emotional control, other days she felt sorry for him because he couldn't just feel his own emotions and be himself. But, on that particular evening she was glad of it. Even though this Rebel group knew him well enough to understand he wasn't some all-knowing deity, they still put him on a pedestal and without his ability to hide his emotions they would soon knock him off it.

He waited silently in his calm until every single member of their cell was seated on the floor. The door closed and he took a breath to speak. The energy in the room shifted as his empathic blue faded into a cloud of black static, which rolled out to the walls like a buzzing storm cloud. His face seemed to age in decades, and she wondered for the tenth time if he was aware of how much his energy shifted when he spoke as Hawk.

His voice was quiet, almost gentle, but at the same time commanding. "Welcome. Thank you for coming at such short notice. The next stage of our attack on the Agency is about to start. Our attack plan..." he paused, and if she didn't know any better she'd think he was pausing for effect. "Is to plant an explosive device in the Ao Council chambers."

There were gasps of surprise and incredulity in the room, and he waited patiently for them to be quiet again.

"As you can imagine this is going to be quite a complicated operation. Our main priority will be to ensure our non-combatants are safe. In the aftermath of this attack, the Agency will come down hard on the Rebels, and those who do not move out of the city beforehand will be taken out."

He paused as if thinking carefully about his words. "The first stage of the evacuation will be moving all non-combatants to the outlying towns, but I will need as many as ten combat members from each of your cells to remain in Arām until the final evacuation to help support the attack. However, I only want volunteers.

"This goes for every single one of you as well. If you do not wish to participate, you are not obligated to remain in Arām. Considering what we are planning to do, I will understand if you wish to opt out of the actual attack. That said, I would like to continue relying on your discretion; we do not want this to leak back to the Agency. I'm sure you each have the diplomacy to facilitate choosing—"

A shimmer of black pulsed out of him like the chime of a grandfather clock. Asha grunted as a bolt of itching static shot through her feet and up her spine. As she swayed under the pulsing waves of static and put her hand to the wall to steady herself, she heard swearing and groaning from some of the other Time Psi in the room.

There were several layers to the pulse, one was sharp and traveled up and down her spine like a cleaver. Another, lighter layer brushed tickling and tingling sensations over the surface of her body. And the most painful layer was the resounding wave, which felt like a giant metal bell, vibrating her very core and seemingly every atom in the room.

There was one final massive bell-chime and the other sensations flitted away into nothing. She sighed in relief and opened her eyes again. Taelin, who stood across the room by the door, looked pale as if he was about to vomit. She gave him a sympathetic smile.

Hawk cleared his throat. "I apologize for the interruption. Unfortunately, we have more pressing issues to attend. Nama, Taelin, I need you to go downstairs right now and start the prep work for a combat mission. I'll give you more instructions soon. Everyone else, go home and instruct your cell leaders to open their evacuation instructions. We'll meet back here again in a week to continue this meeting." He bowed his head formally. "Thank you all."

Asha stood next to him and watched the others slowly shuffle out of the room. Neither she nor David moved until they were alone again. The door closed and she turned to face him. She still felt dizzy and itchy. But he looked just as focused and calm as if nothing of importance had happened. He recovered so quickly from the static waves. She almost wanted to slap him to share some of her discomfort.

He seemed to read her mood. "You alright?"

She smirked. "Nothing a couple of margaritas wouldn't fix. So, what are we doing?"

"While Nama and Taelin are traveling west to Naradān, you and I are going hunting. You have the combination for the weapons store at Rose Road?"

"Yes, Sir," she replied automatically.

"Good. We leave tonight, but I've got something else I have to do first. Can you pack for both of us?"

"Of course." She frowned. "But who are we hunting?"

"Bana. And it's not going to be easy."

She snorted. "No kidding."

* 9 *

Triian Rena sat on her bedroom floor in the dark. She wrapped her arms around her arthritic knees and leaned back against the wall. She knew without a doubt that it hadn't been Little Ghost who betrayed her. The boy would have done everything he possibly could to keep her safe. Unfortunately, no matter who had told Jaran about Wolf and David, she was still on suspension and facing a trial. They'd charged her with releasing classified information to firstly a minor, and secondly an Agent of lower rank. The Council was deliberating, and without her voting against him, Jaran now had the majority in the Council. Ordinarily, the punishment for this sort of offence was a slap on the wrists. However, paranoid and self-obsessed as he was, Jaran would want her convicted and killed as a traitor—if only as revenge for all the trouble she'd caused him over the years.

She didn't want to die, but she didn't regret her decision either. No matter what Jaran had transformed him into, David deserved to know that his son survived, and that poor little boy deserved to not feel utterly alone in the world.

She sighed and pulled her legs closer into her body. Whatever would come, she would try to face it with a modicum of pride and grace—even if she faced death.

In the parlor beyond her bedroom, someone knocked on the front door. There was no empathic sense of the person knocking, not even a sense of their consciousness. This meant it was a person who was trained as an assassin, and at such a late hour, it also meant that the Council had come to their decision. She wouldn't answer it. If they wanted in they were going to have to break into her apartment, and for most people that would take time.

The silent alarm triggered a small red LED on the wall next to her bedroom door. Seeing the blinking light, she stifled a cry of fear with one hand. Whoever the assassin was, they were good. There was neither sound nor sense of their presence, but the door in front of her opened very slowly. A dark shadow moved out of the black and entered her bedroom.

Trying desperately not to submit to her terror, she watched the figure. Death would come at any moment from somewhere in the darkness via a muffled flash, and she wanted to look it in the face. The light turned on above her and she blinked back the sudden bright sheet of white that filled the room. As her eyes adjusted, she saw a dark figure step closer and kneel down in front of her. She looked directly into vivid blue eyes.

A choke of terror escaped her. "They sent you, David?"

"No, I asked to be the one to do it."

She suppressed a sob. "Do you hate me that much for lying to you?"

He wiped away her tears with the palm of one hand. Through the physical touch, she sensed no hatred or hostility. He was utterly calm if not affectionate towards her.

"No, Triian. I'm here to save your life."

"No!" Her eyes widened. "David, you can't defy him like that! Please, don't sacrifice everything just for me!"

He smiled and shook his head. "Don't worry, I have a plan that will work. But you have to completely trust me. Do you trust me, Triian?"

He was open empathically and she sensed the boy she had known, not the nightmare Agent called Enigma.

"I—" a frown flickered across her face. Perhaps he'd been playing Jaran for these last ten years? Perhaps the boy she'd watched grow up had survived Sarah's death? If he really was her little Dobe, there was no doubt in her mind. "Yes, David, of course I trust you."

He lifted one long-fingered hand towards her and she took it. He pulled her up from the floor to her feet.

"I've brought with me a friend who can help make you into a convincing corpse. Her name is Karen Frene."

She blinked at him. "My daughter? You know my daughter?"

"Yes." He grinned. "But first we have to get to your lab. Can you run?"

"Of course." She nodded, starting to feel a little excited. "Do we need some acting, David, like when you were a child?"

He laughed. "Yes! That would help. Come on, we don't have much time."

* 10 *

Karen waited in Triian's lab-room, pacing and unable to calm her nerves. Her mother was sixty-one years old, was that too old to survive the drug? It had nearly killed the man, Taelin, she'd used it on six years ago. Although, this time she had lowered the dose significantly so that wouldn't happen again. Was it enough? Was it too much? Had she adjusted properly for her mother's fitness? What if her mother had an allergic reaction? She'd had only nine years with her birth mother, and it would be intolerable to lose her now simply because she made a mistake with the dosage.

She sighed. As she walked, she passed high tables with stools stacked on top, making them look a little like looming figures in the dim light. She got to the end of the aisle and turned around again.

There was a scream from outside. It was the kind of scream that crawled up your spine and made your whole being shiver—someone was dying. She turned to look across the room. The person screamed again, closer this time. The lab-room door opened and her mother entered.

A feeling of absolute terror jumped inside of Karen and she cried out from its suddenness. There was no thought. All she knew was that her mother was terrified and Karen stepped towards her, trying to ease that intolerable fear.

"Stay back!" Triian yelled. "Karen, stay back! I don't want you to get hurt!"

Someone else came in through the doorway and Karen turned to see a stranger with David's face. Ice blue eyes glanced at her for a moment and he turned to grab Triian.

The illogical terror dropped away and Karen could think again. She knew suddenly that the feeling had probably been her mother broadcasting empathically as a part of the ruse. There was a security camera in the roof above Karen, and this was all an act for that camera and David's superiors.

Karen gripped the hidden hypodermic needle in one hand and waited.

Her mother and David struggled for a few breaths before he pulled her into a headlock. She seemed to be choking. She fought against him for a few moments, before passing out in his arms. That was Karen's cue.

She ran towards them across the room. "What are you doing? Let go of her!" she cried out, trying to unhook his arm from around her mother's throat.

"Stay back!" he barked.

"No! Let go of her!"

Using his shoulder, he pushed her so she slipped and fell backwards. When she turned over again, her mother was lying on the ground and David was striding away. Karen crawled towards her mother's limp form and checked her pulse. A strong heartbeat pushed against her fingertips and Karen tried not to show her relief in any way that the camera could see.

With her body between the camera and the needle, she pushed the one-shot dose into her mother's arm. When it was done she dropped the needle in her jacket pocket and pretended to start doing CPR.

There was a click and she felt the cold barrel of a weapon touch her temple.

"Step back from her," said a hostile voice.

She looked sideways into David's face. He barely even looked like himself. In fact, the look of abject hatred in his eyes was like something out of a nightmare. Trembling from the shot of real terror that flared up through her spine, Karen lifted her hands and got to her feet. She understood in that moment why he needed such drastic measures to hide who he really was. If this was the man his superiors knew, then the brave, kind man that *she* knew would likely be immediately killed if his deception was ever revealed.

Footsteps came towards them down the hallway and others entered the lab. People in Agency suits, lab-coats and off duty colors all looked curious and concerned at the woman who lay on the floor. One younger woman wearing a white lab-coat stepped in through the doorway and cried out, running towards Triian as if to help her.

David's voice was filled with icy venom. "No one touch the body. She was a traitor."

The woman stopped immediately. Wide dark brown eyes stared in shock. The woman turned away with a hand over her mouth. Karen waited at barrel's end for the official medical team to arrive.

Her mother would remain in a near-death state for about forty minutes. That gave them ample time for the EMT's to do the formal declaration and move Triian's body to the basement morgue. Before dawn, after the fuss had died down, she and David would get her mother out of there to the Rebels. Karen knew she might never see her mother again, but at least she'd be alive.

* 11 *

Triian woke with a terrible pain in her head. Her body refused to move no matter how she pushed at it with her mind. Eventually, she managed a pained moan.

A cool hand brushed her face and she felt the owner empathically push a calm sense of safety towards her.

"You're OK. The drugs haven't worn off properly, you'll be able to move soon—promise." The woman sounded young and Triian felt an openness to her that meant she couldn't possibly be an Agent.

"David!"

"Mmr?" a groan answered.

"Your friend, she's waking up."

Triian pushed against whatever it was that held her limbs and she felt her hand twitch. Her face wrinkled up in concentration and after three attempts her eyes finally opened. Above her was a blurry face with bright blue eyes.

David smiled down at her. "How are you feeling?"

"Head hurts." Her voice creaked. "But... I'm free aren't I?"

His smile lit up his eyes. "That you are."

Feeling oddly frail, Triian struggled to sit upright and David grabbed one arm to help pull her into a sitting position.

A young woman stepped around him and handed her a glass of water. Triian smiled, looking up into an innocent heart-shaped face and a pair of dark brown eyes that shimmered slightly with a layer of night-vision purple. The girl was a hybrid, part-Tolan, part-Aranan, and her returning smile was so affectionate that Triian found her own grin widening.

She took the glass of water. "Thank you... um?"

"Nalana," said the girl with a little chuckle. "I'll let you guys talk." She had an odd trace accent to her voice, as if she'd spent time in South Rona or perhaps Naradān in her childhood. The girl scampered out of sight.

The space around Triian was completely empty except for the couch she sat on—which smelt as if it had had a past life as a sponge that was never rinsed. There were windows to one side of her, but they were covered with old stained towels, probably to block off the cold. The only light came from several candle holders that burned in the corners of the room. A dark-haired woman, wearing faded black combat fatigues, sat on the carpet opposite her with her back against a flaking wall.

Triian frowned sideways at David. "How can you do all of this without getting caught?"

Mischief lifted into his eyes, making him look very young. "Can you guess?"

She shook her head. "I don't know. I'm too tired for guessing games, how about you just tell me?"

"I am Hawk."

She snorted, expecting him to be joking, but the grin on her face dropped when she sensed a sad patience in him.

"You... you're serious? Hawk?" She stared at him for a moment. "What, are you looking for a horrific death, boy? You know better than anyone what Jaran would do if he—"

"I can handle him, Triian. Besides, I'm a 20/5 Time Psi."

Her jaw dropped. "A twenty? How are you not insane?"

Across the room from her, the other woman laughed. "The jury is still out whether he's a madman, matron. But sane or not, he's effective."

David laughed, not offended at all by this woman's insult, and Trii sensed that whoever she was, she and David were very good friends.

"So," still grinning, David glanced sideways at her. "How does retiring in Aramān with your nephew Tiras sound?"

"That sounds perfect. But first, what about my daughters?"

"With your 'death' Karen will lose her job in the labs and she'll be safe as a civilian. I'm keeping an eye on Gwen and Cassandra. However, they are on the run so I can not guarantee anything. But you have my word that I will do everything I can to keep Gwen and your granddaughter alive."

He was empathically open to her—the first time, really, since he was a boy. She could see behind his eyes a very strong man (perfectly sane too), and she sensed the pain he was in over his son. Her heart filled with a deep affection for another of her adopted waifs, and she touched his face with one hand.

"I trust you, boy. You know, your mother would be incredibly proud of you."

He scoffed. "I think, first and foremost, she would be horrified that one of her sons was a Rebel."

"Maybe, but you're doing the right thing and she would understand that. Your father has turned the Agency into something it wasn't ever meant to be, and I believe you can stop him. Just be careful and stay alive. That little boy of yours desperately needs you. He's too much like you were at his age. Without you, he'll never have a sense of belonging anywhere." Feeling a deep shaft of guilt, she looked down at her hands. "I'm sorry I couldn't tell you about Little Ghost. Your father threatened—"

"No," he interrupted. "You don't need to apologize to me, Triian. I understand and you are completely forgiven. Now, do you feel strong enough to travel tonight?"

She nodded. "I think so."

"Good, there's a van outside waiting to take you to a private airstrip." He offered his arm to help her stand and she took it. "Tiras says he's bought some cake sprinkles for you, so you can feel at home when you get there."

She laughed. "That's my good grand-nephew."

* 12 *

8 Meha 3010
The next morning
Naradān (south west of Arām)
On the border between Arana and Rona

Ducking down into the small gap between two half-completed cars, Lilān swore a string of the most offensive Ronan obscenities she knew. Bullets dented and penetrated the car to her left, and a moment later more hit to her right. She was surrounded. After three years on the run from the Ronan Special Guard, the Rona-Abān and more recently the Aranan Agency, it was stupidly ironic that it was a kid and the pursuit of a loaf of maka bread that were going to be her downfall. So much for her plans to get to Arām and join the Psi Rebels—she'd barely even gotten over the border.

Lilān reloaded both of her weapons from clips in her pants pocket. The reverberating booms and metallic chinks of gunfire and ricochet tried to get at her through the metal on either side. She thanked all that was good in the world that she'd run into a factory that made proper metal cars, and not those mostly-plastic things from Basān, otherwise she'd be dead already.

She threw the spent clips behind her and put her weapons back in their holsters on her thighs. Shuffling towards the front of one car, she had to see how bad it was. North, over a blue car bonnet and towards the front of the factory building, four suited Aranan Agents had cover: two to her left, behind a yellow forklift, one next to the main exit, behind a large red shipping crate, and the fourth stood in a doorway to her far right.

Gunfire sounded and she ducked. There were at least four more in the south end of the factory that she'd seen on her way in. By now they'd probably found ample cover in amongst the machinery.

"Right," she said quietly to herself. It was time to play hard-ball.

Crouching close to the south-side vehicle, she gripped the bottom of it with both hands, added most of her kinetic strength, and lifted the entire car up onto its side.

Grabbing her last grenade from a jacket pocket, she pulled the pin and threw it south over the tipped car towards the back end of the factory. She ducked and covered her ears. The explosion rocked the foundations of the building, and came with a few satisfying cries of fear and pain, as well as a hail of metal and wood debris.

That'll sort 'em for a while, she thought with satisfaction.

With the south end clear for the moment, she turned north and drew both weapons. Firing with the accuracy Goid had taught her as a child, she hit the Agent in the doorway and he fell with a choked scream. She ducked for a moment and came up again. Pushing hard with her mind, she slid the yellow forklift away from two Agents and took them out before they could run away. The fourth, an older Aranan near the exit, seemed a little smarter than his companions and had slipped back behind the cover of the shipping crate. Unfortunately, the crate was a little too big for her to move kinetically, and she wasn't desperate enough yet to waste bullets on the hope that a lucky ricochet through the metal would get him.

She sighed and sat back, waiting for the next wave of Agents. It was only a matter of time before she'd be overrun, but if she was going down, she would bring as many of these tween-sized Aranan Agents with her in the process.

* * * * *

Taelin clambered up the fire escape ladder behind Nama. They were about three stories up and would be sitting ducks if the Agency saw them on the side of the old brick factory. But, it was the way Hawk had suggested, so they were doing it. They got to the top of the ladder and climbed onto a metal balcony. Taelin looked around him as they both caught their breath. The factory was high up enough on the hill overlooking Naradān city to see right across the towers of the central business district and, in the distance, a sliver of blue on the horizon.

Naradān was a quiet sprawling city built on one side of the massive river that formed the entire western border between Arana and Rona. The city had fared a lot better in the Hundred Year Depression than Arām by trading with the South-Ronan cities over the river. The trading was so successful and free-flowing that there were as many Ronan faces as Aranan in the crowds of the central city. It seemed like another world to Taelin who had never seen a Ronan up close before. They were very tall, averaging over two meters—at least a head taller than him. Some of the men were so broad across the chest they were two Aranan men wide. Taelin smiled at the city below them. They were like ebony giants, beautiful and fierce like their pioneering ancestors.

Nama patted him on the back and he turned to survey the window behind them. There didn't seem to be any immediate way in. With the unblemished white metal window frame sitting in crumbling brickwork, it would seem that the fire exit balcony was much older than the window.

So much for the safety of the workers in a fire, he thought cynically.

Taelin shrugged. "Maybe we need to just—"

The balcony vibrated as a fairly loud boom sounded from downstairs. Obviously, explosives were now a part of the battle below.

"Yep." Nama lifted the butt of his rifle and smashed the window.

Whoever used to work in the office beyond had left a mess of discarded papers in their panic to get out. Metal filing cabinets hugged all available walls with many of their drawers still open. Official documents lay crumpled in a chaotic storm around the only desk in the room. Behind it, another window overlooked the factory floor below.

They approached the second window and stared at the carnage below. Next to him, Nama whispered a curse of absolute surprise. One side of the factory floor below them was scattered with bodies and rubble from what must have been a grenade. By his count, there were at least fifteen bodies lying around two shot up vehicles—one car on its side. A Ronan figure sat crouched between the two with a number of discarded clips around them and their weapons aimed at the ceiling. They seemed ready for more.

Taelin blinked. "They almost don't need our help."

"They will soon." Nama patted him on the chest. "Come on."

The office sat above a steep stairwell, which dropped into near pitch blackness. For a moment as they descended, Taelin felt like he was floating down into an abyss, and then the sounds of gunfire led them back towards the light into a long corridor.

At the end of the hall an Agent lay dead in the doorway. The man was probably only barely out of high school—a young face stared blankly at the wall with his neck in shreds and body lying in a pool of blood.

Nama knelt over the young man to check his wounds. "Crack shot. Whoever they are, they're good."

The carnage on the main floor looked worse from ground level. Bodies and bits of flesh were strewn across the concrete, and the brick wall opposite them had chunks of shredded metal embedded in it. To their far left, machinery and the dead were blotted together in the twisted aftermath of an explosion. No one was coming in from that direction for a while. To their right was a flat concrete expanse with more dead bodies and massive crates of whatever the factory made, spread between the Ronan and an entrance to the building some twenty meters away. All was quiet for the moment.

"Tae, keep under cover. They don't know we're friendly yet."

He smirked back at Nama. "Of course."

A single shot fired and a bullet hole appeared in the wall right next to his ear.

"Hai da!" Surprised, Taelin ducked back.

Nama shuffled around him closer to the doorway. "We're Rebels, we've come to help you!"

"I'm not that stupid!" Bellowed a voice from outside.

"No, really. My name's Nama Ree, this is my friend Taelin. Hawk sent us to help you."

"Ha!" The Ronan fired at their doorway, embedding a few more bullets into the brick wall near their faces. "What would Hawk want with me?"

"How the Nuth should I know? Maybe he's in need of a one-person army?"

There was a snorted laugh. "Funny or not, you come in here, I'll shoot you."

Nama seemed to see something. Turning in the other direction, he stepped out of cover, lifted his rifle and fired three times towards the entrance of the building.

Taelin stretched to look in that direction and saw two Agent bodies on the concrete. Standing in front of him, Nama realized he was out of cover and his eyes widened over the barrel of his rifle. Taelin held his breath. There was a moment of silence but even though Nama was in plain sight of the Ronan, no gunshot sounded.

"Rebels, y'say?"

Nama lowered his rifle and turned around to face them. "Yep."

"Come on out, other person, I ain't gonna shoot ya."

Taelin stepped nervously in behind Nama.

The Ronan strode towards them with two large hand guns aimed, but Taelin sensed no immediate hostility. She wore dark pants and a t-shirt that was speckled with tiny purple flowers. Over top was a full-length trench coat that blew out behind her as she walked. She had two holsters strapped on the side of each thigh like Asha preferred, and she wore a dark backpack. Her thick black hair was brushed from her square face into a pony-tail. Strong and yet graceful, she walked with purpose. Taelin's mouth opened—she was beautiful.

She grinned. "You men got an escape route or do you intend on dying here with me?"

"Taelin," Nama elbowed him, and only then did he realize he was staring. "Go upstairs ahead of us, let me know what you see out that window."

Blushing as he closed his mouth, Tae turned back towards the stairwell. "Right."

"So, Mr. Rebel," her voice was tinged with an open friendliness. "You happen to have a grenade, on you?"

Nama laughed. "No, what for?"

"I prefer to exit with a bang and not a whimper. Ah well." Taelin climbed back up into the darkness, and her voice dimmed. "What was your cute friend's name again?"

* 13 *
In the mountains above Epa City
About the same time

"Daddy, if we were the princess in the tower, would Mommy be the prince who comes to rescue us?"

Bana glanced over the top of his book and lifted an eyebrow at his daughter. "No, my dearest. Mommy isn't coming back." He kept his voice gentle. "But we can be each other's prince. How does that sound?"

His ten year old daughter giggled at him from across the room. "You're funny, Daddy."

Long curling blond hair bounced around her face as Gusa laughed. For a moment she seemed just like a young Lii sitting there in the corner of the room: all mischief and joy, like an elfin princess caught in the body of a person.

Tears drifted into his eyes. *Oh, Lii, I miss you so much.*

Gusa; who was developing into a fairly high-rated empath even at the young age of ten, immediately sensed his sadness. She got to her feet and practically dive-bombed across the floor to give him a full-body hug.

He laughed and wrapped his arms around her slight form. "I'm alright, Gusa, I was just thinking about how much I miss Mommy."

Her blue eyes were sad and her bottom lip lifted. "I'm sorry for talking about her."

"No, it's OK." He smiled. "Talking about her helps us to keep her memory alive. Sometimes that memory hurts, but we need to feel it so we don't forget her." He kissed the top of her head and let go of her. "You stay here. I'm going to check the perimeter now, OK?"

"OK, Daddy." She shimmied off his lap and returned to her corner of the room, where she curled up again in the nest of blankets with her precious book of fairy tales.

The middle room beyond was dusty and cold. Broken windows let in not only the sunlight, but the autumn chill. Outside, a few stories below him was the dark slate of a church roof and the surrounding overgrown graveyard. Crumbling tombstones poked out of long grasses and from behind old twisted trees. The occasional carved weeping angel struggled with the greenery as if Mila, nature herself, had trapped them there forever.

Other than the ghosts of the past and the power of nature to swallow even death, there didn't seem to be any visual, telepathic or empathic sense of another presence nearby. Though, of course if a high ranking combat Agent was within immediate range, Bana wouldn't sense much of anything anyway. But it was the principal of the thing—he had to at least keep out the accidental threats.

He strode to the stairwell entrance. Jogging down into that spiraling pitch blackness always felt as if he was being swallowed whole by some great whale.

The murky vaulted church below the parsonage was broad and long—bigger than other small-town churches he'd seen before. The darkness of the broad room was cut into long dusty sections by colored light from many stained glass windows. The place smelt of dark stone dust and dry wood. Broken pews were scattered about as if a mob had left the place in a hurry and scrambled over everything in their efforts to get out. Tall wax-encapsulated candelabra lined the edges of the room; some of them still had half-melted candles in the tops of them. At the darkest end of the room, most of the altar decoration was gone, except for a lone silken cloth that lay crumpled on the floor in front of the ancient wooden pulpit.

The only way into the building was through the front doors and he kept them bolted and locked. Bana strode down the central aisle towards its gothic entrance and checked the doors. The bolts were still in place, as well as the long wooden bar over its center.

There was a secret exit behind the altar in the dark, but it was one way—a ladder led down to a tunnel that was carved into the bedrock and came out at a cottage a few kilometers down the hill. The trap-door was locked from the inside at both ends. Even a PK would have to know what the inside looked like to unlock both bolts, so it was fair to say that he wouldn't need to check the tunnel because it was almost certainly secure.

He swept around from the front doors to the far end of the church and another doorway, which led to a back room. There had once been a kitchen and storage room out in the back. But there must have been some kind of fire because the entire back wall was black with soot and only rubble and twisted metal remained of the kitchen. In amongst the debris was probably another door but no one was getting in or out that way any time soon.

He turned back the way he'd come, heading to the stairs and up to his daughter.

Stepping through into their room, he looked towards her corner. "Hey, honey, what do you think—"

She wasn't there. Her book was there and her blankets. He turned. Even their emergency bag was still next to the door. The only thing missing was his daughter and she would not move from her position without telling him.

Before his shock lifted, he grabbed her book from the floor, stuffed it into the emergency bag and pulled it onto his back. He took his secondary weapon from under his chair and turned, taking off the safety and loading the chamber.

He reached out tentatively with his mind. *"Gusa?"*

She wasn't in the three-room parsonage. She wasn't down in the church or even in the tunnel underground. Reaching further and further, she wasn't anywhere within a five km radius of him, or if she was, she had to be unconscious or dead. Probably the latter, he realized with a flare of grief. If someone was after him, it would be strategically sensible to take out the non-combatant first, and leave him upset and confused, thereby, also a better target for hunting.

His eyes narrowed. Well, whoever they were and no matter how good, they had a fight on their hands.

* 14 *

David watched Bana check the inner perimeter of the church. He was hidden in the shadows behind the altar, only visible if someone got in a good shot with a torch or was practically on top of him. Bana moved from the front door, back down the old stone church, around the rubble and broken pews, and passed right next to him to check the back room. When he got out of sight, David shuffled deeper into the shadows to put his back against the wall, so that, upon returning into the main church Bana wouldn't see his shadow from the different angle.

Stepping back into the church, Bana walked between the wall and the altar, within a hairs-breadth of David, but did not sense nor see him in the dimness. David held his breath and stilled any emotional reactions. If he felt remotely present in the moment, at such short range the sensitive empath would feel him and the situation would degrade to a shooting match very quickly. He had to take Bana by surprise and give him no option but to comply.

Bana made his way back to the stairs and out of sight. David waited for the static to flare in behind his shielding as the signal that it was Time to move. When it came—reverberating backwards and forwards in the relatively small mental space inside his shield—David got to his feet and followed Bana up the spiral staircase.

As he climbed, the light level dropped to almost pitch black for a few twists and he touched the stone wall with one hand to steady himself. When it returned, the light was like a bright sunrise at the top of the stairs.

He heard Bana off to his right. David lifted his weapon from out of his holster and approached the doorway. Bana had already discovered his daughter was gone. His body movements were quick and deliberate—not yet the grieving father and therefore, probably more dangerous.

David waited next to the other door. Footsteps came towards him and he lifted his weapon barrel into Bana's face as the man stepped through.

* * * * *

The tiny room they were using for a bedroom was dim but dry, and like the rest of the parsonage, it had wood floors and old dark-stone walls. Asha gently lowered the unconscious girl onto one of the two cots. Gusa would take a number of hours to wake from the sedative, but she would live. The girl looked so much like her mother it was almost creepy. Her blond hair framed an angular face, and Asha bet the girl had bright blue eyes as well. Asha knew that the likeness must pull on Bana's heart some days.

She felt a little guilty about drugging a ten year old girl, but if Gusa was anything like either of her parents she would have been difficult to subdue in any other way.

She lifted a couple of blankets around Gusa's shoulders and brushed a thread of blond from the girl's face. As Asha got to her feet again, she sensed the lightest touch of Bana searching for his daughter telepathically—that meant David would be close and needing back-up soon.

Sliding sideways along one stone wall towards the door, Asha kept herself physically silent and psychically invisible. The doorway came out right next to the stairwell and she glanced around the edge to see what was going on. She saw David lift his weapon as Bana walked into the barrel.

"Weapons." The growl that came from David was more in tune with his alter ego "Enigma".

A snippet of fear flickered through her. He was probably still in hunting mode, and with all that had happened over his son his control might have slipped. This would make him very dangerous.

Lifting her own weapon towards Bana, Asha stepped into sight towards the two men. "Please, Bana," she said quietly. "Hand over your weapons."

Bana's dark eyes widened. "You're with him? Of all the Rebels, you're the last I expected to be a spy."

"Weapons," growled David with Enigma's voice.

"No." Bana was oddly calm. "Where's my daughter?"

She sensed a rising rage from David and stepped forward. Dropping some of her empathic shielding, she let Bana sense the serious fear in her.

"Bana, please give me your weapons. David's a little cranky today, but I assure you he's not here to kill you, right David?"

The black eyebrows on Bana's face came together into a frown, but he seemed to sense that she didn't have any hostility towards him. He handed his weapon to her and she looked sideways at her old friend.

"David, can you put Enigma back in his box now, please?"

"Of course." David dropped his handgun, engaged the safety and put it away. The icy rage she had sensed eased somewhat as her friend slipped back into his own body language.

"Now isn't that better?" Asha let out a long sigh and put away her gun. "So, now that we're all disarmed, Bana, I'd like you to meet Hawk."

"What?" Confusion flared up and fell into disbelief on Bana's face. "There's no way—wait, where's my daughter?"

"She's in the other room, sedated."

Bana walked past both of them, fearless and without care for any threat from them. She and David followed. They both understood that Bana wouldn't listen or do anything for them until he knew that his daughter was OK. In the other room, he sat down on the floor next to Gusa's cot. For several silent minutes, he stroked her sleeping face. Asha watched impassively, knowing that he'd need a little time to absorb the new information.

Bana looked back at them over his shoulder. "Let's just say for the moment that I actually believe he is Hawk, which I don't, what do you want?"

"We're going to attack the Ao Council, and need your help to do it." The hostility of Enigma had completely disappeared from David's voice, leaving behind his normal calm and direct cadence.

"Attack the Council?" Bana snorted. "That's impossible."

"Actually, it's *quite* possible. The plan is to get a small-scale explosive device into the Chambers—I can do that myself. What's going to be almost impossible is *getting* the explosives."

"By the Old Gods, you're actually serious." Laughing slightly, Bana got to his feet. "He really is Hawk?"

She smiled at him. "Unfortunately, so."

"You know," Bana turned to address David. "You being Hawk is even more frightening than you being Enigma." Bana sighed and wiped his face with one hand. "But, before we go any further with this, I need to know how you intend on making sure Gusa is safe."

"She'll be safe with my daughter and the other Rebel children. We'll be evacuating them out of Arām fairly soon. They won't even be near the explosion or the aftermath."

"OK." He seemed to be taking it all fairly well. "So, where exactly is this impossible explosive?"

"Kamo," David took breath. "We are going to try and get the Rona-Abān to trade with us for it."

Bana snorted. "Even if we could find them, they're violent terrorists who kill indiscriminately. They'll shoot us on sight before any offer can be made."

"Exactly," there was the edge of a smile in David's voice. "It seems impossible. Are you interested?"

* 15 *
That evening
(8 Meha 3010)

David leaned forward over the Rose Road kitchen table with a lit match and touched the flame to the wick of one white candle. "For Sarah." He lit the second candle. "For Wolf."

He had a son. Tears came into his eyes and the minutest of smiles lifted into his face. He'd lit candles every year on the eighth for ten years and he never thought he'd celebrate the date of her death with anything resembling joy. "Happy birthday, son."

There was a knock at the door. Outside, Asha's mind was open and he sensed that she knew exactly what day it was.

One corner of his mouth lifted. *"Come in, Asha."*

He looked over the candle flames as she stepped inside and closed the door behind her. She seemed tense and perhaps a little uncomfortable, but he'd asked for her to come so she had come.

"You alright?" she asked cautiously.

"Yeah." He shrugged. "It's the eighth. Hey, I'm sorry for scaring you earlier."

She smiled and walked towards the other chair in front of him. "That's OK, I think it helped keep Bana in line, anyway."

He nodded and watched the dancing flames of the prayer candles. He wouldn't ever tell her it was part of the plan. She disliked it when he manipulated her, even for the greater good. So he would let her believe that his control had slipped.

"I can go if you want to be alone."

He glanced up at her and saw that she was uncomfortable again. He kept his voice gentle. "No. Despite the date there are things that need organizing. Besides, I wouldn't mind the company right now." He let the silence permeate them for a moment before taking a deep breath. "I need you to lead this mission in Rona. I think Heth has my scent after Triian's escape, if I leave now I won't be able to run interference."

"Of course." She leaned her elbows on the table and looked at him through the flames. "You really want to let Xak go to Rona with us?"

He smiled. "Five years of training and being a combatant Rebel, and you still don't think he can do it?"

"No, he can do it." She shook her head. "But this is the RA and he's just a boy."

"He's nearly twenty, now, Asha."

"Yes, but he doesn't understand that just because we're right doesn't mean we'll win."

He sighed. "Without him we won't get the explosives."

"Even if he dies getting them? Even if all of us die getting them?"

He shook his head. "This is bigger than you can possibly imagine, Asha. I'm very fond of Xak, you know that, but his life is no more important than all the others who have died in this conflict, nor all of those lives we'll save with the explosives. It's a—"

"A matter of numbers, I know. I've heard this speech before, David. But I still can't understand how you can be so cold."

David stood abruptly and turning his back on her, he paced away from the table. He spoke over his shoulder. "It's not coldness. I do what is necessary, that is all."

"Even if it means killing nearly as many as you save?" she barked.

He turned around and glared at her. "Even if it means everyone I care about dies. If you only knew the scale of this, Asha—"

"Well, then show me, David!" She got to her feet. "Show me! Because I need to know what we're fighting for if I'm going to lead them into Rona and their almost certain deaths just so you can kill your so'then father!"

That fire that he loved about her blazed in her eyes, and he knew that he'd have to show her something or lose her.

"Sit down, Asha." His voice came out as a whisper and he moved back to his own chair. They sat with the table and his prayer candles between them. "Give me your hand." He opened his mind to her and they slipped into the mindscape behind his buried mental shield.

Fresh air brushed across his face and he could smell the long summer grasses around him before he opened his mental eyes. In front of him a breeze danced in Asha's long black hair and flashes of summer sunlight brought out the small flecks of red and blue in her curly threads. Eyes, which were often so dark they were cobalt blue, shimmered like velvet blue pearls in the light.

The valley around them was wide and framed on all sides with tall mountains that symbolized the mental shield.

"What now?" she said looking around her. She wore a long blue dress made of something light and airy that shimmered in the breeze.

He smiled at his beautiful friend. "Look up."

Above them, there was a black rip in the vivid sky blue. It was jagged like a scar from a knife fight. It had been there in his mind since Sarah's death. It was the source of everything Time Psi-related. An icy wind blew through the gash, bringing with it threads and curls of black static.

The gash snapped open to swallow them in an ocean of tingling space. He heard Asha take a shocked in-breath, and then he felt a presence step in behind him, hidden from Asha's senses. The Founder, the source of his faith and determination, stood with him as he had since Sarah's death. He was an unseen figure made up almost entirely of black static energy. A broad hand rested on David's shoulder and he let his control of the situation be handed over to the Founder—he would know best how much she could see of the future.

He felt the Founder's voice speak through him. "This is bigger than the Rebels, Asha. If we don't do what must be done, this is what will happen."

The static cleared and they found themselves hovering in a low orbit around Planet Shadow. It was a beautiful blue and green planet, with shimmering clouds and vast oceans, humming and teeming with life. Directly under them, was the great mega-continent of the Five Nations. On the far south-eastern coast sat Arana, with the broad hook of Arām's massive port directly under their feet as they hovered in the silence of space.

Below them a pulse flowed through Arana like a drop of water hitting a still lake. Ripples of black and red spread across the country, annihilating everything green and blue in its path.

Asha, floating beside him, let out a cry of absolute horror.

Other ripples met the first bringing together more areas of black and red, as fires ripped through the entire planet, burning away the green and blue, and replacing it with black. When the fires were gone, the planet Shadow was gray and rusted orange. Without water, without life. The entire planet was dead.

David felt Asha let go of his physical hand and he opened his eyes. She was on her feet and pacing the length of his kitchen.

"The whole planet." Her voice broke. She stopped pacing and leaned over the table. There were tears in her eyes as she stared down at him. "The *whole* planet?"

"Yes."

"The whole planet!" she bellowed. "Every time you said the scale of this was bigger than I could imagine, I thought you were talking out of your ass!" She wiped her face with one hand. "I thought you were just being a pretentious a'kenān."

He smiled. "Unfortunately not."

"By the Old Gods... this is..." She dropped back down into her chair again and looked at him over the candle flames. "How can we..."

The shock had lifted and her tanned face was starting to go pale. He got to his feet and, grabbing a glass from under the sink, he filled it with tap water and put it on the table in front of her.

"How..." her voice broke and she cleared her throat. "What causes it?"

He let his voice become very gentle. "It's better that you don't know, Asha. But I promise you we can stop it, and one part of stopping it is taking out the current Ao Council."

"This is massive." She shook her head. "I can't get my mind around it."

He put his hand on her shoulder in the hopes of lending her some of his calm. "You can handle this, Asha. You are the strongest person I know. But, now that you know the scale of this, you also know why we have to go to Rona, no matter the cost."

"I do." She swallowed. "I wish I didn't though."

One corner of his mouth lifted. "That's exactly why I haven't shown you before now."

She seemed to gain control of her emotions again and looked up at him. "OK, well... we'll need a few weeks prep time for this mission, and some gear. Is there anything I need to know before you go back to the Tower tomorrow?"

He shook his head. "No, I don't have much information, I only know that if you're to succeed Bana and Xak must be on the frontline." He smiled, giving her as much affection as he could muster for her to sense empathically. "Do you feel like some ice-cream? I think there's some left in the freezer."

She snorted. "Ice-cream solves everything, right?"

Chuckling, he made his way to the little refrigerator. "Yes, ice-cream and coffee."

* 16 *
Five weeks later
17 Pala 3010

David stood in the Cathedral bell-tower, leaning over the stone wall as he looked northwards out across the city. To his right the sun was starting to rise, flaring a miasma of rainbow colors into the dense air, and slowly pushing back the colorful clouds of the nearby nebula from the sky. The city was fairly quiet so early in the morning, but he liked it. The silent peace of it eased the raging agony inside of him.

On the western horizon sat the bright point of light, which was their nearest star, Elata. The name meant "hope" and "light" in one of the old languages. One day, he would visit that star. For some reason, it had called to him since he was a small boy. All year round, it was the brightest star in the Aranan sky and the easiest astronomical body to identify in amongst the billions of stars and vast colored clouds over which their solar system hovered.

He sighed and brushed his face with one hand. He should be going to Rona with the others. He should have gone to rescue his son from the desert the moment he was sent there. He should have killed his father years ago, if only for his own personal vengeance for the continued cruelty, but also because of how much better the Agency would be without Jaran Cowdy senior in it. But the knowledge of seeing the future changed everything. If he lost control, even for an instant it could spell disaster for everyone. That cost was too high for him to be so selfish and simply do what he wanted. But still, some days it was hard to moderate his actions.

He hoped the others would be alright. Asha's group was already in the Ronān city of Kamo. They had to get the explosives from the Rona-Abān, but there was a good chance that some or all of them would die getting these explosives. Knowing that cut at his heart, but if they failed to get them, there would be no stopping the Threat from destroying everything.

It was a month away from his ten year anniversary of becoming Hawk. This was neither a thing to celebrate nor commiserate over. The ten year anniversary was what it was, but the time had gone fast. Five more years and it would all start in earnest. He still had so much to do, but he'd get it done—he couldn't not.

He sighed and let his thoughts drift back to Asha and the others. Because he wasn't involved, he couldn't see much of what would happen in Rona. He had only a vague sense that it wasn't good. If everyone did their job they'd get the explosives, but at what cost? He couldn't even guess. He took one last look at the fading night sky, and turned to the trap door that led back inside.

It was time he got back to the Tower to continue wrestling with Heth's suspicions. Heth was a good man, but when the time came, he'd probably have to escape the Agency or die with David's father in the explosion because he was too good at his job. The identity of Hawk had to stay unknown for a further five years, and left to his own devices Heth would no doubt figure it out.

* 17 *

City of Kamo, Rona
Later that morning

Asha watched out of the window through the detached rifle scope.

The hotel room they had rented was themed in a yellow and gold palette. The double bed that sat against the wall behind her had a threadbare bedspread with a gold mosaic pattern. The walls were papered with lines of white-gold flowers and vertical stripes, and the faded yellow carpet was littered with stains of every perceivable variety. Even the curtains that framed the floor-to-ceiling windows were buttercup yellow. She liked yellow, as a color, but not that much.

It was a cheap and fairly nasty hotel. But it was oddly luxurious to be somewhere that was warm, dry, mostly clean, and had actual furniture. Asha smirked. A "one-star" hotel was a luxury for her—that was amusing.

However, the target of her attention wasn't the scummy room, but the ancient manor house standing across the road from it. The house, with its beautiful cream stone walls was probably several hundred years old, and had, until recently survived the barrage of time quite well. Unfortunately, its entire third level had crumbled in on itself, and the outside of the east wing was almost completely black from soot. Despite the relatively recent fire damage, Asha thought the old building still had much of its historical pride left as it stood tall and ancient over its contemporary neighbors.

Behind her, Lilān came in from the bathroom and Asha glanced over her shoulder at their new Ronan recruit.

"You sure they're in there, Lilān? Why would they come back here?"

"Yep, I'm sure." The broad-shouldered woman grinned at her. "It was Mena and Goid's family estate. Trust me, if Mena is still alive they're in there. Are *you* sure about the boy? They're gonna kill him the moment they see him."

Asha snorted. "They're certainly going to try."

They'd been lucky that a hotel had been built so close to the target residence, at least she and Lilān had somewhere comfortable to keep an eye out on proceedings. The others had no such luck by being in an abandoned house next door and a park on the other side of the property.

With Lilān ready, she spoke into the radio.

~ "Sound off."

~ "One Two." Nama replied.

~ "Three Four." Taelin's voice was clipped and tense. She hoped she hadn't been selfish bringing her brother on this mission.

Bana and Xak had their own radio ear pieces, so upon hearing their sound off, they would know that everyone was ready and they could approach the house. She shuffled down into a more comfortable position on her belly and re-attached the scope to the rifle. Behind her, Lilān grabbed the binoculars off the bed.

"Here we go. May Lady Krena smile on us today."

* * * * *

Mena's old family library was dusty and half of the books were so water-damaged from the fire that there was little use in even trying to read them. Their family had collected those books for ten generations and it was all destroyed by the Ronan Special Guard in one night of merciless killing.

"What are we going to do?" Mena paced past his little brother, Goid, who sat slumped in a lawn chair watching him.

"Nothing. We've lost, Mena."

"No!" He turned and pointed at his brother's dark angular face. "Not as long as I breathe!"

"Brother." Goid's black eyes were sad. "There's only a small number of us left, there's no money for another year, and only enough explosives for one more bombing. What more can we do?"

"Parliament House!" Mena snarled. "The Aranan Embassy! Half of this so'then city if we processed and rationed it well enough!" He was yelling and only when he heard his own voice echoing off the high stone ceiling did he realize. He cleared his throat. "They destroyed our family and they will pay for this humiliation. Look at this house, Goid. Don't you remember what it used to look like? How many died in that fire? The history they've destroyed?"

"I was five." His little brother sounded bitter. "Of course I don't."

"The Rona-Abān was created to right that wrong, and the other wrongs that the Guard has committed. The Malan Family, *our family*, has protected this city for over five hundred years, so, it's our responsibility to keep fighting. You may not understand that but I will not give up until our victory—or my very last breath."

"Mena!" someone called from down the hall. "You better see this!"

Walking back past Goid, Mena strode out of the library and down towards the front parlor of their family manor. Above him, white marble stairs spiraled up to the left and right of the main door and for a moment he saw it as it used to be: a house filled with elegant antique furniture and a history as old as the city itself. He heard the sounds of his other siblings laughing upstairs in the old play room. The scent of cigar smoke came to him from the den where his father and uncles would talk business all day, and he heard the echoes of their mother playing complicated concertos on their grand piano in the main sitting room. He saw in his mind's eye, the servants flitting about in formal uniforms keeping the house running at peak efficiency. He smiled at the memories, and sighed. It was all gone now.

Brushing off the painful ghosts of his past, Mena stepped through the doorway of their old den. A part of him wished that his father and uncles would be sitting there smoking and talking business. Instead, the den walls were black, the air permanently filled with the scent of smoke and mildew. High velvet curtains that were ripped, melted and burned, hung ineffectively over the dusty glass. Ayren, the youngest of their group stood behind a thatch of intact curtain and stared out at the front yard.

"What is it?" barked Mena.

"Trespasser." The thirty-year old turned a rounded face to him and his dark eyes looked tense. "What do you want me to do?"

Through the window, Mena saw a young Aranan man wearing gray clothes. He was in his late teens, perhaps early twenties, with black and red streaked hair.

Mena lifted an eyebrow at Ayren. "What do we usually do with trespassers?"

Ayren smirked. "Yes, Sir."

* 18 *

Being careful to hide his psychic presence, Bana followed Xak down the driveway at a safe distance. They wanted the Rona-Abān to see Xak, but not the larger man with the assault rifle following him.

Bana stuck close to a fairly high and overgrown hedge that lined the long graveled driveway on one side. Ahead of him by about ten meters, the boy confidently strode down the middle of the drive. Bana only sensed a snippet of tension in the young man—the boy had learned how to mask his fear well. He'd seen some of what Xak could do, but he still wasn't sure if he was ready for this kind of combat.

They neared the metal gates leading to the house and Bana stopped behind a pillar of stone to watch. Xak, with his long black and red hair cut at odd angles around his face, should have already been spotted by any inhabitants. The young man pulled open one gate and stepped into the cobbled area in front of the manor house.

The house must have once belonged to a fairly well-to-do family. But, like many when the Ronan Government enacted a law stating that Psi were a threat to national security, the Special Guard must have locked the family in their own house and lit it on fire.

Bana understood why the Rona-Abān existed. He even understood why they bombed government facilities. What he couldn't understand was that in the last three years since a traitor in their midst nearly wiped them out, why they continually targeted schools and other civilian places. Targeting non-combatants was no way to win a war and, certainly, no way to make a point about justice. They'd changed from freedom fighters like the Rebels, to terrorists focused solely on revenge. This made them unpredictable and dangerous, which made *him* very nervous.

Watching the boy, Bana hoped again that Xak had the stones for this. The young man walked to a point in the cobbled entrance, halfway between the gates and the front doors.

With his shoulder to the cream-colored stone, Bana lifted his weapon in the direction of the house.

It couldn't have been more than a minute that the boy waited before muffled gunshots fired from out of the manor house. Xak dodged expertly out of the way as bullets ricocheted off the cobbles around him. A full three minutes went by as someone (or many someones), fired at Xak and the boy dodged, unhurt, out of the way. He looked a little like he was tap-dancing across the courtyard for their entertainment and not for his own survival.

The gunfire stopped and soon after, the front door opened. Two tall Ronan men wearing jeans and dark long-sleeved shirts, stepped out with their handguns aimed at Xak. Bana moved into sight so that they knew Xak wasn't alone. The two men flinched, but did not fire.

"This is private property. What do you want?" barked the elder of the two Ronan.

"My name is Xak," the young man said confidently. "This is Bana. We'd like to talk about the possibility of the Psi Rebels trading with the Rona-Abān."

"What makes you think you have anything we want?"

Bana stepped forward. "We can get you the one who betrayed you."

The elder of the two men snorted. "You can bring the traitor back here to Kamo?"

"No, that would be too complicated. But we *can* give you the transport and the means to go to Arām and kill him yourself."

The man lifted an eyebrow at him. "What do you want in return?"

"Explosives."

The man smirked. "Aside from Kid Dodgy here, what's to stop us from just killing you here and now?"

A rifle shot fired from the neighboring house where Nama was hidden, and a bullet pinged off the stone at their feet.

Bana was unable to suppress his smirk. "We're not complete amateurs."

The two men looked at each other and he sensed a thread of telepathic conversation between them.

The elder spoke. "Come back at dusk, with an offering of weapons and ammo for us, and we might negotiate." He turned his back on them. "Now, get off my property."

* * * * *

Mena walked away from the Aranan men, and Goid followed. He deliberately turned his backs to them, without fear or pause, to show them he was not intimidated by their ridiculous approach. Mena let his brother step inside first, before entering their old parlor and closing the door behind them.

"Ayren!" he bellowed.

The young man's long dark face peeked out through the den doorway. "Yeah?"

Mena pointed behind him with a thumb. "Follow those fools home."

"Yes, Sir."

He and Goid made their way under the left-hand grand staircase and returned to their library.

His brother looked back at him over one shoulder. "What do you think they really want?"

"I don't know," Mena sighed and brushed at his short black hair with one hand. "But we'll see how bad they want it tonight." He sat down on a plastic lawn chair in the middle of their wrecked library. A frown drifted into his face. "But their offer might give us the opportunity to kill two birds with one stone."

"What do you mean?" His brother handed him a beer bottle from the ice chest between them and sat down.

"That Aranan preta."

"The one who wants to buy the Bank?" Goid took a swig from his beer—he'd been drinking a lot lately.

"Yeah." Mena's jaw tightened for a moment. *Egotistical a'kenān, won't get the last of my family legacy.* "When Ayren comes back, send Jo out to find him."

"Of course. Only one problem," his brother took a mouthful of beer and glanced sideways at him with black eyes. "We can't afford to give these Rebels any of our explosives."

Mena laughed. "Ha! We don't have to, we only need to play along until we get what we want. They're just cocky fools playing with guns."

"I guess." His brother shrugged. "That other guy seemed to know his way around his assault rifle."

"Perhaps. It just means when the time comes, we kill him first."

* 19 *

Taelin stood in what had probably once been a grand private library. Books sat in rows from the white marble floor to the vaulted ceiling on every available wall. Wooden bookshelf edges were carved with swirling cloth and little painted figurines dancing across the in-between spaces. Mildew peppered the faded book covers with green spots and sections of the cream stone ceiling were marred with tongues of black from long dead flames.

Despite his fear and awareness of how dangerous these people were, Taelin felt a flicker of sympathy for the family that must have died in the house.

"Do not feel pity for us, boy." The eldest Ronan, whose short black hair was gray above his ears, stared intently at him from across the room.

Taelin sensed something indescribably dangerous about the old man. He swallowed and tightened his grip on the weapon at his waist.

Lilān and Asha had to stay behind at the hotel, leaving the four men to show a unified Rebel presence in the Rona-Abān manor.

All of Taelin's instincts told him to get out of there as soon as possible. He hoped the RA would trade, so this business could just be finished with and they could go home again.

There were four lawn chairs in the middle of the room, two on their side and two on the other, facing the first pair.

The eldest Ronan, who made Tae's skin crawl, sat down. Another man, with a similarly square face and body, but at least ten years younger, sat in the second chair. The elder Ronan indicated with one broad hand that someone should sit on the remaining two chairs.

Bana came around the front, and then, clearing his throat tensely, Nama took the last chair. Next to Taelin, Xak shuffled closer. Empathically the young man seemed tense, but otherwise calm. However, Taelin knew the boy's body language well enough after six years to know that he might be able to block his emotions empathically, but he was still really rather afraid. Taelin understood completely.

"This is my brother Goid. I am Mena." said the elder Ronan.

"Weren't you supposed to bring weapons with you to start the trade?" Goid was oddly relaxed, as if he was half drunk at a party and not in the middle of tense negotiations.

"We only have two spare autos right now," said Bana firmly.

That was his cue and Taelin lifted the spare auto off his back. Xak did the same and together they put them on the ground between the two sets of chairs.

Bana continued. "However, once we have an idea of how much you require, we can arrange for more to be brought across the border within a few days."

"Fine." Mena seemed emotionally neutral. "Would you tell us about these arrangements for us to get our traitor?"

"The Rebels recently acquired a private jet," Bana matched tone with the elder Ronan. "So we can fly across the border without any official problems. Once in the country, we have accommodation and transport, and we're acquiring the information on where your traitor is within the Agency as we speak. Once in Arana, you'll have the information to be able to find him. After you've killed him, we can transport you back to Kamo. I'm sure, if you add this to the offer of more weapons and ammo, you can appreciate how much of a good deal this is simply for us to acquire some explosives?"

"A good deal indeed." Mena grinned. "How much do you need, and what kind?"

The man seemed suddenly pleased with the deal, but Tae still sensed the constant thread of danger underlying it all.

Bana didn't seem to notice the danger and smiled. "Small. Tactical. With an approximate kill radius of ten meters."

Amusement flickered around the old man. "That's a very specific kind of explosive, but we just happen to have some. How soon can you get some of us to Arana?"

Bana shrugged. "Just after lunchtime tomorrow?"

Mena got to his feet and offered Bana a hand to shake. "I believe we have the beginnings of a deal."

"Excellent." Bana stood and took the older man's hand.

"Goid has a list of the weapons we want. It's a fairly modest list, considering our numbers. I'd only ask that if we have people under your care in Arana, that we should have the same number here under our care."

Bana bowed his head formally. "I will discuss this with my superiors and get back to you in the morning."

"Good. Before you go, would you like some food? Perhaps a beer?" Mena seemed too friendly all of a sudden.

Bana shook his head. "No, thank you, Mena. We really should get back to organize your weapons." Bana bowed formally a second time. "Mena, Goid, thank you for your hospitality."

They left the house quickly—but not so fast that it looked like they were retreating. The graveled driveway

seemed ridiculously long to Taelin, and he had to fight
his instinct to just break out into a run.

The road beyond was quiet but dim. None of the
street lights in the area were working. As they crossed
the road, Taelin noticed an odd-looking Ronan woman
staring at them. She was dressed as if she was going
out or "street walking", in a short skirt and low top,
with long colored stockings, but her hair was a mess
and she wore a pair of old running shoes instead of
heels. She held a cigarette between two long coal-
colored fingers, but did not take a puff from it. There
was something alien about her, icy and oddly terrifying.
Warning bells went off in the back of Taelin's head and
a sense of immediate danger shot through him.

He telepathically tapped on the other men's minds.
*"I think we're being watched, lady on the corner.
Something dangerous."*

"Right," said Bana's deep, red mental voice. *"Taelin,
you and Nama go right at the next intersection, tell
your sister to get out. Xak and I will go straight. If she
follows you, lose her before you return to the fall-back
location near the jet."*

"Yes, Sir," he replied without thinking. Bana wasn't
the leader of this mission, but in the absence of Asha
the man's confidence almost demanded that he
became that leader.

* 20 *

There were no street lamps in the area where Xak
and Bana walked, so it was dark. Abandoned buildings
towered over them and there seemed to be no one else
around. Xak forced himself not to look back at the
strange old woman who followed them down the street.
He didn't want to get creeped out or submit to his
instinct to run, but she followed with an intensity that
unsettled him like nothing else.

"What are we going to do? We can't lose her." Xak
wasn't much of a telepath, he was told he was barely a
2, but it was enough to be able to communicate with
Bana or any other telepath in range.

"I'm not sure." Rumbled Bana's deep voice in his
head.

"*You're not sure?*" Xak baulked. "*Aren't you supposed to be ex-Ao? Can't you fly a helicopter and take out people in the blink of an eye like some action hero?*"

Next to him, Bana chuckled out loud. "*Movies aren't real life kid, you should know that. But, no, it's not a lacking in skill but information. I can't sense what she's thinking or feeling, but she doesn't seem to have any psychic shielding. It's like she doesn't exist. I've never come across anything like this before. She could just be a madwoman, but she could also be a highly trained assassin. I prefer to know what we're facing before we escalate this to combat.*"

Xak snorted. "*What do you suggest? Turning around and talking to her?*"

"*Actually, yes.*" Bana stopped walking.

"*Oh, great!*" Sighing, Xak turned around as well.

The woman walked towards them at the same pace as she had been for the last half-hour. She was an odd collection of things. Her hair was pure white and dark face wrinkled as if she was very old. But the bright colored clothes she wore were young, more than that, it was as if someone had put an old woman's head on a young woman's body—it was creepy.

As she neared them, Xak looked into her dark eyes. All he saw inside was static. It flowed out of her and towards him like a tsunami of icy water. The wave of black static hit him and he flinched back, stumbling from the force of it. He heard a terrible rushing in his ears.

Bana seemed to grab him and something snapped in his head. The world stopped flowing and rushing, and an old woman stood in front of them.

Xak blinked up at the considerably taller figure. A thin, heavily lined Ronan face stared back down at him. Her black eyes seemed hollow, but then she smiled, filling that empty chasm in her eyes with a caramel flame. The static pulsed gently around her.

Strange or not, Xak sensed at that moment that she meant them no harm. Relaxing, he smiled awkwardly back at her.

"Um, hi?"

"Whirly man and fire dancer must listen to Old Ana," she said in a lilting, childlike voice. "Leave little lamb to the wolves. Protect each other, or die yourselves." She nodded as if to accent a wholly logical point she was making. "Or die yourselves."

She walked past them and Xak watched the woman shuffle back into the night-time shadows. He stared after her, his mouth slightly open in his surprise. There was silence between he and Bana for a good minute.

A broad hand touched Xak's back. "What... was that all about?"

"I don't know." He shrugged. "She was a Time Psi though. Really powerful."

"But mad, right?" Bana smirked. "Mad as a meat axe?"

Xak laughed, releasing the odd tension in him. "Probably."

* * * * *

It was pitch black and freezing cold by the time he and Bana got back to the old cottage. It was surrounded in overgrown brush and in an abandoned part of town, but not even five minutes walk to the private airstrip where the Rebel-controlled jet sat refueling in a hanger. The cottage itself was relatively intact, although, from the outside it looked about ready to crumble away into a broken pile of flat slate rocks at any moment.

It seemed oddly welcoming to Xak as they walked up the steps and across the balcony. He opened the front door and much warmer air brushed his face like a welcome hug. Inside, light flickered from a fire on the right side of the room, illuminating the small space with a comforting glow.

Nama and Taelin sat to his left on one of the hand-made bunk beds and Asha was crouched down tending to the fire in the old hearth. Lilān sat at a table in the middle of the room, facing the door. One of her massive handguns sat at her place setting, barrel also facing the door, as if she were guarding the house. She looked up at them with those big black eyes of hers and

Xak tried not to show his discomfort under her powerful gaze.

Asha stood. "What happened?"

"Crazy woman; harmless," answered Bana as he closed the door and walked around Xak. The older man picked up a loaf of maka from the table, ripped off a chunk of it and threw it behind him to Xak.

He caught it and took a bite—he was ravenous. "Yeah, Time Psi lady," he said with food in his mouth. "If she's still remotely sane we might be facing trouble with the RA."

"We already know that trouble's coming." Bana leaned over a chair.

"Yes," agreed Asha. "It was too easy. Trade negotiations don't even go that smooth between Rebel cells."

Xak pulled a rough wooden chair out from the table and sat down. "So, what should we do?"

"What do you think, Lilān?" Asha glanced sideways. "You're the expert with the RA, what *should* we do?"

Lilān grabbed the remaining loaf from Bana. "Mena will kill every last one of us when he gets what he wants. He may even kill us before then if he finds out I'm the one helpin' ya."

"What kind of ex-family are they, then?" Xak gasped.

She shrugged. "Mena is a zealot, to him a deserter is just as bad as a traitor. Personally, I'd vote to get the Nūthen out of here. But, if you want to keep on, I'd suggest being careful and smart."

"Well," Nama stood up and approached the table, leaning on the back of an empty chair. "Do you have any ideas on how to do that?"

"Yes," she said, biting into the food. "It's just like a game of Strategy, except the Lord piece is the explosives you want and their Lady piece is Mena. It's all about being smarter than they are, and Mena is very smart. But he does have weaknesses we can use. For example, he will not move if his little brother Goid is under threat."

* 21 *

Approximately 9am,
The next day

Goid sighed and crossed his arms over his chest. The intersection in front of the Malan family bank was crowded with people. A set of marble steps guided clients to the broad entrance, and great white columns lifted the roof far above everyone's heads. It was the oldest bank in Kamo (probably one of the oldest in all of Rona), and had been in their family for many generations.

Most people thought rather highly of the building, but Goid disliked it. It always seemed to him to be such a pretentious establishment, with pretentious employees who were always looking down their noses at people, simply because they had the money and everyone else didn't.

Goid stood on the street opposite the old bank, the others of the task group were situated at various points around the intersection, waiting. The target was an Aranan businessman. He was a mid-level manager for the Mega-Corp-Conglomerate, which was the most powerful corporation in the Five Nations. In Goid's not to so humble opinion, the MCC were even more pretentious than his family bank.

At the top of the stairs, their target walked out of one large door. The man was young, perhaps only barely in his twenties. He wore an expensive gray suit and blue striped tie. He was one of the lucky ones to be born a Norm. Without any Psi or Talent abilities, he was free to live the life he wanted. Walking next to the Suit was a little girl, perhaps four or five years old. She was tiny, about the size of a Ronan toddler. A flare of wavy dark red hair covered her little head and shoulders like cotton wool.

Goid frowned. He hadn't known the Suit had a child with him. He watched the Aranan take his daughter's hand as they started to cross the road. The girl reminded Goid of his own children—all killed by the Guard.

He sighed. Unfortunately, from Mena's point of view, taking the child as well as her father would be a strategic advantage. Goid knew, however, what that would mean for the life of that little girl.

He felt a stab of guilty dread. Reaching into his long woolen jacket, he took a quick swig from his hipflask. A trail of liquid cut its way through his mouth and down to his stomach, burning away the guilt and dread. He put the flask back into the jacket and signaled with one waved hand for the others to get into position.

The intersection was very wide and crowded with people. It wasn't too hard for his group to dodge around pedestrians and surround the lone Aranan man and his child. When the others were in position around him, Goid stepped in close behind. He lifted his weapon and touched the back of the man's suit jacket with the barrel. The young man seemed like the kind of person who had probably never even seen a gun before, but he still stiffened at the touch of it and stopped walking.

Without saying a word, Goid took his elbow and guided him towards a waiting taxi—one of those still loyal to the RA.

* * * * *

Mena stared down at the unconscious Aranan man, who lay on the floor of their old servant quarters. He had an oddly content expression on his young white face and looked a little like a boy in his father's disheveled suit—perhaps a boy pretending to be a businessman.

Hate seethed in Mena and his eyes narrowed. This boy didn't even deserve to be in their servant's quarters. He was worse than these Rebels, he was a Norm; only one step away from being Guard. He was practically a dog and his little whelp too. Mena wondered how the dog could sleep at such a time and brushed his mind with a telepathic hand. Inside a simple, innocent mind were mental blocks and checks, carefully constructed to keep him asleep until the right mental trigger would wake him. Goid must have forced the dog to sleep.

Mena sensed his little brother walking towards him down the hall, and turned around. "Why did you knock him out?"

There was alcohol on Goid's breath as he approached him. "Blubbing like a baby. Wouldn't shut up. Thought if he was bruised he'd draw too much attention in Arana, so I did the next best thing."

Mena nodded. "Smart. And the brat?"

"Play room with Jo. Gave her some of Rena's old toys—happy as a lark."

"Good. Those Rebels will be here soon, make sure everything's ready."

His brother looked a little uncertain. "You sure we should let them so close to the explosives? We could use a decoy?"

"No." Mena shook his head. "They might be smarter than they look. A decoy could be dangerous."

"But—"

"Just do as I say!" Mena barked.

He closed his mouth and sighed. "Yes, Sir."

Mena watched his little brother walk back the way he'd come. As he went, Goid pulled out their father's old silver hipflask from a jacket pocket, and took a quick gulp of its contents.

Mena narrowed his eyes. Since Goid's last child was killed by the Guard, he'd started to drink far too much and have bouts of uncontrolled violent behavior with his kinetic ability. It could serve as a dangerous distraction.

"Goid, give me the flask."

His brother turned around, frowning at him. "It's just a little whiskey, can't a guy—"

"No." Mena said firmly. "You're drinking too much and it's getting dangerous. Give me the flask and stay sober from now on. I'll give it back to you when you return."

His brother sighed again and took it out of his back pocket. Mena grabbed the flask. As his hand brushed Goid's, he sensed frustration and humiliation. Mena didn't pull rank with him often any more because it was insulting to Goid's self-respect. However, RA business-sense had to come first over their personal issues. Sober, Goid was much better able to handle himself. He'd need his wits to keep the dog in check, while also watching for betrayal from the Rebels. He would also need to kill the traitor if the dog couldn't do it for them.

Besides, by Mena's logic, he could always apologize later when Goid returned, but if Goid was killed because he was drunk, any apology would be useless.

* 22 *

Nama slowed the car to a stop at a vast eight-lane intersection. He sighed. He didn't like this. Not one bit. Everyone knew the story of the RA. How three years ago, a traitor in their midst made a deal with the Agency and his government for immunity, and nearly wiped out the RA. After that, they started attacking not only government buildings but schools. The Rona-Abān became killers of children.

He didn't understand why they couldn't just get these explosives in some other way. He honestly would have rather tried to attack the Armed Forces than the Rona-Abān, despite the risks. At least the Armed Forces had honor and rules of engagement. Not so with the RA.

The lights changed and he shifted the massive car into first gear.

Kamo was a huge city, the largest in all the Five Nations. Most of the buildings were massive and made of some kind of strange creamy yellow stone from a quarry in the southern mountains. The streets were filled with giant men that towered at over a head taller than him. Everything, the cars, furniture and even the buildings were oversized. They made him feel like a child in an adult world.

He knew the feeling was just from culture shock, but combined with the imminent danger posed by these revenge-obsessed RA, he felt rather disheveled and scattered.

He sighed again.

"Taelin." Asha sat next to Nama in the front passenger seat. "I'll need you to stay in the car while we make this transfer."

In the back seat, Taelin snorted. "No argument from me."

"Nama, I need you to be my gun hand."

He nodded once. "Yes, Ma'am."

Asha had been tense and distant for the whole mission, and while Nama was sure he wasn't the only one to notice, he trusted that she would to do her best to keep them safe.

They turned into the street where the RA's broken manor house slouched in the centre of some large overgrown gardens. Nama pulled the rental car into the graveled driveway. At the end, the high metal gates were open wide. He steered the overly broad car in through the gap and parked it in front of the entrance.

A number of armed Ronan women and men were stationed around outside, all watching them warily. Nama counted seven, but none of them seemed to be the Malan brothers.

Asha got out of the car first. Nama left the keys in the ignition, and got out as well. Bana and young Xak stepped in behind them and as the four of them turned, the front door of the manor opened.

"Ah, you're here," said Mena in such a convivial tone of voice that Nama imagined they were being greeted for a grand dinner party and not an armed trading of resources.

"Welcome. I am Mena." He approached Asha, and Nama had to forcibly suppress the sudden urge to put a weapon in the old man's face.

Asha, mirroring the man's friendliness, took Mena's offered hand. "I am Asha. Thank you for accepting this trade agreement, Hawk sends his thanks and regards."

Mena's eyes widened and he seemed genuinely surprised. "You know Hawk?"

"Yes, I am his representative. Are your people ready?"

"Of course."

The older Ronan turned and his younger brother came out of the doorway. He carried someone over his shoulder. The figure was obviously unconscious, but too small to be a full-grown Ronan.

"Unfortunately," Mena continued in an almost bored tone. "Our second man had far too much to drink last night." He sighed. "He's a little worse for wear, I'm afraid."

"Will he be alright for this mission?" Asha asked.

"He'll do what's necessary when the time comes." There was a snippet of danger in the older man's voice, and Nama fought to control his unsettled fear. Something else was going on and whatever it was, it wasn't good.

Asha lifted an unimpressed eyebrow at the man. Turning, she addressed the younger Malan and pointed at the vehicle behind them. "Please, take a seat in the car. We won't be a moment."

The younger Malan brother passed them, likely to get in the car, but Nama didn't see because he continued to watch the old man warily. With every bone and instinct, Nama did not like Mena Malan.

Once the car door slammed, Mena bowed his head formally, somehow pulling off the perfect humble bow, but at the same time still having an air of condescension in every movement.

"Would you all like to come in and see the explosives?"

"Yes, thank you, I will come in, but my people will stay here." Asha glanced sideways at Nama. Before he could verbalize any objections, she spoke with a gruff voice. "Stay here."

"But—" he said telepathically.

"No. Mena's brother is in our car, so they will not kill me. But they may kill Taelin if he's left alone."

Sighing, he bowed his head. "Yes, Ma'am."

Nama turned around, collected the other two men with a firm glance and walked them back towards the car. Asha had already gone inside by the time he turned around again. He sighed and touched the minds of the three other Rebels, including Taelin, so they could all communicate without being overheard.

"What is Asha doing, going in there by herself?" Inside the car, Taelin was not happy.

"Protecting us." Nama corrected his friend. *"They won't hurt her because we have Mena's brother."*

"But, she shouldn't—"

"I don't like it any more than you, Tae. But she's the boss."

Bana's voice was deep and calm in his mind. *"She knows what she's doing, Taelin. She'll be fine."*

"What he said," interjected Xak. *"It's Bana and I going in there that you've got to worry about."*

Nama grunted and looked sideways at the young man. *"With your dodging and Bana's training, you two just have to keep your guard up and you'll be fine."*

Xak lifted a dark eyebrow at him. *"You sure?"*

"Kid, you can dodge a bullet at point blank range. I have no doubt you'll be just fine."

Unseen behind Xak, Bana frowned at him. Being an empath he would have sensed the niggling fear and doubt in him. But his lie was meant for Xak to keep him focused, not for anyone else.

The boy was good with combat missions and was developing into a very effective combatant Rebel, but he did at times psych himself out with his own doubts. So, he often needed a pep-talk to get him focused. Knowing this about the boy, Nama was unapologetic about lying because it would keep Xak alive.

Nama watched the front door and the scattered RA members who stood around them and the car. The RA were all silent and unemotional. They guarded the entrance of the manor house without any apparent anxiety, as if the four Rebels were of no importance what so ever. Despite their disinterest, they still outnumbered them and could easily kill the four men if things came to blows.

He waited tensely for Asha to return.

Lilān had given Asha a small crude hand-held testing device to authenticate that the RA did in fact have explosives. When she came outside again, Asha lifted the device so that they could see the bright orange strip on its square faceplate. Orange confirmed that there were definitely explosives present—though it couldn't discern the type.

On the top step, Asha smiled at Mena and shook his hand. "I believe we can proceed." She glanced back at them and the car. "Xak, Bana, come on up."

The two men moved from beside Nama towards the house entrance. They would stay with the RA until Goid and this other person returned from Arana.

Nama didn't like it, but again, he wasn't the boss. He just hoped his ill-ease was nothing more than his own culture shock and paranoia.

* 23 *
A few hours later

Bana stood in front of a broad window and looked outside. They were in the second story of the old manor house, and the window looked out over the cobbled entrance and driveway. The high metal gates outside were closed. A twitch of instinct yelled at him that he and Xak should take the girl and run like a Wraith out of Nūthen. But he was too disciplined to listen to it or let it alter his behavior in any manner that others may sense or see. He stared across the driveway and over the road to the hotel window, where he knew Asha was standing with binoculars.

"The girl can't be any older than about five."

"This doesn't change the situation, Bana."

He sighed and brushed at a thread of black hair in his eyes. *"I know, I know, there's more at stake here than us and this little girl. But you have to admit it's a surprising complication."*

"What? That the RA wouldn't kidnap a child to get what they want? No, not surprising—disturbing. We're just going to have to hope this girl's father and Goid can get it done."

The little girl was giggling loudly behind him, playing some kind of game with Xak. Bana was reminded of Gusa and wiped at his face again.

"We could withdraw?"

"No. We can't withdraw. If you can save her, save her. If you have to leave her behind to save yourselves, do so."

He frowned. *"But, Asha—"*

"No, Bana! We can not withdraw. We can not fail to get those explosives. And if I have to choose between keeping you and Xak alive over the life of that poor little girl, I choose you two. Your orders stand!"

He sensed through their mental connection that she was just as conflicted as he on this issue, but that something else was at work. He knew her well enough to realize whatever it was that she wasn't telling him, it was big. He trusted her, and, oddly enough, he even trusted Hawk, so it was something he would have to simply accept.

He sighed. *"Fine, OK. Orders stand."*

"Anything else to report?"

"No," he mentally went through his checklist. *"Psi shielding in the external walls, I've counted ten others in the building in addition to Mena, and you have my objections. I did wonder about the boy, though."*

"Xak? What about him?"

"I think he's really scared, even though he's doing a pretty good job of hiding it empathically. I'm just a little worried that when the shooting starts he's going to drop the ball because of nerves."

There was a mental sigh. *"Look, Hawk trained him. Xak has the skills and the instinct for combat, and he's a 15/5 Time Psi. He can do it. He probably just doesn't know that you now know he can do it."*

Bana suppressed a snort. *"What? You're suggesting I give him a pep-talk like some sports coach?"*

There was a grin in her mental tone. *"Something like that."*

He rolled his eyes. *"Right. Any news for us from your end?"*

"The jet is in the air, should get there late afternoon. If all goes well, you'll be out of there by morning. Report back in an hour?"

"Yes, Ma'am."

* 24 *
Back in Arām, Arana

Nalana was putting away the food supplies in David's little ailing refrigerator when the front door of Rose Road opened and slammed closed again. She sensed a wave of annoyed frustration, and turned to see David standing in the little green kitchen.

She smiled. "Bad day?"

"You could say that." His voice was quiet and gentle despite the storm of emotions around him. He sighed.

"What are you doing here? Weren't you supposed to evacuate with the children?"

"I'm not leaving the city until you do."

"Nalana Yen—" his tone was correcting but she refused to let him bully her into submission.

"No, David," she interrupted. "I may not be able to shoot people but someone needs to give you support. These are hard times." She leaned over the Formica bench top and turned on the kettle. "Now, what's gotten you all angry like this?"

He sighed as if he'd lost an argument and sat down at the table. "The Agent in charge of finding Hawk has got my scent because of Triian's escape. I just spent four hours being verbally interrogated by him." He put his elbows on the table and wiped his face with one hand. "I should be in Rona helping Asha, not here playing word games with Heth Pallen."

She gave him a gentle smile. "So this has nothing to do with Wolf?"

His bottom lip twitched and he put his hand over his mouth to cover it. "It has everything and nothing to do with him. It's so difficult to focus knowing he's out there suffering."

She sensed a deep well of sorrow come out of him. It was so intense that she walked across the room to wrap her arms around his shoulders. He shuffled in his chair to face her and returned the hug. Nalana poured a calm sense of self into him like water into a glass, and he physically relaxed. The anger and frustration around him cleared away, like a sunbeam through a gap in storm clouds.

"You're a good friend, Nalana. Thank you."

She let go of him and smiled. "Even Hawk needs a hug sometimes."

He chuckled. "Too tr—"

Mid-word his body language tensed up and he closed his eyes. The temperature in the room dropped and every surface of skin on her body that faced him tingled and itched. She'd felt the sensation before—it meant he was having a vision. Something pulsed in the air like a pressure change and a shiver ran up her spine, making all the hairs on her back and neck stand on end.

"Hai di'chena!" he gasped. Vivid blue eyes looked up at her. "Where's Ren?"

"Back at base, why?"

"You and he need to go to Rona. Right now." He got to his feet and strode back towards the front door. "Come on, I'll drive you to the airstrip and we'll pick up Ren on the way."

She followed him, frowning at his back. "But Ren still thinks you're a spy! He'll flip out if he sees you!"

"I don't care. Without you two, people are going to die."

* 25 *
Just before midnight
Kamo, Rona

Mena paced across his old family library in the candlelight. It was midnight and Goid was overdue in contacting them. More than overdue, he was unaccountably late. They arrived in Arām mid-to-late afternoon. They should have received the needed recon from these Rebels, trapped and taken out their traitor and already be on their way home again. Goid should have contacted them on the satellite phone at least three times already if the plan had gone ahead. The last communication had been five hours ago when they confirmed they'd arrived in Arām and were transferring to Marakan. He paced back towards the door, past his brother's chair and the ice chest containing Goid's favorite beer. Something was very wrong; Mena could feel it in his bones.

Had the Rebels betrayed them? Or was Goid just late because there had been complications? But could complications cause his brother to be out of touch for so long?

Mena stopped pacing at the library door and sighed. No, it wasn't likely that Goid would remain this long out of contact without there being something very wrong. It was more likely that the Rebels had betrayed them and killed Goid. They probably wanted to break his spirit and take the explosives for themselves. Or perhaps they weren't even Rebels at all, but actually working for the Agency or the Guard to wipe them out properly this time. Either way it wouldn't work. Such a blow would only strengthen his spirit not break it.

He strode out of the library, into the broad white-stone parlor towards their old den at the front of the house. Young Ayren stood in the darkness watching the entrance outside. He was a good guard dog. Not particularly smart, but loyal and unquestioning.

"Come on, Ayren, this little dance with the Rebels is over."

* * * * *

Asha sat at the tiny hotel table cleaning her handguns with an oiled cloth. Her unsettled feeling had very suddenly intensified at about eight o'clock that evening and she'd spent the last four hours keeping herself busy in an attempt to calm her nerves.

The others knew she was tense, but if her brother sensed how afraid she really was it would be over. Taelin simply would not cooperate when she was that scared. Without Taelin she didn't have Nama, and Lilān wouldn't follow her orders if there was dissension in the group.

If they all went on strike like that, the only way she'd get them to follow her again would be if she broke David's trust and showed them what he'd shown her. But David kept things from people for good reasons. She didn't always agree with what he did or how he did it, but there were always consequences that she couldn't possibly predict. Consequences which he could predict and did with astounding accuracy. Knowing the scale of this entire thing of David's, she knew that if sharing that vision with them was a mistake, it would likely be a monumental mistake with a cost that she couldn't yet fathom.

Besides, she couldn't possibly choose between her family and her loyalty to David's cause—such a choice would probably destroy her. Therefore, she wouldn't let her fear be sensed and risk everything.

She put her second handgun down on the yellow tablecloth, next to its mate and folded the cleaning rag. In front of her, the radio crackled with a new signal.

~ "Hello? Asha?"

Her eyes widened and she stared at the black box on the table. Nalana's voice couldn't possibly have just come from the radio. It didn't have the range to get a signal from Arām.

~ "Asha, this is Nalana, are you there?" Her young voice sounded terrified even over the static. ~ "You have to get Xak and Bana. Right now."

She grabbed the radio off the table. ~ "Nalana? What's going on? How are you here?" Behind her, she sensed Lilān get up from the nearby bed.

~ "There isn't time. Hawk says you've got to go in now."

She lifted her handguns from the little hotel table and put them one at a time into her thigh-holsters, then Asha strode across the room to kick Nama and Taelin's feet where they lay asleep on the floor.

She brought the radio back to her lips. ~ "We'll send someone to pick you up."

~ "No! No, Asha, go rescue the others right now! Ren and I will get a ride to you with the pilot. Please, go right now—just be careful."

Sighing, she lifted the radio back to her mouth. ~ "He sent you two because it's going to be bad, didn't he?"

There was a whimper. ~ "Yes."

"Hai di'chena." She covered her mouth for a moment with the bend of her wrist.

For Nalana's sake, Asha made her voice as strong and calm as humanly possible, and pressed the radio send button.

~ "When you get here, stay in the car until one of us comes to you. Don't worry, we'll get them out. It'll be OK."

Looking around at the confused faces of the others, she dropped the old radio into its sling on her belt. "Everyone, grab what weapons you can carry. We're going in, right now."

* 26 *

Bana stood at a round antique bathroom vanity. The mirror above it was square and had a beautiful dark metal frame, with mythological creatures—what the Ancients called "scorpions"—dancing around the edges of it. He wiped his hands on a battered gray towel laying over the edge of the vanity, and stared at his own face in the mirror.

He looked terrible. His eyes were red, the skin around them was mottled from lack of sleep, and his loose black hair fell around his face in messy unwashed threads. He sighed and turned back towards the door.

The RA members, at least those he could sense through the Psi shielding in the walls, were scattered all over. Most of them were downstairs, perhaps guarding the premises. Bana touched the ornate brass door handle, about to go back to Xak, but stopped. Those in the house he could sense moved from their individual locations throughout the manor house. Their motion was all at once as if an alarm had been tripped.

With his hand still resting on the doorknob, he waited to see where they were going. Some of them gathered in groups of two or three downstairs, likely guarding the doors, but about half of them started to converge on the main stairwell.

Something was going on and whatever it was, it wasn't good.

The stairwell was between where he was standing and Xak, so he couldn't get back to the boy without being seen. Xak could certainly look after himself for a little while. But a person could not dodge *and* fire a weapon simultaneously. Without the capacity to defend himself, it would only take one mistake and Xak would be killed. He had to get to the boy as soon as possible. Once together, they could plan an escape route or at least create a defendable position until the others came in to back them up.

Unfortunately, there was no way to contact Asha and the others to come in and help them until he could get to a window or some gap in the Psi suppressant external walls. Bana pulled out his primary weapon from the holster in the small of his back and opened the door a little. It was crunch-time and he hoped with all his might that the boy was as good as Asha claimed.

Bana glanced down the hall towards the stairwell. Three men were heading in his direction. They did not look friendly. With the brush of a delicate telepathic hand, Bana sensed that two of them had mental shields. He grabbed the mind of the third and squeezed with all his might. The man roared in agony and dropped to his knees. Bana gripped his mind a little tighter. An agonized whimper came from the younger man, and then he flopped face first onto the marble floor. If he wasn't dead, he would be soon.

The other two backed away from their companion— likely having never seen a telepathic attack of that strength before. Taking advantage of their surprise, Bana stepped out of the bathroom doorway, gun up, and with one shot each, killed them both.

* * * * *

Xak was asleep when he sensed the shafts of silver trajectory racing towards him. Bullets. Bullets were coming straight for him. His body tensed and rolled out of the way as he came out of a deep sleep. His instinct got him to his feet and demanded he skitter sideways. He did so, and gunfire became the first thing his fully-conscious mind understood. Someone was shooting at him and to stay alive he had to let his instincts take over.

Standing in the doorway, the old man, Mena, held the young auburn-haired Naomi in his massive arms. The little girl should have woken up from all the noise, so Xak could only assume she had been telepathically forced unconscious. The old woman's words flittered through his mind and he knew now exactly what she had meant. If he chose to help the little girl he and Bana would die.

There were four people with guns, all aimed at him. Xak stared at them for a moment. They seemed uncertain.

"Just kill him!" roared the old man.

Xak moved even before they started firing again. He danced across the floor, dodging the lines of silver bullet trajectory. He had to choose to live. To do that he had to let go of any doubt and fear, as well as any regrets and just let his instinct dodge. He couldn't save the girl, all he could do was save himself.

Xak would have laughed had he been watching the situation on a screen. A gunfight in a room like that? The walls were painted with a vibrant green forest of massive trees, forest animals, wraith creatures and fae figurines in flight. Boxes of toys filled most of the central space and a brightly painted play house sat in the far corner. The little girl, Naomi, had loved that play house, probably because none of the adults could get in there with her. She had played peek-a-boo with them for most of the afternoon.

A line of silver flared down near his foot. He lifted it up as the bullet that followed the trajectory blew through and knocked his sneaker off as it brushed past. He had to focus. Had to focus on him staying alive. He couldn't think about the little girl or his fear or even his doubt. He had to simply focus on nothing and let his instinct guide his body or he would be killed.

The old man roared again over the gunfire and Xak's feet flickered left and then quickly right. They were trying to trick him into dodging one way and into a second line of gunfire. They were smart terrorists. But he simply had to be faster, at least until Bana could get there to help him.

He watched the old man turn out of the play room with the little girl still in his arms. The door closed behind him.

* **27** *

Staring down the barrel of his handgun, Bana made his way across the broad stone hall towards the stairwell entrance. He walked silently and within a bubble of no-thought and no-emotion, so that he was essentially invisible to those RA who were telepaths or empaths throughout the building. It wasn't much of an advantage, but it might help him survive that much longer in such an impossible situation.

Gunfire sounded from the play room and he hoped that Xak could hold on. He had to cross the stairwell before he could get to the boy, but, in a way the constant gunfire was perhaps a sign that Xak was dodging well. It was silence he'd have to worry about.

The stairwell was an open area of the second floor. Two stone staircases led up to a balcony that looked down on the grungy parlor below and the front door. He stopped at the edge of cover to sense out where the enemy was within the building. There was a handful of RA in the corner of the house with Xak, but the rest seemed to be downstairs.

"Ba... na?" Taelin's mental voice was scattered and dim but recognizable.

He reached for the wisps of his mind. "Tae! Send back up! Now!"

"We're coming... hold..." his mental voice faded and came back again, mid-sentence, "... front door."

Someone was coming upstairs towards Bana. He let go of the wisp of Taelin's voice and stepped out into view of the RA woman. He fired before she saw him, splattering her white shirt with blood as she fell back down the stairs. Bana sidestepped across the open space of the stairwell balcony, watching for his next target.

Gunfire continued to come through in a steady stream from the play room, and as he cleared the balcony, coming back under some cover of the wall, the play-room door opened. One figure held the child in his arms as a second lifted a weapon. Bana fired first, and the young man dropped to the ground like a rag-doll.

Bana stared down the barrel at Mena, who brought a gun from behind him up to the head of the little Aranan girl. Bana wasn't sure if he should shoot the man and risk killing the child, or wait to see what Mena would do.

The old man watched him with calm dark eyes. Bana sensed a personality who believed himself to be better than others, and he knew instinctively that this man would kill without remorse or pause. The girl in Mena's arms wasn't a child to him, she wasn't even sentient, an attitude which made trying to save the girl difficult.

Mena's black eyes seemed to shine mockingly at him. "Look at us here, come to conflict. This is why you don't betray the Rona-Abān."

Bana frowned. "We haven't betrayed you."

"Then where is my brother?" With a knowing cynical smile on his face, Mena walked towards him.

Something about the old man made Bana's skin crawl, and he instinctively backed out of reach. But even as Bana moved away, he aimed his weapon.

"Give me the girl."

"No, not until I hear from my brother," said the old man, his dark eyes still mocked him. "Your boy is good. But how much longer will he last before he makes a mistake?"

Bana re-gripped his weapon. This was the choice that crazy old woman had spoken about. Xak or the girl. Protect each other or die. He swallowed and dropped his weapon.

Mena grinned at him and backed towards the stairs. "Tell your leader if my brother isn't returned to me in one piece, this girl's life is forfeit."

* * * * *

The bullet grazed Xak's face as he arched his back to get out of the way. It carved a burning hot line across one cheekbone, before embedding itself into a painted tree in the wall behind him. Xak was getting tired and the bullets were coming closer. He didn't have much time left. Pulling out of the back bend, he flipped sideways and skittered far to the right.

At least they were sort of following a pattern—they'd chase him with bullets, then try to trick him, get frustrated and then chase him with bullets again.

A silver line cut through his left shoulder and he barely managed to duck out of the way in time before the accompanying bullet arrived. His shirt ripped and another burning hot line of flying metal touched his skin. He cried out as the bullet ripped muscle and surface flesh as it went past. He stumbled, his shoeless foot tripping in the bed-clothes on the floor. As he fell,

Xak rolled sideways and hoped that he would have enough momentum to get back onto his feet.

A smaller sounding weapon fired and the silver shafts of potential trajectory disappeared from around him. But there wasn't time to process that because he rolled hard into a wall. His forehead smacked into the painted surface, bringing with the impact a bunch of stars and a microsecond of darkness. He lay on the ground stunned for a few seconds.

Gunfire went off around him, but he wasn't hit by any bullets. Then all was quiet again. Xak coughed, blinking repeatedly as he cleared away the fog in his mind. A long dark face came into his field of vision.

"Xak? Are you alright?" Bana's booming voice echoed in his head and all Xak could do was stare.

After a few seconds, he blinked and finally got his voice to work. "I think so."

"You're bleeding."

"I'm alright." Putting one hand to the wound in his arm, Xak pushed against the nearby wall and got to his feet. "We—"

His head spun and he reached out for something stationary. Bana steadied him with one hand and through their touch Xak sensed that Bana, who'd been almost cold towards him since the man had joined their group, was genuinely concerned.

He smiled. "I'm OK. Just a little beat up. What do we do now?"

"The others are coming. I think we need to get to the front door. Can you—"

A deep nausea lifted out of Xak's spine into his stomach. He felt the color drain out of his face, the world spun around him and he swayed on his feet.

Bana grabbed him again. "I got you, kid."

Xak knew he was fainting, but couldn't do a thing to stop it.

* 28 *

Had the situation not been as serious, Lilān would have been grinning like an idiot as she set up the rush-job "explosives" on Mena's front door. She'd never liked the way Mena behaved towards everyone else in the RA. He acted like some kind of Lord looking down his nose at his subjects. However, in the old days, she'd tolerated it because there was no other choice. It was either be with the RA or be hunted down by the Guard. But now she could bring that high-horse mamon down on Mena's head with one little home-made device.

She'd put the explosive cocktail together from things she found in the hotel room and the cleaner's supply trolley on their first evening back in Rona. She hadn't done it because she expected to use it, but because she was bored with waiting around and doing nothing.

It wasn't technically an explosive device, more like a destructive chemical reaction involving flammable and chemically reactive liquids. Oh, and some good old fashion shrapnel, but it would be enough to get Mena's attention and perhaps break down their front door.

Lilān dropped the powdered triggering agent that was wrapped in an old cloth into the bucket of chemicals and turned tail.

Asha was crouched behind one of Mena's older, sturdier cars and Lilān dove behind it. She grinned sideways at Asha. "Should go off any minute now."

Tight-lipped, Asha nodded and handed her an automatic rifle. The woman was doing a good job seeming calm and composed, but Lilān had watched her long enough to realize that a quiet Asha was a tense or upset one. However, as long as she was still in control, Lilān would follow her orders because she'd also come to realize that Asha was a good, strong and loyal leader—and person. In fact, if Lilān hadn't been interested in Taelin she'd have already propositioned Asha—boss or no.

A watery pop sounded as the chemical reaction burst the plastic bucket. The liquids and all of her home made shrapnel flew in several directions, shredding the wooden surface of the front door and embedding into the stone wall. At the same time, the chemical reaction reached its flash point, igniting the flammable liquids in a satisfying boom and whoosh of flames that covered the stone walls, stairs and door. The wooden entrance; having already been shredded by shrapnel, quickly crumpled under the heat of the flames, leaving a gaping, flaming hole at the front of the building.

The two women got to their feet behind the old car and aimed their autos at the now burning front of the building. Answering weapons-fire came out at them through a window to one side. Next to her, Asha turned slightly and fired at them.

* * * * *

Nama's jaw tightened. It was very dark at the back of the manor house. The moons, stars and nearby nebula that would normally be in the sky lighting their way, were covered over by thick cloud. Nama was lucky to have fairly good night vision—certainly better than Taelin's—but it was still almost pitch black around them. Gunfire came from inside the building. Hearing it and not being able to move yet made it difficult for Nama to keep still. His finger tapped on the metal of his auto just above the trigger.

He and Taelin sat crouched down under the windows next to a back door. Abandoned trash cans had been pushed over onto their sides a long time ago, and lay haphazardly around them.

Nearby, Taelin sighed. *"I can't get to Bana again. The Psi suppressant is too thick to penetrate on this side."*

"Don't worry we'll get in there any—"

A boom sounded from the other side of the building. It had to be Asha and Lilān. Without saying anything, they both strode up onto the stairs and readied themselves to enter. Nama opened the door that Lilān had already unlocked for them, and stepped inside with his weapon up.

The room beyond was an old kitchen, obviously disused and badly damaged from some fire a long time ago. The cracked and blackened crockery wall and floor tiles had once been white or perhaps an off yellow. A lime green bench-top stood against the nearest wall and a second sat in the middle of the room. Inside the opposite wall was an old iron range oven, the type that everyone used two or three hundred years ago before electricity.

On the opposite corner to them, a man in dark clothes was in a doorway with his back to them. Unhooking his silenced weapon from the holster at his side, Nama lifted it, aimed, and pulled the trigger. The man dropped to the floor.

Nama couldn't sense much of anything beyond the room they were in, which meant that even the internal walls must have Psi suppressant materials in them.

He turned to look behind him. *"Tae—"*

"Hall beyond is clear." Taelin had his hand on the wall, likely sensing out the spaces around them through his PK ability. *"Room to the right has three people in it."*

Nama smiled at his old friend. *"Thanks. You ready?"*

Taelin lifted his hand from the wall and nodded.

* 29 *

There was the boom of an explosion downstairs. It didn't sound particularly big, but Bana guessed it was probably the Rebels.

He ripped a length of material from the lining of his leather jacket. Xak lay unconscious on the ground in front of him. The boy had lost a lot of blood from where a bullet tore through the top of his arm, but it had only shredded skin and muscle. It was a messy wound and would probably leave an interesting scar, but it looked as if everything damaged would grow back again. Bana wrapped the material around his wound, and carefully knotted it to stem the bleeding.

The boy was covered in bullet grazes and burns, but only the arm actually had pierced skin. He'd lost one shoe and the dark gray rags that served as his t-shirt were filled with little burn and rip holes from bullets that had missed him. Xak wasn't particularly injured, so the shock of pain, blood loss and being attacked had probably been the cause of him passing out. Though, the boy had tried to fight it before he fainted.

Bana smiled. Xak definitely had the stones for combat despite his age. If he was Bana's son, he'd be very proud of the brave young man.

"Bana?" Taelin's voice was scattered oddly at the edges, but clearer than before.

He sat upright and looked towards the door. "Yeah, what's going on? I heard an explosion."

"That was Lilān at the front door. We're in the building, how are you two?"

"I'm fine, Xak's been shot. He'll be OK, but he's unconscious. We're fairly secure in an upstairs room, north-east corner."

Taelin sounded tense. "OK, as long as Xak's unconscious, stay where you are, we're making a path through the building to you."

"Right-o."

* * * * *

Asha and Lilān stood either side of the blackened front doorway, their backs to the stone. The smell of burnt chemicals and smoke surrounded Asha. It took some focus for her to not cough from the acrid smell.

They were ready to go inside, but simply waiting for a clear signal from Taelin. Asha couldn't sense much of anything, even with physical contact on the stone. Her kinetic ability was more about force and less about spatial senses, at least, compared to her brother's skill. As much as she didn't want Taelin there in case he was killed or injured, they couldn't have pulled off that style of attack without his talent of getting around the Psi suppressant in the walls.

Gunfire sounded through the doorway next to them. Ronan hand-cannons seemed to argue with the smaller Aranan weapons. There was silence for a few moments and she sensed her brother connect to her mind.

"Clear!" His mental voice was kind of scattered and patchy, like a slightly out of tune radio signal, but it was strong.

She tapped her weapon. When Lil glanced back at her, Asha signaled with one hand for her to go in first.

Lilān lifted her weapon and stepped in through the doorway. Half a breath later, Asha followed her.

A smoky haze hovered above them closer to the roof, and at least five bodies lay sprawled in different positions across the old stone parlor floor. Asha glanced sideways at Lilān. She felt a half-suppressed sadness, but nothing that would indicate Lil might switch sides.

Across the massive parlor stood her brother and Nama with their backs to a wall. Both men looked tense but calm.

"There's three more bodies in the dining room," said Nama in a quiet but clear voice.

"OK, secure the—"

"Traitor!" A gunshot fired from above them and next to Asha, Lilān dropped to the ground.

Lifting her weapon to start firing, Asha skittered sideways towards a nearby doorway at the foot of the stairs. Bullets followed her as she ran, until finally one of her shots hit their target. The woman on the balcony above her cried out in pain and fell back.

Asha stood in the cover of a doorway panting. A shaft of pain cut its way through her shoulder and up into her neck. She'd been hit, and judging by the building agony, the bullet had broken her collarbone.

"So'then!" she swore.

"Asha?"

"I'm alright!" she barked.

Edging around the doorframe, she glanced above them. The body was unmoving and she sensed nothing from the figure, so they were likely badly injured or dead. She couldn't see anyone else or sense anything. She lifted her weapon up to aim at the balcony.

"Nama," she barked again. "Get the explosives. Tae, check on Lil. I'll cover you."

The two men moved immediately, Nama turning away towards a far doorway and Tae running up to where Lilān lay on the ground in front of the entrance. She watched the balcony, concentrating on staying upright even through the pain of the gunshot wound.

"She's alive." Tae's voice was clipped and tense.

She swallowed and lifted her gun-arm up some more. "Glad to hear it. Can you sense anyone else in the house?"

He sighed. "No, but I thought it was clear before too."

Her knees weakened under her and she found herself slipping slowly to the floor.

"Asha!"

"I'm alright." she croaked, as her gun hand dropped as well. "Just need to sit... is all." She couldn't really think any more. The agony and a terrible spinning in her head were dragging her down. Her eyes closed.

"Asha! Stay with me!"

* 30 *

Voices spoke below him in the parlor, but Ayren couldn't hear their words. He stood in the doorway of their little secret corridor and stared out at his sister Jodina's body on the balcony. Her dark eyes were wide and unseeing, but at the same time she stared right into him. She was dead. His sister was dead. Killed by these Rebels. She'd landed at a funny angle with one arm buried underneath her, the other flung back over her head. With all her limbs at odd angles like they were, it looked as if she'd broken every bone in her body. He knew she was dead and so wouldn't be feeling anything, but in his shock he desperately wanted to go to her and make her comfortable.

Mena had escaped out through the back tunnels with the girl. He'd instructed Ayren to bring the others to one of their old buildings once the Rebels were dead. Obviously, Mena had under-estimated their enemy.

Ayren couldn't sense any other RA left in the building. Just him and these Rebels. He was afraid. He wanted to escape out of the building and find Mena, but he knew it wasn't likely that he'd be able to do so without being killed. He was only safe at that moment because of his odd Talent for not being sensed by other Psi unless he chose to be.

He gave his sister one last long glance and stepped back into a hidden corridor behind the Play Room. He would be safe in there for a little while.

The secret passage entrance was hidden from immediate view by the architecture of the main upstairs hall. At first glance, it looked a little like someone had widened that end of the hall to let in more light from the windows. The door was hidden around the corner where the hall opened out—it was simply smart design. Ayren had always liked how all the secret parts of Mena's house were put in plain view and were only really "hidden" to people who didn't stop and look carefully around them.

The passage was narrow, dark and very dusty. It was lined on both walls with thick Psi-suppressant stone, so it made a nice place to sit in the dark and get away from the psychic noise of the world. Ayren was technically a telepath, but he was mostly only a receiver. He could hear the noise of the city for many kilometers around him, but couldn't do much more than that. He'd never really learned how to block the noise off, so having a place to go and be alone just with his own thoughts was nice. Mena allowed him to go to the passage any time he needed a break. Despite his frightening hostility, Mena had treated Ayren better than some of the other RA, and as such had earned Ayren's respect and obedience—an obedience Ayren sometimes regretted.

He had two choices. One was to hide in the darkness and wait for the Rebels to leave. But Mena would probably call him a coward and a traitor for not fighting. The other option was that he could try to defend the house and risk being killed.

Ayren sat down in front of the secret panel that led into the back of the Play Room. He couldn't go up against those on the ground floor—there were at least three of them. The two in the Play Room didn't know about the secret door, and the surprise would give him quite an advantage. But two against one were still bad odds. He stared at the door, frowning deeply.

If he showed cowardice Mena would probably kill him. But if he attacked their enemy, it was quite likely that *they'd* kill him too.

He sighed and got to his feet. It was better to die bravely than to die with shame.

* * * * *

When consciousness found Xak again, it felt like his entire body was one big throbbing bruise. He groaned and cracked his eyes open.

A long face with dark eyes and hair, smiled down at him. "Welcome back to the world of the living, kid. How do you feel?"

Xak only managed to moan in reply.

Bana chuckled. "That bad, huh? Well, kid, you did good. I'm impressed. You've certainly got more stones than I had at your age. Do you think you can stand?"

"Sure," he mumbled and started to sit up. His body ached all over, and not just where he'd been nicked by bullets. With a little help from Bana, Xak managed to get to his feet. The taller man pulled Xak's uninjured arm over his shoulder and steered him towards the door.

"The others are downstairs—"

Bana turned suddenly, pushing Xak down with one quick shove. As Xak landed, he heard two gunshots go off in quick succession.

He rolled onto his stomach and looked around. Bana lay on his back nearby, not moving. Crawling up to him, Xak touched his neck to find a pulse. Bana was breathing, but had a nasty, bloody gunshot wound in his chest. Further across the room, was another body.

Grabbing Bana's gun, Xak clambered to his feet to make sure the shooter was dead.

The man lay in front of an open wall panel—a secret door—the lines of which had been masked by a particularly wide painted tree-trunk. The man's black eyes were still open, but as Xak got closer, he saw a bloody wound in the middle of his forehead. Bana was definitely a good shot.

The door behind him opened and Xak spun around with Bana's gun, aiming at the figure that stepped inside.

Nama dropped his weapon. "It's just me. You alright?"

Xak swallowed. "Bana's hurt bad."

* 31 *

Nalana ran after her uncle and Nama, lugging one of the heavy medical cases under one arm. Nama's fear was thick in the air and she found that it was slowly leaking into her. He hadn't said who was hurt or how bad, just that they needed to run.

The long graveled driveway ended at a pair of high metal gates, which were open wide. A massive white stone house rose above her as they ran towards it. It seemed overbearing, as if it was looking down at her with a contemptuous hatred.

She ran through a blackened front entrance and stopped there. Many bodies lay haphazardly on a white marble parlor floor. All of the bodies were Ronan.

"Nala, go in there." Nama pointed to a room on her right. "Ren, upstairs with me."

She nodded and turned away as Nama led her uncle towards a nearby grand staircase. The room off to the side had fewer bodies, but was almost completely ruined by mould and aged scorch-marks on the walls. Two bodies were stacked on top of each other in one corner. In the middle of the room lay two of their people. Taelin sat between them, one hand on each of them to stem their bleeding.

"Tae?" she said uncertainly.

The face that turned to look up at her was afraid and lost. Taelin's dark blue eyes were red and shimmered with a line of tears.

She dropped down in front of Tae and leaned over to check injuries. Asha was unconscious, but breathing evenly. She was shot in the shoulder, and as Nalana lifted his hand from the wound to have a look, she figured that the bullet had probably broken Asha's collarbone. Their new recruit, a Ronan woman who Nala had only met a couple of times, had a pretty bad stomach wound. Her breathing was rapid and her dark face was oddly gray.

"Keep holding pressure, Tae."

Nalana shuffled on her knees to Lilān's head and placed both of her hands on the woman's shoulders. The healing energy flowed out of her hands immediately and pulsed into the pain and injury.

Through her senses, she felt that the bullet was very close to a major artery. Lilān wasn't lost yet, but if they moved her and the bullet pierced the thin arterial lining, she would bleed-out very quickly.

"We need Ren down here as soon as possible."

Her healing ability couldn't do a lot for their type of injury except support peripheral body systems and lift away some of the pain. But she could at least ease the stress on their bodies while they waited for Ren.

She shuffled sideways and placed her hands on Asha. Under her fingers, broken bone throbbed back at her angrily. Asha's face, which had been screwed up from the pain, relaxed somewhat as the flow of buzzing healing energy moved into the bullet wound. She sensed that small pieces of metal shrapnel had spread out and embedded themselves in the underlying bone and muscle of Asha's shoulder. But despite the damage, Asha was in a better condition than Lilān.

"Is Asha..." Taelin's voice wobbled and trailed off.

"She's OK." She looked up, making sure to get eye contact with him. "The bullet has broken her collarbone and shattered on impact, but she's fairly stable for now." The energy in her hands shut off and she went into the medical bag for supplies. She sighed. "What's going on upstairs?"

"Bana." Taelin shook his head. "It didn't look good."

Her bottom lip twitched and she nodded.

* * * * *

Xak leaned over, using his weight to maintain pressure on Bana's chest wound. He sniffled, but couldn't stop the tears that ran down his face. Bana had saved him. He should have sensed it. If he had, then Bana would probably not be dying there in that ridiculous room.

He knew why he hadn't felt the man—because he could only sense those things he could change—but he still felt as if it was his fault. He should have somehow been better. And now Bana was dying. If he died before Ren got to them that smart humorous young girl, Gusa, would be an orphan.

Xak's whole body ached. And the longer he sat there putting pressure on the wound, the worse the pain in his body got. But he wouldn't let his own injuries stop him from doing everything he could for Bana.

The big wooden door at the front of the room opened. He looked up at Ren and Nama, not hiding the tears on his face.

Ren's gray eyes were sympathetic. He kneeled down in front of Xak. Warm, gentle fingers lifted Xak's hands from the terrible chest wound. Ren carefully cleared the bullet hole of torn material and placed a hand either side of the mess.

Xak sensed the old man's light healing energy pulse out of him into Bana. Healing energy had an undertone of white static to it. Xak had often wondered how seeing the future had anything to do with the body's ability to heal quickly like that, but no one had been able to answer him—it was just one of the many mysteries of Time Psi genes.

Xak's hands were sticky with blood, so he wiped at his tears with the crook of his elbow. Under Ren's hands, Bana's breathing didn't change. It was still quick and shallow. His face was very pale.

He leaned forward. Bana's breathing should have changed already, that was always the first thing that happened when Ren healed someone. Xak glanced up at Nama and swallowed. He didn't know what it meant. But it couldn't be good. Panic started to rise inside of Xak, *what if Bana dies?*

"Calm down, young Xak." Ren's deep rumbling voice was quiet. "It's OK."

Bana let out a long, deep breath, which sounded very much like a sigh. His breathing became even, just as if he were sleeping. Between Ren's large wrinkled hands, the skin parted and Xak could see the head of a bullet come out and roll away into the folds of Bana's jacket. Another two pieces of metal pushed out after the first, and the tension in Bana's limbs released. Peace came to the older man's face and Xak knew his friend would be OK.

Xak closed his eyes and lowered his chin. "Abe Kashān, thank Nera."

"Stay with him, Xak." Nama stood at the doorway. "Ren, we've got two more people to help downstairs."

Ren stood up again, with a little grunt of pain from his bad knees. He dropped a comforting hand on Xak's hair and Xak felt a little calmer inside himself.

"We'll send Nalana up to you. You've got a few severe burns that could use some attention."

* 32 *

The box seemed too big to Asha. But she was aware that she was high on painkillers so everything looked wrong to her befuddled brain. She lay in an airplane chair, the seat pushed way back so she could rest, but not so far back that any pressure was put on the broken bone.

She watched the crate of explosives they'd taken from the RA, which sat in the aisle next to her. It seemed too big. She frowned at it some more.

David wanted to put something small in the Ao Council chambers. The crate was big enough to almost hold a tween-aged child. Far too big to put under that big ugly black table in the Council chambers and not be seen. She mentally shrugged. Perhaps there was more in the crate than they needed.

She started feeling a twitch of pain that developed over two or three seconds into a pounding spike of agony. She let out a moan and closed her eyes. Nalana's hands reached over to her from the window seat, and dropped gently down on either side of the agony. Warm pulsing static flowed into the pain and eased it out of her.

"Oh, thanks, Nala."

She sensed a flare of affection from the young woman. "Any time, hun."

Asha opened her eyes again and let her mind flutter over the crate some more. They'd managed to succeed in David's plan without anyone getting killed. It would be a while before their injured, including herself, went on any combat missions but they were all alive.

Thank the Old Gods.

Beyond the crate, lying in the second aisle of seats was Lilān. Her face was turned away so all that Asha could see was the back of her pitch black hair and a lone shoulder peaking over the line of gray blankets. Lilān had done very well, considering she'd grown up with the RA and they had been her family. Asha had honestly expected the giant of a woman to not come in with them to assault the house. But, she hadn't even needed to ask.

Asha smiled numbly at Lilān. She was quite attractive and Asha would have asked her out already if Taelin hadn't been interested in Lilān first.

A moan came from across the aisle and it took a few seconds for Asha's foggy brain to realize that Lilān was waking up. Next to her, Nalana climbed over the back of her seat and around Asha to get to Lilān.

"You're alright, Lilān. Just rest, you've been shot."

"No, kidding, I've been shot!"

Her voice was broken and tired, but still forceful and Asha smiled at the woman's tenacity.

"That a'kēna, Jo! Sisters, my ass!" Lilān's anger degraded into a grumbling mumble in one of the Ronan dialects, and by her tone she had to be swearing something wicked.

Asha chuckled, but flinched as her laughing created a shot of pain through her shoulder and lung. "Oh, ow."

The grumbling stopped and Asha sensed Lilān's attention shift onto her. "So, did we win? Did we get the boys and the explosives?"

Asha swallowed, Bana was still unconscious and poor Xak was very upset, but they were alive. "Yeah, we got them. Explosives are right next to you."

Lilān's face turned towards her and dark eyes dropped to the crate between them. "So'then Nuth, that's the wrong kind."

In her surprise Asha tried to sit up, but grunted. "What do you mean it's the wrong kind?"

Lilān's voice lowered into a growl. "I mean it's the wrong so'then type of so'then explosives! That's the stuff used for mining. That amount'll blow up the whole so'then building not a so'then room!"

"Well, can't we—"

"No, it's the wrong kind! Look, you can't even refine much—it's not reactive enough in small doses. You'd have better luck only killing them by throwing a so'then grenade at this Council o'yours."

Nalana, who was still hovering over Lilān, looked across the plane at Asha. "What does that mean?"

"Kiddo," answered Lilān for her. "It means Mena was tricking us all along and if Hawk still wants to use this stuff in the Tower, he ain't just going to kill his target."

Asha swallowed back her sudden grief. "It mean's that a lot of innocent people are going to die, Nala."

Lilān looked at Asha across the cabin. "So, Hawk won't back down?"

Remembering the vision of a dead planet, Asha shook her head. "No, he *can't* back down."

* **33** *

Two days later
Kamo

David watched the old Ronan man below him in the alley. Night time shadows and the biting rain gave him the stealth to be unseen where he stood crouched on a fire-escape. One major advantage that Aranan physiology had over Ronan was night vision. Ronan people had almost no night vision. Even if David had been standing in the alley level with Mena, instead of above him, he wouldn't have been seen by the old man.

Mena stood under an awning in the curving alley, trying to keep from getting wet in the midnight downpour. The tension in his shoulders and his tightly balled fists told David that the man was not only cold, but fearful. One edge of David's mouth twitched upwards. A fearful target gave him a significant advantage over the taller, stronger man.

David hadn't been able to find the girl—it didn't seem to be on his path to find her—but he had found every other Rona-Abān left in the city. There had only been five RA left after the firefight at the manor. Each of them had been frightened and inexperienced, making it an easier hunt for him. However, he wasn't going to attack *this* man without first watching him for a while. He needed to know what kind of man Mena was before he could judge the best angle of approach.

Below him, a Ronan child wearing a faded white t-shirt and jeans ran towards Mena through the shadows. The boy held an older-style metal torch and the artificial light flickered back and forth through the pounding rain as he ran.

"Gred, what have you found out?" barked Mena from under the awning.

The boy stood in the rain, not even attempting to get under cover. "Sir, they's all dead."

"What?"

The boy shrugged. "Dead, Sir. Shot in th'head. Cops say it weren't the Guard neither, gun's too small."

"Fine. Keep listening for more information." The man's voice was condescending as if he was talking to a trained serving animal and not a sentient being. "Here." Mena took a small package from out of his dark wool trench coat. The boy snatched the package from his hands and skittered away, back towards the street, taking the dancing shaft of torchlight with him.

David climbed over the edge of the fire-escape rail without making a sound, and dropped himself onto the concrete below. There was no artificial light in the alley, making almost everything a night-vision gray. But where occasional shafts of light touched the edges of brick, there were pockets of red that faded into the gray like a special filter on a camera.

David's footsteps were silent against the pattering rain. He closed the gap between him and the tall, broad Ronan man.

Mena, like the rest of his people had to die. Not just because he'd betrayed the Rebels, though, that fact made the situation at least mildly enjoyable. David lowered himself into his Enigma persona, the more arrogant and hostile the better. He made sure he was still in the pitch blackness when he spoke, but close enough to Mena to seem as if he had appeared out of nowhere.

"Mena Malan, I presume?" He kept his voice icy and hostile, but not quite growling yet.

The man managed to suppress his surprise well, but his body still stiffened as he looked around him for the source of the voice. A frown crossed his square features.

"No, you didn't imagine me." David flicked on the pen-sized ambient lamp he held.

The man stepped back into the wall, only then realizing how close David had managed to get to him without being sensed.

The fear on Mena's face dropped into an angry defiance. He was being played and he knew it. Mena went for a weapon in his coat. David dropped the tiny lamp and grabbed Mena's wrist. With his thumb and fingertips triggering pressure points, David used the pain to redirect Mena's arm long enough to reach into the man's coat and take his weapon.

David stepped back out of Mena's visual range and started stripping down the man's hand-cannon. Once he'd completely taken the gun down to its collapsible parts, he threw the pieces back at Mena.

The old man couldn't see David, and only seemed to get angrier. "Hiding in the dark! What are you? A Coward?"

"I am Hawk."

"Mamon!" Mena bellowed, as he lunged blindly towards his voice.

David stepped to one side and kicked the man's knees out from under him. "Why did you try to kill my people? I thought we had a deal."

"You betrayed us first," Mena growled from the grubby pavement. "Where is my brother?"

"He failed." David said through gritted teeth. "*We* can not be held accountable for *his* mistakes."

Mena man leapt to his feet with his broad arms wide in an attempt to get a hold of him, but David simply moved out of range again.

Mena dropped his arms and glared at the dark. "You know, you won't find the girl."

"I'm not interested in the girl." David lied coldly.

Black eyes tracked to the location of his voice and the old man frowned. "You want to trade again? Is that what you want?"

"You have betrayed us." David let a deep undertone of hostility into his voice. "You tried to kill some of my best people. You never had any intension of fulfilling your part of the trade. And soon, when things get hard enough for you, you will betray us to the Guard to gain a short term advantage. It will not only get you killed, but many of my people. The logical conclusion is that I can not let you live, Mena Malan."

The man's eyes widened. He turned, but didn't have time to escape because David punched out, triggering a number of pain centers in the man's back, and then he cracked some ribs with a quick jab-punch. The old man cried out in agony and dropped to his hands and knees on the dirty pavement.

"You can't do this!" he gasped.

David took his weapon out from his jacket and put the barrel to the man's forehead. "I already have."

Part Five

* 1 *
About a week after leaving Kamo
Back in Arām

Lilān was still getting used to the low ceilings of Aranan buildings. Even sitting on the carpeted floor, she still felt boxed in from above—in fact, boxed in from all sides. Everything was too small for her, vehicles, clothes, utensils, bathrooms, even the blankets and cots on which she slept. She wouldn't ever complain out loud, but she didn't feel particularly comfortable anywhere at the moment and it was getting on her nerves.

Only those who had been there in Rona were in the meeting. Nama and Taelin sat against the wall to her left. Nalana; the healer girl, sat by the door. Bana lay in the corner on a cot because he wasn't able to walk around yet, and sitting next to him was Xak, still with burns on his face and arm in a sling. Sitting across from her against the opposite wall was Asha, and a man Lilān didn't know. Supposedly, this man was the "great" Rebel leader, Hawk. He commanded a lot of respect from the others, but Lilān didn't know the blue-eyed twerp from a bar of soap. She didn't care if he was the Founder himself, after Mena, she wasn't going to give anyone respect without their first earning it.

"Look," she said as she lifted her legs up under her. A shaft of pain shot through her stomach and she grunted. "I can refine it as much as possible, but this explosion is still going to be too big for what you want. Mena humped us, he humped us hard."

Hawk frowned at her. "Is there any way we could make the right explosive from scratch?"

She leaned her head back on the wall and sighed. "I could make the triggering device out of a car radio, no trouble, but the explosive chemical you want is too hard to make on the fly. Even if we had a lab and a bunch of technicians. But, given a few months, I might be able to find a supplier here in Arana that we can—"

"We don't have the time." The man's voice was quiet even though he interrupted her.

Asha, sitting across the room from Lilān, looked sideways at him. "Why, not? If we do this now with these explosives hundreds of innocent people will die."

Hawk got to his feet and paced away from them towards a window covered with graying towels. He sighed. "It's Heth Pallen," he glanced over his shoulder at them all for a moment. "He's the Agent in charge of finding Hawk. He's very close to finding proof I'm involved. When he finds it, there won't be anywhere the Rebels can hide. It has to be done very soon or it'll be too late for everyone."

"The other Rebels aren't going to like this development." Nalana spoke up from the door.

Still with his back to them, Hawk sighed again. "We can't tell them."

Sitting next to Lilān, Nama grunted. "Of course we can't. They'll mutiny on us."

"I'm tempted to mutiny myself," added Taelin on the other side of Nama. "There has to be another way of doing this. We can't—"

"It must be done, so it will be done." Hawk turned around to face them.

Lilān sensed a flicker of danger in the man's deliberate movements, and she instinctively tensed up.

"The loss of innocent lives is regrettable, but it's going to happen regardless."

His voice was too calm and Lilān wondered what was underneath all that ice, whether he was mad and egotistical like Mena, or if something else was responsible for his uncompromising manner.

"Lilān, will you refine it as much as possible for us, please?"

She nodded. "I'll do my best. But I'm going to need some gear and a cool dry environment."

The man nodded slowly. "Compile a list and give it to Asha, I'll supply everything you require. But I need to know, once it is refined as much as possible, how much damage will it do?"

She folded her arms across her chest and thought for a moment. "Well, anyone in the immediate levels around the explosion will be vapor, no doubt about that. If we shut off the gas before hand you'll have less damage. If your Tower is steel-reinforced like it should be and the explosion isn't anywhere near the load-bearing foundations, the building will probably stay upright, so those people above and below will be alright if they can get away from the fire." She sighed. "Essentially, it's not going to be pretty, even after I refine it."

"Tokāto—" the girl healer stood up, she covered her mouth with one hand and went towards the door. "I need some air."

Hawk sighed. "Give me a moment." He walked through the small group of Rebels to the door and followed outside.

There was silence for a long while. Lilān waited for the spell to lift, but it didn't. She smirked across the room at Asha. "So, what, do those two grapple in bed or something?"

Asha snorted, and Lilān's gambit on easing the mood paid off as most of the rest of the room laughed at her as well.

"So, that's a no, then?"

Taelin grinned at her and she felt her heart flitter. "That's definitely a no, Nala's married to Marius, and Hawk's a priest."

"A priest?" Lilān's snort degraded into a cackling laugh. "So'then Nuth! No wonder he's so uptight! He needs a roll in the sack to loosen those butt chee—"

The door opened and she shut her mouth, even as the others continued to laugh. Hawk looked around the room, and lifted an eyebrow at Asha.

"What's going on?"

"Don't worry, just a joke at your expense." Asha answered with a grin, and then cleared her throat. "So, what's next? How do we minimize the collateral damage?"

He glanced around for a moment with an uncertain frown on his face, but shrugged and paced to the other side of the room.

"Misdirection," he said as he sat down.

They were all quiet again.

Lilān tipped her head on the side and frowned at the young man. "What, you mean deliberately lure folks out of the Tower?"

"Yes." The man's coldness lifted into a mischievous half-smile and Lilān saw some of the man underneath the mask.

Not so uptight after all, she thought as she mimicked his half-smile.

"Tiras can help!" blurted Asha.

"Yes," said Bana from where he lay. "If some high-profile Rebels go to a large public place with cameras, we could get a lot of attention from the Tower."

Sitting next to Bana, young Xak sat forwards. "With Liz and the others, we could—"

"No, Xak." Hawk's voice was gently correcting. "You and your friends have had enough risk. I'd like you guys to help by shutting off the gas to the Tower. No combat. Lilān," blue eyes lifted to stare at her. "How long will it take to refine the stuff?"

She shrugged. "I don't know, a few weeks. A month at most. Just obtaining and setting up the gear will take some time."

"OK. Asha, I need you to continue planning ways of getting people out of levels eight through twelve of the Tower and organize supplies for Lilān. See if the old Ronan Embassy building is adequate." He got to his feet and smiled down at Lilān. "You should at least be comfortable."

Asha frowned. "What are *you* going to do?"

"I've got to stall Heth."

She smirked. "Good luck."

* 2 *

The next day

Taelin sat on the soft cream carpet. Autumn sunlight poured through the wide windows over his back. He should be enjoying the warmth and light, but he couldn't stop his raging thoughts. He sighed, took another mouthful of Nama's homemade beer, and put the bottle back down on the carpet between them.

"Do you think he could be mad?"

Nama grabbed the bottle and took a swig of his own. "Who? Hawk?"

"Yeah," he nodded. "I mean, I know Asha jokes about it all the time, but what if he actually is insane?"

Nama shrugged. "If he is, he's a good pretender. Why?"

"We're helping him kill..." he sighed. "You know... There are hundreds of innocent people..." he trailed off again, struggling to get his head around it all.

"Yeah," grunted Nama.

On the outside Nama didn't seem to care. His yellow eyes stared off into space and his face was clear of any emotion. But Taelin sensed a shaft of confused grief in his old friend.

He glanced sideways. "How do we make it right?"

"Make what right?" Someone walked into the room and Tae looked up into Nalana's heart-shaped face. She sat down on the carpet next to them and added another two bottles of homemade beer to the space between the three of them.

He shrugged with one shoulder. "This bombing thing."

"Don't you dare!" she said, suddenly angry.

Both he and Nama stared at her, surprised at the vehemence in her voice.

He frowned. "What do you mean?"

"Don't you dare make this right! We're helping to kill innocent people and that's not right, not by any measurement. If you make it right in your head you're no better than the Rona-Abān!"

Taelin sat back and stared at her. "But—"

"It's not right," she interrupted. Her voice softened and Taelin sensed a pulse of sadness. "But it is necessary. That's how you can accept that it's going to happen. It's not right but it's necessary."

She sighed and grabbed one of the bottles she'd brought with her, taking a long swig of its contents before putting it back down on the carpet.

"Necessary," said Nama quietly. "OK, I think I can handle that."

Taelin lifted the bottle to his mouth. He wasn't sure if it was enough for him, but he guessed it was the best he could do considering their situation. What could he do exactly? Take back what happened in Rona? Perhaps try to stop David from doing this? Neither of those options were possible, he just simply had to figure out how to make peace with it and get on with doing what he had to do to survive.

The three of them sat, drinking Nama's bitter home-made beer in solemn silence. The fight against the Agency wasn't what he thought it would be. It wasn't a heroic battle for freedom. There were more Rebels than there had been before, and they'd certainly won a great deal more victories against the Agency under Hawk, but it wasn't a joyous victory for the "right side", as he'd hoped. Taelin hadn't even wanted to fight in the first place, but had done so to protect what was left of his family.

Oddly enough, he trusted David, despite all of the hidden agendas and deceptions. He knew with every inch of his instinct that David was doing what he believed was right, but like his sister, Taelin often wondered if there were better ways to do things, certainly without needing to kill innocent people.

Nama cleared his throat, bringing everyone's attention back to their little second floor sun-room.

"So, Tae, you going to help out or evac with the others?"

"I'm staying. Mall?"

"Yeah. Why not, sounds like fun."

Nalana took a long gulp of beer. "What's the mall?"

"Star mall," said Nama between mouthfuls. "Tiras and I will go in and play tag with the cameras to get people's attention. Raha will hack into all their security systems and play havoc like we're after something important. All with the hope they'll send an army of Agents over from the Tower to stop us. Just before it goes down, we'll evac. out of there."

"Yeah, it's basically just doing a bunch of pranks," Taelin winked at Nalana. "So it should be lots of fun."

She laughed. "That does sound like fun."

"So," Taelin smiled sideways at her. "When are you going to evacuate, Nala?"

The smile on her face lowered into a determined scowl. "When I'm good and ready!" She took the fullest bottle of beer from the floor and got to her feet.

"Hey, I was just—"

She left the room, slamming the door closed behind her.

Taelin sighed and took another gulp of beer. A moment later Nama did the same.

* 3 *
17 Aracan 3010
Two and a half weeks later

Jaran's office was too much like an altar to his own genius for David's liking. Awards and commendations, every promotion certificate his father had ever earned, and even the potted plant he'd been given as a wedding present, were all on display. The self-worship cluttered the walls and every available surface. To David, it all seemed uncomfortably garish. He would have already made several disparaging remarks about his father's lack of public humility that morning, but he just didn't have the energy to devote to their customary insult-sparing as well as arguing with him.

"He is my son, *I* will go and claim him." David crossed his arms over his chest and glared.

From behind his desk, Jaran snorted. "No, you're needed here. Heth is using every opportunity he can to discredit you."

"Heth is a petty little man grasping at straws," David growled. "I will not dignify his harassment by allowing him to stop me doing my job. I am going to get my son and the new A1 intakes, and if he has a problem with me doing my job, he can sit on it and spin!" He turned away from his father and stalked towards the door, stopping to growl over his shoulder. "If you're so worried about Heth, why don't *you* deal with him? I have better things to do with my time than letting his little witch-hunt rattle me."

David slammed the door behind him and kept up his act of an enraged person down the length of the level ten hallway to the elevator. People saw him coming and hurriedly stepped into side rooms or turned completely around to avoid him. No-one wanted contact with an angry Enigma.

Underneath his outer persona, David wanted to skip down the hall. He wanted to crow from the top of his lungs and grin like an idiot. He'd finally managed to get all of the kids from his Primary Players list at the desert training base *and* Wolf onto the next intake list. He could now legitimately go and get his son from the desert, and do his job as Hawk by protecting the other children.

As he moved to enter the elevator, those who had been waiting in front of it stepped back out of his way. He turned around, glared at the five terrified faces standing in the hall and pressed the button. The door closed and he was alone in the elevator with the security camera.

The edges of his mouth twitched up. *"Not long now, son, I'm coming."*

* * * * *

About lunchtime
West of Epa, deep in the Great Desert

David's stomach tightened as the helicopter approached a squat off-yellow building. The Ao facility was constructed in an ugly box shape with an open air exercise yard hugging the north wall. His jaw tightened. Despite all of the good that had come out of his experiences there, he still hated the place.

Like many other desert facilities, the helicopter pad for incoming traffic was located on the roof above the control room. As they hovered down towards the landing pad, David looked through the glass at his feet and saw the Head of the facility waiting for him. Agent Brea's square face was pulled into a cruel glower. It was the same expression as the last time David saw the man, which was thirteen years ago (almost to the day), on his own Agency-sanctioned escape from Nūthen.

When the helicopter was on solid ground, David pulled open the door. Upon seeing him, Agent Brea's eyes widened and his mouth opened.

Observing Brea's genuine fear, caused a malicious spark of glee to shoot through the core of David, but he kept his face emotionless. He approached the man who had repeatedly broken his bones and bullied him mercilessly. Brea was older, skin spotty from sun damage, and wisps of white hair orbited an otherwise bald head, but he otherwise looked the same as he remembered him.

"Agent Brea, how nice to see you," he said in a hostile, but polite tone.

The man swallowed and took his outstretched hand. "Hello... Sir."

David lifted his chin. "I've come to take the next A1 intake back to Arām. I have the list. E.T.A. for the transport helicopter is approximately ten minutes." He paused, waiting for Brea to invite him inside.

The man seemed afraid, so much so he probably wasn't thinking straight.

The corner of David's mouth lifted mockingly. "May we proceed?"

"Oh! Yes, please come in. They're having lunch at the moment. Standard lock-down procedure?" Brea indicated the stairwell door, and his outstretched arm shook.

"Yes." David strode past him. "If you give me the access card I'll go down there myself."

"Of course. Do you need an escort? Sir?"

He looked back over his shoulder at the older man. "Just direct me to the stairwell, I know the way from there, Brea."

The man simpered. "Of course, Sir."

* * * * *

David stood in the doorway, staring at the noise and bustle of children eating lunch. No one had sensed him yet so they were in their natural state of misbehavior. Half of the long room was filled with grubby wooden picnic tables, the other half was taken up by the food line and kitchen.

One corner of his mouth lifted slightly and he reached to touch the doorframe. His fingertips found a mark; the Ancient letter "dena" carved into the wood. It was his tiny rebellion against a system that had tried to suffocate him. Sitting on either side of his symbol were the ancient letters, "shan" for Asha and "reda" for Araian. It had been their little pact to stay friends forever, and not let the world crush them. He sighed, swallowed back the memories and dropped his hand again. He had more important things to focus on than the past.

Wolf sat across the room with his back to David, eating. The boy had made friends with almost all of the children on his Primary Players list. This was good, mostly because they'd helped to protect him, but it also made acquiring the children much easier. The six of them sat at the same table talking and laughing animatedly. His eyes hovered over each child for a moment and eventually returned to Wolf's back.

He brushed the surface of his son's mind with gentle fingertips and the boy instantly turned around. Wolf's oval face tightened as he suppressed his reaction, but his silver eyes gleamed at him.

His son was alright. He'd been protected and now the boy would be safe at the Tower until the bombing.

Taking a deep breath, David dropped all of his emotions again and became the professional Agent that was required to complete the job.

* 4 *
That evening
Arām City Church of the Founder

David sat on the edge of the Cathedral bell tower, one shoe hanging a meter or so over the black roof-shingles, his other foot rested on the ancient stone of the bell tower. He stared out at the flickering lights of the city and the bright orange double full moons low in the sky. Such a celestial event as a double full moon, as well as its harvest orange only happened once in a lifetime.

He put a broad hand on the head of the stone gargoyle next to him. It sat inside the tower and stared out at the city, as it had for a thousand years. The real gargoyle creatures still existed elsewhere in the world, but there were none left in Arana since the Reformation massacre wiped out most of them.

The modern Church called them Wraiths. David preferred the more neutral word of gargoyle. Nalana called them Mern, but she also called whales Mern, just to confuse matters.

David felt a kinship with the original tribe of gargoyles that used to live on the Cathedral roof. They were not soulless creatures of the Darkness and

Destruction like the Modern Church taught. They were intelligent, and loving—more so than most humanoids. So few people knew the truth about the real gargoyles, just as so few knew the truth about Hawk.

One corner of his mouth lifted in amusement. Of course, the main difference between him and the gargoyles was that his mask of lies and deception was mostly of his own making.

He sighed, stroking his hand gently over the nose and neck of the old carving. Tomorrow was the eighteenth of Aracan—the day of the bombing. Tomorrow he would die simply because there was no one else who could get the explosives into the Ao Chambers. The original plan involved an amount small enough to hide unseen under the table. Unfortunately, there was too much explosive material to follow that plan. Someone would have to carry it in and then set it off manually.

So, he *would* see the look of betrayal on his father's face before he died, after all.

To his far left, the trap-door under the ancient brass bell opened. Nalana's heart-shaped face looked tense and a little frightened. She still hadn't lost that touch of fear of him. A thing which, if he was honest with himself, pained him every time he saw it in her eyes. No matter what he had said or done since, he could not erase her memory of him capturing her all those years ago. He glanced away from that fear.

"I figured you'd be up here," she said.

One corner of his mouth lifted. "Big day tomorrow."

"I guess so." She sighed. "Are you going to do what I think you're going to do?"

He brushed her mind with a telepathic hand and looked sideways at her. "Yes."

"Why?"

"It has to be done by someone. Why not me?"

"Why not someone else?" She sat down on the stone ridge in front of him and folded one leg under her.

He shook his head. "I can not ask this of anyone else, Nalana. Besides, who would you recommend? Taelin? Asha? Nama? Who deserves to die?"

"No." Her voice was firm. "No, David. Don't do that, don't redirect this. There's always another way, you of all people know that to be true. There has to be someone else who can do it. We need you alive and so does your son."

At the mention of Wolf becoming an orphan, a shaft of despair came into his heart. It rose so quickly that a tear dropped from one eye before he managed to suppress it. He swallowed and wiped his face with one hand.

"There is more at stake here than Wolf and I." His voice wavered.

"Yes, there is, but the whole world, humanoids and Mern needs you for the next thing that's coming."

He frowned at her. *Did she know?*

She continued. "I know there is someone else who can do it for you, if you just stop being stubborn and look into the future to see who it is."

He faked an amused smile. "And how to do you know with such certainty, oh wise one?"

She glowered at his sarcasm. "Ha ha. No, my nan told me that you would save us all, and not from the Agency. This thing tomorrow can't be your last act as Hawk, so there must be another way."

His mouth opened. "How—"

"You're just being pig-headed and deciding to fall on your sword!" A stubborn pout lifted into her lips. "I don't know why you have trouble valuing your own life, but I won't let you throw it away without looking for another solution. If it's the only solution, then I'll leave it be. But I'll never forgive you if you die and you could have saved yourself. And," she crossed her arms over her chest. "I'm not leaving you alone until you look, even if I have to stay here all night."

He chuckled. "Alright, I'll look. But you have to promise that you'll leave the city on the next evac truck in the morning. Deal?"

She nodded. "Deal."

He took a deep breath, releasing all the tension in his body. Closing his eyes, he asked the wordless question that Nalana wanted. The static shivered over the front surface of his body, bringing goose-bumps to the back of his neck and an odd vibration up his spine.

When the vision shifted away from him again, he sighed and opened his eyes. "Nalana," he made his voice very gentle. "The one who can replace me is an innocent."

"So is your son!"

He sighed. "I'll think about it." He lifted one eyebrow at her. "Look at you, the Champion of the Innocent insisting I sacrifice an innocent in order to save my own skin."

She snorted. "It's not just your skin I want to save. It's my own and everyone else's."

"What do you mean?"

"You know what you're really stopping, David. This isn't just about the Agency, there's something bigger coming and that's what you're really stopping."

One side of his mouth lifted. "Exactly how much do you know, Nala?"

Her mouth tightened and he sensed that she was sad. "I know my own part in it and I know that you need to survive beyond this despicable bombing, if only you'll just save yourself." She sighed and the tension in her shoulders dropped. "Now, will you come downstairs and have a hot drink with Father Andrew? He misses you."

David smirked. "Yes, mother."

* 5 *
Later that evening
Rose Road

Asha was slowly putting together a herb tea with one arm, when David strode through the front door of the Rose Road safe-house.

He had a look of determination in his vivid blue eyes. "It needs to be postponed until the nineteenth."

Asha put a scoop of herb tea into the teapot and frowned sideways at him. "Why?"

"It's the ten year anniversary of the rise of Hawk." He smirked. "Call it poetic timing."

She snorted. He wasn't the type to focus on poetic-anything. "No, really, why?"

"I need more time." She sensed regret even though there was no shift in his expression.

"You're not going to do anything stupid, are you? Like make Wolf an orphan?"

"I haven't decided." He sighed. "Either way, I need more time. Let's just leave it at that."

She shrugged. "Right."

He approached her and lifted the kettle from out of her hand. "Let me do this for you."

Turning from the bench, she sat down at the little table and absently put her free hand over the aching collarbone.

"So," he looked sideways at her, as he poured hot water into the tea pot. "Is Raha's program finished?"

She shrugged with one shoulder. "Yeah, should be done any minute, I'll go and get it later. He said the file will take some time to recompile on the other end, but it should work a doozy."

David smiled. "That's good. Tell him thank you."

"Of course." She cleared her throat. "So, can I finally tell him about Toma?"

"No, Asha," he finished pouring hot water into the tea pot and put the kettle down. "I shouldn't have told you in the first place. Tom is more at risk of discovery than I am in all of this. Raha can be told about his cousin when it's time for Tom to escape and not before."

"Right, right." She sighed. She didn't have the energy to argue with him.

David lifted the teapot and two mugs onto the table, and sat down opposite. He looked across the table at her and there was a different expression in his eyes. The edges of his mouth twitched upwards slightly—he was excited about something.

"So, what else is going on?"

A grin burst into his face. "I got Wolf today."

"That's great! How is he?"

An un-veiled boyish joy lit his eyes. "He's good. He made friends with a group of kids who kept him safe."

"Are they getting out too?"

He nodded. "I'll do my best. I just have to get them all into one classroom, which might prove somewhat difficult. The eldest of the six is almost two years older than Wolf."

She smiled. "Have you hugged him yet?"

David swallowed and looked down at his hands. "I haven't been able to get him alone. Enigma wouldn't show affection, even to his son. It's difficult."

Asha glared at him. "I don't care if it's difficult, that boy needs love, and love comes from hugs and kisses and tickling. It comes from closeness, not distance. So you figure it out, even if you have to drop your Enigma face for ten seconds. That boy needs to know you love him, especially if you're not coming back."

He stared at her for a long moment, his mouth open. "I—" he closed his mouth and nodded. "You're right. You're absolutely right."

She winked at him. "Of course I'm right. Now pour the tea!"

* 6 *

18 Aracan

David watched Wolf from the edge of the training mats. The combat gym was overly tall and wide compared to the other training areas of the Tower. Its walls, floor and angled ceiling were covered with wood paneling, and the lighting was set up in such a way that if one didn't look too hard, one could assume that the windows at ceiling height actually let in real sunlight. Someone had gone to a great deal of effort to create an atmosphere of not being in the Tower, and it was for this reason that the room was one of David's favorite places in the building.

None of the children Wolf's age were any challenge for his advanced combat skills, but those at his level were at least ten years his senior, and therefore legally too old to spar with him. The age and skill imbalance had caused a great deal of difficulties for David while he tried to source an appropriate interim sparring partner for his son.

Wolf faced his opponent with a fierceness that surprised David. His son had Sarah's stubbornness and David's focus. It was a beautiful thing to behold from the perspective of a combat trainer. As a father, however, it still saddened him that his son essentially never had a childhood.

The older boy, wearing a gi and belt two ranks below Wolf's, looked afraid. The corner of David's mouth lifted—that fear meant Wolf had already won.

The older boy went in for a sudden, but off-target punch. Wolf deflected the strike and pulled him into a throw with barely a momentary shift in his footing.

The older boy hit the training mats hard and lay on his back without getting up. He seemed to be winded, or perhaps overwhelmed by his own humiliation.

David stepped into the territory of the training mat and, still in his uniform navy-blue suit, dodged in through Wolf's defenses and went for a strike to the face. He felt the flicker of static as the boy sensed the blow and dodged away. A much smaller fist flew back at David, but he adeptly dodged and redirected it.

They sparred backward and forward for some minutes, testing each others boundaries and style of combat. The boy had a good instinct, and fought with a confidence many people didn't develop until their mid-twenties. David stepped back and dropped his arms out of their sparring position so the boy would know it was time to stop.

He bowed formally. "Wolf."

"Dad." The boy returned his bow, a touch of mischief played at the edges of his mouth.

David smiled affectionately. "You'll have to train with me until we can find you a more suitable training partner."

"Fine with me, Dad." Wolf said "dad" like it couldn't possibly be said too many times and David suppressed his grin. Wolf was cocky too.

The older boy hadn't moved from the floor and David glanced at him coldly. "Nacha, you can leave now."

"Yes, Sir." The young man got to his feet, bowed and skittered quickly out of the room. When the door was closed, David glanced around him in an effort to sense if anyone was watching them or listening in digitally on the otherwise empty room.

"We can talk this way. I can mask you." Wolf's voice rang with the sharp mental taste of a very tight private telepathic frequency.

David nodded and took off his suit jacket. "Let's start slowly with the Twenty Primary xeka moves and go from there."

The boy got into the first position and David into its mirror. They started the slow dance-like series of positions that beginners were taught before they entered the sparring phase of their training.

"Wolf, I'm getting you and your friends out of the Tower, but I'll need your help."

"What do you need me to do?" The boy performed a perfect round-house kick at one-quarter speed.

"Keep your friends together." David captured the boy's leg with a deflecting xeka and slowly spun him around with a twist of his body. *"It's going to happen quickly and anyone who is left behind will die."*

The boy adeptly flipped sideways and landed on his feet again. *"The bombing?"*

David swallowed. *"Yes. It's going to be bigger than I intended it to be, but it's still going ahead."*

"Are we going to become Rebels?" Silver eyes shone at him from behind a slow jab-punch.

David smiled and redirected the jab sideways and down. *"Yes, I may not be able to come, but you and your friends are going to be Rebels."*

In his surprise, the boy failed to shift into the next position, breaking the flow of their movement. They both stepped back into the first position and started again.

"May not come? Are you going to die with Jaran?"

"I'm sorry, if I can't get someone to take my place there won't be a choice."

Wolf's mouth tightened. *"I won't leave without you."*

"Son, I'm doing everything I can to come with you. But, if I can't get someone else to do it, I must take their place."

"You are not meant to die with Jaran." Wolf stepped back out of position, his arms down and fists clenched. "Father," his physical voice was clipped and very formal. "I need a bathroom break."

David swallowed and bowed to allow their "sparring" to end. Wolf also bowed and turned away immediately. Even at ten, he had already learned to keep up appearances despite his true emotions.

He watched his little form leave the room, and sighed. He'd upset the boy. He didn't want to lie or manipulate his son, but it seemed he would need to learn a different kind of tact with him.

David waited silently with his hands clasped behind his back and his body absolutely still. He knew Wolf was probably crying in the bathroom, but he couldn't go and find him without possibly revealing to someone else why he was crying.

At his best guess, Wolf was gone for thirty minutes. When he returned, his little oval face was red and patchy, but his silver eyes were determined and not sad.

"Close the door, son." David said quietly.

The boy did as he was told. The moment the door clicked closed David gently wrapped his arms around Wolf and lowered his shielding enough for him to sense his feelings.

"I'm sorry for upsetting you, son. You deserve more than you've been given. You deserve a better father than I and you deserve to have your mother. I love you, I will always love you. I will do everything in my power to come with you tomorrow. But you must promise me that you will get yourself and your friends out of the building when I tell you. Yes?"

"Yes, Dad."

He lifted Wolf into his arms, opening his empathic shielding even more so the boy could sense the depth of his love for him. Wolf started to cry again and wrapped his arms around David's neck.

"It's alright, son," he whispered. "I'm here."

* 7 *
19 Aracan 3010
Early morning, the day of the bombing
Arām Agency Tower

Toma Aria brushed a dark thread of hair from his eyes. He sat cramped into the little stationery cupboard adjacent to David Aenan's office. On the laptop screen in front of him, the code his cousin Raha had created for their purposes was seventy-five percent compiled. He wished it would hurry up, today was not a day where slow computers were good things.

He sighed. *Not long now.*

"Tom? Is it done?"

He looked up from his laptop. David stood in the doorway of the tiny cupboard-like office. The muscles in his face and shoulders were tense, but those amazing blue eyes of his were steady and calm.

Tom smiled. "Almost. Are you ready?"

"Yes," he nodded. "Everything else is on schedule. Do you have the last of those stickies?"

Tom lifted the manila folder from his desk and handed it to him. "Of course I do."

One corner of David's mouth lifted. "I'm going to miss you, old friend."

He got to his feet and opened his arms wide. David stepped into the hug.

"Me too." Tom grinned. "But I won't miss the stickies."

David snorted. "I'm not surprised." Their hug separated and David smiled at him. "Alright, do you need anything else before I go?"

"No, I'm fine. Just be careful."

David turned in the doorway with a sideways smirk on his face. "Always."

The door in the main office closed and Toma was alone again. He sighed. Ten years and two months they'd been working from that office, and it was about to be over.

Toma had secretly penned thousands of yellow sticky-notes for David, whose handwriting was atrocious and easily recognizable. He certainly wouldn't miss the stickies, or the fear of discovery that had haunted him all these years, but he would miss David's company and the rush of helping others get free of the Agency.

Toma turned back to his laptop. The program shouldn't take much longer to compile from Raha's text file. Its function was simple: to find the air conditioning systems for all of the kindergartens on levels eight and nine of the Tower, shut them off, and register an unbreakable error message. He hoped his cousin was just as amazing with code on this project as he had always been. It wasn't that Tom doubted his cousin's ability, but a lot was riding on the success of the program—not the least of which were the lives of about a hundred and fifty under five-year-olds.

* 8 *

Asha stood watching the street below her. At that height from a neighboring roof, the individual ochre cobbles below melded together into one flowing spinning design that covered the entire intersection. She lifted the binoculars.

The street was cordoned off by dark Agency vehicles and police tape, framing Star Mall's northern entrance in an oblong semi-circle. By her count there were two teams of eight Black Suit Task Force Operators, and their high-ranking superior. The CO would be sitting in one of the black vans opposite the entrance with his or her radio co-coordinating their search for and the capture of two Traitors, Tiras Malar and Nama Ree. On the Agency's Top Ten Most Wanted list, Tiras and Nama were second-equal underneath Hawk—much to Tiras' amusement.

Asha smirked. *I bet Tiras is having fun with all this attention.*

Dropping the binoculars, she glanced back over her left shoulder across the roof-tops through a gap in the skyline that was the City Park. The Agency Tower building was angular, domineering and covered in dark blue glass. Being the tallest skyscraper in Arām, it always seemed to her to be a bully kid glaring down at the other buildings.

Another encrypted radio broadcast chattered in her ear-piece on the Agency radio channel, and she looked back at the Star Mall entrance below. Her left arm was strapped to her body and made completely unusable, in an effort to ease her infuriatingly aching collar bone.

She mentally grumbled. Ren wasn't able to heal bone as quick as he could flesh, so she had to heal the old fashioned way with time and patience, and she was quickly running out of the latter.

She would have preferred to participate directly in their "Misdirection" mission inside the mall. However, being a spotter was better than evacuating with the non-combatants and doing nothing at all.

There were teams of Rebels all around Arām causing distractions at many different public places with the hope of drawing out people from the Tower. There were two teams at other malls, one team outside the Cathedral, and another two up on the elevated motorways in front of the traffic cameras. At their best guess, all of the teams could save as many as a hundred people, if they were lucky. There were also other, smaller teams helping with the last escapes or attempting to minimize the damage, like Xak's team who were shutting down the gas line to the Tower.

Her lips tightened. Unfortunately, the misdirection missions wouldn't be enough. Not near enough to stop even half of the potential innocent deaths from this explosion. There could still be as much as five hundred people still in levels eight through twelve when the explosion occurred.

She sighed. At least they were trying, and those Agents who were lured out would have their lives. Asha shook her head. She had to focus on those they were going to help and not the hundreds of people they couldn't save or she'd go crazy.

Over the garbled Agency channel in her ear, she heard a radio buzz in three long channels of concentrated static. This was a signal from Tom in the Tower that it was about to happen. Touching the earpiece, she buzzed the channel once to let him know that she'd received the message. She flicked stations to the Rebel frequency and spoke into her headset.

~ "All stations, evac. I repeat, all stations, evac."

* * * * *

Star Mall

The Star Mall was considered to be one of the best malls in all of Arana. Nama felt it was more like a pretty rabbit warren made of shining glass and steel. There weren't enough exits and there were far too many angles from which a threat could come at him. But smashing cameras from wall sockets and breaking shop windows had improved his liking of the mall significantly in the last hour.

Nama lifted the wooden bat and swung it at another camera on the wall. It shattered on impact, spreading chunks of dark plastic and glass across the polished wood floor.

He laughed. "This is fun."

"Told you, didn't I?" Tiras spoke over his shoulder, as he too destroyed another camera.

They were in a public corridor of the mall, near to the parking building entrance. Nama put the bat through the window of a men's clothing store, and grabbed a black fedora hat from the display.

He dropped it down onto his head and turned. "Hey, Tiras, what do you think?"

Further down the hall, Tiras winked at Nama. "Sexy! I think it suits you. But it's time we move back downstairs."

Nama nodded. As they turned towards the car parking entrance, he wondered if the other Misdirection Teams were having any luck throughout the city.

~ "All stations, evac. I repeat, all stations, evac." Asha's voice was completely icy cold in his earpiece. She was using her very serious "commander voice", as Taelin called it.

~ "You're single aren't you, Asha?" Tiras' replying tone was playful and flirting.

Asha's laugh was almost a girlish giggle. ~ "I am if you grab some alcohol on your way out."

Tiras laughed. ~ "I'll hold you to that!"

Nama smirked at his companion. ~ "Now, now children. Behave."

As they ran down a second hall, Tiras grinned back over his shoulder. ~ "Never!"

Laughing, Nama followed him through a door, out into the car parking building, and down a concrete parking ramp to the next level. While he ran, Nama shoved the handle of the bat awkwardly into the belt of his jeans and brought out his handgun.

On the next ramp, which brought them down to the ground floor level, they had to dodge around an abandoned car with its doors open and the keys still in the ignition. One of the TFO teams must have forced the civilian owners out at gunpoint. Nama took note of its location in relation to the exits in case they needed another escape route.

He and Tiras approached the ground floor mall entrance and he heard a distant boom that could be the Tower. He gritted his teeth against a shot of dread and fear that wanted out of him. He swallowed and forced himself to refocus. There was nothing to be done now, just continue to do what was needed to survive.

Tiras opened the mall entrance door for him. With his weapon up, Nama walked through and almost into a man in Agency fatigues. They both flinched back. The fear was instant in the young man's gray-blue eyes, but he still lifted his automatic rifle into Nama's face.

"H... hands up!" the boy stammered.

The radio on the TFO's bullet proof vest started to buzz away loudly. Nama guessed it was probably a voice telling this man that he had to withdraw and get back to the Tower immediately.

Nama re-gripped his handgun and stared coldly at the boy. "You have two choices, kid. You can continue all this and die, or you can leave now and see if your family is OK. I won't shoot you unless you give me no choice. So just go."

The TFO slowly lowered his rifle. He moved back cautiously until he got to a corner in the corridor, then he turned and ran. Nama stared at his receding figure, and quietly hoped the kid's family and friends hadn't been in the Tower.

"Nama! Come on, we've got to go!" yelled Tiras from behind him.

He dropped his gun hand and turned the other way. The broom closet with Taelin and Raha was down the hallway, and past it was an emergency fire exit that led out to the street and his van. They would pick up Asha and the desert kids, and then they'd get out of the city.

* 9 *
Close to the Agency Tower

Xak watched Liz close two big metal doors and pull a heavy chain through their handles. Beyond the doors, and down a stairwell into a subterranean level in the sewers, was a massive valve that they'd needed the three women's combined kinetic thrust to switch off. The gas supply was now cut to the Tower as well as to the entire block around it. They just had to lock it all up again and they'd get back to the pick up point.

Levi was out with another team so it was just him, Jai, Nick and Liz on this mission. The four of them were down a short alley between buildings, which ended at a dirty brick wall and the sewer access.

He glanced up above them. Broad white-stone apartments climbed high above their heads. Clothing and linen hung in the air in layers and attempted, perhaps futilely, to get dry in the dim space between buildings. A gray feline skulked around on a fire escape several stories above them. Above the feline, a window was open and bright yellow curtains flittered in the breeze. Out on the same fire escape, a line of potted flowers filled what little space existed between the window pane and the fire escape ladder with a multitude of cheerful colors.

Xak felt strangely nervous. Scared even, and the feeling kept him distracted and unable to focus on any one thing at a time.

"Lock!" called Liz from the door.

His attention came back to where it should be and Xak fetched the massive padlock from his pocket. He handed it to Jai, who passed it to Nick and then to Liz.

"Thanks." Liz brushed back some of her ever increasingly long blond hair from her face and pulled the padlock into place through two heavy metal chain links. There was a "click" as the lock pulled into place and Liz turned around to face everyone.

"Alright, time to go, we've got to meet Nama and the van soon."

She strode past Xak. The others walked after her and Xak stepped in line last. He followed the trail of women out of the dim alley and onto the street behind the Tower. The road beyond was a one-way service lane behind the massive Tower building. Xak had never seen the Tower from that angle before. All of his visions and dreams had been from the plaza on the other side, which faced the main public entrance.

He stopped walking in the middle of the lane and looked up. The Tower building was so tall from that angle. It looked like a square obelisk of tinted glass and concrete that reached up and touched the sky with its very peak.

Space and Time rumbled around him, tumbling and twitching in every atom of the air. Reality shook with multiple static waves and ripples. His skin tingled so badly from the feedback that it felt as if he had insects crawling up his face.

He held his breath. *This is it.*

"Xak!" called someone from one side of him, but he didn't respond. He was moments away from the event around which his entire life had revolved for the last ten years.

The pulsing static flowed up the Tower, causing shivers to eddy through his spine. The sensation peaked at the base of his skull and became almost painful. A boom sounded and fire blew out of the glass building far above his head. The ground shook as the impact wave shimmered down to the street and out through the concrete.

He sensed threads of terrified mental screams, which were cut off abruptly. His mouth opened and he stared. Glass fell towards him, but in his horrified shock he was frozen to the road. Massive shards shimmered in the air and he knew that when those shards hit they would kill him, but his body wouldn't move.

"*Xak!*" a voice called out again.

Something like big invisible hands grabbed him. He was pulled sideways so hard that what air was in his lungs, was forced from him with a choked wheeze. As he flew, he heard the tinkling crashes of glass smashing on concrete behind him.

When he landed roughly on the sidewalk next to the others, tears were running down his face.

"By the Old Gods," he whimpered. "What have we done?"

Liz knelt down next to him and her smile was gentle. "Come on, Xak," she offered him a hand to help him stand. "We have to go now."

* * * * *

There was a deep sense of ill-ease inside Taelin and he stared out through the back of Nama's van at the road. On the horizon, surrounded in shorter skyscrapers, the Agency Tower Building was on fire. Massive black clouds of smoke billowed out and filled the air around it. Numerous ambulance and fire service sirens blared as they rushed towards the Tower.

Taelin swallowed. They'd done that. Together, the Rebels had done that. He wondered how many people would be dead by day's end.

His father had always taught him that violence was a weak person's defense. He used to say that if you couldn't find a peaceful resolution to a situation you weren't trying hard enough. But, his father had lived in a different world, a different Arām. He also had the police department to help hide him and his family. However, in the end, all of his father's words had meant nothing because the Agency still found them. Taelin wondered if what they had done would make a difference at all in Arana, or if it would simply make things worse for the Rebels. Had, in this case, his father been right? Was it a lazy person's action? Or had there really been no other choice but to strike back at the Agency in such a horrific fashion?

He swallowed and stared out through the glass at the burning Tower, watching it as it got further and further away from them.

"Tae?"

He turned from the back-door windows to look across Nama's crowded van. His sister sat with her back up against the front seats. He sensed over the muted shock of the desert kids that Asha was worried about him.

He gave her a little smile. "I'm alright."

He really wasn't, and the knowing smile on Asha's face suggested that she knew he wasn't either, but he didn't want to talk about it in the confines of the van. If they managed to get out of Arām before the Agency shut down the city, they would have an eight hour car journey on their hands. It would not be helpful to start the journey with any more melancholy atmosphere than was absolutely necessary. He turned back to watch the burning, smoking silhouette of the Tower grow smaller and smaller as they traveled away from the carnage.

* 10 *

On the day of the 3010 Bombing, there were ten classrooms for under-five-year-olds; all located on level eight and nine of the Tower building. Inexplicably, an hour before the explosion, all of the air-conditioning units for each of those ten classrooms failed simultaneously and could not be restarted by tech-support.

The classrooms became hotter and stuffier as the hour crept on. It eventually got so bad that every teacher pulled rank on their supervisors, and evacuated their students to the empty teaching labs on level twenty. The very last class to evacuate upstairs left fourteen minutes before the explosion ripped through levels twelve, eleven, ten, nine and eight. Because the servers were located on level eleven, no one ever discovered the virus written by one Rahan Aria and planted on the Agency system by his cousin Toma Aria. Officially, it was forever thought of as an extremely fortunate "Act of Divinity".

Toma Aria, who had been the personal assistant for an undisclosed high ranking Agent, also became one of the most public heroes of the day. Tom, being a fairly low rated clairsentient, had sensed fire was coming and was cutting all of the locks on the old fire escape doors at the time of the explosion. The open fire doors enabled those survivors of the initial explosion to escape the resulting flames that swept through some of the upper levels of the Tower building afterwards. His actions saved approximately two thousand women, men and children from dying that day with those lost in the initial explosion.

Outside, as emergency crews were putting out the fires, and evacuating and treating the survivors, a number of those Agents evacuated to the street went missing. They drifted off, one by one, from the crowd of their fellow Agents and disappeared. As a group, about twenty ex-Agents, all covered in soot and dust from the explosion, met as strangers at a large open access point to the sewers. A single person welcomed them to the Psi Rebels and directed them all to go down into the sewers, where together they made their way through an ancient underground tunnel network towards the ocean. Ironically, their path through the sewers also happened to be the same journey that the survivors of the Reformation massacre followed when they evacuated the city just over a thousand years before.

The newly escaped Rebels were taken north up the coast on an illegal trawler to the small mountain-city of Shada. All those missing in the bombing, including the people who escaped the Agency that day, were declared killed in the explosion or the fire, and were never pursued by the Agency.

Further out, near the edge of the Arām city limits, Nama Ree drove his little white van and the remaining Rebels of his Cell out of the city. Five minutes after they passed through the boundary line, the temporary Head of the Agency ordered the city to be completely blocked off from the rest of Arana. The new Head started the search to find the Rebels responsible for the horrific bombing that killed almost four hundred people, including all but one of the original Ao Council, but to no avail. In the five years following the bombing, no Rebels directly responsible for the Bombing were ever found.

The 3010 Arām Agency Tower bombing became the kind of event where everyone knows where they were and what they were doing when it happened.

* 11 *
outskirts of the city of Peera
south west of Arām

Taelin sat out on the balcony of an old farmstead and watched the sun set over the scrabby abandoned fields. There was something inherently peaceful in the sound of the wind in that place, and he needed that feeling to seep into his body and ease the pain inside him.

The farmstead had been stocked up with food and other supplies by one of the Peera Rebel Cells a few days earlier, so at least they could stay there for a while. David had said the Agency would try and hunt every Rebel down after the bombing, so each Cell had to hide, no matter where they were in Arana, until the grief-soaked search eased.

Taelin swallowed and wiped at his nose. The last count over the radio for the bombing had been over two hundred dead. It was horrific. He wasn't sure what to do with this feeling inside him, or if he'd ever feel differently in the future. It felt like a terrible mistake that he should have somehow tried harder to prevent.

The front door opened and he looked back to see his sister Asha standing on the balcony. She approached and passed him a mug of hot chocolate. Her smile was sympathetic. She knew how he felt about all this, probably even better than Nama.

He took a sip and leaned sideways on the balcony rail. "I don't know if what we've done was worth it."

One corner of her mouth lifted up just like David, but her eyes were gentle, not mocking. "Taelin, I know it seems awful right now. And it really is. I'm upset and grieving over what we did too. But, trust me when I say that it was worth it. By doing this thing, the Rebels have helped to save far more lives than we took."

Taelin frowned at her. "How is that possible?"

Her dark blue eyes were sad and she touched his arm. "Just trust me, Taelin. Can you do that?"

He stared at her for a moment, fighting with his own childlike need to understand, and his instinctive sense of absolute faith in her. His trust won the argument and he smiled. "I trust you."

"Good." She dropped her hand from his arm. It was then he sensed that she was worried about something else.

"Is something wrong?"

She sighed and shook her head. "I haven't heard from David yet."

"You expected to?"

There were tears in her eyes when she glanced up at him, and the shock of understanding pushed the air from his lungs.

"W... was he the bomber?

"I don't know." She shook her head. "Last we talked, he hadn't decided."

"What are the Rebels going to do without him?"

"I have no idea."

The rushing wind filled the quiet that descended between them, and they stood side by side on the balcony, watching the sunset.

Bright oranges and yellows played in long wisps of cloud. As the sun eased out of sight, the orange shifted into red and eventually purple. Stars flickered on and filled the entire darkening sky with little points of light. The sun sunk away and the sky became dark. Stars expanded into the flickering rainbow mass of nebula above them.

When it was as dark as it was going to get on a clear two-moon night, Taelin sensed the approach of an unknown mind. He felt the telepathic equivalent of a knock on the door.

"Asha." Taelin touched his sister's shoulder and let her into the conversation.

"Who are you?" He frowned.

"It doesn't matter who I am, Taelin Kān," said a woman's voice. *"Hawk is asking for transport. We're trapped in Arām and we need to get out of the city before the Agency finds us."*

The other mind was calling from far beyond the limits of his senses. Whoever she was, she was a very powerful telepath.

Taelin frowned. *"I don't know you, how can I know for certain that you're from Hawk?"*

There was a mental sigh. *"Hold on."* The woman kept a touch on his mind, but he sensed that she stepped back for a moment.

Taelin felt Nama's mental energy join the conversation just as the woman returned.

"He wants to know if Asha is there?"

"I'm here. Who are you?"

Another sigh came from the woman and Taelin sensed that she was extremely tired. *"It doesn't matter who I am. The pertinent point is that Hawk needs someone to come back for us."*

Asha's mental voice was firm and emotionless, despite the anticipation Taelin could sense empathically. *"I'm not ordering anyone to go anywhere until you prove that your message is from Hawk himself."*

There was another long pause. *"He says to tell Nalana that her skin is saved."*

Nama pulled away from their connection, and Taelin waited for him to pass on the message to Nalana. A squeal emitted from inside the farmstead, and the front door banged open.

Nalana ran towards them with a massive grin on her face. "It's him! It's him! He's alive!"

"Alright," Asha said, laughing. *"How many of you are there?"*

"Eight children, five adults."

"Nama?"

The front door opened. Nama was wearing his new black fedora hat and mirror shade glasses. He grinned at them. *"I'll be there by morning. Where does he want me to meet him?"*

For more information, news, stories, books, history, games and other Time Speaker Universe squee, please visit the website:

www.keyanadrake.com

www.ingramcontent.com/pod-product-compliance
Lightning Source LLC
Chambersburg PA
CBHW030932020726
47498CB00001B/213